The Fish That Climbed a Tree

Kevin Ansbro was born of Irish parents, and has lived in Malaysia and Germany.

He is married, and currently lives in Norwich, England.

BY THE SAME AUTHOR

Kinnara

(Paperback and eBook)

The Angel in My Well

(eBook)

The Fish That Climbed a Tree

KEVIN ANSBRO

2QT Limited (Publishing)

First Edition published 2018
2QT Limited (Publishing)

Settle, North Yorkshire BD24 9RH United Kingdom

The author has his own website: www.kevinansbro.co.uk

Cover Illustrations by Kevin Ansbro

Printed in Great Britain by
Lightning Source UK

A CIP catalogue record for this book is available
from the British Library

ISBN 978-1-912014-32-3

For anyone with a library in their head
and love in their hearts.

"Do not go gentle into that good night but rage,
rage against the dying of the light."

Dylan Thomas

"There are more things in heaven and earth,
Horatio, than are dreamt of in your philosophy."

William Shakespeare

PROLOGUE

Due to his being dead for the past decade, Ulysses Drummond could only look on in horror as his son was doused in petrol. Then, in no more than one darting second, a blowtorch ignited the puddle at his boy's tethered feet, twisting him into a human bonfire.

Henry's skin began to move; he felt his eyes boil and, while his body spat and crackled, his assailant, Pascal Makuza, gloried in his terrible death.

CHAPTER ONE

For a Light to Shine, Darkness Must Exist

Twenty years earlier: 1997

Quite why the newly incumbent Reverend Ulysses Drummond wore an eye patch was the subject of much speculation when he was appointed vicar of St Cuthbert's Church in the London borough of Hackney. One of the most promising lines of local tittle-tattle was that he had lost his left eye in the first Gulf War while seeing action there as a young lieutenant with the British Army. The less interesting reality was that he'd withstood the heat of battle and returned home unscathed, only to carelessly skewer his eyeball on a bamboo cane while pottering about in his parents' greenhouse.

Having only recently progressed beyond his thirtieth birthday, he looked far too young to be a vicar but had nevertheless replaced tortoise-headed Reverend Crabtree, a man seemingly as old as Methuselah and heavily peppered with dandruff. Distinct from other clergymen, Ulysses cut a dashing figure and was impossible to ignore, given that he was tall as a lamppost and carried the smile of Zorro. In truth, he was as easy to spot in a crowd as a lighthouse on a cliff.

Of more pressing interest to some of the more flirtatious women of the parish was the status of his marriage to Florence, a diminutive and noticeably pregnant English rose, whose pretty head barely reached the height of his armpits. To the acrid dismay of those gossips, Ulysses was as devotedly in love with his little Florence as Paris was with Helen of Troy. Then, when they presented themselves at their first church 'meet and greet', amid the smell of burning candles and musty hymn books, the star-crossed couple set about winning over any doubting Thomases and even succeeded in charming a chorus of unseen angels down from the rafters. Pretty soon they were accepted into the fold, organising raffles, fêtes and a whole host of fundraising events that brought their fractious community closer together. Ulysses even became something of a local celebrity, having famously performed an exorcism on a teenage girl who was formerly inclined to tear off her clothes and scream obscenities at her parents each time there was a full moon.

It didn't go unnoticed that Florence and Ulysses were collectively the product of good breeding and it was widely thought that their privileged upbringing might not have prepared them for the lawlessness that existed within the fringes of their new community, namely drug dealing, knife crime, sexual assaults and robbery. Those in the know nodded wisely, confident that a dose of harsh reality would soon dull the shine of their idealism.

One moonlit night, following a tip-off from a parishioner, Ulysses interrupted a gang of thieves who were enthusiastically stripping sheets of lead from the church roof. One of the robbers, astonished to see a one-eyed priest shouting up at him from the graveyard, lost his footing and plummeted onto a gravestone that broke his worthless head in two. It was, therefore, somewhat ironic that the man was later buried in the same place he'd met his untimely death, with Ulysses overseeing the service.

The couple were ancestrally favoured with an unassailable positivity that stretched back several generations. Ulysses, for instance, was thus named after one of his forebears, the empire-moustached Captain Ulysses Drummond who, after fortuitously surviving an ill-considered cavalry charge towards Russian cannon in 1854, decided that he would be the first man ever to swim across the English Channel to France.

Slathered in porpoise fat, and brimming with the confidence of a madman, he waded into the sea trailed by two clueless men in a rowing boat who were equipped only with a brace of gas lanterns, an insufficient picnic basket and a compass. Because he'd inauspiciously set off against the incoming tide, Captain Ulysses spent several profligate hours managing only to swim parallel to the shore while achieving a forward distance of just one mile. Exhausted, hypothermic, stung to buggery by jellyfish and unable to call out to his wingmen, who had both fallen asleep through boredom, he saluted the moon and sank deep beneath the waves to sleep with the fishes.

Florence, although having to contend with swollen breasts and a stomach that had grown to the size of a small planet, still radiated a nimbus of happiness everywhere she went. It was noted by all that, for some mystifying reason, butterflies were drawn to her alabaster skin in the same way moths are beguiled by a flame. Nobody could have imagined that her reliably sunny disposition prevailed in spite of a past tragedy that had left her invisibly shackled to heartache.

Nine years earlier, on the exact same day that she had fallen in love with Ulysses Drummond, Florence had hurried back to the student house she shared with best friend, Poppy Jennings. She was altogether giddy with excitement, eager to tell her confidante about the charming Sandhurst army cadet, with his preposterous name and raffish smile. But alas, Poppy was silent as a cloud, nestled under her duvet beside an empty pill bottle and a tear-stained suicide note.

The next evening, with Florence's address scribbled on a scrap of paper and innocently unaware of this calamitous occurrence, Ulysses rang her doorbell in eager anticipation of their first date. Instead he found Florence wretchedly alone, sharing the quietened house with a black cat and a broken heart.

More recently, she had suffered the anguish of a third miscarriage, which had left them hesitant to try for another baby. So it was a matter of great joy, and no small measure of discomfort, that Henry, plump as a partridge and slippery as a bar of soap, cascaded into their world. The midwife and the obstetrician, thinking alike, each expelled a loud gasp as it was instantly apparent that Mother Nature had generously conferred on this newborn infant a man-sized penis.

"Our Lord must have had a whole lot of baby plasticine left over when he made this one," said the midwife, her eyes bulging as she clamped his umbilical cord.

Neatly swaddled in a blanket, wrapped up like a burrito, the well-endowed baby was presented to his mother, her wet face a picture of instant adoration. Ulysses wept for joy from his one remaining eye. Henry, for his part, arrived on this planet with the same look of bewilderment that would inhabit his podgy face for the rest of his life.

While ancestors murmured in the afterlife, the caterwaul of a police siren drifted through the windows of the delivery room and Ulysses made a solemn pledge to his newborn son: "Welcome to the world, my darling Henry. I faithfully and heartily promise that I will be there for you, always."

CHAPTER TWO

Know Thyself, Know Thy Enemy

Ten years later: 2007

It was unkindly whispered by many that Master Henry Drummond presented quite a comical figure with his Dickensian riot of wavy hair raked into a side parting and his lips plump as sausages. In addition, he had a porcine nose, the eyelashes of a girl and goodness-knows-*what* stuffed into his pants.

Henry, who bore a dimpled stoutness befitting a Mongolian prince, was standing upon the vicarage driveway on the morning of his tenth birthday. He was momentarily lost in wonderment as he watched a dark flock of birds sweep balletic patterns in the sky.

"A murmuration of starlings, Henry, a fine start to the day!"

His father had exited the vicarage wearing a swashbuckling smile and a cable-knit cricket sweater that accentuated his black shirt and clerical collar. To Henry, he looked every bit as magnificent as a buccaneer with the morning sun reflecting off his leather eye patch.

"OK, birthday boy," his father said, clapping hands together. "If you've collected all your bits and bobs, I'll get you off to school."

Florence, squinting into the sun and shadowed by a white butterfly, had returned from posting letters and splayed her arms for a hug, which Henry reluctantly plodded into.

"Ooh, what's this you're reading?" she asked, noticing the hardback novel barely contained by his satchel.

"*The Three Musketeers*, Mum. It's rather exciting. D'Artagnan is travelling to Paris to join the King's Musketeers. It really is ace."

Henry had developed into a most peculiar child. He was socially awkward, not that he seemed to care two hoots, and had an old-fashioned air about him. The boy spoke as if he belonged in the Victorian era and, even at the age of ten, considered himself something of a bibliophile, having a particular fondness for books about whales that were able to swallow ships and mongooses that could kill cobras. He conjugated verbs as easily as other children gathered swear words, and it was this precociousness that left him friendless with most boys his own age.

"Gosh, you'll be reading Dostoyevsky next," Florence quipped. "Right, off you go, Pumpkin. Enjoy school and you just might have a lovely birthday surprise waiting for you when you return home. Come on, give your mum a nice kiss."

Henry scrunched his face and tensed up. "I don't like kisses."

"Oh, thanks! I love you too."

It quietly saddened Florence that their son wasn't

disposed to return her affection; the boy was well intentioned but wore his standoffishness like a cloak. She nevertheless entertained the idea that this quirk might be reversed should he ever mature into a doting teenager.

Ulysses walked to his car with a stride pattern not dissimilar to that of a giraffe. Before grabbing the door handle, he couldn't help but notice the two sinister young men parked directly across the road from the vicarage. One was as black-skinned as a Kalamata olive and presented a mouth full of skeleton teeth; the other was a stony-faced white lump, Eastern European, he guessed. Both stared none too subtly in their direction. Both were trouble, for sure.

Ulysses glanced at Florence and saw by the concern on her face that she had noticed them too. "Darling," he said. "I'm just going to pop over the road, find out what those two guys are up to."

"Please don't, Ulysses, they look rather threatening."

"Probably nothing. A friendly chat is always best in such circumstances."

"Oh, for heaven's sake, just ignore them."

"Can't do that, Florence. I'll be back in a tick."

"Christ, you are infuriating at times."

"And don't take the Lord's name in vain." Ulysses walked away with a smirk that made Florence want to slap his face.

As he began to traverse the road, his fingers interlocked so as not to appear combative, the black fellow's rictus smile spread wider. He even fluttered a playful wave as their black Toyota four-wheel drive thrummed to life and crept up the road.

Henry scowled at his mother. "Why are you so angry with Dad?"

"Because he never listens and he only ever sees the good in people, even when they're amoral toe-rags."

Ulysses returned with a shoulder shrug and an unruffled countenance. "See, just some hoodlums casing the street. Nothing we haven't seen before."

"You saw the toe-rags off, Father," Henry bubbled. "I should imagine that they were scared."

"Ha! Doubt they were scared, Henry. Men like that are never fearful, and 'toe-rag' is not a description to be used willy-nilly."

"Point taken, Father."

It was at this moment that a khaki glob of bird shit dropped from the sky and splattered Ulysses' eye patch, prompting wife and son to collapse into mild hysterics.

"Don't know why you're laughing, you devils. This is widely considered to be a very good omen," Ulysses retorted.

"Good?" said Henry.

"You heard me. Today will be our lucky day."

*

While driving his battered Volvo estate to Henry's school, Ulysses sang *Nessun Dorma* with great gusto, and also purposely out of tune, to the accompaniment of the stirring aria that emanated from the speakers. His son sat po-faced throughout, comedic irony making as much sense to him as a piano does to a horse.

For some baffling reason, Ulysses' and Florence's Christian beliefs hadn't filtered down to Henry from their shared gene pool. Their progeny, a boy given to questioning absolutely everything, had determined that believing in God was every bit as absurd as supposing there were mobs of leprechauns giggling in hedgerows. So today he stared at the gilt-edged Bible sitting before him, thick as a blacksmith's anvil, with his usual irreligious scepticism. He had in mind though a burning question that he had hitherto been aching to ask. So, summoning the boldness of D'Artagnan from his duffle-coated being, he took the plunge.

"Father, why on earth did you leave the army to become a vicar?"

"Wow, that's a very good question, Henry, and one that I'm happy to answer." In that moment, Ulysses' facial expression changed from jovial to reflective in the blink of one eye.

"OK, the potted version. So, whilst on foot patrol in Iraq, my platoon was ambushed. We came under heavy machine-gun fire. Rocket-propelled grenades were exploding all about us and we could barely see the enemy for all the smoke and dust that was thrown into the air. Bizarrely, despite a hail of bullets fizzing past my ears, I remained wholly unscathed. Then suddenly I was out of ammo and simultaneously knocked unconscious by a terrific blast. When I came to, all noise had ceased. I called out to my men, none of whom answered. It transpired, sadly, that I was the only one left alive."

Henry, guilelessly unable to grasp the true horror of war, was transfixed. "Wow! Everyone else dead. So how come you were still alive?"

"Ah, only God can answer that, Henry. But as I lay there in the dirt, out of the smoke appeared an Iraqi officer with pistol drawn. He gazed down at me and said, in the most perfect Oxford English, 'Play dead, old chap.' He then fired a few rounds into the ground next to me. With my ears ringing like church bells, I heard him say, 'Go with God.' Then he simply smiled and ambled off to join his troops."

Henry was awestruck, his eyes as wide as duck eggs, "That's amazing, Father! You are the coolest."

"No, Son. There's nothing *cool* about war. In fact I'd urge you to remember that the two most powerful warriors in earthly existence are love and understanding."

Henry folded his arms and frowned. "Um, you still haven't told me why you became a boring old vicar."

"Well, I thought that would be self-evident, Henry. Remember that the officer said, 'Go with God.' Our Lord sent an angel that day, one who not only spared my life but also showed me the true path."

Henry immediately wondered if his father had completely taken leave of his senses and gone stark raving mad. Surely this hypothesis was completely absurd? But what misgivings he had, he magnanimously kept to himself.

"Father?"

"Yes, Henry?"

"Have you ever actually garrotted anyone?"

"Ha! No, can't say that I have. Oh, you really are priceless."

*

There was a throng of chatty mothers at the school gates, wearing an array of tracksuits, business suits, burkas and saris. Ulysses snuck into a parking place and switched off the engine before pressing his hands against his son's chubby cheeks. "Be a blessing to someone today, Henry."

"I will," said Henry, enjoying the woodsy scent of his father's cologne. "You're the best."

"So are you, Son. So are you."

As Henry left the car, some of the other boys scowled at him and pulled faces as was their daily habit. One, upon noticing Ulysses' eye patch, then launched into an enthusiastic impersonation of a pirate, hopping about on one leg while shouting, Arrrgh, shiver me timbers, with a throaty inflection.

"Make sure you've got your inhaler, Henry," Ulysses called out, prompting a thumbs-up from his son.

"Yeah, make sure you've got your inhaler, Hen-ry-y," the boys mocked in gleeful unison.

As Ulysses drove back to the vicarage, stopping off on the way to buy some birthday balloons, his mind returned to the two miscreants in that black Toyota.

CHAPTER THREE

Perchance to Dream

Escaping post-genocide Rwanda in his mid-teens, Pascal Makuza, shepherded by a cut-throat smuggling gang, arrived in London in 1994 after a perilous journey that took him across land and sea. In Rwanda Pascal was himself both victim and villain, press-ganged as an eleven year old into a Hutu death squad by men who, for fun, had sliced off his upper lip and fed it to a dog.

Drunk on whisky and high on drugs ransacked from abandoned pharmacies, Pascal and his adoptive militia were bussed into Kigali to slaughter the ethnic Tutsis who had been deplorably abandoned by Western peacekeeping forces and foreign governments. Armed with a machete, Pascal discovered after his first kill that he had an unimaginable capacity for evil and eagerly hacked at men, women and children, whether they pleaded for their lives or not.

Under a hot African sun, the prevalent orchestra of crickets was drowned out by the screams of the dying and those soon to be dead. Even under the hazy canopy of dusk, as the disappearing sun seared silhouetted treetops, the killing continued. A panicked throng of citizens, who had fled to the imagined sanctuary of a Catholic church, were butchered *en masse* under the mournful gaze of a crucified Jesus mounted high upon an apse wall. Within days, every dusty road and scrubby field for miles around was strewn with flyblown, raggedy bodies, many with their eyes pecked out by vultures.

Now aged twenty-four, and perfectly at ease on some of London's meanest streets, Pascal had progressed from the street gangs of the local Pembury Estate to gangsterism, burglary and extortion under the tutelage of Yuri Voloshyn, a twenty-six-year-old Ukrainian who remains unpunished for the rape and murder of a barmaid in his home city of Odessa.

Yuri, a human rhinoceros more accustomed to breaking bones than polite conversation, had been drawn to Pascal because of the boy's clinical zeal for violence. Theirs was entirely a marriage of convenience and especially surprising, given that Yuri was formerly a member of a racist skinhead gang in his youth.

He had first noticed the African, fresh out of prison, competing for money at an illegal bare-knuckle event in a Victorian warehouse by the docks. Despite being a wiry teenager, Pascal took on three brutish Irish gypsies one after another and destroyed each one in a blur of fists and elbows. A person such as this was uncommonly useful in Yuri's line of work.

Although the Ukrainian was a thug of unremarkable height, he stood as solid as a sea wall; anyone other than a circus strongman would have found him as difficult to heft as a stocked refrigerator. Yuri looked a decade older than his age, with blond hair shorn to a suede-like surface and a face as scarred as a butcher's chopping block.

Pascal, though, was by far the scariest looking of the two. The absence of his top lip meant that the cage of his long teeth eclipsed most of his other features, hanging from exposed gums like a necklace of metatarsals. Vitiligo added to his minacious appearance, pink islands floating on a black ocean of skin, and he possessed a powerful frame that was at odds with his bat-like head. Since coming to England he had developed an athletic body and now trod London's pavements with a boxer's swagger. Acting on a whim, he'd lately taken to varnishing his fingernails in lurid colours, hoping in some part to wrest a snide comment from his associate that never came.

With Yuri driving a stolen Toyota Land Cruiser, the two men toured the tree-lined roads of a prosperous part of Hackney, which were in sharp contrast to the streets in the concrete jungle where they lived.

Pascal bounced about hyperactively in his seat. "I like it. A lot of money here, yes, Yuri?"

Yuri merely tilted his head and blew a plume of cigarette smoke from his mouth; vocabulary, in his view, was an unnecessary chore. When they'd first arrived in the country Pascal mostly spoke Kirundi and colonial French and Yuri his native Ukrainian. Now they conversed in a Pidgin English forged on the unadorned streets hidden from London's tourists.

The big, ivy-clad vicarage on Sowerberry Road, with its arched windows and secluded position, caught their attention and prompted them to pull over for a better look. Yuri was also distracted by a smiling lady in a floral print dress who was returning to the vicarage after posting letters. He was hunching his bull neck to observe her in a side mirror when Pascal burst his deviant daydream.

"Look, Yuri," he sneered, while the cosmos eavesdropped

on their conversation. "We see here a happy family: a pretty mother, a fat little pig and his father, the priest."

The lady in the summer dress rejoined her family and at the same time cast a quizzical glance in their direction.

"Oh, so petite, Yuri. I think you like her, yes?" Pascal murmured.

The thinnest of smiles graced Yuri's cuboid face and he grunted in agreement, causing a feather of cigarette smoke to curl from his lips.

They remained in the car, absently watching the family milling about in their driveway when, most surprisingly, the rangy clergyman strode purposefully towards them, causing Yuri to grin with amusement. But so as not to precipitate conflict, he sharply woke the car's engine and steered away from the kerb.

See you later, my friend, Pascal mused, as he offered this impudent priest a mocking wave.

*

London had recently suffocated in the grip of a humid summer that brought with it air as thick as an ogre's breath. With storms forecast for later in the day, Florence made the most of the early sunshine to hang laundry on the line. Returning to the kitchen, she left the back door ajar so she could gather in the washing in the event of a sudden shower.

Once inside, she spotted something dark on the quarry-tiled floor. At rest against a skirting board, on its back with its little legs in the air, lay a recently deceased mouse. Bagheera, their cat, must have carried it in.

The mouse had, for some reason, met its death pulling a funny face at whosoever should discover it, which caused Florence to crack a wide smile. After slipping on a pair of rubber gloves, and with a great deal of care, she carried the rodent outside, granting it an unfussy burial and a personalised eulogy.

"Sleep, little one," she soothed in a liquid voice, "perchance to dream."

Her benediction done, she checked the sky. Although sunlight was still gliding across the lawn, an ominous mountain of dark cloud had risen in the distance. Without warning, the garden sprang to life. A sudden violent gust of wind shook trees and billowed Ulysses' trousers, causing them to flap their legs like dancing Cossacks. With the smell of jasmine in her nostrils, Florence righted upended flowerpots, tucked windblown hair behind her ears and scampered back to the kitchen.

In readiness for the task of making a chocolate cake for Henry's tenth birthday, she donned her favourite apron, the one with 'Kiss the Cook' emblazoned across it, and climbed upon a dining chair to reach the baking ingredients stowed in a high cupboard. She would have loved to organise a party for her son but, because of his widespread unpopularity, sadly there was no one to invite.

Bagheera slunk in unannounced, sprang onto the chair and began curling in and out of her legs, issuing an emphysemic purr.

"Come along, Baggy, you're getting in the way," Florence coaxed, prodding him with her foot.

Stepping down, she sensed a physical presence behind her. Anticipating that Ulysses had returned with the party balloons, she spun round with an expectant smile. Instead of her husband, there were two gloved men, the same ones she'd spotted in the black car. They sat themselves calmly and comfortably at the large dining table as if they were invited guests. Her heart flapped like a trapped bird and Bagheera shot out of the doorway.

"Get out! Get out!" Florence shrilled. "How bloody dare you come into our home uninvited!" The sharpness of her anger, though, was blunted by the alarm in her eyes.

Pascal giggled. The sound was high and bird-like, almost feminine.

"Lady, be nice," he said languidly. "It is my opinion that you are not being very friendly."

Still facing them and finding it hard to control her breathing, Florence surreptitiously felt for a large kitchen knife she knew was resting on the worktop behind her.

"Chaps, my handbag is in the hallway," she said evenly. "If you allow me to fetch it, I'll gladly give you all of the money in my purse."

Thinking on her feet, she made a cursory mental inventory of any household items that could be of some worth to them.

"Who say we want money?" asked Yuri, gruffly.

Terror rose inexorably from the pit of her stomach. "Now look, m-my husband will be home any minute." She glanced hastily over her shoulder. The knife was out of reach.

"Oh no, not your husband," Pascal chuckled, interlacing his fingers behind his head and leaning back so that only the chair's hind legs touched the floor. Yuri remained anchored to his seat, imposing as a sphinx.

Florence, in her desperation, weighed up her options but no solution that could have possibly worked sprang to mind. The stocky man's blue eyes bored into her, a cat studying a goldfish; cruelty dwelled in the African's beetle-dark stare. She realised that if she made for the back door, they'd cut her off easily. Her only hope was to pacify them.

"Guys, please, it's my son's birthday today. I just want to be left in peace to get on with the things that I need to do. I'm a good person, my husband is too. We truly only have love for people."

Pascal's eyes brightened. "That indeed is good, lady, but now you have seen our faces. How do I know you won't run to the police?" With that, he withdrew a sharpened machete from his jacket and placed it on the table. An unseen number of his Rwandan victims, ghostly and invisible, funnelled into the kitchen, electing either to dissolve into the fabric of the walls or bunch together in the ceiling.

At the sight of the machete a shockwave tore through Florence's body, forcing her heart to beat through her chest and her legs to buckle. Then the driveway woke to the maraca rattle of gravel under the tyres of her husband's car. Before she was able to scream out, Yuri had approached her, a lion upon an antelope, and clamped her mouth in a vice-like grip.

*

When Ulysses arrived home he half-expected the black Land Cruiser to be parked across the road again, so he was relieved to discover that it was nowhere to be seen. He stepped from the car and scrabbled to clasp the ribbons of four helium balloons that had grouped against the underside of the roof.

As he approached the front door, fumbling with keys, he heard the sound of breaking glass, followed by an almighty crash, emanating from the back of the house. Pascal had hurled the microwave oven through a kitchen windowpane, knowing that this would bring his prey running into a snare.

With balloons bobbing behind him, Ulysses dashed to the back door, where he was met by the sight of his wild-eyed wife swamped in the bear hug of the Eastern

European. Before he had time to assimilate this shocking reality, he registered a noise behind him. Pascal had crept from his hiding place in the garden and, with a savage swing of his machete, severed one of the vicar's Achilles tendons.

Ulysses threw his head back and bellowed like the Minotaur. His body spasmed and his fingers clawed in physical shock, releasing the balloons skyward. The Rwandan ghosts wailed from their spectral frieze and howled in consternation as their countryman continued his attack, swinging the heavy blade into the Englishman's other ankle and forcing him to collapse in an untidy heap in the doorway.

Florence writhed and kicked, her muffled screams barely leaking through her captor's gloved fingers while Bagheera yowled helplessly from a tree branch.

"Pascal! This is not plan," Yuri barked, his voice rumbling like a volcano. "Remember, we agree just rob this place. Not be stupid."

"But I do not like this piece of shit," Pascal griped, tapping his victim's head with the flat part of the blade. "Walking to the car like he is some kind of hero."

Yuri relinquished his hold on Florence, allowing her to rush tearfully to her husband who was writhing about in agony.

Ulysses pleaded from underneath her, as she desperately sought to shield him with her body. "Please … nnnng, please, argh. Please, please for the love of God don't hurt my wife."

Yuri, who had anticipated only a morning of rape and robbery, could see where this was headed and sought to dampen his associate's murderous intent. "Pascal, be smart. We make robbery and we go. Easy, yes?"

For a moment, Pascal's expression mellowed.

Yuri was relieved that his charge was becalmed and seemed ready to see sense. "We tie them up and we take what we can, yes?" Yuri reasoned. "We have not left DNA. We tell them if they describe our faces we come back to kill their boy. Good plan, I think."

Barely had the words left his lips when Pascal raised the machete over his head and hacked the blade some way into Florence's neck, screeching as he did so.

"No-o!" Yuri roared, but it was too late. A second and a third strike in quick succession saw the vicar and his wife horribly mutilated and mortally wounded.

"Fuck! You are fucking stupid!" Yuri shouted, taking care not to step into a spreading lake of the victims' blood as he stretched for the doorjamb. One of Florence's severed fingers, still wearing her wedding ring, slid silently down the wall.

Yuri stood on the outside looking in and grimly surveyed the scene, concerned about incriminating evidence. He pulled Pascal forcibly towards him, seeking to rescue the situation. "Hide that in jacket," he instructed, indicating the bloodied machete. "Do hood like this, same like we do when we arrive."

The men draped their hoods over their heads, tying the drawstrings to conceal their faces should any CCTV cameras capture their likeness. Then they fled the scene as storm clouds started to crawl across the sky.

While the tide of their fevered breath ebbed and flowed, Florence and Ulysses faded in each other's arms. A whirl of butterflies flittered about their bodies and the heavens grumbled high above. Their lives passed before them, death extinguishing final insensate memories of first kisses and childhood picnics until only the faintest whisper of their earthly love remained.

CHAPTER FOUR

There Are No Comets Seen

"Well done, Henry, you have been an absolute star," said the police detective, whose tie was tucked deep into his shirt. "You mark my words, we will catch these bastards."

Henry recalled that he'd earlier addressed the murderers as toe-rags, much to his father's disapproval. 'Bastards' seemed to him to be the very least they should be called given the circumstances.

The detectives at Hackney Metropolitan Police Station, working with a sketch artist, were tongue-tied with admiration for this tearful, doe-eyed pudding of a boy who, on his tenth birthday, spoke with such clarity about the two men he'd seen parked outside the vicarage; the same men who went on to slaughter his mother and father. Unable to recollect anything memorable about one of the bastards, he was at least able to describe the nightmarish black fellow and his skeleton teeth. No sooner had this verbal portrayal been given than the detectives were nodding at each other, instantly knowing who their man was. And, thanks to Henry's eloquence and keen memory for detail, the artist was able to sketch a compelling likeness of Pascal Makuza.

"Just got news that your grandparents are in the building, Henry," the lead investigator soothed. "They'll be with you real soon. In the meantime, can we get you anything?"

Henry, sitting despondently and hugging his hardback novel for comfort, barely managed to shake his head and instead continued to gaze at the floor. Then he wept bitterly for the umpteenth time that day.

*

Ulysses' grief-stricken parents, Constance and Leonard, were the first to put themselves forward for the role of Henry's guardians, given that Florence's bohemian parents had some years since upped sticks and emigrated to Bali. Because Henry had no immediate family to speak of, they were the most obvious appointees.

Constance Drummond was an extremely tall woman who drove a disproportionately small car. Leonard, whose eyes were as melancholic as a bloodhound's, was the proud owner of a grey walrus moustache that overspread a rather lugubrious mouth. Arriving at the police station, having driven through a torrential downpour, they were led by the senior detective to a room where Henry was in the care of a child welfare officer. Sitting forlornly in his duffle coat and clutching a scuffed leather satchel, he looked very much the human incarnation of Paddington Bear.

*

"Shouldn't take much more than an hour to get there, Henry," his grandfather shouted above the noise of rain and windscreen wipers, referencing the drive home to Epsom. It was an altogether claustrophobic journey, what with Henry squished against a large suitcase in the rear of their tiny car and his gangly grandmother cramped against the steering wheel, rather like a giant praying mantis.

With his mind in neutral, Henry thumbed through the pages of his book and gazed vacantly through rain-lashed windows.

His grandparents' house was a mock-Tudor affair, wooden-clad, with white stucco walls and spangled with leaded windows. The interior décor, in keeping with their marriage, was a manifestation of substance over style. Prior to collecting Henry, they'd passed through the police cordon at the vicarage to pack some of his belongings into the suitcase now accompanying him on the ride. Bagheera, they were told, was nowhere to be seen but they would of course be contacted should he ever turn up.

"Let's get you inside, Henry," Grandmother said stoically, her voice choking. "This is your home now."

Henry spent most of that evening sitting with his guardians, sipping mugs of hot chocolate while dutifully listening to their homespun attempts to offer support. It was all white noise as far as he was concerned; he writhed inwardly in the throes of overwhelming grief and they might just as well have been talking to him underwater. He either observed his grandmother's lips moving or insensibly studied the fine-lined whorls on his palms. More often than not, a solemn silence ensued where heads were collectively bowed and tears stifled.

When night fell, Henry asked to be excused so he could retire to bed. Pausing at the living room doorway and evoking the spirit of a desolate David Copperfield, he allowed a parting comment to hang plaintively in the air. "If it wasn't for you, Gran and Grandad, I would be all alone in the world and then where would I be?"

His allotted room was the same one that Ulysses had

occupied as a teenager. Of some comfort to Henry was the fact that much of his father's paraphernalia was still in residence. Sleep didn't arrive easily and was further hampered by an unseen bluebottle that feathered his nose and bugled in his ears. Wide awake, Henry slid from his bed and walked to the window, hoping to catch sight of his father and mother in the same way that he once looked out for Father Christmas and his reindeer.

"I miss you so much," he croaked, staring into the firmament, his voice strangled by tears. But only a luminescent moon hung, taciturn and lonely in the sullen sky. His parents were nowhere to be seen.

*

It was still blackboard dark when Henry woke to the crushing realisation that things had cruelly remained the same. Understanding this, he trawled the duvet over his head, curled himself into a foetal position and sobbed as quietly as he was able, not wishing to wake his grandparents.

After gaining some composure, he switched on a bedside lamp that barely fulfilled its effulgent purpose and sought solace in the quivering shadows of his father's room. Suspended in time, the air stirred to the echoes of teenage dreams and undefiled aspirations. Ulysses' memory was very much evident in this museum of sports trophies, dinosaur models, beer steins and musty books. An acoustic guitar plastered with Greenpeace stickers, an old favourite of his father's, stood poised in a far corner.

Henry slunk from the bed to clasp a framed photograph of his parents that his grandmother had placed on top of a chest of drawers. He touched the glass that encased their smiling faces in the hope of achieving some kind of necromantic connection, sorely regretting not kissing his mother when she'd last asked him to. Then, in the half-light, he talked to the stars and beseeched his parents to plan their miraculous return.

For the next hour, he padded about the fringes of the room in his pyjamas seeking comfort from anything that had once belonged to his father, inhaling the smell of cardigans, mothballed wardrobes, rugby shirts and fusty shoeboxes. His fingers found the main light switch, illuminating a room he hadn't had the heart to explore earlier. The walls were daubed with a dark-blue paint that formed the backdrop to a gallery of faded sci-fi posters, record sleeves and other ephemera. Pinned to a large corkboard was a miscellany of rock-concert tickets and a monochrome photograph copy of the ill-fated Captain Ulysses Drummond, with his moustachioed face and inescapable stare. Directly underneath was a faded photograph of two different medals: one, it was stated, was the Crimea Medal, the other a Military Cross.

The bluebottle had become trapped behind a curtain and was buzzing furiously. Henry opened the window and gently shepherded it into the cool morning air.

Cautiously, the flower of a new dawn bloomed in the distance; at the same time, a throat-clearing cough preceded a knock from the other side of the bedroom door.

"Henry, we heard you moving around. May I come in?" his grandfather asked, his shadow shambling in the light that stole under the door.

"Oh, sure," answered Henry.

Leonard skulked into the room as if he were walking barefoot on broken glass. "How are you, my boy?"

"Uh, I'm OK," Henry shrugged.

"Now then, the bathrooms are both free should you need to freshen up. Then we'll see you downstairs for breakfast. That's if you're up to eating anything—"

"Grandfather, whose are these medals?" Henry asked.

"Ah, one was awarded to your ancestor, Captain Drummond, after the Crimean War. The other belonged to your father, not that he ever showed any interest in it."

Henry, despite his grief, was fascinated. "Um, and where are the medals now?"

"Oh, in a drawer, safely tucked away, my boy. You're very welcome to have them. A keepsake of sorts, I suppose."

"I'd like that," said Henry softly, showing the first shoots of recovery.

"Then they're yours," his grandfather smiled, camouflaging his own sorrow. "I shall fetch them just as soon as we've all eaten breakfast."

*

Florence who, together with her husband, had posthumously spent the entire night keeping a watchful eye on their son, was now on the far side of the world, unable to feel the sea breeze that jangled the wind chimes on her parents' Balinese veranda. She so wished that she could kiss them, wrap her arms around their shoulders and thus liberate them from their grief. Instead, all she could do was observe the loneliness of their anguish as they lay huddled together on a bed swing under a quivering mosquito net.

*

Just as Henry was leaving his bedroom, he felt sure he heard the distinct twang of a guitar chord being strummed and stopped in his tracks. Standing as still as a gecko, he listened intently but only silence reigned. Concluding that he must have imagined it, he continued his walk to the bathroom.

CHAPTER FIVE

The Four Horsemen of the Acropolis

2008

Shortly after his eleventh birthday, and a year after his parents' funeral, Henry awaited his first day at an all-boys' boarding school with the same sense of dread that condemned men take to the guillotine.

St Jude's College, founded in 1879 and named after the patron saint of lost causes, was a large Gothic structure with its own chapel. It was originally intended for the education of the sons of middle-class Anglican clergymen and was the choice of Leonard, who had boarded there in the 1950s. Ulysses, similarly induced, was also schooled at St Jude's prior to his training at the Sandhurst Royal Military Academy.

Henry and his grandparents had recently been given a tour of the campus by the llama-faced bursar, Mr Panmure, a man blighted with the canker of bitter disdain.

"All animals are equal, but some animals are more equal than others," he bleated, quoting Orwell, his cleverness impressing nobody but himself. Dressed in a tweed gamekeeper jacket most notable for its ink-stained breast pocket, he held court in his fusty office, speaking in clipped sentences, never once allowing Constance and Leonard to finish a question. He was also a man fond of using Latin words where plain English ones would have sufficed.

"You'll be interested to learn that my great-grandfather once played against a visiting cricket team captained by Sir Arthur Conan Doyle," he boasted in his cut-glass voice, wafting a bony hand vaguely in the direction of the sports field.

Henry could tell by the frosty look on his grandmother's face that she wasn't interested and that she would have loved to hit Mr Panmure about his elongated head with Conan Doyle's cricket bat. Irked by his mournful arrogance, she was keen to get a word in edgeways.

"I'm sure that Henry will be a credit to the school," she ventured.

"Quite," Panmure sneered.

"Quite?" she queried, fixing him with an icy stare and drumming her fingernails on his desk.

"Mrs Drummond, it is my firm belief that if Henry applies himself whilst he is here, and does precisely what he is told, then he might one day be deserving of his place in this estimable institution."

"One day? How dare you?! He's fully deserving of his place already," she bristled.

Gnawing the air with his brown teeth, Mr Panmure remained inexorable. "And to that, madam, I would say, *labor omnia vincit*. This, you might wish to know, means 'hard work conquers all'."

Constance's nostrils began to flare. "And to that I would reply, *maxima voce vas vacuum fecit*. This, you might wish to know, means 'an empty vessel makes the loudest sound'. Good day, Mr Panmure!" With that, she shot from her seat with the rapidity of a dolphin leaping from the sea and stormed off, leaving Henry and Leonard to follow in her wake.

Henry noticed that when his grandmother drove from the school that day, her car seemed to be even less capable of accommodating her long limbs. It was almost as if her bitter dislike for Mr Panmure and his maddening monologues had puffed her up like a prawn cracker. Henry heard her spit words that he couldn't readily find in his pocket dictionary, so he surreptitiously wrote them down for further investigation. Leonard, with more sangfroid than his wife, sat quietly and wondered if all mention of the reputable Drummond name might now be struck off the school register.

"How dare he?" Constance fumed. "The contemptible, pompous prig! If I have any say in the matter, Henry, you will not be returning to that vipers' pit ever again."

Henry didn't answer and instead heaved a quiet sigh of relief.

Yet now, a month later and in a complete turnaround of events, Constance was extolling the virtues of the school to Henry as she drove her tiny car along the tree-lined driveway on his inaugural day. Behind the scenes, Leonard had somehow persuaded her not to break from the proud family tradition of Drummond boys attending St Jude's.

"Be careful not to recite poetry in the presence of your contemporaries, Henry, as they're hardly likely to share your enthusiasm," Constance cautioned.

As a coping mechanism, Henry had taken to comfort eating cheese triangles directly from their foil wrappers, but all too soon the fearsome building was upon them, looming like the Parthenon. Having recently read *Tom Brown's Schooldays,* Henry immediately envisaged himself being roasted in front of an open fire by a Flashmanesque character dressed in a tailcoat. He recalled on his tour of the school an abundance of closed oak doors, all with the same ominous look about them, and arrived at the realisation that no amount of processed cheese triangles was going to quell his fears.

Fidgeting with the biscuit crumbs in his trouser pockets, he noticed with cursory interest that the huge building boasted more brick chimneys than there were funnels on the *Titanic* and began to feel nostalgic about his former school, even though everyone there disliked him.

Constance parked in front of the school's pillared entrance and secretly doubted that Henry would last a week in such a place. "Keep smiling, Henry," she chirped, seeking to lift his spirits, "and you will be sure to make lots of new friends."

Constance was a pragmatic woman who made a virtue of recovering from life's tragedies with the minimum of fuss. She saw some benefit in moving on from her son and daughter-in-law's murder and had encouraged her grandson to do the same. It was with this precept in mind that she saw Henry off with the briefest of hugs and an airy wave. She then watched him struggle with his suitcase, cutting a lumpen, forlorn figure until he disappeared from plain view, brusquely shepherded into the main hallway by the odious Mr Panmure.

*

For the continuance of their time at the school, the pupils were divided into house groups, each one numbering approximately forty boys. These were named after a clutch of historical British war heroes and Henry was summarily enrolled into Nelson House.

In due course, despite unnaturally smiling at everyone as if his young life depended on it, the only friend he made that day was Bertie Cheng, a bespectacled Chinese boy who had also spent his entire first day beaming at all and sundry in the faint hope of kindred fellowship. After exchanging pleasantries, Henry swiftly discovered that Bertie was one of those boys who started almost every conversation with the word 'so'.

"So, my parents are in Hong Kong," Bertie explained. "So I'm in England all on my own."

"Mine are both dead," Henry countered, as glum as a fish. "I guess that makes us both orphans of some kind or another."

"So, omigod, how did they die? Like, that must have been awful for you."

"Yes, Bertie, *awful* is the perfect adjective. They were, um, murdered in cold blood, but unfortunately their killers were never brought to justice."

Henry went on to explain that no one had been jailed for their deaths, despite the police knowing only too well who the perpetrators were. Pascal Makuza and, by association, Yuri Voloshyn were brought in for questioning and placed in custody but the absence of any substantial evidence, and the fact they supplied corroborated alibis, meant that the police were forced to drop all charges against them.

"When I'm older, Bertie, I intend to see that these savages get what they deserve," vowed Henry, though he didn't the vaguest idea how he might one day put such an ambitious plan into action.

After eating dinner in the communal dining hall,

Henry and his new-found friend strolled about the lawned grounds in the failing light, discussing everything from literature to *Star Trek*. Henry was delighted to discover that Bertie had mastered the Klingon language with the same fervour that Muslims learn the Quran. In addition, his friend was indiscriminately friendly with everyone he met and had the kind of smile that would brighten the gloomiest of days.

Unfortunately, the realm of their quietude was about to be besieged. Towards them, with three cohorts in tow, strode Sebastian Fox-Gudgeon, the most conceited and over-privileged twelve year old ever to wear the school's burgundy blazer. Sebastian, who was starting his second year at the school, had earlier identified Henry as being a person he would rather like to humiliate. Here was Henry's Flashman brought to life.

"Hey! New boy! I need to have a word with you," Sebastian brayed with his customary air of entitlement, flicking back a flop of preppy hair.

"Um, w-who me?" Henry stuttered, with the sinking realisation that it was he, and not Bertie, who was being addressed.

"Yes, of course you. Wow, aren't you just a fat thing? What's your name, boy?"

"Um, Henry. Henry Drummond."

Henry optimistically offered a speculative handshake, which was casually ignored. Before he could ask the boys their names, he was being talked over.

"We have a first day tradition at this school, Drummond, the tradition being that we baptise any new boys by throwing them into that pond over there. You are a new boy, therefore we will be chucking you into the pond."

Swamps of perspiration appeared under each of

Henry's armpits. This wasn't quite the warm reception his grandparents had cheerily told him to expect; in addition, he was becoming more than a little annoyed by the older boy's unwarranted belligerence.

"Why the heck would you want to throw me into a pond?" he asked, his hackles raised.

"Just think of us as the Four Horsemen of the Acropolis, Drummond."

"It's the Apocalypse."

"What?"

"It's the Four Horsemen of the Apocalypse, you dimwit."

"Whatever."

Then, without further ado, the boys manhandled Henry, dragged him kicking and yelling to the edge of the pond and, on the count of three, hurled him into its malodorous water. Henry scrabbled to the bank, splashing and spluttering, wondering why on earth someone would want to do such a wicked thing.

"Ha! Welcome to St Jude's," Sebastian chuckled, while at the same time high-fiving his boot-licking sidekicks.

"You're still a dimwit!" bleated Henry, his voice falsetto as he tried to fight back tears.

"Hey! Was that absolutely necessary?" Bertie shouted at the bullies with noble outrage. "Henry's mother and father were murdered only a year ago."

"I really couldn't give less of a shit," Sebastian chuckled. Then, to chasten Bertie for his opposition, the Four Horsemen of the Acropolis launched him into the pond as well.

*

That evening, having both suffered mild stomach upsets from swallowing pond water, Bertie and Henry were sent to Mrs Murphy, the school matron, for a check-up.

"Ah yes, Sebastian Fox-Gudgeon," she sighed. "Keep him at arm's length, boys. He's as tricky as a reel of Sellotape that one."

CHAPTER SIX

Who Lifteth the Veil of What Is to Come?

Facing the shimmering majesty of the Taj Mahal at the first wink of dawn, Florence and Ulysses sat together upon the same white marble bench that supported Princess Diana's bottom during a famous photo shoot back in 1992. Their human consciousness had continued into death but not the physicality of their earthly bodies, which continued to rot in the ground. Therefore they were unable to feel the warmth of the Indian sun, even though it was already hot enough to evaporate the clouds in a mackerel-skinned sky. Nevertheless, the two were able to gaze upon the mausoleum and its perfect reflection in the mirror of the central canal.

"We often said that we'd come here one day, though I never pictured it as being under such unusual circumstances," said Ulysses, placing a weightless arm across Florence's spectral shoulders.

"How tremendously beautiful it is," his wife remarked,

as an orange-hued butterfly danced about her mirage, as if to steal her secrets.

"Whoa, that is truly amazing," said Ulysses. "Even now the butterflies enjoy your company."

The complex was closed to the public today and only a small team of gardeners were present, clipping hedges and sweeping leaf cuttings into rattan baskets. Florence patted her husband's intangible hand and silently rehearsed the same thorny question that had so often caught in her throat. "Darling, do you not think that perhaps it's time we moved on to the next phase? Henry has his own life to lead and we're of no use to him anyway."

"Yes, the thought has crossed my mind, of course," Ulysses admitted, furrowing his brow. "Thing is, I promised faithfully on the day he was born that I would be there for him always. We really must stay together, Florence. We need to keep watch over Henry."

"But in the meantime we're trapped in this other dimension because of your stubbornness, when common sense and nature tells us to head for the light, which I should imagine is what everybody else does."

"Florence, please let's not argue. I truly believe that God himself will come to guide us."

"But you also believe that he's going to come to you with a mane of white hair and a Leonardo Da Vinci beard. Just think about how unrealistic that sounds."

"I'm sure that people said much the same to poor old Moses, back in the day. Faith is not like a raincoat, only to be worn on drizzly days."

Florence stilled him with a fierce look. "Ulysses, you exasperate me as much in death as you did in life and your flippancy isn't helping matters."

"I know, I know, but please trust me on this one for just a little longer."

Florence fixed him with her Mona Lisa eyes and raised an eyebrow to let him know that he needed to give this matter some serious thought. Then, with a seismic shudder, the bench and the ground beneath their feet fell away, dissolving to reveal an ocean of stars. The Taj Mahal, along with its central canal and geometric gardens, folded in on itself and disintegrated into the vastness of the galaxy. Florence and Ulysses, touched by the kiss of Heaven, once again found themselves within the corridor of the Aurora Borealis, walking on nebulae and heading toward a mesmeric phosphorescence of celestial light.

CHAPTER SEVEN

The Girl with the Butterfly Tattoo

Five years later: December 2013

Beneath a low, milky fog, a sparkle of winter frost veneered the lawns of St Jude's. The oak trees had shed their leaves, revealing the inky thumbprints of crows' nests in the crackle glaze of dark branches. And it was against the backdrop of these denuded trees, and into the teeth of an icy wind, that Henry walked alongside Bertie, each snorting plumes of powdery breath from their nostrils as if they were blazered dragons.

"So, I shan't miss the cold when I'm in Hong Kong next week," said Bertie, blowing into his hands, his teeth rattling like castanets.

"And I'm really not looking forward to this presentation today," Henry grimaced, hugging a leather-bound copy of *Crime and Punishment* to his chest.

Henry, now aged sixteen, had finally grown into his chunky frame, sprouting both upwards and outwards until he resembled a lumbering bear. Upon his spotty chin there existed a paddy field of wispy hairs, each barely as long as a cow's eyelash, and his diction had grown more suited to the modern age; sharing a dormitory with a cauldron of boys has a way of forcing even the most unsociable of fellows to be less standoffish. In the same intervening years, Bertie had not only become captain of the school chess club but approached theoretical physics projects with a zeal that would have bested Sir Isaac Newton. Though self-confident and garrulous in the cloistered seclusion of each other's company, the boys remained taciturn and uncertain in the public domain.

Books had given wings to Henry's mind, and today he was due to receive a prize for winning the prestigious Young Fictioneer Short Story Competition, in the fifteen-to-seventeen age category. He'd speculatively written a sci-fi yarn about an Englishman who falls asleep in his London flat but then impossibly wakes up in a similarly sized apartment in Barcelona. Although he was somewhat embarrassed by the piece, the judges had loved it and unanimously declared it to be their worthy winner.

This was the last day before the winter break, which meant that there were no lessons to attend. Henry had brought his father's war medal into school for the week so that he could flourish it in Ulysses' memory at the end of his acceptance speech. And, although excited that one of his literary heroes, renowned sci-fi author Fergus Munro, would be on hand to present the award, Henry was nervous at the prospect of having to speak in front of the entire school.

"So, I can't believe that you'll be actually meeting Fergus Munro," Bertie gasped. "He and Neil Gaiman are my heroes. You must introduce me, although I'll most probably get tongue-tied in his presence."

"You and me both," Henry replied, pulling a panicked face.

Once inside the warmth of their oak-panelled dormitory, Bertie and Henry shook themselves like ducks, unwound their scarves and hung their blazers on hangers. Bertie rubbed his frozen hands together briskly as if he might ignite a small blaze.

"Hey, Bertie, I don't think that I've shown you my father's medal."

"Medal?"

"Awarded for bravery," said Henry proudly, turning to the locked drawer by his bed.

"Cool. Let me see it," his friend marvelled, keen to view it at close quarters.

But to Henry's horror, it was clear that the drawer in question had been forced open. "No, no, no-o!"

"What?"

"My father's medal … someone has filched it!"

"So, it's gone?"

"Yes, it's bloody well gone. What the hell? I seriously do not believe this!"

*

Sebastian Fox-Gudgeon stepped from the pawnbroker's shop, blazer hooked over one shoulder and £100 of cash in his hand. He knew via a Google search that the medal was worth a great deal more but hadn't wanted to be too greedy.

"You are quite the cash cow, Henry," he said out loud to no one but himself and kissed the banknotes as if they were a hard-earned sports trophy.

*

The award presentation descended into farce as the secretive Irish author Fergus Munro, whose real identity was possibly only known to his family and publisher, addressed his giggling audience disguised in a floppy fedora, dark glasses and a joke-shop moustache that worked loose and jigged about his top lip like a leaf caught in a cobweb.

To Mr Panmure's annoyance Munro cracked a risqué joke, which caused the assemblage to laugh even louder, and then went on to make it abundantly clear that he had enjoyed Henry's story.

"Let me tell you, I know published authors who can't write as well as this lad," he declared passionately, to which the whole school cheered and stomped their feet as if attending a rally for world peace.

Once the ceremony had run its course and the local news photographer had taken his last shot, Henry was surrounded by a small posse of pupils intent on congratulating him. Despite their laudation, his lumpish lips were deeply downturned, causing many to remark that he bore some resemblance to one of those sad circus clowns.

"Good God, Drummond, what's up with you?" exclaimed Sebastian, with a flash of perfect teeth and a flick of his mane. "You look as if you've fallen into a bucket of tits and have come out sucking your thumb."

"So, someone has stolen his father's war medal," explained Bertie.

"Ah, I see. Hmm, a valid reason to be glum. Tell you what, Henry, how about I treat you to a fast-food lunch? Try to cheer you up, eh?"

Henry was stirred from his despondency by this unexpected act of human kindness. Sebastian only ever addressed him by his first name when he wanted something and, despite the boy's father being a wealthy stockbroker,

Henry had never seen him dip into his pocket for anything other than a handkerchief.

"Thank you, Sebastian, that's very kind," he said guardedly.

"Not at all. Come along, Cheng, I'll pay for you too. You freaks have caught me in a generous mood today."

Henry and Bertie shared a quizzical look, not quite believing what they were hearing.

It was Sebastian's idea to eat at the Burger Wizard restaurant, which was easy to reach via a short cut through the woods and a scramble over a drooping section of the perimeter fence. The route was a dank, foul-smelling one, a clandestine rat run caked in leaf mulch and littered with crushed beer cans and muddied porn magazines.

"Sebastian, I'm not altogether sure that this is a good proposal," said Henry, knowing that unless you were in the school rugby team it was not a sensible idea to venture into a popular fast-food restaurant wearing the St Jude's blazer.

"Why?"

"Because any number of brutes from the high school would love to beat us up, that's why," Henry reasoned, while Bertie nodded in tacit agreement.

"Nonsense," snapped Sebastian, encouraged by the sound of his own voice. "What would we be if we allowed the hoi polloi to dictate where we come and go?" With that, he strode through the diner's plate-glass doors with the resolve of a crusader, his two lunch guests following on nervously.

"I am nothing if not misanthropic," declared Sebastian as they set an abundance of packaged food on a Formica table top.

"I think you mean philanthropic," said Henry.

"God, you are so perdantic."

"That would be pedantic."

"See! You're even perdantic about the word perdantic."

As expected, the volume of Sebastian's privileged enunciation caught the ears of two teenage boys and a girl who immediately began to stare coldly in their direction.

"Oh look, the plebs have taken their snouts out of their troughs," Sebastian declared loudly.

"Sebastian! Could you please keep your voice down?" implored Henry, his voice lowered to a hissing whisper. At the same time he couldn't help but gawp at the beautiful girl with her hip clothes, Gothic eye makeup and woollen beanie hat. The girl smiled back, still managing to retain her badass stare.

"Whatchu lookin' at posh boy?" barked one of the lads, jabbing a hand that featured a gaudy ring on each finger.

"Er ... um, nothing," Henry blustered. At the same time, Bertie fixedly gazed into his milkshake carton as if it contained all the unknown secrets of the universe. Henry decided to employ the same tactic and tried to become invisible, but the boy was suddenly at their table, staring straight into his terrified face.

"You throwin' shade my way, bruv?"

"Um, um, I don't even know what that means."

"You takin' the piss, posh boy?"

"No, absolutely not. I come in peace."

The girl's black-lipstick smile widened; a stud piercing in her nose caught the light.

Sebastian, who had become uncommonly quiet, had somehow managed to sidle out of the exit unnoticed and was hoofing it up the pavement like an Olympic sprinter. In the meantime, the other delinquent had sprung to his feet with eyes blazing.

"You two are taking proper liberties, innit?" he stormed. "I'm gonna slap you rich boys stupid."

Bertie and Henry, despite having the athleticism of hedgehogs, scrambled for the door. Bertie, squawking like a terrified hen, managed to escape his pursuers by suicidally racing across a main road that was alive with speeding traffic. Henry, though, had only managed to trot the length of the restaurant's car park before he was out of breath and in need of his inhaler. He gave up on his hapless getaway and instead decided to have a lie down on the tarmac, where he was captured by the girl.

"I got this!" she shouted across to her friends in the middle distance. They stopped in their tracks. "Pretend I'm hurting you," she whispered.

"Huh?"

"Pretend I'm hurting you, you geek, otherwise they'll come over and they *will* hurt you."

She proceeded to lay siege to his body, pulling her kicks so that there was barely any venom in them.

"Aghh, you *are* hurting me," Henry squealed, rolling about on the ground as she continued her simulated assault. "Not the face! Not the face!" he shrilled.

After one final toe punt into his buttocks, she exhaled a puff of breath and threw him a secret smile. He noticed, peeking through trembling fingers, that her cheeks were as speckled as a robin's egg.

"You did great," she said, with a furtive wink of her vampirish eyes.

Henry, who was on his back resembling an upended turtle, caught a glimpse of a butterfly tattoo on the girl's exposed midriff. The sky above was an atlas of clouds and the sun radiated behind her head like Krishna's halo.

"You're cute. We must do this again sometime," she breezed, before scampering off to join her friends.

An unnatural smile spread across Henry's face. It seemed to him that this young lady was a heroine straight out of a cyberpunk comic. She'd unlocked from deep within something he had never known existed and, for the first time in his abstemious life, he was stupefied by infatuation.

CHAPTER EIGHT

Till It Be Morrow

"Promise me that we'll meet on the other side, darling, and please let it be soon," urged Florence, no longer able to ignore the compelling draw of the light.

"I promise," said Ulysses, as the leaden chains of despondency dragged across his being. He looked into the celestial sphere hoping for divine intervention but all he saw was a crescent moon, idly reposing in its silver hammock.

Ulysses could hardly blame his wife. For six years their nomadic, spectral existence had flown in the face of natural progression and it was as instinctive to step into the light as it was for a newborn baby to suckle. Besides, Florence wanted to reunite with her grandparents and to once again hug her best friend Poppy, whose unaccompanied death had haunted her for so long. As things stood, Ulysses and Florence were no more real to each other than reflections in a mirror.

Drawn by the same geomagnetic forces that guide salmon to their birthplace, Florence stepped from an ocean of phantasmal darkness into a hallway of iridescent light.

Howling like a tempest, a legion of tortured souls lamented her departure. She looked back at Ulysses, at first with a countenance of despair but then with an air of serenity. And in the blink of an eye she was gone.

CHAPTER NINE

Execution Dock

East London: 2017

Natasha Shaw woke to find herself bound and gagged, her brain peculiarly slow to comprehend the danger she was in. Cloaked in absolute darkness, she was drowsily aware of vehicular movement and the drone of engine noise; there was also the unexpected stench of motor oil that filled her nostrils and seeped into her lungs.

Now that the sedative effect of the propofol in her bloodstream was starting to wear off, she came to the terrifying realisation that she was somehow trussed and held captive in the back of a moving van. Panicked, she wondered how long she'd been here. Minutes? Hours? The flashbacks came in fits and starts: her car – the African devil with the horrific teeth – his leather gloves – a hypodermic syringe.

Then all at once, in the present, there was silence. The vehicle she was being transported in had stopped. Her hearing was sharpened and each sound bled into her consciousness. She heard hushed voices and the screech of a gull, followed by the rattle and hum of what sounded like an automated roller shutter. The engine restarted and there was further movement for a few more seconds before the unseen shutter whirred and clattered once again.

The van doors were yanked open, flooding her coop with a jarring brightness that shrank her pupils. Natasha twisted her supine body, saw the filthy mattress she'd been lying on and caught a second glimpse of the African maniac who had ambushed her earlier. Another man appeared, the driver of the van, and she was immediately unnerved by the faint smile on his stony face. She could sense that this thug, like her husband, enjoyed seeing terror in a person's eyes.

The man flattened a fly that had settled on the van's interior light and, in its demise the insect, as delicate as a blown filament, flickered its last memory of flight.

*

In the ten years since realising they could actually get away with murder, Pascal and Yuri had added contract killing to their list of nefarious activities. Within the criminal underworld their reputation as men who could be relied upon to get the job done grew exponentially with each clinical execution.

Their target, Natasha Shaw, was the perma-tanned wife of Frankie 'The Dentist' Shaw, a wealthy East End gangster boss whose violent rise to power had earned him more enemies than friends. The Albanian mafia, not realising that he customarily wore a bulletproof vest under his Savile Row suits, had already failed in their attempt to murder Frankie in broad daylight and decided to target his wife instead. It was expressly requested that Natasha be defiled at the time of her murder and that photographic evidence of this be sent to her husband.

Yuri and Pascal had rented a small lockup warehouse in Wapping, East London, where they stored contraband and stolen goods. It had also become a useful place to torture people without their screams being heard. The warehouse was near the Thames, not far from the site where fifteenth-century pirates were once hanged at Execution Dock, their ropes deliberately shortened to induce them to dance for the crowds like marionettes, kicking their legs until they met their maker.

*

Earlier on the day of Natasha's capture, twenty miles away from their lockup, the men had tailed her white Range Rover at an inconspicuous distance until she turned into the one-track country road that led to her palatial home in Harold Wood. Yuri paid scant attention to Pascal's incessant chatter and drove with a look of grim determination, his calloused hands strangling the steering wheel. This was their golden opportunity, nothing around them but trees and fields. Polka dots of poppies, scarlet against green, lined the grass verges, a sight better suited to poetry books than a kidnapping. The killers were pumped with adrenaline and excited by the prospect of what was soon to come.

"Oh, you have got to be bloody kidding me!" shouted Natasha into her rear-view mirror as the grimy van behind her shunted the back of her Range Rover. Without a second thought, she pulled over to a mudded, tyre-flattened part of the verge and killed the engine.

The passenger from the van, grotesque-looking and probably African, was already out of the vehicle and approaching with a penitent look on his unpleasant face.

No sooner had her window whirred down than Natasha was giving him a piece of her mind. "What the hell were you two idiots doing? This wouldn't have happened if your mate hadn't driven so bloody close."

"Sorry, so sorry, Madame," the man muttered, nearing her door.

The hedgerows, silent until now, anxiously rustled their leaves and began to whisper warnings while tremulous clouds scurried behind treetops and birds trembled in the trees. Natasha noticed with sudden alarm that there was a ragged line of pink scar tissue where the man's top lip used to be and, in that same moment, a hypodermic syringe flashed into view. His gloved hand moved quick as a cobra strike and the needle was jabbed efficiently, deep into her arm, before she had time to react.

Invisible to the human eye, Ulysses stood on the grass verge in the jittery company of Pascal's Rwandan ghosts. He, of course, found that he was every bit as powerless to intervene as they were and had no option but to watch the men drag the woman's limp body to their van. Despite roaring at the universe and beseeching his god to grant him some human ability, his protestations went unanswered.

*

Still lying on the dirty mattress inside the van, Natasha's terrified eyes peered out at the brightly lit warehouse, looking for clues as to why she was a prisoner to these two men.

His shadow falling upon her, the burly one clambered into the van, rocking it on its suspension. He was breathing heavily, his stale breath reeking of cigarettes and vodka. The percussion of Natasha's heart drummed loud inside her skull and the distant echoes of nails being driven into scaffolds ghosted into the warehouse. Wielding a large hunting knife, the man cut away the duct tape that bound her legs and loosened the gag, which she spat from her mouth.

"Frankie will kill you for this," she raged, assuming that these men must have at least some idea who her husband was. Rather than alarm him, her threat elicited a quiet chuckle from his hulking silhouette. She grimaced and squealed under his weight as knees as hard as sledge hammers pinned her ankles to the mattress. Cold steel touched her thighs as the man cut the dress away from her body with his knife. She desperately wanted to shove him in the chest and claw at his face but her wrists were still tightly leashed together.

The African peered into the van in the way that someone would casually regard a hot-dog stand, vitiligo giving his skin the mottled hue of a lobster shell.

"Your husband, he cannot help you," Pascal hissed, cradling a fire extinguisher in his arms. "You see, I like to kill, and my friend here, he likes to *rape*." The word crept from his mouth like a lizard.

Yuri, holding Natasha's phone in his meaty hand grunted, "What is passcode?"

"W-what?" she stuttered, her mind scrambled.

Her failure to answer prompted Yuri to slap her hard across the face. "The passcode for phone. I will not ask again."

"Oh-h, it's one, nine, seven, four."

After noting down the numbers Pascal, whose proclivities had never included carnal desire, sat on a folding chair and listened to rap music through headphones as his associate battered and sodomised their sacrificial lamb in the back of the van.

When Yuri was done, he dragged the traumatised

woman from the vehicle and discarded her on the concrete floor where death sniffed at her broken body. Then he took explicit photographs of her with her own phone, the tattered dress ruched up above her naked waist. These would be shared with the gold-toothed gangster bosses who had hired them and would also be texted to Frankie Shaw's personal phone. Sweating and out of breath, Yuri then used his own mobile to call the Body Snatcher, a man who specialised in the disposal of dead bodies.

Pascal, who had lapsed into a lassitude of boredom until this point, promptly came alive. With a ghoulish smile on his face, he doused the woman with petrol as she begged for mercy then he switched on an industrial extractor fan and reached into a green canvas bag for his blowtorch.

"Body Snatcher is on way," Yuri announced, as casually as if he'd ordered a pizza.

*

London was under a canopy of darkness by the time the Body Snatcher prepared to leave the warehouse. He punched in the key code, his grisly cargo already bagged up and thrown into the back of his van. Yuri and Pascal trusted him enough to lock up and had earlier taken their leave after paying him the agreed sum of cash.

Under a thin crescent moon that hung like a toenail clipping in the night sky, the man was relieved to rinse his lungs with the damp, brackish air that drifted in from the Thames. He wasn't best pleased that his nostrils, skin and clothes were polluted by the smoky, charcoaled climate of the warehouse; it was an unnecessary add-on to the precise list of things that he had to deal with.

As a phlegmatic man, predisposed to discipline and diligence, he was less than enamoured by the African's incautious method of execution. Setting fire to a victim was as messy as it was inefficient; in his view, a loose cannon such as Pascal was a serious liability in his line of work. Yuri, on the other hand, was more measured and clinical, a person that the Body Snatcher could at least do business with. In truth he intensely disliked both men but the risk-to-reward ratio was weighted solidly in his favour.

Those two donkeys would've probably dumped the body in the river, he thought as he drove towards Tower Bridge against a glimmer of luxury wharfside apartment blocks lit up like cruise ships above the black mirror of the Thames.

*

Once his initial irritation at not being able to get in contact with his wife had remoulded itself into consternation, Frankie Shaw instructed his chauffeur to drive him home from a restaurant he owned in London's West End. The illuminated dome of St Paul's Cathedral moved slowly by in the city's passing nightscape as a stream of red and yellow lights drizzled across the windscreen and roof of his black Bentley.

"I got a bad fucking feeling about this, George," he muttered, loosening his tie. "Tash never takes this fucking long to answer her phone."

Because the capital was placed under a threat level of 'severe' after recent terror attacks, there was a strong police presence in Central London. Distracted by all that was happening, neither Frankie nor his driver spotted the Albanian hitman who was tailing them inconspicuously on a motorcycle.

Frankie heard his phone ping and was relieved at first to see that finally it was a message from Natasha. Not yet aware of the devastating content of the text, and of the fact that he would also be dead before the night was through, Frankie Shaw opened the first of four photo attachments.

CHAPTER TEN

Voltaire

Four lonely years had elapsed since Ulysses had watched his wife walk into the sanctuary of light, drawn by the reins of time through a whirl of butterflies. Thereafter, he'd had to contend with the maddening susurration of lost souls as they rustled past like leaves in a wind. He'd failed to keep his family together and the weight of God's silence tested the vestiges of his faith. Indeed, it began to dawn on him that his wait for God was every bit as misguided as Madame Butterfly's wait for Pinkerton.

Bagheera had meanwhile died from a liver tumour and unexpectedly appeared at Ulysses' feet one day, his only companion as he traversed the galaxy in godforsaken isolation. With a vagrant's aimlessness, Ulysses negotiated the extremities of the Earth's globe, hearing the whispers of lost souls in mountain ranges and the howls of men drowned at sea. He sought solace by returning to the tranquil confines of St Cuthbert's church and, like Ebenezer Scrooge, gazed upon his own gravestone.

Now, moving as near to the light as he dared, there suddenly opened up in front of him a brightly lit aquarium, as expansive as an ocean, that stretched higher and further than his eyes could see. In advance of this, spreading rapidly under his feet, was a marble floor that soundlessly continued to extend into infinity. Upon this polished surface, an endless array of brightly coloured armchairs and sofas appeared from nowhere. Marine life of all sizes, from plankton through to blue whales, swam in the vastness of the aquarium, filling the air with a lament of subterranean echoes.

Ulysses sank into a chair, bathed in blue, rippling light. He was gathering his thoughts when a man, dressed in eighteenth-century finery, approached him with an impish smile upon his powdered face.

"*Bonjour*, Ulysses, ça va?"

Ulysses, though bewildered, stood to receive the gentleman, who greeted him with an extravagant air kiss to each cheek. He knew French well enough to reply with a bewildered, "*Je vais bien merci, et vous*?"

"Oh, we can dispense with the French, my dear Ulysses," continued the man, who wore a shoulder-length Cavalier-style wig and whose face radiated a great intelligence. "My command of the English language is sufficient, having once spent some time in your noble country. Please allow me to introduce myself: I am François-Marie Arouet, though you might know me better as Voltaire."

"Really? Voltaire?" mumbled Ulysses, slumping back onto the seat, all at once awestruck to be in the presence of such an historical icon.

"At your service," twinkled the Frenchman, lowering his head like a courtier and flicking back his coat tails to sit opposite. "So, tell me. What do you think of your surroundings?"

"Completely and utterly astonishing. It's just beyond words—"

"But not beyond your imagination, Ulysses. All of this is but your own vision. None of this exists. Illusion is the first of all pleasures, my friend."

"Doesn't exist?" Ulysses spluttered.

"Of course not. All that exists is yonder. For you, Paradise awaits." Voltaire leaned forward on one elbow. "Allow me to say, Ulysses, that I, as an angel, have been designated to appeal to you lest you make a most terrible mistake."

"You're an angel?"

"An archangel, no less."

"But I've been waiting—"

"Yes, but waiting for what, or whom, exactly?"

"For a message from God."

"Ha! So there we have it. A good man held back by the shackles of earthly belief."

Ulysses' eyes glazed over for a moment, as if he were communing with spirits. "So you're telling me that God doesn't exist?"

"Of course God exists. But God is no more a man than you are a snowflake. God is nature. Nature is God. It is interesting to me that the faithful stop praying the very minute they enter Paradise."

"And what about the evil that exists in man. What about the men who killed my wife, and me?"

"Trust in nature, Ulysses. There exists a cosmic balance. Remember only this: Paradise was made for tender hearts, Hell for loveless hearts."

Ulysses, listening keenly, steepled his fingers. "And beyond the light is Paradise, you say?"

"Most certainly!"

"Oh, God, I need time to think this through." Ulysses rubbed his temples with his fingertips while Bagheera settled happily at Voltaire's feet.

The philosopher adopted a more serious tone. "And this is why I am here to offer you counsel. You want to play at being Morpheus yet your wife and so many others yearn to be with you. Your namesake, Captain Ulysses, and the men who died fighting alongside you all want to embrace you, my friend. A new beginning awaits."

"And if I delay for too long?"

"Then you might remain a *fantôme,* a ghost."

"Please, how much longer do I have?"

"Who knows? But wouldn't it be so nice to hold a loved one again, to smell the perfume of fresh flowers and feel a raindrop on your skin?"

"Yes," gasped Ulysses, feeling himself waver.

Voltaire stood up, kissed Ulysses on both vaporous cheeks and wished him luck. Bagheera, acting upon feline instinct, followed him.

"Do you see? Even your cat should have made his way to Paradise but he found you first," concluded the Frenchman. "You are the fish that got away, *mon ami*. But be very careful because sometimes a ghost does not know how to be anything other than a ghost."

CHAPTER ELEVEN

When Henry Met Sally

In addition to leaving boarding school with commendable exam grades Henry had also, in his seven years at St Jude's, learned to play a violin badly, fasten a bow tie, lay cutlery for a state dinner and converse in Latin. However, ambassadors' parties and palace invites seemed an unlikely proposition right now as he sat watching evening television with his grandparents, sipping lukewarm tea and eating a triangle of buttered toast.

"The Gettysburg Address!" Henry's grandfather shouted, in answer to a question posed in a quiz. Coffee foam dripped languidly from his moustache, much like suds from a mop.

"Oh good grief, Leonard. How horrid," Constance whined. "Please, please just gaze into a mirror and give that monstrosity a wipe."

When the quiz show finished Leonard, with a biscuit crumb trembling in his damp moustache, switched channels to catch up on world events. At that moment, to Henry's great surprise, Sebastian Fox-Gudgeon's imperious face appeared larger than life on a national news broadcast.

"Quick, Grandad, put the volume up. I know this chap!" Henry blurted, almost choking on his toast.

Sebastian, under a barrage of photographers' flashlights, was filmed being escorted into a Bangkok airport terminal by a contingent of Thai police and a grim-faced official from the British High Commission.

"Ah yes, this is the infamous young wretch who stole his father's credit cards before trotting off to the other side of the world on a spending spree," his grandmother explained. "And you know him, you say?"

"Yes, he attended St Jude's. He was in the year above me. You might even say that we were friends—"

"Huh! He's clearly not the best kind of friend."

Henry had seen neither head nor tail of Sebastian for more than three years. The older boy had absconded from school on the eve of his final exams and now here he was in the nation's living rooms, blowing kisses to reporters and mugging to cameras as if he were a rock star rather than a runaway brat.

Henry regarded the handcuffs on Fox-Gudgeon's wrists. Not since the time when Bertie Cheng had surreptitiously filled Sebastian's Evian bottle with Turkish tap water on a school trip to Istanbul had Henry derived such a measure of *schadenfreude* at a fellow's comeuppance.

*

Bertie Cheng made sure that his expensive education was put to good use. Immediately upon his return to Hong Kong, he'd ingeniously set up a highly profitable blog network that saw him shortlisted for a Young Entrepreneur of the Year award. Meanwhile twenty-year-old Henry, in his own parallel universe, had recently secured a position as a trainee journalist for the *Hackney Chronicle*. The newspapers' premises were a short distance from the vicarage in which he had grown up, and he'd purposely targeted that newspaper, hoping to use it as a means to rekindle local interest in the unsolved murder of his parents some ten years earlier.

Much of Henry's time at St Jude's had been spent moored in the safe harbour of the school library, lost in the majesty of Tolstoy, Shakespeare, Tolkien, Márquez, Steinbeck and Orwell. He was equally inspired by Austen, Woolf, the Brontës, the legendary Scheherazade and a legion of sci-fi authors. It was to the exasperation of his grandparents that he chose not to further his education at university and instead spent the best part of the next two years in his bedroom, anchored to his laptop, tap-tap-tapping on a keyboard while writing his seminal sci-fi novel, *Planet Foretold*.

Driven by literary aspirations beyond his years, Henry dived into an ocean of spectacular creativity, creating downtrodden characters worthy of a Victor Hugo novel and displaying a gift for personification that Charles Dickens might have envied. In his novel, the protagonist, a warlord turned altruistic nation builder, populated an uninhabited planet with a diaspora of grateful people whom he'd freed from a galaxy of tyrannical rulers. Imbued with the philosophical disposition of Genghis Khan, Henry's principal character proves to be as philanthropic as he was militant.

There were celebratory days when Henry read through his work and considered it a sci-fi epic to rival any previously written; at other times he thought himself deluded and saw only trite, pretentious drivel where he'd previously seen sublime prose. He often squabbled with his inner voice and forced himself to rewrite entire chapters, boiling down his overblown narrative by culling a plethora of adjectives, adverbs and similes. He created hostile planets and kaleidoscopic galaxies that he imagined would enthral future readers, but also castigated himself for using bizarre synonyms that no one but an accomplished lexicographer could ever have heard of.

It was here in the inauspicious sanctum of his bedroom, hemmed in by thesauri and with screwed-up balls of scribbled notepaper strewn about his feet that he dreamt of becoming Henry Drummond, renowned sci-fi author.

*

On the morning of what was to be his auspicious first day at the newspaper office, Henry was happily wallowing in the bathtub when his grandmother rapped loudly on the bathroom door in the manner of an impatient debt collector.

"Henry, it's nearly six-thirty, shouldn't you be making a move?"

He listened half-heartedly, mesmerised by the head of his penis as it bobbed on the water like a marker buoy. "I don't have to be there until nine, Grandma. There's plenty of time."

"Are you sure?" she asked crisply. "You're not the most practical of boys and it wouldn't look good if you were late for your first day."

"Grandma, you're talking as if this will be my first time on the London Underground. I've lost count of the number of tube trains I've ridden in."

"Agreed, but school trips to art galleries and museums with teachers shepherding you around don't quite count, do they? Look, please don't imagine that we're keen to get rid of you, Henry, but might it be a good idea to find yourself an apartment nearer to your place of work?"

"Relax," he reassured her, draping a wet flannel across

his face. "I've researched the journey online. There are only two train changes and the entire journey should take less than ninety minutes."

"Famous last words, Henry. Don't say that I didn't warn you."

*

With his yak-like hair still damp but combed into a presentable side parting, and sporting a tight suit he had once worn to a cousin's wedding, Henry pedalled to Epsom railway station on his grandmother's bicycle, complete with a wicker basket attached to its handlebars. After securing it to a rack, taking two puffs of his inhaler and pouring some coins into the proffered hat of a homeless person, he caught the 7.34 train to Vauxhall and was in his seat with minutes to spare. Happily tucking into a slice of fruit cake topped with marzipan, he felt that anything was possible. A self-satisfied smile inflated his face and he basked in a rare moment of smugness. Despite his grandmother's misgivings, he'd proved himself to be the master of his own destiny.

The train was full and, apart from a lantern-jawed businessman who wanted the entire carriage to know how much money he was earning by way of a loud phone conversation, the journey was straightforward and agreeable. A montage of pebble-dashed houses, metal fences, playing fields, overhead cables and sooty walls dashed by. Henry was in London before he was able to finish the third chapter of *Great Expectations*.

The Underground platform, with its shiny ceramic tiles, howling gusts of stale air and confusing map diagrams, was an altogether tougher proposition than the overland leg of the journey. Nevertheless, with the help of an obliging Rastafarian who seemed to know London's rail network better than most people knew their own faces, Henry was soon sharing a northbound tube train with a miscellany of indifferent people who stared into their phones and not at each other.

Even Henry, although born with the intuition of a sloth, couldn't help but notice that when the train made its next squeaking stop a loud collective gasp billowed from the mouths of all its regular passengers. Herding together, each one began to mutter 'Mad Sally, Mad Sally' under their breath, as if performing some type of Gregorian chant. Then, as the doors whooshed shut, the source of their unease was revealed to him. Mad Sally, a prune-skinned, unwashed lady of indeterminate age, had boarded the train and was causing passengers to part like the Red Sea as she tilted and floundered with the bearing of the Hunchback of Notre Dame.

"Blaaarghh!" she shouted.

"My kingdom for a horse!" she bellowed.

Because so many people had hastily vacated their seats, Sally was granted ample room to take the weight off her bunioned feet and spread out her plastic bags. Sitting opposite Henry, she looked him up and down, lifted one buttock to discharge a reverberant fart and then fell as quiet as a library.

Henry pretended to be fascinated by the cuffs of his shirt and ignored her unremitting gaze, prescient of the fact that he was in the eye of her storm. She stared at him, and only at him, knowing it was only a matter of time before he relented and looked her way.

Henry realised that he shouldn't make eye contact but he felt sorry for the lady. He reasoned that she was possibly someone's mother, perhaps even a grandmother, and that she had seen better days. The eyes of the entire carriage were upon them; it was a Mexican standoff and most people had their phones set to video mode in eager anticipation of something that they could later share on social media.

Of course, curiosity got the better of Henry. He looked up and their eyes met. As well as an impish grin, Sally was in possession of Frida Kahlo's eyebrows, a face as round as a sunflower and a solitary tooth that stood like the last skittle in a bowling lane.

The carriage was hushed. Nobody wanted to leave and one man even ignored his stop so as not to miss anything.

"You!" Sally suddenly bellowed in Henry's direction.

Me? mouthed Henry, too self-conscious to say the word out loud.

"Yes you, you piss-ridden lump of lard! Who else d'ya think I'm talking to?"

The audience was enrapt, each person delighted to be on the outside looking in. An anxious mouse, hearing its owner's raised voice, popped its head above one of Sally's coat pockets, looked left and right and disappeared again. By this time, more than twenty phones were aimed towards Henry and his new friend.

"Blaaarghh!" she blurted, pulling a face at the empty seat next to him, directing her soothsayer's finger as if there were someone there. Henry, in common with the rest of the carriage, even looked to where she'd pointed, an unavoidable reflex action.

"A-hah," Sally cooed, her watery eyes suddenly wise as Galileo's. "You don't see whatsisname, do ya?"

"Er, who's whatsisname?" Henry asked.

The gawk of those in the gallery switched from one side to the other as if they were umpiring a tennis match.

"Your father, that's who!" she replied, with a triumphant grin.

"Um, m-my father? You can see my father?"

"Well 'course I can, you pillock. Look at him sat there, lanky streak of piss with that stupid eye patch across his face."

Henry stared at her dumbfounded, his mouth turned to sand.

"Yeah, and he wants you to know that he's seen Bagheera the cat too."

"Bagheera—" Henry repeated weakly, his jaw hanging like a sporran.

"And for that snippet of information, you may kiss my hand," Sally said, closing her eyes and theatrically holding her fingers out as daintily as a countess.

"Um, er, righto," he faltered, courteously leaning forward to put his plump lips onto her grimy mitt. He felt, given the circumstances, that it was the very least he should do. The spectators roared and cheered then broke into a spontaneous round of applause.

As a finale, Sally lowered her voice, leaned forward and looked him squarely in the eye. The carriage hushed. In a calm voice that wasn't quite her own, she said, "Be a blessing to someone today, Henry."

*

A little later, still befuddled by the preternatural event that had occurred, Henry caught the wrong tube train for the final leg of his commute and travelled for thirty minutes in completely the opposite direction before realising his error. In the blind panic that ensued, he became lost, muttering and gibbering at every rail map, barrier, escalator and theatre poster that he passed on his circuitous route to the correct train.

Wide-eyed and flustered, he arrived at the newspaper office some two hours later than he was supposed to, incurring the unbridled wrath of his boss, Mr Crabtree, a splenetic and apoplectic news editor whose thunderous mouth revealed a rattling graveyard of yellow teeth.

With each of his unintroduced work colleagues smirking at him from the sidelines, and bearing the toe-curling ignominy of such a public lambaste, Henry arrived at the sudden realisation that his grandmother's scepticism was fully justified. He urgently needed to find himself an apartment in the area.

CHAPTER TWELVE

Amber Manette

Amber Manette, a curvaceous young lady with mermaid eyes and a bone-china complexion that might have been painted by Titian himself, found herself staring at the all-too-familiar door with a great sorrow in her heart. Her mind was in a tangle; this was the day in which she was moving into the bay-fronted semi-detached house bequeathed by her beloved grandmother. On the one hand she was profoundly grateful for such an inheritance, one that she couldn't have afforded in her own right; on the other hand, it had only come into her possession as a result of her grandmother's untimely death.

It was on a humid afternoon in June that Pamela Manette's jaunty life came to its unforeseen end. Amber's grandmother was walking her dog on Hackney Downs when a lightning bolt split the sky and blew her clear from her ankle boots, leaving them smoking like shotgun barrels on a patch of scorched grass.

Of course Sherlock, her King Charles spaniel, couldn't understand why his owner was now lying on her back with her eyes staring unblinkingly up at the sky. He stayed by her side, licking and pawing gently at her face, hoping to wake her from this most unusual slumber. When the paramedics arrived on the scene, Sherlock was still endeavouring to raise her from the dead.

Amber had always loved being in the company of her doting gran, and in her rebellious teens would often stay over rather than spend time at home in the company of her alcoholic mother and lecherous stepfather. The atmosphere at home had become so bad that she'd recently made the decision to permanently cut all ties with her mother.

On this bittersweet noon, while Sherlock cocked one leg and piddled on a row of pink chrysanthemums, Amber struggled to find the front-door key. She was up against a sexagenarian's cluttered keychain that bore fluffy pompoms, a supermarket fob and a 'Best Grandma Ever' emblem that Amber had bought several years earlier.

Impatiently waiting by the small removals van she'd hired for the day was her uncivil boyfriend, Danny, who had proved to be unashamedly delighted to have such a nice house fall into his lap. He was indifferent to the fact that it belonged to his twenty-year-old girlfriend, not him. He'd stripped to his T-shirt, revealing puny arms so intricately tattooed that they resembled two dead rattlesnakes.

"Get a move on, Amber!" he bellowed, tapping the face of his watch. "I need to be down the pub by five o'clock!"

Amber winced with embarrassment, noticing that one of her immediate neighbours, the grim-faced Ukrainian named Yuri, had scowled at Danny as he lumbered towards his BMW.

"Danny, can you please keep your voice down?" Amber hissed, as her boyfriend carried sections of a disassembled pine bed from the van. "Especially in front of *him*."

"Who?"

"Him next door, the Ukrainian. Gran used to say he was a gangster or something of the sort."

"What, that dickhead? He's no more a gangster than I'm a member of a boy band."

"Well, just keep it down, OK? I don't want us to get on the wrong side of the neighbours on our first day."

"Oh, fuck me. Old Twitchy-Curtains is at it now!" snorted Danny, pointing towards the window where Amber's other neighbour, Mr Beardsley, was keeping an eye on proceedings. "None of your business, tosser!"

"Now just stop it," Amber scolded, "Mr Beardsley was very kind to my gran, so rein it in. You're acting like an idiot."

"Yeah? Well you need to shut that trap of yours. That shit ain't cool, you get me?"

"Oh, I get you," she sassed, wishing she'd listened to her inner voice and ditched him long before moving into her grandmother's house.

Amber already had the advantage of knowing something about each of her two neighbours, namely Mr Beardsley, whose house was attached, and Yuri, whose narrow driveway rubbed shoulders with hers. The Ukrainian, whose face couldn't appear any flatter if it were pressed against a pane of glass, looked every inch a gangster and behaved accordingly.

"If it looks like a duck, walks like a duck and quacks like a duck, then it probably is a duck," her grandma had remarked whenever his name came up in conversation.

For a man who didn't appear to be gainfully employed, the stocky Ukrainian seemed to have an endless supply of expensive cars at his disposal and was often found snarling into any number of phones while he smoked Turkish cigarettes on his doorstep. In addition, sulky-looking Eastern European women appeared at all hours, sometimes ringing her grandmother's doorbell by mistake.

In sharp contrast, Mr Beardsley was a retired Scotland Yard police detective who chaired the Neighbourhood Watch and was the appointed treasurer for a local Masonic lodge. Bespectacled Gerald Beardsley, a polite man as meticulous in his appearance as he previously had been in his approach to solving crimes, unfailingly wore a shirt and tie, even while doing the gardening. His silver-grey hair was slicked back in a vintage style and he spoke with a dogmatic inflection that betrayed his Cockney heritage.

Although Amber had always considered him to be the local busybody, she was impressed that he had at least turned up to pay his last respects at her grandmother's funeral, something her own mother couldn't be bothered to do. On that day, when she sought him out to thank him, he furthermore surprised her with some thoughtful words of solace that seemed out of kilter with his deadpan countenance. "Always look to the sky, Amber," he said, "for when the sun goes down, the stars come out."

Danny continued to rush backwards and forwards, lugging kitchen appliances and overstuffed cardboard boxes like a man possessed. Amber carried what she could, giving her boyfriend a wide berth on each short journey. When they shared the load of a large dining table, Sherlock scampered excitedly about their feet, whereupon Danny dealt the animal a hefty kick that sent it flying through the air.

"Don't you *ever* kick my dog again!" Amber shouted, her words dripping with venom.

"I'll kick its teeth in the next time it gets in my way. You need to get rid of the pissing thing."

"I'd rather get rid of you, you heartless bastard. And that's a promise."

Danny affected a puerile expression. "Look, I ain't got time to argue with you, babe. I need to get this done and dusted so I can drop the van back and be down the boozer before the football starts."

Gerald Beardsley, his eyebrows knitted, looked down surreptitiously from an upstairs window and didn't like what he saw.

CHAPTER THIRTEEN

The Wretch with the Suitcase

Constance Drummond was standing in front of a walnut dresser, carefully snipping stamens from the heads of lilies, when the doorbell sounded around seven o'clock in the evening. Knowing that neither Leonard nor Henry would bother to leap out of their seats, she elected to open the front door herself. There she was greeted by a young man with a preppy hairstyle who'd matched a grey linen blazer with a lurid pair of scarlet chinos.

"Mrs Drummond, I presume? Enchanted to meet you," he bubbled, offering a confident handshake that was met with due propriety.

"And you are?" she asked suspiciously.

"Sebastian Fox-Gudgeon, good friend of Henry. Is he at home by any chance?"

"Ah, yes, thought I recognised you," Constance said sturdily. "So, *you're* the loathsome wretch who whizzed off to Thailand with his father's credit cards."

"Ooh, *wretch* is rather strong, I merely—"

"A wretch is what I called you, and a wretch you

undoubtedly are. If Henry has any sense, he'll have nothing more to do with you."

"Understood. Er, may I speak with him … if he's here?"

Constance fixed him with a look that could have curdled milk. "He's upstairs working on his novel. Wait there and I shall fetch him."

She turned her back to him and called for her grandson from the bottom of the stairs.

"Sour-faced cow," Sebastian muttered under his breath as he fussed with a silk handkerchief in his breast pocket. Up high in a tree, a disdainful crow unfurled its wings and cawed at him.

As a result of biting into a fish-finger sandwich just as he was summoned, Henry lumped down the staircase with a moustache of tomato ketchup above his top lip. He approached the doorway with a degree of trepidation but was nevertheless pleased to see Sebastian standing there, albeit curiously with a suitcase leaning against one red trouser leg.

"Sebastian, to what do I owe this pleasure?"

"Hello, Henry, my old geeky chum. I bet you've missed me."

"Um, not especially."

"Ha! Great banter."

"And, er, what's with the suitcase?"

"Father has turfed me out, Henry. Hit me for six. I wondered if I might stay with you until I get back on my feet?"

"Uh, I'd really need to run it by my grandparents—"

"Over my dead body!" squawked Constance, who was unseen but had been earwigging from the living room.

Later, after much wrangling and only because Leonard was fraternally keen to help a fellow St Judian in his hour of need, Constance reluctantly rescinded and had to endure the sight of Sebastian's ridiculous red trousers disappearing up the staircase with his fat suitcase in tow.

"This might be a blessing in disguise," Leonard said, cosying up to his disgruntled wife but being shoved away. "Henry did say that they could look for an apartment together and share the cost—"

"Huh!" Constance harrumphed, folding her arms and looking as cross as an owl.

CHAPTER FOURTEEN

Mr O'Connor

After just four days, the Drummonds had lost all patience with their ungrateful freeloader and the *entente cordiale*, such as it was, lay in tatters. The atmosphere in the house had become fractious and the family collectively felt that Sebastian, with the inclination of a cuckoo, had slyly found a suitable host to exploit.

"He's rather keen on himself and not terribly quick to reciprocate our kindness," Constance remarked acidly. "In fact he's eating us out of house and home without as much as a thank you or a bouquet of flowers."

It didn't come as much of a surprise to Henry to discover that Sebastian wasn't presently in possession of any money so, without daring to tell his grandparents, he was forced to subsidise his fair-weather friend secretly by dipping into his own inheritance. Sebastian, with very little enthusiasm, travelled into London early each evening at Henry's expense, meeting him after work to look at rental apartments in the Hackney area, none of which seemed to suit his highborn standards.

"A converted loft?" he moaned on one such evening. "What do you think I am, a bloody pigeon?"

"But beggars can't be choosers, Sebastian," sighed Henry, who now wished he'd possessed the backbone to have told Sebastian to clear off at the outset. "Two-bed apartments in London aren't exactly cheap and I don't see you bringing any of your money to the table."

This induced Sebastian to sigh irritably. "Now see, there you go again, Henry, with your snide comments. I shall of course pay you back threefold but, through no fault of my own, I find myself financially insoluble—"

"Insolvent."

"Oh, insolvent then! Do be quiet. Anyway, my idiot father is sure to reinstate my allowance once he's calmed down and realised how childish he's being. Then, my sceptical friend, you shall have as much money as you wish."

With night approaching, street lights started to flicker into life under a bat-ridden sky. Henry was browbeaten almost to the point of giving up as they trooped past a cheerless line of fast-food outlets, betting shops and laundromats en-route to their next viewing. Sebastian had earlier dismissed two properties without so much as a second glance but nevertheless promenaded the pavements like a nobleman, entertained by the sound of his own voice.

"Why anyone should choose to live here is quite beyond me," he sneered, kicking a dove that had landed near his feet.

"Well, I must beg to differ, Sebastian. We spent ten very happy years here. It really is quite lovely in parts."

"Nonsense. We're rather too bourgeois for this place. It

appears to be rife with scroungers, illegal immigrants and cat stranglers!"

It was just as Sebastian made his absurd proclamation that they turned the corner into a well-lit pedestrianised street that had been gentrified with an eye-catching huddle of independent fashion boutiques, bijou restaurants and artisan coffee shops.

"Ah, this is more like it, Henry. Why don't you scamper off and buy us both a cappuccino?"

"Uh … have you even seen the price of these coffees?" Henry sputtered, perusing the menu board.

Sebastian rolled his eyes. "Oh, don't be such a cheapskate. I'm fairly certain I've never met anyone as stingy as you."

Five minutes later, despite himself, Henry was handing his burdensome friend a Styrofoam cup of milky coffee that expressed aromatic steam from an oval hole in its plastic lid.

"This next property promises much, Sebastian. When I spoke to the owner on the phone, he said that he is far keener on having desirable tenants than making a profit."

"In that case, Henry, lead the way. Procrastination is the thief of time."

Henry's eyebrows shot to the top of his forehead, so amazed was he that Sebastian had succeeded in uttering one of his ostentatious adages without getting the words muddled.

"And please be on your best behaviour, Sebastian," he urged. "I really, really need this apartment, and the landlord seems to be a thoroughly decent chap."

"You shrewd bastard, Henry. Have no fear. I shall be the soul of discretion."

With coffee cups smoking like church incense burners, and guided by phone navigation, they trudged to the next viewing to the sound of Sebastian carping on about Henry's need to buy himself a car.

"Ah, this is the street," Henry finally announced, pointing to a sign that read Peggotty Road. Sebastian siphoned the last few drips of coffee into his mouth and tossed the empty cup into a gutter.

"I can't believe you just did that, you litterbug!" Henry scolded, before stooping to retrieve it.

"That's what road sweepers are for," Sebastian said airily. "It's people like me who keep them in a job."

When they reached the house, an impressive buff-bricked three-storey terrace, even Sebastian seemed mightily pleased. "Are you entirely sure that we can afford this, Henry?" he asked, oblivious to the fact that his use of the word 'we' had caused his reluctant benefactor to grind his teeth.

Henry unlatched an ornate iron gate, which opened with a bagpipe's skirl, and managed to avoid treading on a moonlit snail that was traversing the chequerboard tiles. The black front door was inlaid with art-deco stained-glass window panels that offered a tantalising glimpse into the warm, homely interior. There were three doorbells, each one held together by Sellotape yellowed with age. Henry took a deep breath and pressed the one labelled *Mr O'Connor (landlord),* whereupon a distant staircase was illuminated and the landlord's slippers, trousers, cardigan and head came into view.

Fergus O'Connor, a robust Irishman with seventy years under his belt and the ears of a chimpanzee, opened the door with such vigour that Henry almost stepped back onto the snail he'd just avoided.

"Good evening, fellas," the man said, scratching a grey

swathe of tight wavy hair that resembled a terrier's fur. "One of you boys is Henry, I take it?"

"Yes, that's me, Mr O'Connor. Please let me introduce my friend, Sebastian—"

"Sebastian Fox-Gudgeon, raconteur and eminent philosopher at your service, Mr O'Connor."

"Ah, so you're a philosopher are you? Then we have much to talk about. I taught philosophy at the University of London for many years."

"Did you?" Sebastian sputtered, the wind suddenly taken out of his sails.

"No, I didn't. I made it up," Mr O'Connor chuckled, winking at Henry. "I can spot a bullshitter a mile off. C'mon, let's get you two indoors."

Mr O'Connor led the way, treading floorboards that creaked like the deck of the *Mary Celeste*. The place smelled clean. A glass-fronted oak grandfather clock tick-tocked dolefully in a corner and vintage movie posters, in black lacquer frames prettified the walls.

"You would both have the run of the ground floor," Mr O'Connor explained, ladling words with a velvety Irish brogue and waving his arms expansively. "There are two bedrooms, a kitchen, a living room and a bathroom. The kitchen is communal, though I rarely use it as I've got a small one of my own in my apartment."

"And who else lives here?" asked Sebastian, with his chin in the air, suddenly horrified at the thought of having to share a kitchen with commoners.

"Oh, just my son and me. He's got the middle floor, I've got the top. He's quiet as a church mouse, so won't be any bother. And that's it in a nutshell. What are your first impressions, boys?"

"I love the place," said Henry enthusiastically. "What about you, Sebastian?"

"Yes, I think it's rather prepossessive," Sebastian replied.

Puzzled by such anomalous word usage, Mr O'Connor immediately looked to Henry, whose vivid smirk told him almost all he needed to know about Sebastian Fox-Gudgeon.

The Irishman, keen to get to know his prospective tenants, invited them to take tea in his penthouse apartment. He'd taken an instant liking to Henry, seeing in his trustful eyes a boy who was always keen to see the goodness in others but was often disappointed. He noticed that Sebastian, walking through the hallway en-route to the staircase, couldn't pass his reflection in a mirror without engaging adoringly with it.

As they followed the landlord upstairs, Henry spotted a row of muddy boots on the first-floor landing. They were laid on sheets of newspaper and huddled together outside one of the doors.

"My son's apartment," said Mr O'Connor forlornly, almost as if his son were no more alive than his boots. "Ah, I'll tell you more about him over that cup of tea."

It quickly became apparent that Mr O'Connor liked to play classical music at high volume, such was the noise booming from his top-floor apartment as they climbed higher.

"Now you can see why I've bagged the top floor," he shouted, referring to the din. "Plus the stairs keep my bones moving. As a consequence, I have the lungs of a Sherpa."

It was a source of much amusement to the boys that when Mr O'Connor flung open the door to his apartment, they marched in to Wagner's *Ride of the Valkyries*, making them feel as if they were taking part in an art-house movie. The Irishman immediately scurried to turn down the volume of the music, his ears jiggling as he dashed.

The living room was dimly lit, furnished with heavy velvet curtains, an upright piano, a profusion of crucifixes, and upholstery depicting a mawkish array of medieval pastoral scenes. The place was masculine and had about it the whiff of chimney soot, spilled Guinness and furniture polish. In addition, Mr O'Connor owned an African grey parrot that could mimic voices and a cat that was born with the face of an owl. Once tea was served the cat took to Henry, purring contentedly in his lap, but hissed at Sebastian if he so much as rattled his teacup.

Henry noted with reverence that the landlord was a literate chap; a large bookshelf was crammed with an eclectic array of novels by every author imaginable. Flaubert, Proust, Poe, Sartre, Plath, Pasternak and du Maurier rubbed dust-jacketed shoulders with Kerouac, Rushdie, Vonnegut, Kafka, Murakami and Lahiri.

Mr O'Connor noticed the young man's fascination. "Now, would you be a book reader, Henry?"

"Is he ever," Sebastian piped up. "And he wastes most of his spare time writing a novel that only his grandparents are ever likely to read, don't you, Henry?"

"Um, yes, I am presently writing a novel," Henry muttered, cowed by the weight of expectation.

"So you see," Sebastian smarmed, "despite looking like an oaf, Henry is exceptionally clever."

"If only I was exceptionally deaf," Henry grumbled.

"A novel, eh? That's grand," said Mr O'Connor, tapping his fingertips together. "I'd love to read it when it's done. What's it called?"

"*Planet Foretold*," said Henry meekly.

"A-hah, sci-fi, I'm guessing. Oh, you and me are going to get on just fine, Henry."

"You were going to mention the situation with your son," Sebastian interjected, his Machiavellian interest piqued.

"Ah yes, my son, Liam. Oh, Jesus, what a mess," Mr O'Connor said, crossing himself. "Daft boy got into drugs, heroin and the like. Ended up in prison, he did."

Henry, hoping to put a positive spin on things before Sebastian could open his mouth again, declared, "Ho Chi Minh once said that it's the people who come out of prison who can build a country."

"Thank you, Henry. It's kind of you to say, but the best I can do is to look after him here and keep him safe. Fair play to the lad, though, he's turned a corner. Been doing grand for the last five years, may the saints guide him." Mr O'Connor remained lost in his thoughts for a few seconds but was soon back on track. "So … important questions, boys. Are you both employed?"

Henry answered first. "Um, yes, I am, Mr O'Connor, as a cub reporter at the *Hackney Chronicle.*"

"And you, Mr Double-Barrel Gudgeon?"

"Not gainfully employed right now but naturally, with my background and high standard of education, I can easily find work in the area. Henry is happy to cover for me."

"And marriage? Either of you boys thinking of getting hitched?"

Both Henry and Sebastian shook their heads vigorously, as if the very idea of matrimony was preposterous. Sebastian, as was his habit, almost blurted out that Henry was still very much a virgin but managed a rare moment of self-censorship.

"Ah, that's sensible," Mr O'Connor cooed. "An ice cream on a hot day has better longevity than most marriages these days."

"And, um, is there a *Mrs* O'Connor?" asked Henry, guilelessly.

"She left me for another man, thank God. Horrible, vicious woman. Kicked like a kangaroo and spat like a camel. Let St Patrick, who drove the snakes out of Ireland, be my witness. That woman was a bloody nightmare."

"Jesus, Mary and Joseph!" squawked the parrot.

Snapping out of his diatribe, Mr O'Connor heaved himself to his feet, hitched up his trousers and stepped forward to offer the boys his handshake. "So, fellas, subject to a month's rent up front and all credit checks passing with flying colours, I'm pleased to say that the apartment is yours."

CHAPTER FIFTEEN

Lily-liver'd Boy

It was with a measure of sorrow that Yuri gazed at the framed photograph of his mother on the living-room mantelpiece. Wearing a silk headscarf reserved for Sunday worship, she was pictured lighting a white candle with a taper.

Their last conversation hijacked his thoughts. "*Come with me to church, Yuri, just like you did when you were a little boy. Please, I'm begging you to give up this foolish gang life, it's breaking my heart.*"

Yuri bitterly remembered laughing contemptuously at his mother as he mocked her faith, this saintly woman who ensured he would never again suffer at the hands of his abusive father and who would have gladly given her last *kopiyka* to help a stranger in need.

Of all the terrible things that he'd done in his life, this disrespect was his one true regret. He was never afforded the opportunity to make amends; his mother, Iryna Voloshyn, aged fifty-three, had dropped dead from a broken heart walking to church that same day.

*

Yuri had seen the girl before, a granddaughter who often visited her grandmother, staying over at weekends and during school holidays. No longer a grungy teenager, she was everything he desired in a woman: white skin, wide hips, a cascade of red, Celtic hair and as full-breasted as a Bavarian milkmaid. He sensed though, in common with most other beautiful women, that she wouldn't be physically attracted to a lumbering hulk such as him.

So, haunted by his obsession, he watched her furtively from an upstairs window that provided a clear view of her garden, garage and driveway. She spent much of her free time decorating her new home, regularly returning from the local DIY store dressed in paint-splattered T-shirts that were taut across her breasts and caused his pants to tighten.

Yuri, whose heart was largely bereft of sentiment, had always quite enjoyed watching Pamela's little spaniel and now it accompanied the granddaughter everywhere she went. The girl and that dog shared a level of happiness that he had once known as a child. He imagined himself sitting at the girl's dining table, eating food she'd prepared for him and sharing her wine. But he could also see himself bunching her red hair in his fists while grinding her face into the carpet and forcing himself inside her.

*

"Hello, we have not met," he said, standing on his driveway as Amber came out of her garage with a bundle of calico dust sheets in her arms. "I am Yuri."

"Oh, hi," she breezed, thinking that he sounded like a robot and looked like a Bond villain. Scrunching the sheets to her chest, she initiated a handshake. "I'm Amber, Pamela's granddaughter."

"Sorry about grandmother. Must be terrible for you," Yuri droned, as if reading slowly from a script.

"Yes, it was."

"And nice dog. His name is Sherlock, I think?"

"Ah, yes. And I'm very fond of him, aren't I, Sherlock?"

Sherlock didn't answer but nevertheless looked up at her with adoration in his doleful eyes.

In a different dimension, linking arms and watching this scene unfold from a park bench in Paradise, sat Pamela Manette and Iryna Voloshyn, who huddled together with a joint look of consternation.

Amber's boyfriend appeared as suddenly as a thunderclap and stomped from the house with a loutish swagger. "Where's that poxy dog?" he blazed. "Fucking thing has chewed my football boots!"

Sherlock hid behind Amber, quivering and whimpering.

Yuri frowned, his brow not dissimilar to a pie crust Danny tried to snatch the dog but Amber, after ditching the dust sheets, pushed him back and squared up to him, prepared to fight if necessary.

"Leave dog alone," Yuri grunted, his voice low and menacing.

"Yeah? What's it got to do with you, shit for brains?"

Yuri positioned himself between Danny and Amber, his yoke-like neck and bison shoulders shielding her from view. "You must be very brave or very stupid, little boy. I wonder which?"

Danny, noticing the man's facial scars up close and seeing the cold menace in his gunslinger eyes, instantly regretted his decision to storm outside.

"Or maybe you make big mistake and remember you are not tough guy after all?"

"Uh, y-yeah, I s'pose."

"And need to apologise to girlfriend, I think?"

"Yeah, of course. I'm sorry, Amber. You know how I

get—" The words fell softly from his mouth, like dead flies from a windowsill.

"Good boy," smirked Yuri, patting him firmly on one cheek with a meaty hand. "Amber, it is good to meet with you."

"Er, yeah, you too, Yuri," she replied, cradling Sherlock in her arms.

*

"Look, please don't think I'm being nosy," began Mr Beardsley after calling Amber over to their boundary fence. "I couldn't help but notice that you were talking with Yuri Voloshyn earlier—"

"Yeah, so?" said Amber, slightly irritated by his daily meddling.

"Well, just be careful," he continued, with an exaggerated grimace. "Yuri was well known to the police even in my day. Let's just say that he's not someone you should get involved with, especially if you're of the fairer sex."

"Oh, I've seen all the tarty girls turning up at his house, Mr Beardsley. I'm not that bothered, to tell you the truth."

"Well, just be careful around him, yeah? The devil doesn't always show his hooves, you know. His house isn't surrounded by all those CCTV cameras because he's worried about getting burgled, if you catch my drift."

"OK, thanks, Mr Beardsley. Gran always said that he might be a gangster."

"Well, you just hold onto that thought," he said, looking over the top of his spectacles to let her know that her assumption was correct. "I shall say no more… Hey, would you look at that. A butterfly just landed on your hair."

Amber allowed the butterfly to flit onto an outstretched finger. "Oh, that happens to me all the time."

Her neighbour shook his head. "Extraordinary. A

real-life Mary Poppins. Anyway, I've said my piece. Be on your guard when it comes to that man, yeah? Catch you later."

"Yup, see you later, Mr Beardsley. Come along, Sherlock."

CHAPTER SIXTEEN

Muddy Boots and Frothy Coffees

"Hi, friends, I'm Liam," said the previously unseen owner of the mysterious line of muddy boots. Despite having moved into their apartment several weeks earlier, this was the first time that Sebastian and Henry had actually set eyes on Mr O'Connor's son, a state of affairs that had largely come about because of his innate shyness.

He was sitting cross-legged on the coconut-fibre doormat, removing two of the aforementioned boots, when the boys came upon him on their way out. Because Liam showcased a riot of long hair allied with the beard of an apostle, his eyes, nose and lips were all that were visible to the naked eye. He spoke faintly and appeared fragile as a china vase.

"Ah, hello, Liam. I'm Henry. Great to finally put a face to the name. And this reprobate is Sebastian—"

"Sebastian Fox-Gudgeon," he snorted, intent on everyone knowing from the outset that he had a double-barrelled name. "Quite a look you've got there, Liam. I should imagine your friends call you Rasputin."

"Um, no they don't, as a matter of fact," Liam faltered.

Sebastian pursed his lips. "Hmm, pity."

Henry shot Sebastian a filthy look and continued to make polite conversation. "So what type of work do you do, Liam?" he enquired, regarding the tiny petals caught up in the nest of the man's unruly beard.

"Oh, I don't work as such. I rent an allotment over at St Kilda's. Not sure if my dad's told you but I'm a reformed addict, so I've switched to a healthier lifestyle and have gone vegan. It's kinda transformed my life."

"Wow, that's impressive," said Henry approvingly. "So are you completely off the drugs these days?"

"Oh, for sure. Weaned myself off methadone too. I needed to repay my father's faith in me and I also wanted to give something back to the community, which is why I donate much of the stuff I grow to charitable organisations. I like to help those among us who can't afford to eat."

"Utter rot!" snorted Sebastian, as per his time-honoured principle of not giving a shit. "No one in London needs to go hungry. Funny how these people can afford mobile phones, yet don't have enough money to make themselves a sandwich. Spongers and freeloaders, the lot of them!"

"Sebastian! That is utterly ridiculous and quite uncalled for," Henry interrupted. "Especially coming from someone who is the high priest of freeloaders."

Liam adopted a placatory stance, not wanting to be the cause of friction between friends. "Guys, guys. Hey, keep cool. Sebastian is perfectly entitled to his views—"

"You bet I am, and you'll find that I'm right." Sebastian canted, with an air of smugness that had taken him two decades to perfect.

Liam padded towards the staircase, deftly carrying a grubby boot in each hand and trailed by a shadow of regret. He turned to quietly deliver a parting statement.

"I'm truly sorry that you haven't got love in your heart, Sebastian. But I hope that one day it will find you, my friend. Things got so bad for me that I had to steal to feed my habit, which is why I ended up in prison. As a result, each day of my recovery has been a blessing. I'm truly grateful for the sun, the earth, the rain, and for life itself. So I wish you both a joyous day."

"Yes, you too, Liam," Henry replied, while at the same time glaring incredulously at Sebastian.

"Bloody hippy," huffed Sebastian, while the front door's painted glass projected cheery colours onto his undeserving face.

*

Today, after much cajoling on Henry's part, Sebastian had secured himself a job interview, namely for the position of waiter at the Café des Rêves in town. It was only after they'd moved into Mr O'Connor's house that Sebastian finally confessed to the fact that his father had disowned him entirely, and that none of the promised funds were ever likely to be forthcoming.

"Your inherent deviousness has put me in a spot," Henry grumbled as they walked into the town centre. "It's hardly fair that I've got to pay the rent for both of us."

"Well, it's a poor show if you can't help a friend in his hour of need," Sebastian said imperiously.

Henry was exasperated. "I suspect Mr O'Connor would be shocked if he knew how sneaky you've been."

"Oh, it's always Mr O'Connor *this*, Mr O'Connor *that* with you," sneered Sebastian. "He's got you mesmerised, like du Maurier's Bengali."

"You mean Svengali—"

"Anyway, you'll soon need to subsidise me no more,"

Sebastian announced with a theatrical wave of his arm. "This sommelier's job is as good as mine."

"Um, you're not going to be a sommelier, Sebastian. The bistro merely advertised for a waiter. To become a sommelier one must have studied, which is a general discipline that has hitherto passed you by."

"Nonsense. My father kept a well-stocked wine cellar, replete with the finest wines that money could buy. Even if I was blindfolded and thrown into a pig pen, I'd know a Pinot Noir from a Château Latour."

Henry, secretly wishing that someone *would* throw Sebastian into a pig pen one day, wished him good luck for the interview and then headed for the second-hand antiquarian bookshop he was inclined to frequent on a Saturday afternoon.

"Hen-ry!" Sebastian shouted from a distance, his bellow surpassing the volume of an Alpine yodel and causing his benefactor to turn on his heels. "Let's meet up at Misto's for a coffee later!"

Visibly sagging like a split sack, Henry assented to Sebastian's suggestion and continued his walk.

*

Micawber's bookshop, huddled between a kitchen appliance shop and a vegan cafeteria, bore some resemblance to Dr Who's Tardis in that it seemed small from the outside but was surprisingly commodious on the inside. Whispering from their compressed pages was a kingdom of once-cherished words, fusty and longing to be read again. Susan, the shop's cordial proprietor, told Henry that in 2011, when hordes of rioters were running amok in Hackney, all of the shops in the immediate vicinity were looted apart from hers. "Not one pane of glass was broken," she recalled. "It seems that even the most volatile of anarchists have an inherent respect for literature."

Henry was inclined to drift towards books as keenly as a duck paddles for bread crusts and, having perused a hodge podge of innumerable bookshelves, some curved like longbows under the weight of hefty tomes, he tottered to the counter with an accordion of paperbacks balanced upon one arm. He thought the labyrinthine bookshop a godsend although, including today's haul, his yet-to-be-read stack of books was already of a sufficiency to fill a suitcase.

"Henry, when on earth are you going to find the time to read all of these?" remarked Susan as she slipped his spoils into a paper carrier bag.

"I don't know. I need help," he croaked.

Dusk was descending on London as Henry left the bookshop to the ding-a-ling chime of the brass bell above its door. He'd just received a triumphant text from Sebastian stating that he'd got the job and was already on his way to Misto's.

Today was the fourth of November and, despite it being the day before Bonfire Night, fireworks were already squealing and fizzing in the darkening sky. A magical, sulphurous, smoky smell hung in the air. Sebastian, who clearly couldn't be bothered to wait for his companion, was nowhere to be seen as Henry approached the coffee shop's cherry-red awning. Either side of its gleaming entrance were two large, neglected flower pots, whose bosoms were once alive with summer geraniums and bumblebees; now they served as a repository for cigarette butts and cysts of chewing gum.

Once inside, Henry scanned the room, searching for Sebastian's supercilious face in the crowd. Suffused with the ambrosial aroma of Arabica beans, Misto's was a buzzy meeting place for office workers, shoppers, students and hipsters. Then, of course, there were the table-hogging theorists who spent hours discussing a multitude of abstract ideas while consuming a minimal amount of coffee.

Sebastian spotted Henry first and loped over, slaloming through a chattering throng of people. "Told you I'd get the sommelier's job, my sceptical friend."

"Waiter's job."

"Whatever. Fact is, I nailed the interview and start on Monday, so hurrah for clever old me. If I had any money, I'd buy you a coffee."

"Oh, I wouldn't hear of it, Sebastian. Please allow me to pay. In fact, I insist," said Henry sarcastically.

Behind the counter was an intricate coffee machine that rattled, steamed, burped and farted under a large blackboard upon which a bewildering menu of coffee choices was inscribed; more options, it seemed to Henry, than there were seats in the place. The servers, an enthusiastic mix of young men and women, worked feverishly to ensure each customer was attended to. So loud were the repeated bangs of fireworks echoing in from the street that the clientele flinched as if under gunfire, clutching their chests in mock terror and chuckling into their cappuccinos.

"May I help you, sir?" asked the vivacious redhead whose radiant smile instantly took away Henry's breath. As he always did in the presence of feminine beauty, he began to sweat profusely as if he had just hacked through a jungle.

"Um, a medium hazelnut latte, please," he replied, noticing she fetchingly filled out her uniform and that her name badge read 'Amber'.

"Any pastries or cakes to go with that?" she enquired

as a reflected starburst of fireworks gilded her fathomless eyes, lending her the appearance of a sorceress.

"Er, um, no, I'm fine, thank you."

"And what is your name?" she asked, charmed by his shyness and with a marker pen poised in her hand.

"Oh, you want my name?" Henry sputtered, experiencing a peculiar type of stage fright.

"Yeah, so I can write it on this cup."

"Ah, I see. Of course, silly me … it's Henry."

"You look familiar, Henry. Do I know you?"

"Um, I really couldn't say," he garbled, only too aware that Sebastian had been childishly prodding him in the back for the past twenty seconds.

"Well, it's nice to meet you, Henry. Emilio will prepare your coffee."

"And what would *you* like, sir?" she asked Sebastian.

"A caffè breve grande, Amber," he purred, attempting to seduce her with his lounge-lizard eyes.

"Sure. Anything to go with that?"

"Your phone number and a French kiss."

"I'll take that as a 'no' then," she huffed. "And your name, so that I can write it?"

"Sebastian Fox-Gudgeon."

"Whoa, easy there, tiger. Just your first name will do."

"Sebastian, *obviously*… Would you like me to spell it for you?"

"Oh, yes please, kind sir. It does sound *so* complicated."

Henry could barely watch as Sebastian actually spelled his name out while she scribbled.

"Who's next?" Amber called out to the queue of customers while at the same time handing the empty cup to Emilio.

When Sebastian eventually received his coffee, it

delighted Henry to see that she'd actually scrawled 'pompous prat' across his cup.

Sebastian's face was a picture. "Clearly a lesbian," he sniffed.

"Aww, she should have added a smiley," Henry chuckled.

CHAPTER SEVENTEEN

Nom de Plume

After a fitful night's sleep, Henry was roused by the dink-dink of expanding central heating pipes, the peal of church bells and the need to empty his bladder. As was often the case, he'd searched for his parents in his dreams but they were always out of reach and forever turning a succession of limitless corners.

Before heading for the bathroom, he plodded to the living-room window and partially opened the Venetian blinds, causing sunlight to stripe his pyjamas. He slipped his hand between the slats to tease open a window and took a deep, salutary breath. A blast of damp air, still redolent with the saltpetre of last night's fireworks, chilled his lungs.

He'd suffered a disrupted night's sleep, awakened around two o'clock by Sebastian's cacophonous return from a local nightclub. A peace-shattering bout of door slamming was followed by the coital squeals of a mysterious *señorita* who, whenever lustfully impaled by Sebastian, wailed, "*Oh Dios, oh Dios!*" at the top of her lungs in fervent Spanish.

Henry, whose equine but virginal penis hadn't yet encountered anything more intimate than the palm of his right hand, sought to drown out the noise of their lovemaking by bunching a goose-down pillow about his weary head. It seemed to him that Sebastian possessed the uncanny gift of being able to beguile women from every corner of the globe: libidinous Russian *devushkas*, amorous Italian *signorinas* and lusty German *fräuleins* all fell for him and ended up groaning and squealing on his mattress, only to be discarded in the cold light of day. He imagined Sebastian standing in front of his map of the world egotistically sticking a marker pin into each one of their countries.

En route to their shared bathroom, Henry collected from the carpet an empty wine bottle and two glasses, one of which bore a frieze of red lipstick crescents around its rim. The life-size cardboard cut out of Darth Vader, intended to gravely guard their living-room door, now saw a white pair of silk panties indecorously draped across its cardboard helmet.

After freshening up in the bathroom and spraying himself with deodorant, Henry changed into day clothes that included a long-sleeved Chewbacca T-shirt and supermarket chinos. Not wanting to be around when the porn stars stirred from their post-copulatory slumber, he slipped into the hallway with a second-hand paperback copy of *The Mote in God's Eye* under one arm, intending to read it in a quiet corner of Misto's coffee shop. He deemed the book to have previously been read on a sultry tropical beach, given that its yellowed pages were as corrugated as a ploughed field.

After soundlessly shutting their apartment door, he spotted Oscar the cat asleep on a sunlit section of the stairs and sensed that the entire house was steeped in a soporific air of laziness. Just as he was about to leave the building, a

Panama-hatted Mr O'Connor bundled through the front door clutching a Sunday newspaper and a bag containing a brace of freshly-baked baguettes.

"A very good morning to you, Henry. Jesus, you're up early. I thought you youngsters didn't surface until mid-afternoon on a Sunday."

"Good morning to you also, Mr O'Connor. Seb is presently in the company of a noisy Spanish nymphomaniac, so I'm off to Misto's to read my book—"

"No, no, I won't hear of it," Mr O'Connor interjected, shutting the door with his heel. "I won't have you paying an arm and a leg for nothing more than a piddly cup of hot milk that vaguely smells of coffee. Pop upstairs with me, m'boy, and I'll fix you a proper breakfast."

"Er, but—"

"No buts. And what's that you're reading? Ah, *The Mote in God's Eye* … the lad's got great taste, so he has. Rather dated now, of course, but unquestionably a true sci-fi classic."

Henry, seemingly with no say in the matter, had no alternative but to follow his landlord up the stairs, taking care not to tread on Oscar whose paws twitched and fidgeted while he chased an imaginary pigeon across an imaginary lawn.

"By the way, I'm dead keen to find out more about this book you're writing," said Mr O'Connor, ascending the stairs at a speed that belied his age.

Oscar, awakened from his quiescence by their passing shadows, sprang onto the banister and promenaded alongside them with the intensity of a flamenco dancer, staring deep into Henry's eyes as if reading his mind.

Mr O'Connor continued, "Y'know, I've read that many books it's a miracle I've not ended up cross-eyed."

"I assumed that, as a man of Christian faith, you'd be attending church on a Sunday morning," Henry confessed.

"Ah, did you not know that God is omnipresent, Henry? He hears the prayers from my armchair just as clearly as any I make in a draughty church. Besides, they're a miserable bunch of buggers at St Patrick's."

When Mr O'Connor unlocked his apartment door, his cat offered such an exaggerated yawn that Henry couldn't help but yawn too. "Um, my novel's still very much a work in progress," he elaborated. "I've written over 100,000 words so far, but I'm nowhere near finished."

"Hmm, well don't go crazy with the word count," Mr O'Connor cautioned. "There's a lot to be said for brevity. You wouldn't want to be boring your readers to death, now would you?"

The air was soon thick with Vivaldi. Mr O'Connor clumped into his galley kitchen after directing Henry to the sofa. The youngster watched him grabbing mugs from a Welsh dresser that was equipped with an array of blue china among which was a grim-faced plaster bust of Ludwig van Beethoven. No sooner had he sat down than Oscar, with a whiff of sardines on his breath, settled into his lap where he purred contentedly while licking a fishy paw.

Mr O'Connor called out from the kitchen. "Now you just relax, Henry, and I'll fix you a proper coffee. I could rustle you up a bacon sandwich too, unless you're a vegetarian?"

"Not vegetarian and yes, a bacon sandwich would be lovely."

"What a nice day!" squawked the parrot.

By the time he'd eaten everything put in front of him Henry, for some cathartic reason, had told Mr O'Connor all there was to know about his parents' murder and also outlined his plan to use his position as a junior reporter to rekindle local interest in the case. In doing so, his mind flashed back to the African with the skeleton teeth whose sinister smile was forever imprinted in his memory.

"Oh, sweet Jesus, I remember it very well, Henry. Oh, terrible, terrible business. God, I'm so sorry for your loss. Yes, you must do everything in your power to bring those vicious bastards to justice. That's assuming, of course, that they're not already banged up in prison."

Not customarily inclined to baring his soul, but finding Mr O'Connor an agreeable confidant, Henry opened up to his landlord, even going so far as to say that he retained his mother's perfume and his father's cologne bottles just so he could recollect their smell from time to time.

Drawing from a well of secret thoughts, he continued. "Despite being agnostic, my most treasured possession is my father's Bible, a big, heavy thing with a gilt edge. I found out, some months after his death, that he'd written a message inside. It read, 'Be a blessing to someone today, Henry'. This was something he routinely said to me each morning before school."

"God, that's a swell thing for you to have as a keepsake, Henry."

"It is, but do you know what is truly unpardonable?" Henry sniffed, his eyes dewy with remembrances. "I never once told my parents that I loved them."

Mr O'Connor allowed a silence to pass between them. He saw that the lad was caught in a moment, ambushed by the saddest of memories.

"Ah, Jesus, don't beat yourself up, Henry. They knew full well that you loved them. It's instinctive for a parent."

Henry sought to regain his composure by changing

the topic and went on to summarise the novel he was writing, all the while thinking that his cherished story line sounded completely ridiculous when explained out loud. Nevertheless Mr O'Connor remained interested and every so often trotted off to the kitchen to replenish their coffee cups.

Henry was astonished that his landlord seemed to possess an inexhaustible knowledge of the science fiction genre but, despite continually being entreated to refer to him by his Christian name, Henry couldn't break the habit of addressing him formally.

"If you don't mind me asking, Mr O'Connor, how is it that you have an encyclopaedic knowledge of sci-fi when none of your books fall into that genre?"

Mr O'Connor threw him a roguish smile, like that of a bandit who had snuck into a palace. "Now that's because you haven't seen my sci-fi shelves," he chuckled, rising from his armchair. "Come, take a look."

Henry followed him into a roomy office, furnished with a large computer monitor, a wraparound desk and an expensive-looking leather chair. Stacked from floor to ceiling, on every available inch of wall space, was a shelved collection of almost every notable sci-fi novel ever written.

Henry gasped and immediately found himself at a loss for words. He ran his fingers down the spines of various books as if their visionary secrets could somehow be transmitted into the neurons of his brain. He was especially pleased to see that Mr O'Connor was also a fan of Fergus Munro, and that there were entire shelves devoted to the author's work. Munro, in his pomp, was a prolific writer, producing novels as easily as most men produced flatus.

"Oh wow, you've read all of Fergus Munro's books. I've actually met him," Henry said proudly.

"Really?" remarked Mr O'Connor with a puzzled frown.

"Yes, he came to my school to present me with an award for a short-story competition that I'd won."

"You were at St. Jude's?" asked Mr O'Connor enigmatically, as a grin spread across his face.

"Er, yes," answered Henry. "How did—?"

"Dear mother of God, *you're* the boy who wrote that fantastic little story about the fella who fell asleep in one country and woke up in another!"

"Um, er, yes… I don't quite follow—"

"*I'm* Fergus Munro, Henry, *I* gave you that blasted prize. Jesus, can you believe it? Talk about a small world."

Henry's plump-lipped mouth was agape as he struggled to assimilate what he was hearing. He recalled Fergus Munro's farcical appearance at St Jude's: the fake moustache that flapped about like a tethered bird; the dark glasses, and the Irish accent. *Omigod*, he thought, as realisation kicked in.

A rattle of laughter burst from Mr O'Connor's mouth, like air released from a balloon. "Ha-ha! Priceless. Ah, will you just look at yourself? God in Heaven, you look like an oversized goldfish, with your mouth hanging open."

"I can't believe it," babbled Henry, his speech restored to him at twice the speed. "I am such a huge fan of yours. I even follow you on Goodreads. I especially liked *Alien Triumvirate,* where Kitchiru body-swapped with his ailing grandmother in the fourth chapter but most readers don't realise this until much later in the book. Superb piece of deception."

"Well, thank you Henry, but that was written back in the 1980s. Christ, I'd die of embarrassment if I were to read it again. It's young Turks like you who'll move the genre forward."

"I would never in a million years have made the connection," marvelled Henry, "even though you used your actual Christian name."

"I did, and 'Munro' is my ex-wife's maiden name. Jesus, that woman had witchcraft in her eyes and a tongue sharp enough to cut paper."

Henry was star struck. "Gosh, this is such an honour, Mr O'Connor."

"Yes, well let's just keep this a secret. I don't particularly want any of my most ardent fans finding out where I live, ringing my doorbell and camping on my doorstep."

"Uh, yes, of course."

"And, if you are daft enough to have kept any of my books, I'd be only too happy to sign them any time you want."

"Oh, wow. That would be amazing," Henry trilled, ruefully remembering the shabby T-shirt that Terry Pratchett had autographed, only for his grandmother to unwittingly gift it to a charity shop.

"And, if one day you achieve great literary success, my boy, don't ever allow your self-esteem to get the better of you. Remember *this*, that wherever you climb you will be followed by a dog called 'ego'."

"Gosh, that's an excellent line. Did you just make it up?"

"Don't be daft. It was Nietzsche, I believe."

CHAPTER EIGHTEEN

An Englishman, an Irishman, an Indian and a Jew Go into a Bar

Mr O'Connor persuaded Henry to join him for drinks at The Hanging Pirate, a public house just a brisk stroll from Peggotty Road. Henry secretly couldn't wait to email Bertie to tell him that he was living under the same roof as the legendary Fergus Munro.

"You'll find us an unorthodox bunch, Henry," Mr O'Connor grinned. "Three old farts from vastly different backgrounds getting together each Sunday, swapping anecdotes and putting the world to rights."

"Sounds most agreeable," said Henry, infinitely happier in the company of older men than with lads his own age.

"Collectively, we are an Irishman, an Indian and a Jew. Sounds like the beginning of a racist joke, but it's perfectly true. And one of them, my pal Vishnu, is an agent who pitches authors' work to publishing houses so he's a great person for you to get to know."

Henry almost had to pinch himself. He was walking alongside one of his childhood heroes, chatting as if they were old friends. Not only that, he was also about to meet an influential literary agent. Such days were the stuff of fantasy.

Fergus, affable as ever, cheerily heralded every pedestrian and dog walker who came their way. As they walked by a graffitied wall that shouted "MIDDLE CLASS SCUM GO HOME", Mr O'Connor described Hackney as it was in the seventeenth century, long before the urban sprawl of London had gobbled it up.

"It's difficult to imagine, Henry, but this used to be a rural parish at one time. Samuel Pepys himself would come here to escape the stench and squalor of London. But by the time Charles Dickens was swanning about the place, it had all changed from green to grey."

"If you don't mind me prying, why did you stop writing books?" Henry asked. "I read that you were working on a new novel, one which I couldn't wait to read, but nothing ever came of it. Instead you announced your retirement from writing."

"Ah, a very sore subject, my boy. I'd spent four damn years working on my magnum opus, *The Sea at the Edge of Time*. It was to be my crowning glory, the novel that would place me in the pantheon of literary gods, but my deranged wife soon put paid to all that."

"By leaving you for another man?"

"Oh God, no. He's welcome to her, whoever he is. No, much worse. When she left, purely out of spite, she took my laptop with her. I wouldn't have minded were it not for the fact that it had the whole damn novel on it."

"No-oooo!" Henry wailed, holding his head in his hands. "Didn't you have it backed up on a portable hard drive or a memory stick?"

"Oh yes, but she took those too! She knew the best way

to hurt me, right enough. Honest to God, that woman sucked all the writing out of me. Four years of blood, sweat and tears all gone in a puff of smoke."

"Omigod, I could cry for you. That's truly dreadful. I'd be utterly beside myself. Crikey, I am so, *so* sorry."

"Extremely kind of you, but in a way I can't blame the woman for looking elsewhere. I was almost adulterous myself in my preoccupation with writing. I even continued to write after Liam was sent to prison, which proved to be the lit match in her gunpowder barrel."

"Couldn't you have asked for it back, once she'd calmed down?"

"I'd have loved to, but we've seen neither hide nor hair of her since she upped sticks and vanished. I haven't the faintest idea where she is. My publisher suggested I get the police involved but I didn't have the heart."

Henry shook his head. "Gosh, I can totally see now why you gave it all up."

"Ah, Jesus, it was my best work yet," Fergus said ruefully. "My last shot at literary greatness gone forever. Lady Macbeth herself couldn't have been more wicked."

The Hanging Pirate stood at the confluence of two roads, preceding a jostle of red-brick houses. Above its chimneypots, the glass spires of The Shard gleamed in the hazy distance and pricked the sky. A coterie of smokers, resembling birds on a wire, huddled together outside the pub, jigging on the balls of their feet in an attempt to stay warm.

Fergus flourished an arm as if casting seed. "Now this isn't one of those trendy gastropubs for the bruschetta brigade, Henry. It's a good old-fashioned English boozer."

"Suits me fine," said Henry, allowing Mr O'Connor to walk through the door before him. In that instance he felt a gentle, reassuring hand on his right shoulder but when he turned on his heels in certain anticipation of someone being there, he gazed upon nothing but an empty street.

Mr O'Connor's friends were already barnacled to their favourite table like two old clams. Henry followed his landlord, treading the same oak floorboards that Victorian cut-throats once walked upon.

"Well, if it isn't our fellow inebriate, Fergus O'Connor," cheered a bow-tied elderly Indian gentleman whose dyed hair was black as panther fur.

"And he's brought a fine young man with him," greeted a bald-headed, bespectacled Jewish man, as hunched as a heron. "Fergus, introduce us to this young rascal."

"Fellow gargoyles, this is Henry, one of my lodgers… Henry, the gentleman to your left is Vishnu, and the other one is Reuben."

"Come closer so I can get a good look at you, m'boy," demanded Reuben, squinting over the top of his wire-rimmed glasses.

"He really is as blind as a bat," explained Vishnu.

"I can see perfectly," snorted Reuben. "A hawk would envy such eyes."

"A hawk would go hungry and crash into trees with such eyes," Vishnu quipped.

"And this coming from a pensioner whose hair is the colour of black boot polish."

"At least I have hair. In which decade did your shiny head last see a comb?"

Henry was instantly delighted to be in the company of such an entertaining trio. "So, what would you chaps like to drink?" he asked, placing his fingers on the sticky table top.

"Ah, a polite, well-spoken boy. A *mensch* we have here,"

said Reuben approvingly. "As a good Jew, I drink only moderately, but in your honour I shall have a large glass of the house red."

"That'll be his third so far," revealed Vishnu. "And I'd like another pint of this draught lager, please."

Mr O'Connor helped him to ferry drinks to their table and Henry instantly felt at ease with this triumvirate of wisecracking septuagenarians. The pub was timeworn and venerable; dark, polished table tops shone like conkers, and motes of dust danced in what little sunlight streamed through the bottle-glassed, mullioned windows. Either side of a tatty dartboard were framed sepia photographs that nostalgically depicted a London that had long ceased to be. A large portrait of a young, fresh-faced Queen Elizabeth II hung behind the bar, next to a display card that held bags of salted peanuts.

"Henry, may you have the health of a salmon," Reuben toasted.

"And may our penises be harder than our hearts!" Vishnu shouted, eliciting a raucous cheer from a nearby table.

After clinking their glasses together Mr O'Connor, while the thought was still fresh in his mind, addressed his Indian friend. "Vishnu, I've already mentioned to Henry that you're a literary agent. Well, let me tell you with no word of a lie that this boy here is a better writer than I was at his age."

"He's very likely better than you are now," said Reuben with a catlike smile.

"You cheeky bugger! And me a distant relative of George Bernard Shaw."

"And possibly a distant relative of an ape, judging by those ears."

Vishnu, seeking to restore order, slid his chair nearer to Henry. "So, in which genre do you write, Henry?"

"Um, sci-fi."

"Sci-fi, eh? Now, within its pages are there floating cities and newly-discovered aliens who can somehow speak perfect English?"

"Er, no."

"Good. So, have you got anything prepared, a manuscript that I could read?"

"Uh, nothing that's finished—"

"Perhaps a few chapters, then? I wouldn't usually show an interest – the vast majority of writers are pathologically deluded as to their ability – but if Fergus says that someone's good then I sit up and take notice."

"I'll email his first three chapters to you tonight," said Mr O'Connor, realising that Henry was far too sheepish to push himself forward.

"OK, it's a deal," agreed Vishnu. "But I warn you, Henry, if your work is dreadful, I will tell you. This business is already saturated with writers who wouldn't know their syntax from a Tampax. Life's too short to drink bad wine or to read substandard books. So consider yourself forewarned."

"Uh, OK, thank you for the opportunity, Vishnu," said Henry with a worried gulp, at which point Mr O'Connor flashed him a reassuring wink.

By midday, the bar staff were rushed off their feet and the boozy air was suffused with the smell of gravy and roast potatoes. Amid the throaty chatter of lunchtime drinkers, one loutish voice could be heard above all others from a heavily-tattooed youngster whom Reuben instantly recognised.

"Feh! Just look what the cat dragged in?" he groused.

"I'm surprised he dares to show his face, that revolting momzer."

"Oh, for the love of God, let it lie, Reuben," urged Mr O'Connor.

When Henry looked towards the object of Reuben's ire, he was stunned to notice that Amber, the demi-goddess from the coffee shop, was standing by the loudmouth's side, albeit reluctantly it seemed.

"Why does that guy make you so angry?" asked Henry.

"We had a fight two years ago," Reuben huffed. "Me and that schmuck, we had a full-blown fistfight."

Henry was incredulous. "You had a fight?"

"You heard me. We got into an argument. He got lippy. He asked me if I wanted a fight so I thought I'd teach him a lesson he'd never forget. Seizing the moment, I pushed the idiot out onto the street so that we could fight properly, man to man."

"Omigod, you beat him in a fight?"

"Of course not! What, are you stupid? I'm an old man and he's young and strong. What do you think happened? He punched me about the head until I saw stars, but still I was victorious."

" Er, how come?"

"Because he broke his fist on my skull and also because an upstanding group of lads piled out of the pub and gave him the thrashing he so richly deserved."

"Yes, but now your fighting days are over, aren't they, Reuben?" said Vishnu, massaging his friend's geriatric shoulders.

"Oh, I don't think that they ever began," Reuben sighed.

Amber recognised Henry from his visits to the coffee shop and acknowledged him from a distance with a guarded wave. Reuben, despite having the impaired vision of a mole, noticed this discreet gesture. "Oh-ho, the schmuck's pretty girlfriend has her eye on you, isn't that so, Henry?"

"Um, I sincerely doubt it," Henry mumbled, his face flushing scarlet.

"Then I'll fight you for her," Reuben chuckled. "I still retain the sexual desire of a young man, if not the body. Oh, wait! She's coming over, she's coming over!"

Amber strode purposefully towards their table; the contrast of her oceanic eyes against pale skin made them all the more striking. Though rooted to his seat, Henry felt himself drawn to her gravitational field.

She stopped beside Reuben's chair. Getting onto her haunches, she held his onion-skin hands and looked him squarely in the eye. "Sir, I have just found out that my idiot boyfriend picked a fight with you the year before I met him. Please know that, as of now, I want nothing more to do with him and that I am so, so sorry for his behaviour."

"No need to be sorry, my dear, he is what he is."

"Well, thank you."

Amber kissed Reuben on his liver-spotted forehead and then stormed out of the pub, ignoring the protestations of her querulous boyfriend.

"So, the girl is smart too," said Reuben with a twinkle in his eye.

CHAPTER NINETEEN

The Ultimatum

Before she had even begun her shift at Misto's on Monday morning, Amber was summoned by a bony index finger belonging to her weasel-faced manager, Mr Rickets. "Amber, I need to see you in my office," he whined, the sound of his voice reminiscent of a mosquito in flight.

"Oh, is something wrong?" she asked, all at once noticing the downcast expressions of her co-workers.

"Leave your apron to one side and follow me," Mr Rickets instructed, walking to his Lilliputian office as slowly as an undertaker.

"Please sit down, Amberrr," he mewled, elongating her name. The wispy fringes of his hair were brushed forward, emulating the laurels of a Roman senator. The thinnest of smiles stretched his snail-skin lips. "Do you know why I have invited you into my office?"

"Uh, no, actually I don't."

Amber had often wondered how an inept individual such as he was able to secure a managerial position. The man expected excellence of everyone else, yet was bereft of it himself.

From his desk drawer, Mr Rickets' reedy hands produced a polystyrene coffee cup that plainly bore the words 'pompous' and 'prat' in large letters. "Scribed by your fair hand, I believe," he said with an unctuous smile.

Amber was flabbergasted. "Oh, for crying out loud. So that arrogant posh boy has had the nerve to put in a complaint?"

"A complaint we take very seriously, Amber. I can't have my staff insulting our valued customers, now can I?"

"But he was a condescending git!" she protested.

"That's as may be," Mr Rickets continued. "But the welcome news here is that he has magnanimously offered to drop this if you grant him a personal apology—"

"Apologise? You've got to be kidding me! There is no way I'd ever apologise to that idiot."

"Are you sure about that, Amberrr?"

"Positive."

"Then it is with regret that you leave me no alternative but to terminate your employment forthwith."

"What? You can't! Seriously? Just for *that*?"

"Precisely for that."

"That's just pathetic!"

"Now keep a lid on your emotions, Amber. We could end this amicably, or we could end it acrimoniously. All that you require is contained in this envelope, including a glowing reference from me. I must say that I've been very pleased with your work."

"Oh, that's marvellous. I'm *so* pleased that you're pleased," Amber replied sarcastically. With that, she snatched the envelope from his skinny fingers and left the premises through a cordon of hugs and kisses from tearful colleagues.

*

"You're home early, Amber," said Mr Beardsley, when she knocked on his door to collect Sherlock. At his suggestion, she'd been leaving her dog in his care most days while she was at work.

"I got fired from my job, Mr Beardsley," she grimaced, almost too embarrassed to mention it. "This upper-class twit of a customer was being obnoxious, so I wrote 'pompous prat' on his cup. Trouble is, he complained about it to my manager, the sneaky sod."

Amber thought that this might cause her neighbour to at least crack a smile, but he remained impassive.

"Foolhardy, Amber. Still, hardly enough reason to give you the boot."

"Exactly."

"Listen, sometimes when one door closes, another one opens." He breathed on his spectacles and wiped them with a cloth. "I know a couple of catering managers over at the Olympic Park who are in my Neighbourhood Watch group, so I reckon I could swing it for you to get a job in one of their restaurants. How does that sound?"

"Aww, that would be amazing! Thanks, Mr Beardsley, I'd love for you to put a word in. And thanks too for looking after Sherlock."

"Look, it's my pleasure. I'll get on the phone sharpish, see if I can get you an interview, yeah?"

"I really, really appreciate that. Thanks, Mr B, you are a diamond. Come along, Sherlock."

*

In the span of only five hours, Amber lost one job and gained another. Mr Beardsley called to say that he'd set up an interview for her with a friend who managed the ¡Arriba! Mexican restaurant in Stratford. The eatery was sited within the Olympic Park development. Amber drove straight there and was offered a full-time waitressing job on the spot.

The joint was a riot of reds and greens with hand-painted menus, cactus motifs and strings of dried chillies adorning mustard-coloured walls. Much to her relief only the male waiters were required to wear sombreros, but she was served notice that dancing to *La Cucaracha* whenever birthday cakes were sent out was part and parcel of the job.

At times, Amber didn't quite know what to make of the enigmatic Mr Beardsley; on the one hand he was captiously quick to tell her if her music was too loud, or if her lawn needed mowing; on the other hand, he'd come across as a good Samaritan, a guardian angel, even. She'd seen him pugnaciously berate drivers for leaving tyre tracks on his grass verge but also witnessed him doing the weekly supermarket shop for an old lady who lived in a neglected house on the opposite side of the road.

"What shall we buy Mr Beardsley as a thank-you gift?" she asked her dog while dunking an oatmeal biscuit into a mug of tea. "We can't buy him a bottle of whiskey or a crate of wine because he doesn't drink alcohol. So what d'you reckon, Sherlock?"

Sherlock looked at her, his ears raised in the expectant hope that he might one day decipher his mistress's puzzling language.

"Tell you what, how about we bake him a nice cake?" Amber said this regardless of the obvious fact that spaniels aren't universally known for their cake-making skills. "And, I think that today is the day that we finally tell Danny boy to sling his hook. What d'you think about that, eh?"

Sherlock liked the upbeat tone to her voice and beat his tail enthusiastically.

"Yes, you'd like that wouldn't you, Sherlock? So, we're

agreed then. It's high time that we gave him his marching orders."

Sherlock issued an enthusiastic bark.

Amber knew well enough that the execution of such a plan was easier said than done. She'd fallen out of love with Danny several months ago but had allowed him to pollute her new home like a medieval plague. She'd really only stood by him through force of habit; they mostly slept in separate bedrooms and only the ghost of their happiness remained. When they were a legitimate couple, one of many bones of contention was his snide insults about her recent weight gain; she'd began to comfort eat after her grandmother's death and had therefore gained several pounds. Also thrown into the mix was the fact that Danny was as morbidly jealous as Othello, pathologically suspecting Amber of being sexually unfaithful with any number of imagined men, leading him to screen her private text messages and to follow her secretly on girls' nights out. And yet, duplicitously, it wasn't uncommon for him to sneak into her bed in the early hours, smelling of booze and women. But finding out yesterday that he'd actually stooped so low as to pick a fight with a harmless old man was the final straw.

She hadn't seen Danny since she'd abandoned him in the pub and hadn't responded to his subsequent phone calls and texts. He wasn't happy, evidently, and had decided to skip work at the construction site, his latest text confirming that he was coming over later to collect his tools and work clothes. Amber knew only too well that Danny would have lathered himself into a petulant frenzy and was therefore prepared for the histrionics and threats that were sure to follow.

As expected, awash with spit and bile, it was a wrathful

Danny who approached Amber's house that evening. The chime of her doorbell was immediately followed by a succession of loud raps announcing his unwelcome arrival. Mr Beardsley's curtains twitched.

"Hello, Danny," Amber said flatly, upon opening the door.

"What you did down the pub was bang out of order!" he seethed, as a moth battered itself against the porch light above his head.

Amber was unbowed. "Are you going to come inside and discuss this like an adult or just stand there throwing your toys out of the pram?"

Danny, bedevilled by inadequacy and inundated with rage, brushed past her and continued his tirade in the hallway. "You made me look a complete mug in front of my mates, you bitch."

"No, you made yourself look stupid, you idiot. What the hell were you thinking, picking a fight with an old man? What sort of person are you?"

"You wanna watch your mouth, darling. You're already skating on thin ice as it is."

Rats scrabbled about in Amber's stomach but she was determined not to show fear. "Oh yeah? So what're you going to do, tough guy? Beat me up like you did that old man?"

Her windpipe was suddenly in the grip of Danny's left hand; he slammed her into the wall, knocking a framed photograph of her grandmother to the floor. As his other fist primed to punch her in the face, Sherlock valiantly bit into his legs.

"Go on … do it," Amber taunted, her strangulated voice resembling that of a Dalek. "I'll … show my friend, Yuri … what you've … done."

The mere mention of the man's name was enough to make Danny relinquish his grip. Amber leant back against the wall, clutching her throat and gasping for air. Sherlock cowered behind her, his sad eyes peeping out from behind her ankles.

"Ah, so that's it!" Danny blazed, his face contorted with disgust. "You're screwing him, you fucking whore!"

"Yeah, didn't you know? I'm sleeping with him and also half the men in London too, you sick bastard."

Danny made as if to punch her but instead slammed his fist into the wall, causing a knuckleduster of blood to foam from his shredded skin.

"If I ever find out that you're sleeping with him, I swear to God that I will kill you *and* your shitty little dog."

"But it's OK for you to screw around, is it?"

"Well, maybe I wouldn't need to screw around if you'd taken more care in your appearance, you fat cow!"

"Oh, nice! And while we're at it, I found out today that my gran's jewellery has gone missing. You really are something else, you absolute arse!"

Her grandmother glowered up at Danny from her photograph on the floor.

It didn't come as any surprise to Amber when the clamour of their argument was interrupted by the sound of the doorbell. "Aw, great! I know who this is," she sighed, making for the door and opening it without pause.

Mr Beardsley's solemn face seemed ghostly under the austere glow of the porch light. "Amber, I heard raised voices." He looked beyond her and stared at her boyfriend.

"Oh, do one!" snarled Danny.

"Is everything OK here, Amber?" asked Mr Beardsley, choosing to ignore him.

"Yeah, yeah, I'm so sorry, Mr B. You will be pleased to

hear that this doomed relationship is coming to an end. I promise that we'll keep things civilised from here on in."

"Fine, but if things get out of hand I'm calling the police, yeah?"

"It won't come to that, Mr B."

"Young man, you need to calm down," instructed Mr Beardsley, fixing Danny with a hawkish stare.

"Yeah, yeah, jog on, Grandad," Danny sneered.

"My eyes and ears are open at all times, Amber," said Mr Beardsley, correcting his spectacles with a finger prod.

"I've got this, Mr B. And I'm truly sorry," she replied.

"Goodnight, Amber."

Embarrassed, she closed the door and stared Danny right in the eye.

"I want you out of this house and out of my life, Danny. I've put up with your crap for far too long."

"Yeah? Well I ain't going anywhere, sweet cheeks, so you can think again," he taunted, slyness leaking from every pore.

"I'll give you until the end of this week. If you're not gone by then, I'll change the locks. And let's not forget the help that I can get from my neighbours, yeah? And yes, you can take that as a threat, Danny."

"Ooh, I'm so scared," he grinned.

CHAPTER TWENTY

Verity Fox-Gudgeon

Verity Fox-Gudgeon's satnav had capably guided her Aston Martin to her son's address on Peggotty Road. She'd purposely parked at a spot where she could discreetly watch the house, expecting to observe her son leaving for his evening shift at Café des Rêves within the hour.

It had come as no surprise that Sebastian's emails to her were typically unapologetic and all about himself. He'd vaingloriously boasted about his sommelier job at a fashionable French restaurant, which Verity took to be a flight of fancy from the first moment she'd read it. A quick internet search confirmed her suspicion that the restaurant wasn't all he'd professed it to be, but at least she'd discovered a list of its opening hours.

As anticipated, it wasn't long before he emerged from the amber glow of the house and set off for work on foot. Once he had disappeared from sight Verity, all sleek hair and French stilettos, approached the house and, after opening its squealing gate, selected the doorbell that read *Mr O'Connor (landlord).*

Fergus O'Connor's Irish eyes almost popped out of his

Gaelic head when he opened the door to such an attractive and elegant lady. While 'The Impossible Dream' from *Man of La Mancha* boomed anthemically down the staircase, he rubbed his fingers on his cardigan just in case this mysterious glamourpuss might want to shake his hand.

"Hello, how can I help you?" he chirped.

"I assume that you are the landlord?" Verity asked, peeling off her black leather gloves. Her perfume hung in the air like a genie cloud.

"I am," he replied guardedly.

"Then I should like to ask for your considered opinion of Henry Drummond. I'm rather interested in helping him and want to know something of his character before I do."

"Oh, he's a fine young man. Polite, smart, thoughtful—"

"Trustworthy?"

"Absolutely... Look, to whom am I talking?"

"Verity Fox-Gudgeon, Sebastian's mother."

"Ah."

"Yes, *ah* indeed, Mr O'Connor. Irksome little shit, isn't he?"

"Well, Jesus, I really couldn't say—"

"No need to spare my feelings, Mr O'Connor," she said with precise enunciation, fixing him with feline eyes. "I'm well aware of his many character flaws. We spoiled him from childhood, you see, so have no one to blame but ourselves. It is an inescapable truth that we have created a monster."

She paused momentarily to vent a despondent sigh and then continued.

"Now, the reason for my visit is that I should like to give Henry some money as I have no doubt that he must be out of pocket because of my rat of a son."

"Well, his door's just there," said Mr O'Connor,

instantly comparing Verity to Miss Havisham and Henry to Pip. "I'm guessing he's at home. Spends most of his free time in there, pecking at his computer keyboard."

Henry, who had been enviously gazing at an email attachment from Bertie Cheng showing him on a rooftop bar surrounded by a clutch of Miss Hong Kong contestants, answered the knock at the door and was surprised to see Mr O'Connor standing there with the kind of woman you'd expect to see at a couture show.

"Henry, allow me to introduce you to Mrs Fox-Gudgeon, Sebastian's mother," Mr O'Connor said, making his eyebrows dance. "Now then, I shall leave you both to have a chinwag. Great to meet you, Verity."

"Likewise, Mr O'Connor."

Verity held Henry in her gaze. "Hello, Henry. I'm especially pleased to meet you."

"Oh, um, hello, Mrs Fox-Gudgeon," sputtered Henry, his face blessed with the same look of bewilderment he was born with. "Please, er, come in. Could I offer you a tea, or a coffee? We only have instant—"

"No, I'm fine, Henry. This shouldn't take long," she said, before launching into a monologue. "Now, my son has been bombarding me with emails and texts, all of which amount to nothing more than a series of begging letters. We have no intention of bailing out the ungrateful little shit but, knowing that he is something of a parasite, I am certain that he must be taking advantage of your generosity. So tell me, Henry, exactly how much rent does he owe you?"

At that point Verity produced two bundles of banknotes from her handbag, each secured by thick elastic bands.

"Oh, but there's really no need, Mrs Fox-Gudgeon," Henry protested.

"There absolutely *is* a need," she replied. "I don't see why you should subsidise my freeloading son. So tell me, how much are you out of pocket?"

"Um, a few thousand," he replied, meekly.

"Fine, here's £10,000 to cover it. And if that runs out, just call me. Here's my business card."

"Oh, no, Mrs Fox-Gudgeon, that's far too much—"

"Not at all. And it's of the utmost importance that you only contact me by phone. His father would go bananas if he knew about this. Understood?"

"Understood."

"And especially don't tell Seb about the money. I'm his mother and I can tell you that he's not to be trusted."

"Uh, OK."

"And Henry—?"

"Yes, Mrs Fox-Gudgeon?"

"Thank you for your kindness. He really doesn't deserve it."

"I know."

CHAPTER TWENTY-ONE

We Are Each Our Own Devil

Ulysses found himself hopelessly adrift within the confines of a yew-hedge maze, the leaf tips of which were lit by a Communion-wafer moon that rested on the black tongue of night.

"Ulysses, you appear to have lost your way," greeted Voltaire, appearing from nowhere, gliding an ornate walking cane along the hedge wall as he approached.

"Voltaire. Oh, thank heavens you're here. I badly need your help. I've been desperately trying to find my way to Paradise but have somehow become disorientated."

This admission seemed to please Voltaire, who tucked the silver-topped cane under one arm and produced a guileful smile. "So, are you finally prepared to admit that you've denounced God, my friend?"

Ulysses was confused by the Frenchman's mixed messages and at the same time wondered why Voltaire's accent had disappeared. He noticed that his companion now cast two shadows and exuded a sulphurous smell.

"H-hey, wait. You're not Voltaire, are you?"

Voltaire's eyes darkened and a vibratory snarl like that

of a lion emanated from his throat. His smile revealed a tongue bustling with cockroaches and a previously unseen serpent slithered from the lining of his coat. Then, with much hostility, the hedges began to shake, sending a screeching colony of bats flapping into the sky.

"Come, allow me to show you the way out," purred the imposter, his eyes mirroring the moon.

"No, I'm not coming! Just who the hell are you?" Ulysses blazed.

"Ah, interesting that you used the word 'Hell', my friend. Do you believe in Hell, hmm?"

"Look, I haven't got time to waste and I need to get back to my wife, so just tell me who you are."

"Oh, I think that you know my name, Ulysses… Look upon me and say it. *Say* it."

Ulysses took a deep breath as the penny drop of realisation set in. The name fell from his mouth like a stone: "Satan."

"There. That wasn't so difficult, was it? Of course I'd have settled for any number of other aliases."

Satan, drawing close to his prey, traced a fingernail across Ulysses' eye patch and then hissed into one of his ears. "You are but a calf separated from the herd, Ulysses. I've been tracking you for quite some time now, waiting for you to weaken. And just where is your precious God now, my lost, abandoned friend?"

As the eyeless gargoyles of Hell crawled from the earth and licked their rancid lips in eager anticipation of a soul squandered, Ulysses pressed his hands together and prayed with all the intensity he could muster. The ground trembled and fractured then disappeared from under his diaphanous feet. It was with a huge sense of relief that he once again found himself hoisted high into the corridor of the Aurora Borealis and under the flight of meteors.

CHAPTER TWENTY-TWO

Honour among Thieves

As night rose from its grave, the Body Snatcher collected the van from his brother's pig farm in the Kent countryside and headed for London, having earlier received a call from Yuri Voloshyn. The city twinkled in the approaching distance, hypnotic and shimmering, like an unchartered galaxy. There was another charred corpse to be collected. Had they given him ample warning, as per their gentlemen's agreement, he could have left a lot sooner. As it was, he was going to be a few hours late because Pascal had apparently jumped the gun, setting their captive alight almost as soon as he'd bundled him onto the floor of their lock-up.

"Useless twats," the Body Snatcher smiled to himself. "They'll just have to wait."

*

The Body Snatcher held a phone to his chin, his breath misting the screen. "I'm outside now, Yuri. Is the coast clear to drive my van in?"

Yuri lumbered to the control buttons, cradling his

phone between neck and shoulder. "No problem. I will open door."

As the metal shutter rattled upwards, the murderers came into view, grinning like two kids waiting for the neighbourhood ice-cream truck to arrive.

"You took such a long time," Pascal complained to their associate as Yuri lowered the shutters once the van was inside.

"Well, that wouldn't have been the case if you'd shown some common sense, now would it, mate? Why you couldn't just throw a plastic sheet down and put a bullet in the man's head is beyond me."

"Maybe I should put a bullet in *your* head?" Pascal rasped, tapping his handgun against a metal pipe, his piranha mouth breaking into a grotesque smile.

"Well, you're very welcome to try, sunshine. The Old Bill would be sure to find some stuff about you in my house if I disappear."

"He do not mean what he say," Yuri interrupted. "Here is money."

Looking on idly, dead pirates huddled in the darkest recesses of the warehouse and cursed the ropes that once stretched their necks.

"So out of interest, who *was* this geezer?" asked the Body Snatcher, pulling away a plastic sheet that took scraps of charred skin with it.

"He was two-faced scumbag pimp who think he can steal our girls," explained Yuri.

"Oh dear. You just can't trust anyone these days."

CHAPTER TWENTY-THREE

Written in the Stars

"Hey, grand news," chirped Mr O'Connor, intercepting Henry as he was about to leave for work. "Vishnu has emailed me to confirm that he loved the first three chapters of *Planet Foretold* and wants to see more. He even went on to say that it was the most exciting piece of writing he'd seen in ages."

"Oh, gosh. That's just great, Mr O'Connor. I'm amazed," Henry gasped.

"Ah, don't be so self-deprecating, my boy. Creativity without ambition is like a bird without wings. You've got a God-given talent there. And now that you've got Vishnu's backing, you'll have at least one foot in the door, if not three."

"This all seems so unreal. To actually see my novel in print would be the stuff of dreams."

"True, but once that happens, do you know what you'll get sick to the teeth of hearing?"

"No—"

"Asinine nitwits piping up with 'apparently everyone

has a book in them'. Jesus, I'd cheerfully strangle every last one of them."

*

The main office at the *Hackney Chronicle* was a convivial, albeit unprepossessing, place of work. Bathed by the acid glow of light panels in a suspended ceiling, the room was a clamorous, utilitarian space, carpeted with nylon tiles and divided by faux-pine screens.

Henry, in his short time there, had impressed colleagues with his willingness to answer phones, fetch cups of coffee and water pot plants; he'd also gained the respect of his bosses with the authorial quality of his reports. But today, with some trepidation, he'd pitched his idea of rekindling interest in his parents' murder to grouchy Mr Crabtree.

"Can't see any reason why not, Henry," was his boss's unforeseen answer. "I distinctly remember covering some of the story myself, and it seemed certain that the police had got their men, but then it all fizzled out. The fact that you're personally involved will drum up a lot of local interest."

Henry was pleasantly surprised. "Thank you, Mr Crabtree, this means a lot."

"Right, get cracking on your presentation and then we'll run it by the legal team. It goes without saying that you can't accuse people outright. In the meantime, I'll oil the wheels by taking it up with the chief."

"I can't thank you enough, Mr Crabtree. I promise I'll make a good job of it."

"I know you will, Henry. Now sod off and get back to your desk."

*

When Henry returned to the apartment that evening,

Sebastian had a peculiar look on his face and seemed especially pleased with himself. "Henry, I think that I might be in love," he declared.

"With yourself, I assume?"

"Oh, do stop dicking around. The object of my affection is Ophelia, a girl I've started seeing. Not quite a debutante but she mixes in the right circles and her parents are filthy rich."

"Which, of course. is the most important thing," said Henry.

"I'm telling you, Henry, this bistro job is the best thing ever. The place is teeming with pussy and I'm also shagging the boss's wife. It's rather like shooting fish in a barrel."

"So where does Ophelia fit in with your boss's wife and all these other ladies that you bring here? They seem to revere you until you've had your wicked way and sent them packing."

"Tarts, the lot of them. They're hardly in Ophelia's league."

"But, come on, it's an ignoble way to treat women, Sebastian."

"Well, we all know that you're a paradox of virtue, Henry—"

"Paragon."

"Paragon then. Look, at least I'm not a twenty-year-old virgin. Nearest you've been to a pair of panties is seeing your grandmother's bloomers on a clothes line."

"Thanks for that."

"And another thing. I wouldn't be seen dead bringing Ophelia to this dump. She's got a swish apartment in Islington, which I'm sure to move into if I play my cards right."

"A virtuous aspiration, Sebastian."

*

Henry, with his hair sculpted into something akin to a squirrel's drey, had reluctantly agreed to accompany his flatmate on a rare night out on the town; he had only been asked because Sebastian was jauntily keen to show off his new squeeze. This was unchartered territory for Henry; hitherto he'd only heard, not seen, any of Sebastian's previous love interests and so spent many a night spent wondering what perversions his flatmate might be sharing with these women as they all seemed hell-bent on screaming the place down in a farrago of global languages.

With Sebastian urging him to 'get a move on' from his adjoining bedroom, Henry was forced to remove a stack of Marvel comics from his wardrobe to gain access to a shirt that might be considered even remotely fashionable.

Sebastian peeked through Henry's opened door and saw him stand on his mattress to retrieve a handful of banknotes from a shoebox on a high shelf. *Hmm, what do you have up there, Henry?* he thought, licking his lips with sly delight.

Sebastian was resplendent in his favourite red trousers. "A night out on the town will do you the power of good," he preached, as they stepped from a taxi. "You can't live like a goat herder all your life, Henry."

A queue had formed outside Dodger's Wine Bar and two bouncers stood like Mesopotamian guards either side of its entrance. Eventually, after being scrutinised as if they were marrows at a horticultural show, the boys were allowed inside. The exposed brickwork minimalism of the joint was offset by ornate Moroccan mirrors, Arabesque wallpaper and kitschy light fixtures; it was a fancy venue pretending to be down-at-heel to satisfy the eco-sensibilities of its modish clientele.

Though Henry felt distinctly out of place, Sebastian was in his element, flouncing through the buzzy throng as if he were the embodiment of Dorian Gray. Henry envied Sebastian his unfaltering ability to attract the fairer sex and was sad that he didn't possess just a scintilla of his friend's rakish charm.

Sebastian kissed the cheeks of a willowy beauty, who greeted Henry with a wide, genial smile. "Henry, I would like you to meet Ophelia. Ophelia, this is Henry."

"Such a pleasure to meet you, Henry. I know so little about Seb's friends."

Henry resisted the urge to say, 'I *am* his one and only friend,' and shook her hand. The thought immediately entered Henry's head that this courteous and magnetically beautiful young lady was far too good for Sebastian.

"Hey, I do believe that Champagne befits an occasion such as this," Sebastian said grandly.

"Um, I'd be happy with a beer," gulped Henry.

"Oh, please allow me to pay," beseeched Ophelia, delving into her handbag.

"Shan't hear of it, hon. It's on me. Wait here and we shall return anon with some fizz. Come along, Henry."

Once at the bar, Sebastian ordered a bottle of Veuve Clicquot then patted his pockets as if he were frisking himself. "Henry, you couldn't just get this could you? I haven't quite got the funds to stretch to a bottle of bubbly."

Henry's voice went up an octave. "So what about the money you get from the restaurant?"

"All gone, I'm afraid. You try living on a waiter's wages and see how far it gets you."

"Then why the heck are you ordering Champagne?"

"Because Ophelia likes Champagne. Oh come on,

Henry, don't dampen the mood. It's always something with you."

"God! You are insufferable," blazed Henry, at the same time taking care to ensure that Ophelia didn't register his displeasure as she looked on.

While Henry paid the barman, Sebastian took the credit for his grandiose gesture by carrying the ice bucket, bottle and glasses with all the aplomb of a royal butler.

"You really shouldn't have. Thank you, Sebastian," smiled Ophelia.

"Not just me, my darling, Henry chipped in as well."

"Thank you, Henry."

"You are most welcome," replied Henry, feigning a smile.

"When one pops a Champagne cork, it should sound like a duchess's fart," announced Sebastian as he opened the bottle.

"Oh, just listen to him," said Ophelia. "Showing off just because he's a qualified sommelier."

"Yes, he's good at that," said Henry through gritted teeth.

Fed up with witnessing Sebastian crowing like a cockerel yet somehow continuing to beguile Ophelia, Henry retreated to the sanctuary of a bar stool where he supped pints of beer in splendid isolation. He found the greasy fingerprints on the brass bar rail hard to ignore and was busily removing them with his handkerchief when he was poked in the arm.

"Hey! Where's your posh prat of a friend?"

Henry swivelled round on his stool to find Amber, the object of his fledgling desire, glaring at him with an avalanche of ice in her mermaid eyes.

"Er, hello, Amber, I don't think that we've been properly introduced—"

"Never mind that." she fumed, her breasts seeming as if they might explode out of her tight dress. "Is he here? I need to give that arrogant sod a piece of my mind."

"Um, may I ask what the arrogant sod has done?"

"He went to my manager a week ago and complained about me writing something on his cup. Cost me my job, the bloody sneak!"

Henry buried his face in his hands, embarrassed but at the same time not at all surprised. "Omigod, I am so, so sorry. I really had no idea."

"Look, I know it's not your fault. You strike me as being less of an idiot. But is he here or not?"

"Uh, he's sitting over there," Henry said, cringing as he spoke. "Just through that crowd of people."

"Thanks. Get me a large glass of Chardonnay and I'll be back in a tick."

Henry, after ordering her wine, could barely bring himself to look as Amber wended through the throng and started to remonstrate with Sebastian. Her voice was inaudible through the sea of conversation but her actions were pure theatre. Henry loved that there was something delightfully unpredictable about her.

Her indignation offloaded, Amber returned requited and with a winning smile on her dimpled face. "His girlfriend seems nice. What's she doing with him?" she quizzed, grabbing the glass of wine and planting herself on a neighbouring barstool.

"I've asked myself the exact same question."

"Anyway, I feel better for doing that. Your name, it's Henry isn't it?"

"Yes, it is. Kind of you to remember."

"Well, I'm Amber." She raised her glass. "Cheers, Henry!"

"Uh, yes. Cheers!"

After taking a generous sip, during which time she noticed Henry's Spider-Man socks, Amber studied him intently as if he were a portrait in an art gallery. "Y'know, I'm still trying to figure out where I know you from."

An apologetic look clouded his face. "Um, I'd be surprised if you knew me from anywhere."

"Bit of a nobody are you, Henry?" she teased.

Amber dug into her handbag for lipstick and applied it with practiced precision. Henry noticed a tiny puncture wound in her nose where a piercing had once existed. He also spotted the orange cummerbunds of a Penguin paperback peeking from her bag: *The Rainbow*, by DH Lawrence.

"I know it's terribly rude to look into a lady's handbag but I'm delighted to see that you're a book reader."

"You cheeky bugger! It's not just posh boys who read books, you know!"

"Gosh, I didn't mean it like that—"

She threw back her head, laughing. "I know you didn't. Ha! You've gone bright red, you wally."

The consumption of four pints of beer had given Henry the Dutch courage to converse easily with this curvaceous princess, otherwise he'd have been a gibbering wreck. He wondered why someone so clearly out of his league would bother talking to him. Her coppery tumble of Pre-Raphaelite hair was burnished gold by a row of industrial downlighters that drooped above their heads like wilted tulips. The tightness of her dress further accentuated her voluptuousness.

"Um, are you here on your own?" he asked, noticing for

the first time a mole on her chin that resembled a small raisin.

"No, I came here with two friends, Naomi and Stacey, but they're being chatted up by two Cockney lotharios. I doubt they've even noticed my absence."

Henry scratched his chin. "And, er, what's the situation with your, um, boyfriend, the one who beats up old men?"

"Oh, cringe! Listen, I swear I knew nothing about that. In any case, I've already finished with the idiot. I live in a house that my gran left me but he's still hanging around like a bad odour until I turf him out."

"But why did you go out with such a chap in the first place – if it's not too rude to ask?"

"I guess that I've always gone for the bad boys," she mused. "But I can't even use the excuse that he was a stud in the bedroom, him and his floppy pencil dick. And there's nothing worse than bad sex is there?"

"Oh, um, I wouldn't know," Henry muttered, his cheeks reddening. "I, uh, have never had a girlfriend."

"You're a virgin?!" Amber blurted out, causing a bartender's eyebrows to almost leap from his forehead.

"Alright, alright, keep your voice down," Henry protested. "No need to broadcast it to the whole wide world."

"How is that even possible?" asked Amber, her voice incredulous and reduced to a discreet whisper.

"Well, just look at me! I'm not exactly an Adonis."

"But you're certainly not ugly. And you've got kind eyes."

"Hardly a compliment. Most of the world's despots have kind eyes."

"And your lips are quite gynaecological. It would be almost indecent to kiss them."

"Thanks! So now my mouth looks like a woman's lady parts."

"OK, so your hair's all over the place, you've got terrible dress sense and you look as though you've been dragged through a hedge backwards, but there's nothing there that a spot of grooming won't fix. Trust me, you're fine."

"You neglected to mention that I'm overweight," said Henry, looking as downcast as an orang-utan.

"Big bloody deal! I'm slightly overweight, in case you haven't noticed. More than half the world is overweight."

"Gosh, you're not overweight, you're, er … comely."

"Comely?"

"Rubenesque, perhaps?"

"Fat, in other words."

"Oh no, far from fat. Plumpish."

"Ha! You are *so* not used to being around women," Amber chuckled.

At that precise moment, just as he swigged a half-mouthful of beer, Henry caught sight of Amber's ex-boyfriend hurtling towards him like an enraged hyena. He had barely the time to comprehend this alarming vision before Danny smashed a bony fist into his face, causing beer and blood to spray in all directions.

"Arrrgh!" Henry spat as Danny continued his attack, this time missing his target altogether with two wild swings.

"You bloody animal!" Amber bellowed, throwing herself directly into the windmill of Danny's fists just as a thickset bouncer tore through the crowd and hefted him off his feet in a headlock. Danny was forcibly dragged along sticky floorboards while a mob of cheering drinkers lined up to throw beer into his strangulated face.

"Huh, whaat?" wailed Henry, with blood and

astonishment dripping from his face. "W-why did he hit me?"

"Danny's just a jealous idiot," soothed Amber, swabbing him with a bar towel. "Probably thought you were shagging me. Are you OK?"

Henry, who would have happily endured a barrage of punches to give his assailant such an exquisite reason to be jealous, said that he was fine. "I don't think that your ex-boyfriend is quite the pugilist he imagines himself to be," he smiled weakly.

While Henry nursed his wounds, Amber sipped her wine and continued to wonder where she'd seen him before. Something about his bewildered expression shimmered on her mind's distant horizon.

Sebastian, with an elastic grin across his smug face, nipped over to enquire about Henry's wellbeing, having watched the fracas from a safe distance. He announced that he would be staying over at Ophelia's and wished Henry goodnight without once making eye contact with Amber.

"You've definitely ruffled his peacock feathers," said Henry, discovering that it was painful to smile with sore lips.

Amber smiled and fluffed up her hair. "So I'm guessing that you two went to some posh boarding school. Am I right?"

"Oh dear, it's that obvious, is it?"

"God, yeah."

"Um, we both attended St Jude's, which is in Surrey—"

"No way!" squealed Amber. "I used to live less than half a mile from that school!"

"Oh, really? Um, it's a small world, isn't it?"

"Omigod, I've just realised where I know you from! You

were the boy I saved from getting a beating outside the Burger Wizard."

"Crikey. So you're the girl with the butterfly tattoo? Really? You look completely different without the vampire makeup and beanie hat."

"How on earth d'you know about my butterfly tattoo?"

"I saw it when you were kicking seven shades of whatsit out of me."

"Oh, you big wuss. You know damn well that I held back."

"For which I was extremely grateful. I've, er, often thought of you since."

"Me too!" trilled Amber, her face lighting up. "Ooh, Henry, do you believe in fate?"

"No."

"Well I do! Everything happens for a reason. Perhaps the universe has thrown us together tonight?"

Henry, though indifferent to such murky nonsense, nevertheless liked the idea of them being thrown together so tactfully nodded his head and ordered more drinks as Amber gabbled about destiny and the spinning of mystic threads. When Henry enquired as to the reason for her butterfly tattoo he heard that, in common with his mother, butterflies shadowed Amber like gulls behind a trawler.

"That's astonishing," Henry declared. "My mother was also followed by butterflies wherever she went."

"See? Fate!"

After draining another large glass of Chardonnay, which she then slammed emphatically onto the bar, Amber gazed deep into Henry's soul. A tress of hair fell fetchingly over one eye. "Do you have a place where we can go, Henry?"

"Go?"

"Yes, an apartment, a house?" Amber was licking her

lips in a fashion that Henry found unnerving. She'd also moved near enough for him to smell the fragrance of her shampoo.

"Er, yes, I, um have an apartment. Why do you ask?"

"I think you know why. I think that it's time for you to take the plunge." She uttered the word *plunge* as if its usage was expressly forbidden in polite society.

Henry's heart began to palpitate and he felt the sudden need to retrieve his inhaler from his trouser pocket. "Um … you've probably had a little too much to drink and slightly lost your mind. Shouldn't you be getting a taxi home? It is rather late."

"What, and go back to that idiot? No thanks! You and I are going to have sex! It's written in the stars!"

"I will if he won't," the bartender interjected.

"Mind your own business!" Amber shouted.

Robustly taking Henry by the arm, Amber eeled through a thicket of elbows and led him out onto the street where a procession of gleaming taxis lined the frosty pavement.

"Careful, mate, that geezer who walloped you is still hanging about," a bouncer warned, nodding in the direction of Danny, who was raging like a madman on the opposite side of the road.

"You're fucking dead, you fucking bitch!" Danny blazed, the tendons in his neck as pronounced as tree roots.

"Quite the little charmer, isn't he?" the doorman chuckled, escorting them to the first available taxi. "Have a great night, you two."

CHAPTER TWENTY-FOUR

The Virgin and the Mermaid

"Dear God, are you man or beast?" Amber gasped, as she caressed Henry's thigh in the backseat of their taxi and found lurking there rather more than she'd bargained for. "I don't know whether to be excited or scared."

Henry, unaccustomed to chatting with females much less being groped by one, wriggled and squirmed then tried to talk about *Star Wars* movies and the order in which he rated them. Amber, though, was not to be denied and pawed at his belt buckle as if bedevilled by carnal desire.

"I can be very naughty," she purred, whispering in his ear. "Can I put my hand in there to keep my fingers warm?"

"Ah, yes, this is where I live!" cried Henry histrionically, leaping from his seat and tapping on the driver's partition screen. This prompted a brief respite from the frenzy of Amber's ardour. "It'll be nice to get out of the cold," he rambled, deliberately delaying finding the key that opened the front door while Amber shoved him and told him to get a move on.

His apartment was cold so he clicked on the central heating and asked his lustful guest if she'd prefer tea or coffee.

Amber stood with her chest pushed forward and her arms intertwined behind her back. "Henry, I appreciate that you're nervous. I get it. But just chill. Which one is your bedroom?"

"Um, it's this one," he mumbled, not quite knowing what to do with himself.

Amber clasped his sweaty hand, hit the light switch and led him into the room, smiling over her shoulder to reassure him. She noticed straightaway a poster of Albert Einstein above his bed; the great man's tongue was hanging out of his mouth like a fish from a kingfisher's beak.

Her voice was full of mischief and promises as she reached for the bedside lamp. "We can keep this one on, if you'd like?"

"Um, yes, I'd, um, like that very much, thank you," Henry quavered, relieved to turn off the main light.

Amber peeled back the duvet. While her shapely shadow danced about the walls of the lamplit room, she slowly undressed, kicking off her heels and allowing her dress to puddle about her feet. With a kittenish smile she unclasped her bra, shimmied out of her panties and slid under the quilt with a coquettish smile and a body built for sin.

"You next," she coaxed. "Or would you rather I closed my eyes?"

"Oh, most kind. Yes, I'd rather you did, if you, er, don't mind?"

"Not at all, "Amber giggled, theatrically fanning her hands over her face. "Would you like me to count to a hundred?"

"Um, no, that won't be necessary," Henry smiled

nervously, as bashful as an Ottoman bride. He undressed reluctantly, folding his clothes neatly until he was as nature intended. Mortified that he was now unable to hide the charcuterie of his generous penis, he looked like a fully-grown version of the bewildered baby who had plopped from his mother's womb twenty years earlier.

"I promise that I'm not peeking," Amber chuckled, while making it obvious that she was. "Yum, yum. Aren't you a big boy?"

"Er, perhaps I should brush my teeth?"

"There's no need."

"You know, I'd, um, previously imagined that when this moment arrived, it would be in a Rococo-style, Parisian hotel room—"

"Henry, just shut up and get into bed."

"Um, OK."

Awash with trepidation, he was suddenly on the mattress, lured like an errant sailor onto a siren's rocky shore. Despite himself, Henry eased himself into uncharted territory and nestled his paunch against the warm, curvaceous softness of Amber's milky-skinned body. She rose above him and kissed his chest, allowing her abundant breasts to caress his belly. He massaged them with no real idea of what he was doing. She nevertheless moaned softly and, under his attentive touch, her nipples grew as big as acorns. His penis, which for so long had languished in the quicksand of celibacy, became as hard as a cudgel in her eager hands. He discovered that her mysterious nether regions were damp as a window-cleaner's sponge.

"I want you inside me," she whispered, slipping her tongue into his ear and sliding her body underneath him so that his weight was pressing down on her. "Oof! God, you're a heavy lump."

"Um, what about, er, contraception?" Henry asked as his tumescence throbbed earnestly.

Amber caressed one of his rosy cheeks. "Relax, I've got it covered."

This was the moment that Henry had long been dreading: understanding anatomically what goes where was one thing, but accomplishing such a feat was beyond his comprehension. He flubbered on top of Amber like a sea lion on a slippery rock, hoping that nature would somehow take its course and that penetration would miraculously happen of its own accord.

"Ow, careful! You're bruising me. It's like being prodded with a courgette," she grumbled. " Here, let me help you."

Amber discovered that easing him in wasn't an easy task but, by spreading her legs akimbo and pulling on his buttocks, she achieved what at first seemed impossible.

"Omigod," she gasped, with a wide-eyed look of excitement on her face.

Henry, after an astonished pause in which he realised he was deep inside her, was all at once out of the traps, his hips thrusting like a well-oiled piston and his testicles shaking like maracas.

"Oh, dear God! Oh, dear Go-od!" wailed Amber in a vibrato voice, her breasts jiggling and her eyes popping out of her head, "Oh-h, it's bloody lovely!"

Their sweaty congress generated a ferment of slapping and slurping noises, comparable to those made by a swimming-pool suction drain. The bed shook as if in an earthquake and Amber's butterfly trembled synchronously on her belly.

"Ooh! Oo-wooh!" groaned Henry, looking up to see that even Albert Einstein was willing him on. Amber grasped at lumps of Henry's flesh and felt as if she were steering a rickety bus on a bumpy goat track.

As he'd feared, Henry reached sexual release all too soon, his flushed face suddenly like that of a man in the throes of electrocution. "Ohhh-ughhh!" he grunted, turning cross-eyed and clenching his jaw before collapsing in a sated heap, just as Amber was beginning to succumb to toe-tingling ecstasy. Given his inexperience, she felt that his inability to delay the firing of his gun was only to be expected and sought to reassure him with a supportive smile.

"Oh, oh, gosh. Uh, I'm really sorry," he gasped, instantly realising that he hadn't performed to the required standard.

"Mmm, no need for apologies, Henry. That was fine for your first time," she purred, kissing his bruised lips. "In fact, I'd say that it was more than fine."

Henry, with a soppy look on his besotted face, for some syrupy reason thought that this was the perfect moment to quote Shakespeare. "Virginity, by being once lost may be ten times found," he cooed, arching one eyebrow like a latter-day Clark Gable.

"Oh shut up, you fool," Amber chuckled, reaching out for a cuddle.

CHAPTER TWENTY-FIVE

The Dead of Night

Amber's wantonness kindled a fire in Henry's belly and in less time than it takes to boil a kettle, he was at full mast and ready to go again.

"Careful, you could have someone's eye out with that," grinned Amber, as his adequacy presented itself once more.

He proved to be a quick learner; their second bout of coitus jockeyed the bed some distance from the wall and left them both gasping for air. Henry resisted the temptation to recite poetry and Amber fell all the more in love with his guileless charm.

Afterwards, while she lay gratified in his arms, she abruptly remembered that she'd left Sherlock alone in the house with Danny. Without delay, she leapt from the bed, hurriedly swapped numbers with Henry and phoned for a taxi. When it arrived, Henry opened the cab door and gamely kissed her goodnight.

Her face was a mismatch of exhilaration and bafflement. "I can't believe I'm actually saying this, but I feel great around you. So you'd better ring me."

"Of course," he replied with unequivocal sincerity.

Only a mist of her perfume remained as her ride vanished into the night and, with the grin of a carefree ogre festooning his face, he lolloped back to his apartment, as light-footed as Eros.

*

Amber noticed, with very little surprise, that although it was one thirty in the morning, most of her house lights were on. She expected Danny to have worked himself into a state of hostile delirium and was therefore prepared for his vitriol. Not before time, she resolved to get the door locks changed in the coming week.

From an upstairs window, and unbeknown to her, Yuri watched her climb out of the taxi and fantasised about ripping off her dress and taking her by force. These urges had become so strong recently that he'd even thought about throwing caution to the wind by breaking into her house while she slept.

"I *will* have you, Amber," he muttered to himself. "This I swear."

Bracing herself for what was to come, Amber walked up the driveway and entered the house by the side door. The main kitchen light was on and for some inexplicable reason there was a conspicuous trail of muddy footprints smeared about the tiled floor. She could hear the TV in the living room and noticed an accumulation of Danny's depleted beer bottles lined up like skittles on the kitchen table.

Sherlock's corduroy dog basket lay empty in one corner and he was nowhere to be seen. Amber took a deep breath and strode towards the living room. Thankfully Danny, dimly lit by the TV, was fast asleep on the sofa with a spilled beer bottle resting on his lap. She walked upstairs knowing that Sherlock preferred to sleep on her bed when Danny was around but, after walking around calling his name, her search yielded nothing. Becoming increasingly anxious, she ran down the stairs and into the living room to shake Danny from his drunken slumber.

"Where the hell is Sherlock?" she shouted frantically as he gazed back with confused, bleary eyes. "Where is he? I can't find him!"

"Huh? Let me sleep, you stupid bitch," he slurred, rolling onto his side.

Amber shook him violently, wanting answers. "No, you will not go back to sleep! Wake up! Wake the fuck up!"

"OK, I'm up, I'm up," he sniffed, remembering where he was. "Ha, yeah, your dog. Well you ain't got a fucking dog no more, you slut."

"W-what d'you mean I haven't got a dog?"

"What I said," he grinned. "Come with me and I'll show you something."

Jaw slackened, Amber followed Danny as he lurched into the kitchen. She saw mud on his shoes and trousers. A cold dread chilled her bones and her heart began to hammer at her ribcage.

"There you go, sweetheart. Have a look out there," he cackled, pointing beyond the window towards a mound of earth that she could just make out in the darkened garden.

"You bastard. Is this some kind of sick joke—?"

"Oh, no joke, love," he smirked. "I bloody warned you what would happen if you pissed me about."

With tears in her eyes and panic in her heart, Amber dashed into the garden. The freshly dug mound was contoured by moonlight. Lying next to it was the spade Danny had used to excavate the soil.

Amber dug frantically in the hope that this was just another of Danny's twisted mind games. At a shallow depth she unearthed a high-density polythene builder's sack. Sealed inside was the motionless body of her dog.

"Please God, no," she wailed, brushing away the soil with her hand. "Oh please God, no!"

Desperate to get air into the sack she punctured the polythene with one of her stiletto heels and frantically tore at it, breaking her nails until she'd made a hole big enough to free Sherlock's head. She blew into his nostrils and pumped his chest but it was obvious that he was beyond help.

Incandescent with rage, Amber grabbed the spade and flew into the kitchen. Danny sat at the table with a triumphant grin on his face. "Little bastard took a while to die he did, thrashing about in that bag—"

From the afterlife, her grandmother screamed for her to stop but Amber could only hear the pounding of a drum in her temples. With a bloodcurdling roar, she swung with everything she had. The shoulder of the blade clanged against the side of Danny's head, caving in his skull and sending him crashing to the floor. He lay there motionless, staring resolutely at the ceiling as a crown of blood spread slowly from his shattered head.

Amber staggered back but before she could comprehend the enormity of what she'd done, the jarring sound of the front doorbell daggered through the house. It was obvious that it would be Mr Beardsley. Dropping the spade, she scampered into the hallway, fighting off hysteria and smoothing her dress as she ran.

Though she didn't want to, Amber knew she'd have to answer the door; her neighbour wasn't the type to throw in the towel. She gathered her thoughts, drew a deep breath, turned the key and opened up.

"Come on, Amber, what the hell is going on?" Mr

Beardsley carped, standing in the porch with his hands jammed into the pockets of his towelling dressing gown. Though Amber looked a frightful sight, he was determined to have his say. "It's almost two o'clock in the bleeding morning. I shouldn't have to put up with all that racket."

"I-I'm so, so sorry, Mr B-Beardsley," she stammered, trying to contain the wave of blind hysteria that coursed through her body. "W-we had a fight. We had a fight. It's all sorted now. I swear to God we'll be quiet. I promise."

Mr Beardsley looked at her askance, his detective instincts kicking in. "Amber, you've got mud and mascara all down your face and more mud on your dress. Are you sure everything's OK?"

"Yeah, yeah, it's all good," she murmured, trying to quell her panic. "It's all too, er, complicated to explain, but Danny's sleeping it off now and he's, um, agreed to leave tomorrow."

"Well, that's music to my ears, Amber. A nice girl like you shouldn't be associating with the likes of him, yeah?"

"Y-Yeah, I agree, totally. Thank you, Mr Beardsley—"

His protective instinct made him reluctant to leave her like this. "Amber, you're shaking like a leaf. Look, if you're in harm's way you can kip round mine tonight in a spare bedroom. I've seen how these things can escalate."

"Oh, you're very kind. I-I'm just cold. Need to put on some warm clothes."

"Well, as long as you think you're safe, I'll turn in. Any more noise though and I'm calling the police, yeah?"

"Yeah, I'll be fine. Sorry about the noise, Mr Beardsley."

Her neighbour cast his beady eyes beyond her, wishing he could see around corners. "OK, night-night, Amber. Be good."

After shutting the door, Amber hurried back to the

kitchen and repeatedly called out to a forgotten god but her prayers evaporated into the night. It was clear to see that Danny was dead; nevertheless she checked his pulse, hoping against expectation that he might only be dazed. The dent in his skull and a sickening puddle of blood suggested otherwise.

"Please God, please God," she babbled, over and over again, while pacing about the kitchen with her head in her muddy hands.

In a panic, and not knowing who else to trust, she grabbed her phone and pressed Henry's number. The call was answered after only a few rings.

"Hi, Amber, you can't sleep either?" he chirped, already missing the musky terrain of her body.

"Henry, please, please listen. I'm freaking out. Something terrible has happened. Please come, I'm begging you. Please! I just don't know what to do!"

Henry furrowed his brow and gripped the phone tighter. "Hey, what's wrong? Has your boyfriend hurt you?"

"I can't talk right now, but please, pleeease come. I'm in terrible, terrible trouble."

It affected Henry greatly to hear Amber in such deep distress. He could barely hear what she was saying through the loud sobs that punctuated her every word. "Amber, hold tight, I'll be there as soon as I can. What is your address?"

"Seventy-three, Ferdinand Road … but Henry, please, please don't have the taxi pull up outside, I don't want my neighbours looking out of their windows."

Henry was already out of bed, slipping out of his pyjamas and tripping into a fresh pair of underpants. "Keep calm and try to relax. I'll be there as soon as I can."

At that point Amber was unable to utter another word and collapsed to the floor in a whimpering heap.

*

As Ferdinand Road came into view, Henry instructed his taxi driver to park at least five houses down from Amber's address. Murky clouds swam in the night sky and a security floodlight dazzled him the second he stepped onto her driveway. Amber, muddy and tearful, was waiting to usher him quietly in through the front door. No sooner had he stepped into the hallway than she threw herself into his arms, sobbing uncontrollably.

"Amber, please don't cry," he said, immediately thankful that Danny was not on the scene. "Whatever this is we can rectify it."

She retreated and began to wring her hands. "I don't think so. Oh, God, I'm in such trouble, such bloody trouble."

"In trouble for what? Just tell me."

She held his face in her muddy hands and looked him in the eye. "Henry, listen to me. Whatever happens, please don't freak out. Can I trust you not to freak out?"

"Of course. What could possibly be so bad that I could freak out?"

Fearfully Amber led him into the kitchen where he was beset by a nightmarish sight that went way beyond his worst-case scenario. "Shit! Oh, God! What on earth has happened?"

Unable to answer, she bowed her head and wiped tears from her reddened eyes.

Henry couldn't believe how much blood had leaked from Danny's head. He assumed him to be unconscious and in grave danger. "Have you called for an ambulance?"

"He's dead," she squeaked, her face contorted with dread, her stomach in knots.

Henry was stupefied. "Dead?"

In fits and starts Amber explained the sequence of events that had led to this grisly occurrence. In her distress, she began to talk gibberish and a stampede of words galloped from her mouth. Henry's emotions ran from pure anger towards Danny to heartfelt sympathy for Amber.

"So what should I do, Henry?" she blubbed. "I can't call the police. I'll go to prison. Please don't make me call the police—"

Henry struggled to catch his breath and took a few puffs on his inhaler. His mind was racing and all clarity of thought had escaped him. Were he in Amber's shoes, he wouldn't want the police involved either.

Amber looked at him with imploring eyes. He was her only hope.

It didn't take him long to arrive at a decision. Inspired by the musketeers of his childhood, Henry was hard-wired for such a moment, predestined one day to aid a damsel in distress. Like his father, he possessed a nobility of character and condemning Amber to a lengthy jail sentence just didn't seem to be the honourable thing to do.

Henry steeled himself to do something he knew he'd live to regret and leapt from the precipice.

"OK, we have to dispose of the body," he announced, placing himself in the mindset of a serial killer. "First thing we need to do is to get him out of plain sight. Is your garage floor clear of clutter?"

"Uh, yes," sputtered Amber, surprised and relieved that Henry hadn't run out of the door screaming.

"Good. We'll wrap him in something and take him into the garage. Then we need to forensically clean this area,

OK? And I'll ensure that your dog receives a dignified burial."

"Thank you, thank you, Henry." Amber sniffed, her eyes puffy from crying. "I don't deserve your kindness. I'm so sorry to get you involved—"

"Not at all. But listen, we need to keep our heads. This is not a time for blind panic."

"I'll stay calm, I promise," said Amber, her survival instincts kicking in. "And we also need to be quiet. My neighbour used to be a copper and the last thing we want is him coming round."

Henry, after ensuring that the security light was switched off, searched the garage hoping that there might be a large Turkish rug in which he could swathe the corpse; instead he found only a pile of paint-splattered dustsheets which he brought into the kitchen. Together, they stripped Danny's body naked, removing a mobile phone, wallet, coins, keys and chewing gum from his pockets. Then they wrapped him until he closely resembled an Egyptian mummy and lugged him into the garage, laying him onto its concrete floor.

Earlier, at the point of death, Danny's soul had left his body in terror and was already sucked into the tormenting storms of Hell.

"What do we do with him now?" asked Amber.

"Clearly he's too cumbersome to dispose of," said Henry, scratching his head. "We'll have to cut him up and put him into strong plastic bags."

Henry surprised even himself by the casualness with which he approached this hideous dilemma. Never could he have imagined that, on the same night he would lose his virginity, he would also become an accessory to murder.

"There are plenty of builders' sacks over there, near the

lawn mower," Amber said, tapping into an inner strength. "I could get on with the clean-up."

"Do you own a saw?" Henry enquired, firmly committed to the grisly task ahead.

"I do. But Henry, please don't even think about it. It'll make far too much noise at this time of night. Could you not return to it in the daytime? We're already into Sunday."

"Yes, of course. What was I thinking? We'll padlock the garage and I'll take care of things in daylight hours. Oh, God, can you even believe that we're having this discussion?"

As Amber steeled herself to mop up Danny's blood, she glanced at Sherlock's empty basket and once again burst into tears.

*

Yuri, hidden from view in the darkness beyond his landing window, gazed down at the sight of this young mystery man, who seemed to have suddenly replaced Amber's boyfriend. He watched with keen interest as the boy traipsed to and from the garage until four o'clock in the morning.

"So, Amber, what is your secret?" he speculated, a faint smile on his lips.

CHAPTER TWENTY-SIX

What Fools these Mortals Be

Henry and Amber slept fitfully in a tormented darkness. Each tried to hang onto the coat tails of slumber but the ragged teeth of dread gnawed at their subconscious and an orchestra of ill-boding whispers rattled their ears. Without any perception on their part, they were accompanied by Sherlock who clambered weightlessly onto the duvet to take up his favourite spot at Amber's feet. When it was his time to go, he tried to lick her face one last time and barked a silent goodbye. Amber's grandmother and Henry's mother kept a vigil from the great beyond.

It wasn't long before the youngsters were roused by a damning sunlight. Quickly adjusting to inescapable reality, Henry and Amber each cursed the contemptible life of the man who, even in death, was likely to be the architect of their downfall.

"What about his family?" asked Henry through bruised lips.

"He hasn't got any family. Spent his life in foster care," Amber replied.

"Well, at least that's in our favour."

"Oh, God, this is going to come back and bite me in the arse, isn't it?" groaned Amber, pulling her hair over her eyes.

"You and me both," said Henry, with a rueful shake of his head.

"Look, I shouldn't have involved you in this. I really wouldn't blame you if you walked away."

"We're in this together," asserted Henry, unearthing a fortitude he never knew existed.

"Couldn't we just throw his body in the Thames?" suggested Amber, with a degree of naivety that Henry found astonishing.

"Certainly not. For a start there are CCTV cameras everywhere and in any case he'd wash up somewhere and it wouldn't take them long to identify the body. No, the way forward is to cut him up and bury him in the middle of nowhere. Then we might just have a chance."

Amber recalled Sherlock gambolling around the garden with a princely look on his face. "I don't regret what I did, you know."

Henry touched the point of her chin, raised her head and held her gaze. "Nor should you."

After Amber had prepared a breakfast of scrambled eggs on toast accompanied by mugs of strong tea Henry, with surprising equanimity, revisited the garage with a bucket of hot, soapy water and some towels. He unfastened the padlock and took care to squeeze through its wooden doors without revealing the grisly secret within. He found the saw that Amber had mentioned but it was a large hacksaw effort with a blade he doubted would be up to the task. Nevertheless, he cleared the floor area around the body and pulled off the dustsheets, one of which had stuck to the corpse's blood-caked head. It tore away with a rasping sound.

Rather than have Danny's insensate eyes stare back at him, Henry rolled over his chilled body so that it was face down. In doing so, an alarming camel-like belch spewed from its throat, causing Henry to nearly jump out of his skin with extreme fright.

It's just an inanimate object, he reminded himself as he stripped down to his underpants, laying his clothes on a packing crate for fear of contaminating them. His plan was to dismember Danny and double-bag the body parts. He began to saw into the nape of the cadaver's neck, causing Danny's head to rock vigorously from side to side in silent protest. Henry retched violently but at the same time was relieved that any blood oozed quite passively, due to a degree of lividity; most of it was absorbed capably by the dust sheets underneath.

Henry found the soft tissue of the neck easy to cut through and only the spine offered any real resistance. Frustratingly, the saw blade snapped in half just as he'd severed the bone, leaving Henry with no means to continue. He stood up and looked down at his gruesome handiwork. The corpse's head lay snug against one shoulder, a tatty rag of raw flesh its only means of attachment. It was then that an unsolicited vision of his own parents, their bodies cleft with terrible injuries, invaded his mind.

Daunted by all that faced him, Henry washed his bloodied hands in the bucket of water, slipped into his clothes and returned to the house.

"Amber, I'm afraid that the saw isn't man enough," he sighed. "We need to get a more robust one from the DIY store. Could you drive me there?"

"Of course," said Amber, consternation furrowing her brow. "You've got a bit of, um, blood on your cheek."

The Nitty-Gritty DIY store was a thirty-minute journey from Amber's house. While she drove, Henry drew up a list of all the things he might need, keeping the macabre details to himself for fear of upsetting her more than she already was.

Amber's disquietude was exacerbated by the fact that she bumped into a talkative work colleague, who was shopping for Christmas tree decorations with her equally-garrulous husband.

"Look, Vanessa, I really must get on," she finally snapped, after having to endure every detail of Vanessa and Brian's tried-and-tested Christmas recipe for the perfect roast potatoes.

Henry and Amber eventually left the store with a trolley containing a panel saw, several packets of cable ties, a scrubbing brush and four large plastic bottles of bleach.

Upon their return, Henry instructed Amber to reverse as near to the garage as possible, thus forming a barrier against prying eyes. After unloading the car, Henry was all at once rooted to the spot in front of the garage doors. A look of abject horror plastered his face.

"The padlock!" he blustered.

"What about it?"

At that moment, Amber saw precisely what had caused Henry such alarm. The padlock, which they'd double-checked before leaving, was no longer there. Icy fingers of terror constricted her throat and tore at her heart; her legs buckled and she leant against the car for support.

Henry gingerly opened the garage doors, fearing the worst. Danny's body had vanished into thin air and in its place was a large damp patch which reeked of bleach.

"Shit, shit, shit! What the hell?" quavered Henry, his neurons firing and his fingers trembling. "What the bloody hell—"

Amber was having palpitations. "Quick, shut the doors and get inside the house," she hissed, trying to keep her voice down and fumbling with the keys.

Once indoors, they stared at each other, wide-eyed and aghast. Henry could hear his heart pounding in his chest and struggled to comprehend what had happened. "What on earth? Am I going mad? How is this even possible? We've only been gone two hours," he bleated.

"Omigod, omigod!" babbled Amber, gesticulating wildly and pacing about the kitchen. "It'll be Yuri, my next-door neighbour. I bet you any money."

"Yuri?" remarked Henry on hearing a name that had haunted his psyche for a decade.

"Yuri, my neighbour on *this* side," Amber said, pointing to the kitchen door with a quivering finger. "He's a bloody gangster, Henry. What on earth have I got you into?"

Henry's eyes were as wide as saucers. "I know him! He was involved in the murder of my parents."

"Your parents were murdered?"

"Ten years ago, on my birthday. Your neighbour – and I assume he's the same man – was one of two people responsible for their death—"

"Are you sure he's the same person?"

"Yuri Voloshyn," said Henry. The name rolled off his tongue like wet toothpaste.

"Oh God, that's him. What are we going to do? I feel sick."

"Right, this is what we'll do. We'll keep our heads down. We'll each go to work tomorrow and just carry on as normal until he shows his hand."

"This is just madness."

"Yes, it is, but we need to keep our heads."

Just then, the house phone rang loudly, causing their hearts to leap like salmon. "Could that be Yuri?" asked Henry, fearing a sudden escalation of their woes.

"Oh please don't let it be him," Amber groaned, walking to the phone with trepidation.

When Amber answered, it was simply Mr Beardsley asking if she was all right after the previous night's argument with Danny.

She somehow affected a casual tone. "Oh, he's gone, Mr Beardsley. I doubt he'll be coming here again." Henry nodded encouragingly as he eavesdropped on the conversation.

Mr Beardsley asked if she needed him to look after her dog tomorrow, while she was at work.

Amber, not quite knowing how to answer this, and fighting back tears, croaked, "Oh, Mr Beardsley, h-he's even taken Sherlock with him."

*

"We need to lose his mobile somewhere," said Henry, staring at Danny's phone and trying to think like a criminal. "The police can easily track this, should they need to. The best idea that I've come up with is to take it across London, remove the battery, smash it up and dispose of it somehow."

To achieve this objective, Amber agreed to drive Henry to Mile End tube station. As they prepared to get into her car, Yuri appeared in his driveway under a cirrus of cigarette smoke. Henry, who had been working tirelessly on his article about the vicarage murder, knew the Ukrainian's face only too well from a grim police mugshot that he'd studied a thousand times over: a face that resembled a thickly-knuckled tree trunk. Despite being ten years older than his mugshot, there was no doubting that this man was Yuri Voloshyn.

"Hey, Amber," Yuri droned, his voice suggesting the sound of a wasp caught in a jar. "I think you have busy night last night?"

"W-what do you mean?" she stammered, her heart sinking to her toes.

"Backward and forward to garage," he grinned. "Maybe you have emergency?"

Yuri continued to study Amber with an intensity that sent blood rushing to his loins and venom to his brain. He flicked his cigarette to the ground where it died a slow death. Then, after giving Henry a sinister wink, he sauntered toward his latest car.

CHAPTER TWENTY-SEVEN

Lies and Alibis

Sebastian returned to Peggotty Road before lunchtime, having spent the night at Ophelia's luxury apartment in Islington, to find his flatmate nowhere to be seen. This afforded him the perfect opportunity to discover what pickings might be found in the intriguing shoebox above Henry's bed. After surveying the street to check that the coast was clear, he crept into Henry's bedroom. The shoebox was in the same place, slotted between a Batman figurine and the leather-bound Bible that had once belonged to Henry's father.

Monitored by Albert Einstein, who could do nothing more than raise his eyebrows and stick out his tongue, Sebastian stood upon the bed and slid the box out, keen to see if there were any more banknotes inside its cardboard coffer.

"Oh, Henry, you really are a twat," he chuckled to himself, staring at a stash of money, which looked to be worth easily more than a few thousand pounds. He pushed the box back into position and retired to the living room to figure out a plan as to how he might acquire some, if not all, of this sinfully neglected cash.

Declaring himself a genius, Sebastian devised a foolproof scheme to steal the money whereby all blame would be cast upon Liam, whom he'd seen entering the house a few minutes ahead of him. With shoes removed, he skulked up the first flight of stairs under the suspicious gaze of Oscar, who hissed at him like a furious python. Sebastian tiptoed toward Liam's door then, after selecting what he deemed to be the muddiest pair of boots from the line, he padded downstairs to the hallway.

After rechecking that the coast was clear, he stood on the doormat and put on Liam's boots. He walked into his and Henry's apartment and, taking care to leave mucky footprints all over Henry's duvet, relieved the shoebox of its entire contents.

Ensuring that the boots were returned to their accustomed position outside Liam's apartment, Sebastian complimented himself on his *fait accompli*. Mr O'Connor's ex-jailbird son would naturally carry the blame for the theft, leaving Sebastian to enjoy all the spoils.

With a self-satisfied grin on his face and wads of cash stuffed into his jacket pockets, he set off in the direction of The Hanging Pirate public house to establish a cast-iron alibi.

*

In the stale, subterranean air of a tube carriage, Henry sat with eyes half-closed and vaguely registered the squeaks, beeps and pneumatic hisses of his Central Line train as it rumbled westbound underneath the streets of London. He'd deliberately left Danny's phone switched on in order to create an identifiable record of its journey, with the intention of making it seem that it was Danny who was heading across town. In a blind panic, he'd made this undertaking without properly thinking it through. The more he thought about it, taking the omnipresence of CCTV cameras into account, the more his logic didn't make sense.

Wasn't it Gandhi who said that all murderers fail in the end? he brooded, as he chewed on his Oyster card. With dread rising from the pit of his stomach, Henry sensed that this misguided piece of subterfuge would turn out to be a fool's errand, given that Yuri Voloshyn seemed to have them at an unspecified disadvantage.

Earlier, in the short space of time available to him, Henry had read online that a mobile phone couldn't be traced once the battery was removed but, wishing to leave nothing to chance he wasn't prepared to take that as the gospel truth. His intention was to transport the phone a good distance away where he'd remove its battery and smash it with a chisel before tossing it into a rubbish bin.

Before he'd gone underground, and while the phone still held its signal, one of Danny's friends, who went by the soubriquet of 'Gollum', sent a truncated text message in barely decipherable English asking Danny if he was on his way to the pub. Henry, though tempted to fill Danny's shoes by tapping out a similarly compressed message, thought better of it.

In a muddled state of conflicting emotions, he reflected on recent events, allowing himself to remember the bare-fleshed deliciousness of Amber's body and the mischievous smile on her face. But, in the blink of his mind's eye, he also recalled Danny's head rocking from side to side and the sickening smell of his blood.

The doors swished open at Oxford Circus, enabling a fresh cluster of passengers to stream in and scramble for seats. Like an old man at a great-grandchild's wedding, Henry sat wearily as the world bustled by. He caught a skull-like reflection of himself in a tunnel-darkened window and then, above the whirr of the train's acceleration, he heard an elegant female voice call out his name. "Henry! Fancy seeing you! What a small world we live in!"

When he looked up, bearing down on him, lively-eyed and optimistic, was Sebastian's new squeeze, Ophelia. In the flickering luminance of the carriage she planted a kiss on each of his cheeks and sat beside him, excitable as a puppy.

"Uh, a small world indeed, Ophelia. What brings you into the murky bowels of central London on a Sunday?"

"I'm meeting my grandparents for lunch and a spot of early Christmas shopping before the madness starts. Anyway, how's your mouth? Looks quite nasty. That guy was a brute – did you even know him?"

"Only vaguely. It was nothing really," said Henry, self-consciously prodding his lips and feeling as if the whole world could see into his dark soul.

"So, what are your plans today, Henry?"

"I'm, um, visiting a friend in, er, Notting Hill," he said, looking up at the route map for inspiration. In the way that a guilty person overeggs a false alibi, Henry proceeded to gabble interminably about an imaginary friend in Notting Hill, describing him in scrupulous detail as he would a character in his novel.

"Oh, gosh, here's my stop," sighed Ophelia, rising to her feet and pushing a tress of hair from her face. "I dearly wish I had more time to talk to you, Henry. I'm greatly concerned for poor Seb. And why are his parents being so horrid to him, after all he's done for them?"

Henry, with his personality manifestly changed

overnight, would have loved to spill the beans and tell her what her boyfriend was really like, but she was already leaving the carriage in a flurry of goodbyes.

The doors closed with a matron's shush and, as the train surged from the platform, Henry looked back at Ophelia who stood time-lapse still while a fog of people blurred past. Seeing only goodness in her heart, he resolved to put pressure on Sebastian that he might set her free to love someone more deserving.

*

Sebastian had never previously stepped into the dark conviviality of The Hanging Pirate and immediately found himself among people he considered to be plebeian and repulsive, with their pints of lager and laddish backslaps.

"Guys, I need to get through," he protested to a group of drinkers who were crowding the doorway.

"Whoo-hoo! Hey, lads, we're honoured by Mr Darcy today," cheered a big-bellied man with more tattoos than teeth. "What part of London are you from, mate?"

"Surrey, actually," Sebastian snorted, finding himself surrounded by the smell of beer and cheese-and-onion crisps.

"Oh, but sire, where are our manners? C'mon, let the geezer through, he's near royalty by the sounds of it."

With that, the men parted like the Red Sea, forming a jocular guard of honour and bowing mockingly as Sebastian passed through with a sour look on his face.

After surveying the room with much disdain, he spotted Fergus O'Connor seated with two other men of a similar age. Concealing his guile, he approached their table with the rabbity tread of an equerry.

"Hi, Mr O'Connor, have you seen Henry? I can't get hold of him and was hoping I might find him here."

"Afraid not, Sebastian. He usually pops in on a Sunday but he's yet to show his face… If you're not in any great hurry, you're very welcome to join our merry band of dipsomaniacs." Fergus made the invitation purely out of politeness, expecting it to be declined.

"Excellent idea," replied Sebastian, secure in the knowledge that his alibi was getting tighter by the second.

Mr O'Connor, wearing a French beret that further accentuated the enormity of his ears, hid his surprise and led the introductions.

"Reuben and Vishnu, this handsome fella is Sebastian, my other lodger."

"Gentlemen, it would be an honour to buy the next round of drinks," smarmed Sebastian with a premeditated smile, whereupon a trinity of orders rang out from flaky-lipped mouths. Mr O'Connor, astonished by his tenant's newfound generosity, wondered if aliens had taken over Sebastian's body and replaced it with something more agreeable.

"Well I must say, Fergus, you've landed yourself another fine, well-spoken young man there," Reuben approved as the newcomer headed for the bar.

"Oh, I wouldn't go so far as to say that," said Mr O'Connor. "The boy's as shallow as a puddle."

Fergus leaned into the centre of the table, beckoning his friends to do likewise, as if he were about to divulge a very dark secret. "Hey, now listen. You two will absolutely love this. The lad has the habit of using fancy words he doesn't know the meaning of. So sit back and enjoy, *amigos*. Sit back and enjoy."

CHAPTER TWENTY-EIGHT

Hassan al-Zahawi

Under an inky, silent sky that was permanently starlit, Ulysses trudged unremittingly towards the light, which now seemed to be fading into the distance like a ship heading out to sea. It was more than four years since he'd last seen Florence and, no matter how far he walked, his destination's beacon remained elusive. The vaporous corridor that had once led him to the gates of Paradise in a tunnel of phosphorescence had almost petered out and only the faintest wisps remained. He had long since arrived at the realisation that he might remain trapped in this astral wilderness, adrift in a field of stars, as lonely as a scarecrow.

Ulysses got down on his knees and held his head in his hands under a bone-white moon. No sooner had he stopped to gather his thoughts than a sea of ice appeared at his feet. Through the ice he gazed upon a shoal of forlorn fish that goggled back at him with protuberant eyes. Even his own reflection sought to pity him.

"Dear God in Heaven, I'm begging you!" he cried out in anguish. "If it's not too late, please, please help me!"

In answer to his prayer, a voice came from up high like the calling of a deity. A man of Middle Eastern appearance, with a military moustache and flowing white robes, strode toward him with a welcoming smile. Ulysses recognised him instantly.

The man stretched out his arms. "Hello, old chap, so good to see you again! Do you remember me?"

"I do!" exclaimed Ulysses, as love returned to his depleted heart. "You were my saviour on that godforsaken battlefield in Iraq. I owe you my life!"

The two men embraced but Ulysses, in his present manifestation, might just as well have hugged the wind.

"Please allow me to introduce myself properly. I am, or rather *was*, Major Hassan al-Zahawi. Yes, I spared your life, Ulysses, but alas lost mine the very next day."

"I'm eternally grateful, Hassan. Your compassion meant more to me than you could ever know. And I'm especially sorry to hear that you lost your own life."

"Not at all, dear fellow. Besides, you weren't responsible for the American missile that blew me to kingdom come. And anyway, Paradise is a most wonderful substitute, as you will hopefully soon discover. In fact, when you arrive there I should like for us to share a more meaningful hug and to drink glasses of sweet mint tea together whilst watching the sun go down."

The halcyon vision that sprung to Ulysses' mind almost brought him to tears. "So, your Paradise is the same as mine?"

"Not quite. We each have our own version of Paradise, the difference here being that people from all cultures live together harmoniously. It's impossible to explain, you really do need to see for yourself. Oh, and here's a coincidence that will amaze you. I've since found out that we attended the same school. St Jude's was my home from home when I was educated in England, though I'd already left for university by the time you enrolled—"

"Hassan, are you at all able to help me get back to Paradise?" Ulysses interjected. "Please, I'm desperate. I feel like I'm adrift in an ocean with no means of getting back."

"And this is precisely why I've been sent to you, Ulysses. Like many others, you are a fish that has slipped the net. Sadly, your soul has rotted with each passing day and, if I may persist with the fish metaphor, it has therefore become much more difficult for you to swim towards the shoreline."

"I miss my wife terribly, Hassan. I've been so, so stupid."

On saying this, their wedding flashed through his mind: him in military finery, Florence, a vision of beauty in an ivory wedding gown, both exiting the church under a glinting arch of sabres.

"Ah, Florence, a most wonderful lady. She misses you too, of course, and she doesn't think that you've been stupid – just headstrong, perhaps."

"Is she OK?" Ulysses asked. The mere mention of her name made their separation unbearable.

"She's fine, Ulysses, but she needs you back. You've left this far too long, so from now on I shall guide you spiritually as much as I am able. The clock of your life stopped a long time ago, my friend, making the task all the more difficult, but with my help you might just make it."

"Is it possible?" Ulysses sputtered.

"Of course! But it's all about belief, old chap. Rather than simply being the fish that swims to the shore, you have to believe that you can be the fish that climbs a tree."

A rare smile broke upon Ulysses' face and, when he gazed into the far distance, the empyrean light was already brighter and perhaps somewhat nearer.

CHAPTER TWENTY-NINE

An Odious, Damned Lie

It was late afternoon when Henry returned home from his absurd cloak-and-dagger trip across London. He'd phoned Amber who, despite reporting everything to be eerily normal, had sunk into a morass of uncertainty. The fact that Yuri was yet to play his hand regarding the disappearance of Danny's corpse greatly fuelled her anxiety. Henry, despite his own stomach being as knotted as a pretzel, assured her that everything would be fine and that she should go to work the next day, carrying on as normal.

"I can't believe how kind you've been to me," Amber sobbed into her phone. "I did say that meeting you was written in the stars."

"Even the time you kicked me around the Burger Wizard car park?" he quipped, hoping to break their disquietude with a little levity.

"Yes, even then," Amber sniffled, a sudden smile changing the tone of her broken voice.

Henry found the house to be uncommonly still. There was none of Mr O'Connor's orchestral *fortissimo* rattling the staircases and his own apartment was similarly quiet.

Oscar followed him inside and proceeded to stare at him with owlish eyes, all the time mewing sagely as if trying to conduct a conversation of great significance. He even pawed at some dried clumps of mud that were strewn about the floor, as if piecing together a feline jigsaw puzzle.

Henry discovered that the mysterious trail of mud led to his own bedroom and terminated with a wagon wheel of boot prints on the duvet. "What the hell?" he muttered, looking down at Oscar, who nodded sentiently in return.

Just at that moment, Sebastian was heard bundling through the main door and into the hallway with Mr O'Connor in tow. Henry assumed they must have been drinking all afternoon because Mr O'Connor clumped upstairs singing 'The Wild Rover' at the top of his lungs and Sebastian entered their flat swaying from side to side as if on the deck of a fishing trawler. More of a surprise to Henry was the fact that Sebastian had what appeared to be a cheery look on his face.

"You'll never guess where I've been, Henry," he cried.

"To church, maybe?"

"Nope, The Hanging bloody Pirate, that's where."

"Ah, they must have changed the name."

"Are you being ubiquitous, Henry?"

"Ubiquitous? No, not at all," Henry smirked.

"Positively verminous in there," Sebastian slurred. "I was cheek to jowl with the great unwashed but have nevertheless arrived home unscathed."

"My hero. I'm incredibly proud of you. Anyway, Sebastian, do you know anything about these boot prints on my bed?"

"How dare you accuse me!"

"Huh? No one's accusing you of anything. I was merely asking you if you knew how they got there—"

"A-hah! I know exactly who's responsible. That bloody tree-hugger upstairs, that's who!"

"That's quite an assumption," said Henry, puzzled as to why Sebastian was so quick to apportion blame.

"Well, he's had the run of the place today and he must know where his father keeps the keys, *plus* he's the only person in this house who wears muddy boots. I rest my case m'lud."

"That's ridiculous. Why on earth would Liam want to jump up and down on my bed in his dirty boots?"

"Who knows what goes on in the mind of an ex-con? And I wouldn't put it past him to have stolen money from you to pay for drugs."

The mention of money immediately made Henry remember the shoebox. He hopped onto his desecrated bed and withdrew the box from its shelf. Alarmed that it carried no weight, he looked inside. "No! I don't bloody believe it!"

"What is it?" asked Sebastian, trying to appear concerned.

"My money! I kept more than nine thousand pounds in this box!"

"What? Who keeps money in a shoe box? That's asking for trouble."

Henry stroked his chin. "I can't imagine Liam doing this, he's such a nice chap—"

"Well, that's where you and I differ, Henry. If you ask me, you're far too trusting. Come on, let's go up there together and confront the sneaky little bastard."

Oscar hissed at Sebastian and pointed an accusatory paw in his direction, but before Henry had time to assimilate the situation, Sebastian was hurtling up the stairs faster than a fireman rushing to a blaze.

"Open up! Open up!" shouted Sebastian, banging on Liam's door. Henry stood behind him urging diplomacy, while Oscar sat on his hindquarters and raised two paws in exasperation.

Liam came to the door, smelling of incense sticks and coconut oil. "Hi, Sebastian, hi, Henry," he greeted them with a trustful smile, running twiggy fingers through his Robinson Crusoe hair.

Henry, utterly startled that Sebastian was so keen to solve the mystery, had meanwhile become very suspicious of his spontaneous vigilante act and started to put two and two together.

Sebastian, emboldened by alcohol, prodded Liam in the chest. "How dare you stand there looking as if butter wouldn't melt in your mouth, you thieving maggot!"

"Huh? Hey man, I have absolutely no idea what you're talking about—"

"A-ha! A liar as well as a thief!"

"Sebastian, you need to stop this right now!" Henry commanded. "Liam, I'm so sorry. I think that Sebastian owes you an apology."

"Do I hell!" thundered Sebastian. "Grab those boots, Henry. I'm positive that one of the pairs will match the prints on your bed."

"Oh, I'm sure they will, Sebastian, but I'm also certain that you are devious enough to have concocted this sham in an attempt to cast poor Liam as the villain. Words fail me. Could you possibly sink any lower?"

Liam stood in his tie-dyed clothes with a look of complete bewilderment on his bearded face while Sebastian was caught somewhere between anger and embarrassment.

"Henry, you need to be very careful," Sebastian warned.

"I could sue you for throwing around accusations like that—"

"Could you really?" Henry interjected, shaking his head in sheer disbelief.

Mr O'Connor senior, who'd dozed off in his armchair dreaming of the green hills of Kildare, was woken by the commotion and appeared at a banister above their heads. "Jesus, you're making enough noise down there to wake the devil. What on God's earth is going on?"

Sebastian made certain that he was the first to answer. "A serious crime has been committed, Mr O'Connor. A great deal of money is missing from Henry's bedroom and your son was the only person in the house at the time of the theft."

"Money missing, as in *stolen*?" the landlord said incredulously.

"Exactly!" Sebastian replied.

"Ah, sure. *Now* I get it," said Mr O'Connor, struck by enlightenment as he tramped down the stairs. "It seems I was right to be suspicious of your sudden keenness to spend time in my company and your unexpected readiness to flash your cash. Dear God, you treacherous snake in the grass. You unscrupulous weasel—"

"Now look here, Mr O'Connor—"

"No, you listen to me, Sebastian. I want you to pay Henry back whatever remains of the money you've so clearly stolen and I want you out of my house, pronto. I used to cry myself to sleep over my darling boy and, as God is my witness, he's surely turned his life around. And you honestly think that you can come here and jeopardise that? Why, you pitiful excuse for a man."

"This is an unwarranted character assassination!" Sebastian snorted, looking to Henry for support. "I can assure you that I don't have his poxy money, so you've made yourself look rather stupid."

"Then I'll call the police, shall I? It won't take them long to find the cash. You're far too stupid to have hidden it sensibly."

Sebastian remained rooted to the spot and frantically sought a way to extricate himself from the jam he was in. His lips began to move as if in silent prayer; it was clear to everyone present that he'd momentarily lost the power of speech.

"What's the matter, fella? Cat got your tongue?" Mr O'Connor asked, seeing that Sebastian had fallen into his own trap. "Come on, the game's over, you malicious wretch. With true poetic justice, you've been hoisted by your own petard."

"Alright, alright, here it is," Sebastian blustered, producing banknotes from pockets in the manner of a stage magician and throwing them to the floor. "Trust me, I have no desire to stay in this dump any longer. My girlfriend wants me to live with her in the lap of luxury, so you can all just go and fuck yourselves."

"Sebastian! You are entirely incapable of basic decency," Henry blazed, as an unbidden picture of Danny's severed head flashed through his mind.

"Ha! I couldn't give a pig's fart for decency! And I don't think you even realise what a pathetic loser you are, Henry. People like you will never amount to anything in this life. And as for that mediocre book of yours … well, I doubt it will ever see the light of day."

CHAPTER THIRTY

A Can of Worms

Two weeks had elapsed since the worrisome disappearance of Danny's corpse and, despite their initial fears, Amber and Henry's lives were untroubled by visits from either policemen or gangsters. In light of this, the couple finally dared to believe that they might have escaped punishment for their crime and, as a result, their relationship flourished with each passing day. Together, they'd imagined a myriad of things that could have returned to haunt them, though none had transpired. Apart from a phone call from Danny's site manager, wondering why he hadn't bothered to turn up for work, it seemed that no one actually cared about his sudden disappearance. Having met Danny's feckless friends, Amber knew that they were precisely the kind of men who would have readily given up on him once they'd failed to reach him on his mobile a few times. And, whenever the teeth of guilt gnawed at her conscience, she only had to gaze upon the joyous photographs of her grandmother snuggling up to Sherlock to know that her lethal retribution was wholly justified.

With Sebastian finally out of his life and Amber working

most nights at the restaurant, Henry was afforded the peace and solitude to press on with what was to become an emotionally devastating end to his novel. Even Mr O'Connor, who had become his *de facto* proof reader and editor, was on tenterhooks to learn the fate of Henry's protagonist, a former galactic savage who had completed the arc from being a young, barbaric warlord to the benevolent and much-loved elderly father of a nation. Henry had already cryptically foreshadowed the penultimate chapter within the words of the very first chapter and hoped that his future readers wouldn't remember this until the shocking *dénouement* was upon them.

*

On the first Friday in December Henry arrived for work at the newspaper office to the usual hubbub of ringing phones and rushed conversations. His colleagues had little time for the frippery of Yuletide decoration. Their only concession to festive embellishment was a small artificial Christmas tree sitting sullenly near the water cooler and a solitary length of red tinsel draped haphazardly around a characterless wall clock. Including Henry's, every single desk had disappeared under a flotilla of celebratory Christmas cards and a heady smell of mulled wine suffused the air.

No sooner had Henry slipped his corduroy jacket over the back of his chair than Mr Crabtree sidled up to him. Henry initially feared the worst; a visit from the news editor usually ended with him being scolded in front of everyone else. But today his boss had something of a carefree air about him; his brown necktie was loosened from its collar and, rather propitiously, his nicotine-stained teeth were framed by an uncharacteristic smile.

"Henry. Good news about your article. We've got the go-ahead from above. Come, let's go my office."

Henry had put a great deal of effort into his report of the failed investigation into the vicarage murder, gaining access to detectives who had worked on the case and also the reporter, since retired, who had written the original article ten years earlier. He stayed true to that facts and was careful not to take any of the interviewees' words out of context. Henry had also written the article in the third person so as to keep it from sounding biased, and only mentioned his own connection to the murdered couple in a footnote at the end.

In addition, he'd spoken with some of the national newspaper reporters and TV journalists who had covered the murder. All were only too happy to help and Henry's hardest task was trying to condense the accumulated facts into a readable story that didn't lose its impact by being long winded. When he entered Mr Crabtree's office, he noticed his own mock-up for the article spread across his boss's desk.

"Come in, close the door," Mr Crabtree commanded. "First of all, Henry, great work. You've treated it as a news story rather than as an editorial and that's important." He slid forward in his leather chair. "Have a look at this," he said absently without looking up.

He directed Henry to a computer screen that was fringed with Post-it notes and revealed a representation of how the finished piece would look. It was a double-page spread with a strong visual impact. Police mugshots of Yuri Voloshyn and Pascal Makuza sat underneath a picture of Florence and Ulysses Drummond, who were smiling for eternity in front of the vicarage. Henry, who to this day resented having a camera pointed at him, had turned his back just as the photographer released the shutter. A clipping, made to look as ragged as a pirate map, showed the original newspaper headline, which screamed *MURDER AT THE VICARAGE* because the original reporter had thought the news story neatly echoed an Agatha Christie novel.

"So what do you think?" asked Mr Crabtree.

"It's perfect," enthused Henry.

The news editor leant back in his chair. "The legal team have cleared it and the chief likes it, so we're going to run the story next Monday. If this article forces the police to reopen the case, or if it pricks someone's conscience to come forward with new information, then all the better."

Henry, although delighted that he was instrumental in reviving awareness of his parents' murder, couldn't help but stare at Yuri's photograph and wonder if he'd opened a can of worms.

CHAPTER THIRTY-ONE

Where There Is True Friendship

A butterfly flittered into Florence's orbit and rested behind her ear like a Tahitian flower while Bagheera snoozed contentedly in the gully of her lap.

"To this day Henry has never believed in God," she said, idly swirling chilled white wine around her glass.

"Doesn't he?" replied Poppy, shielding her eyes from the sun and smiling at her friend.

"At least not the god that Ulysses and I believed in. It all seems perfectly ridiculous now but of course everything is obvious with hindsight."

"I never believed in God when I was alive either," Poppy admitted, ever-mindful of the enduring anguish that her suicide had caused her parents. "But I've seen how your faith has helped you through some bad patches."

"Ha! Fat lot of good it did me. We've both ended up in the same place, regardless. Anyway, cheers to us!"

"Yes, to us!" cried Poppy, as they clinked glasses.

Best friends in life and now best friends in the afterlife, Florence and Poppy relaxed in the afternoon sun on slatted wooden chairs facing a glossy lake. The chairs occupied their favourite spot, a cherry orchard alive with birdsong and scented with frangipani flowers. While they reminisced and gleefully finished each other's sentences, sunshine swam through the branches illuminating the wine in their glasses and making the alcohol billow like oil in water.

As was the norm, each had opted to remain the age they were at the point of death, whereas the more elderly of life's casualties typically tended to choose younger versions of themselves. Indeed, it was such a novelty to spot a pensioner in Paradise that strangers felt compelled to approach them in the way that mothers converge on babies in prams. Poppy remained her twenty-one-year-old self, albeit free from the emotional pain that had caused her to take her own life. Florence decided to stick at forty – 'a wonderful age' remarked the archangel who oversaw her induction. Poppy, a chronic insomniac in her first life, now found that sleep arrived easily, washing over her in a soporific tide that carried with it the flotsam of ambrosial dreams.

A moustachioed man, dressed in a striped Victorian bathing suit, stood in the shallows of the lake. He waved in Florence's direction and called out, his cut-glass voice caught in the breeze.

"Ooh, hell-o," Poppy chirped, lowering her sunglasses. "Who's the beefcake with the porn-star moustache then?"

"He's one of Ulysses' ancestors, Captain Ulysses Drummond. The very person he inherited his name from, in fact."

"Mmm, quite the action man," Poppy purred, watching the man suddenly thrash through the water with aquatic enthusiasm.

"I often see him out there. Which is slightly ironic,

given that he drowned whilst trying to swim across the English Channel."

"Well he can't drown himself now, so hooray for Captain Ulysses!"

"Yes, to Captain Ulysses!" Florence cheered, as they clinked their glasses again.

Despite being able to while away the day with her best friend in such a beautiful locale, Florence couldn't escape the spectre of two potentially calamitous events.

"A penny for your thoughts?" Poppy asked, seeing her friend lost in a troubled daze.

"On my first day here, I was told that all of my worries would become small ones," Florence remembered with a wistful smile. "Thing is, I'm so deeply concerned about Ulysses and Henry that my worries, if anything, have increased."

"Oh, the worry doesn't go away, Florence. Nor the guilt. Just look what I've put my poor parents through. It's terrible for those left behind. If only I could pay them a visit."

"Yes, if only," Florence nodded.

"OK, so what're the latest developments?" Poppy asked, shuffling forward.

"You know that Henry has got himself involved with that girl who killed her ex-boyfriend?"

"Who absolutely deserved it."

"Oh, didn't he just? Well, as if that wasn't bad enough, Henry's now decided to write a newspaper article about the two men involved in our murder."

"No-o!"

"Yes! I kid you not. I just wish he'd let sleeping dogs lie. What on earth possessed him to stir up such a hornet's nest?"

"Love for his parents, perhaps?"

"Well, such foolhardiness could get him killed. He's every bit as stubborn as his father."

"Speaking of Ulysses, any news?"

"One of the angels here, Hassan, the Iraqi guy who spared his life in that nonsensical war, has been sent out to shepherd him home. I just wish that Ulysses had come with me when he still had the opportunity."

Poppy steepled her fingers. "Does this Hassan think he stands a good chance of bringing him here?"

Florence expelled a deep sigh. "He couldn't say. Because Ulysses has left it so long, it's become an almost impossible struggle. He's lost in a universe of wasted opportunities while I'm living the high life. Oh, Poppy, as much as I love it here, Paradise isn't quite Paradise without having him to share it with me." With the words catching in her throat, Florence gazed into the distance and fought back tears.

"Hey, beautiful, it'll be fine," soothed Poppy, encasing her in a hug. "Come on, where's that rock-solid belief you showed in your previous life?"

CHAPTER THIRTY-TWO

Appetition

Amber arrived home from her late shift to the sound of flies buzzing in the darkness of her kitchen. After dropping her keys into a bowl by the door, she switched on the light and was startled to see Danny sitting at the table with a self-satisfied smirk on his face. His skin was now the colour of a dove's wing and the wound in his skull teemed with maggots.

"Hey, Amber, how do I look?" he asked, his bleak eyes pale as lychees.

"I've seen you looking better," she replied coldly.

"Now I'm sure you're itching to know just how I killed your dog, ain'tcha?"

"Please, no."

"Yeah, I'm sure you are," he said contemptuously. "You'd like to know how I stuffed him, yapping and wriggling, into that builders' sack and how I sealed him in with gaffer tape—"

"Stop! Just stop!"

"And how he thrashed about—"

The spade was somehow in her hands again and before

Danny could finish his venomous sentence Amber had swung at his neck, severing it completely. Danny's grinning head tumbled from his shoulders and bounced twice on the floor tiles before rolling under a chair. Flinging the chair to one side, Amber lifted the spade above her shoulders and brought it down with all the power she could muster, flattening his face as if it were pizza dough.

The entire kitchen then went into a tailspin.

"Die! Die!" she screamed, waking with a start and thrashing under her duvet. Disoriented, she stared wildly into the murmuring shadows of her bedroom.

"Sherlock! Are you there?" she called out in vain, only to be met with a shoulder shrug of deathly silence.

The clock alarm sounded at 6.20. Amber slipped out of bed and stretched her arms before swishing open the curtains to reveal a window pane wet with condensation. She wiped the glass with the T-shirt she'd slept in and dropped it into the laundry basket.

While showering, she ruminated for the thousandth time on the extraordinary sequence of events that had occurred only three weeks earlier. She found it hard to come to terms with the fact that, despite killing Danny, there was still no sign that she would be punished for the crime.

She was similarly amazed that Henry, a boy once so cartoonishly timorous, had somehow morphed into a capable man almost overnight. He'd shown himself to be the kind of stalwart she never imagined existing outside of a book or a movie: a noble Atticus Finch of a man who, regardless of the trouble he could be getting himself into, had placed her needs above his own. He'd also made her feel loved again, his selflessness extending to the bedroom where, against all odds, he'd become a skilled lover.

Amber needed to start her Saturday shift at ¡Arriba! by 9am. After eating a light breakfast and setting up an ironing board that whinnied each time it was unfolded, she ironed her uniform, tied her hair back into a tight ponytail and left via the kitchen door. Almost simultaneously, Yuri appeared from his house with two phones in one hand and a drag of deep scratch marks down one side of his face.

"Yuri, what on earth have you done to your face?" she gasped, hiding her trepidation.

"One of my girlfriends, she like rough sex," he said flatly and without restraint.

"Oh," said Amber, thrown off guard, wishing she'd never asked.

"Do you like it rough, Amber?" he leered.

"Um, no, certainly not."

Yuri glanced at the V of her cleavage and noted how taut the uniform was across her breasts. He imagined himself ripping it open, her buttons flying through the air. All at once his cock pulsed like a fibrillated heart.

Precisely at that moment, to Amber's consternation, a police car pulled up in front of her house. Yuri, seeing the alarm in her eyes, chuckled to himself.

"Police have come to get you, Amber. What did you do?" he grinned.

An acid taste rose in Amber's throat and she felt her knees buckle. Two grave-faced police officers stepped from the car and nodded in her direction. Yuri was humming a dissonant tune to himself, which added to her anxiety. But then the officers walked toward Mr Beardsley's house where, out of view, she could hear him greeting the men by their first names.

"Just social visit," Yuri said, punctuating his words with a sinister wink. "Old friends maybe?"

*

"Ah, your novel is just brilliant," gushed Mr O'Connor to Henry after he'd read the final draft of *Planet Foretold.* "Jesus, you make me look like a bumbling neophyte. Your book is a work of rare genius. I could cry an ocean of joyful tears, so I could."

O'Connor, having seized Henry in a vigorous bear hug that almost caused him a whiplash injury, went on to enthuse about all the things he liked in the book, including the devastating twist that had grabbed him like a hidden mantrap.

"Gee, I thought I was wise to all your literary tricks but, even though you'd cryptically alluded to it in the early chapters, I still walked straight into it. Bam! Magnificent, Henry, just magnificent."

"Thank you, Mr O'Connor. I've been a bag of nerves these last two days wondering what you'd make of it."

"Bag of nerves? I don't think you realise just how good you are, my boy. Writing is as natural to you as swimming is to a dolphin. When Vishnu sets his eyes upon this, he'll be rattling the cages of the big beasts of publishing. This novel will set the literary world alight, or my name's not Fergus Munro."

"It isn't."

"Figure of speech, Henry. Figure of speech."

*

Sebastian, taking full advantage of the fact that unwary rich girls often fall head over heels for bastards like him, settled nicely into Ophelia's Islington apartment and made a big show of buying her a bouquet of flowers every other day to hide the fact that he'd been living there rent free for the past two weeks. In a similarly calculated display of feigned generosity he'd bought her a pair of drop earrings that looked more expensive than they actually were and she'd worn them every day since.

Ophelia's parents, keen to meet her much-vaunted boyfriend, had reserved a lunchtime table in a restaurant at the top of The Gherkin's latticed skyscraper. Sebastian, hoping to fast-track himself back into the prosperous life he felt entitled to, probed her parent's online presence and was pleased with the search results. Simon and Harriet Marlowe were luxury property developers whose net worth was over one billion pounds. Photographs depicted the couple wearing hard hats on various development sites and rubbing shoulders with celebrities at glitzy charity events. It delighted Sebastian to learn that they owned a sumptuous villa on the shore of Lake Como and a sleek loft apartment in Manhattan. Tucked away in a corner of one article, mention was made of Mrs Marlowe's fondness for the sonnets of John Keats. Driven by ulterior motives, he'd secretly swotted up on the man's life and his poetry.

Ophelia, who had already slavishly ironed Sebastian's shirt and polished his shoes, was urging him to get ready. "Please, Seb, get out of bed and jump into the shower. I really need you to make a good first impression today."

"Make me a cup of coffee and I'll think about it," he croaked, pushing a flop of hair off his face. "Besides, your parents should take me as they find me."

By the time he'd shaved, showered and dressed time was running away from them and Ophelia was worried they might be late for lunch. Sebastian could see that she was proud of his appearance: he was wearing a navy blue suit and a crisp white shirt with the top two buttons undone. She was putty in his hands once more.

"You look handsome and dashing," she beamed,

smoothing his lapel and plumping up his silk pocket square. "We'll be late if we take the tube. Probably best to call a taxi, don't you think?"

"Who's paying?" Sebastian asked.

"Me, if you're that bothered," she huffed, waving her satin clutch bag.

"Taxi it is then," he smirked.

*

Guided by a platoon of sharp-suited security personnel through an obstacle course of sensors and elevators, they arrived at a restaurant on the thirty-ninth floor whose floor-to-ceiling windows offered panoramic views across London.

"I'm only surprised they didn't ask us to pass a retina scan," Sebastian muttered, as Ophelia waved to her parents who were seated at a linen-clothed table in the mid-distance. Sebastian felt that the space resembled the control room of an air-traffic control tower.

"Mum, Dad, meet Sebastian," Ophelia said brightly, after being greeted with a flurry of parental kisses.

Ophelia's father, a go-getter with a mahogany tan and a mane of greying hair, pumped Sebastian's hand vigorously. "Pleasure to meet you, Sebastian. I'm Simon, and this is Harriet."

"Hello, Sebastian," purred Ophelia's mother, narrowing her aquamarine eyes to get the measure of him. "I trust you're taking very good care of our daughter?"

"Of course. I even buy her flowers every other day, don't I, Ophelia?"

"Oh, he does. He's very sweet."

"Sit, sit," said Simon, with the air of someone who was used to taking control. "Have whatever takes your fancy, the meal's on me. I must say that the lobster ravioli is very good here, as is the braised venison."

"Sebastian's a qualified sommelier," Ophelia said dotingly, as her father put on his reading specs to peruse the wine list.

"A sommelier, eh? Well, in that case I'd be a fool not to let you choose the wine, Sebastian. What do you recommend?"

"Let's see … I rather like the look of the Châteauneuf-du-Pape," Sebastian said in a lounge-lizard voice.

"Then Châteauneuf-du-Pape it is." Simon smiled, warming to Sebastian with each passing second.

Ophelia, noticing her parents' favourable reaction to her boyfriend, smiled at him adoringly and patted his leg under the tablecloth. Sebastian hid his smugness in the way that an undertaker conceals amusement.

The atmosphere around the table was convivial. Harriet had a velvety voice and referred to her husband as 'Simes' for reasons best known to herself. Sebastian, meanwhile, used every trick in his book of charlatanism to win her over. After greatly exaggerating his academic achievements and portraying his own parents as being wholly undeserving of his affection, he won the approval and sympathy of Ophelia's parents, who proved to be every bit as trusting as their daughter.

"You know, there's something rather poetic about the way that parents love their children," Sebastian declared with a smarminess that was hard to rival.

"Oh, do you like poetry, Sebastian?" Harriet asked, her interest heightened.

"Like it? I love it!" said Sebastian, lying through his teeth. "Especially the work of John Keats—"

"Oh, really? I adore Keats," Harriet squealed, clapping her hands theatrically.

"Then please allow me to recite a line," he said unctuously. "*And haply the Queen-Moon is on her throne, cluster'd around by all her starry Fays.*"

"Oh, bravo!" Simon roared, slapping the tablecloth while his wife clasped her hands to her chest and almost cried.

"Seb. Omigod, I never knew," Ophelia gushed. "That was beautiful."

"As are you, my darling," he said, tucking a stray hair behind her ear.

After coffees were supped, Ophelia's parents' misguided affinity towards Sebastian was further enhanced when he generously insisted on footing the exorbitant bill, knowing full well that her father was precisely the kind of man who wouldn't hear of it – which, of course, proved to be the case.

With such a well-executed and entirely successful charm offensive under his belt, Sebastian felt that he had every reason to be pleased with himself. So, on the backseat of their taxi ride home, he opportunistically proposed to his heiress girlfriend.

"I'm afraid I haven't yet purchased the ring, but would you consider marrying me, Ophelia?"

"Oh, Sebastian," she answered, her lips trembling. "Yes, yes, of course!"

CHAPTER THIRTY-THREE

Foxes in a Henhouse

On the morning of the eleventh of December, Pascal's mobile rang three times then cut out. Yuri's name had flashed onto the screen, signalling that he was waiting outside.

Despite earning more money than the average investment banker, Pascal preferred to live in an austere one-bedroom flat on a cheerless council estate. Yuri impatiently tapped his chunky fingers on the steering wheel and looked up at the grim balconies of his sidekick's tower block with their satellite dishes and lines of wet laundry. Five black teenagers cycled around his car. One of them lowered his headphones and tapped on Yuri's window with his iPhone.

"What you want?" said Yuri gruffly, as he lowered the window.

The teen wore a hooded sweatshirt under a puffa jacket, standard fashion for the youths on the estate. "Nice whip, man. Mercedes-Benz, innit?"

"What you want?" Yuri said again, irritation rumbling in his voice.

"Hey, we're cool. You're friends wiv Pascal, yeah?"

"So?"

"So, he's like blood, man. So maybe you can put me on the payroll, innit? Trust me, bruv, I could be useful, I got all the skills—"

"Too young," Yuri grunted, flaring up a cigarette.

"Fuck dat, man," said the boy, sucking on his teeth. "I'm fearless and I'm smart, innit?"

"OK, see me when you are older. Maybe we find work for you then."

"Sweet! You won't regret it. Remember my face, yeah?"

Yuri decided to bring an end to the boy's chit-chat by raising the window. Unfazed, the teenager cycled back to his crew, who greeted him with wide smiles and adulation.

As Pascal appeared from the block, an Alsatian dog charged towards him, snarling as if it wanted to tear out his throat. Pascal laughed at the creature and produced a large knife from his bomber jacket, which he waved at its jaws with the countenance of an orchestra conductor. The hound's terrified owner raced over to leash the animal and apologised profusely to Pascal, who found the whole thing deeply hilarious as did the gang of boys who cheered and whooped from their bicycle seats.

Yuri drove out of the estate while Pascal hyperactively hunted for a radio channel that suited him before switching dashboard buttons on and off, hoping to hit the one that warmed his seat. It was their routine each Monday to collect money from the handful of shabby properties and sleazy businesses they owned in the borough. Many of their tenants were working in the UK illegally so knew not to complain about the cramped, squalid conditions they were forced to live in.

So that everyone could see that he wasn't a man to be messed with, Yuri was dressed in combat trousers and military boots to amplify his fearsomeness. Pascal wore a black tracksuit under a black bomber jacket and had painted his nails to match.

On a grey, overcast day, when it was difficult to distinguish between the buildings and the sky, they streamed past red double-decker buses and white vans through an urban landscape that gazed like an outsider upon the gleaming skyscrapers of central London. Yuri, without knowing it, drove down the same roads where, three centuries earlier, farmers had herded pigs to Smithfield Market only for sadistic drunkards to tumble from taverns to swing them by their tails for a bit of laddish sport.

He turned into a God-forsaken cul-de-sac, sandwiched between a coal yard and a printing works. Ignoring the fact that Pascal had taken to tapping his knife against the glove compartment in time to the music on the radio, Yuri parked outside Zen Massage, an inelegant brothel they co-owned. The premises exterior walls were coated in a white paint that had long since peeled away in patches, exposing an underbelly of dark brickwork. The insides of its grimy windows were coated in a frosted film to suggest privacy and an A4-sized laminate, embellished with Clipart holly, bore the message 'A Happy Xmas to all our customers'.

Yuri pressed the intercom button adjacent to the rotted door. They stared up at the CCTV camera and were buzzed through.

"Morning, gents," said Muriel, the unsmiling brothel manager who spent each day squirrelled behind a reception hatch staring into a stark hallway. Her salt-and-pepper hair was tied back into a tight bun, her garish make-up lending her the appearance of a pantomime dame. Her eyebrows were as thin as fish bones and vertical creases, caused by a lifetime of sucking on cigarettes, rose above her lips like tiny railings.

"We had a good week, boys. There's nearly ten grand there," she said matter-of-factly, thudding five large wads of cash, one by one, onto the counter. Muriel, a King's Cross prostitute before the area was regenerated, was as grim-faced as a Russian general but as loyal as an imperial guard.

"Is new girl here?" asked Yuri, while Pascal packed the takings into a holdall.

"Yes, she's in there with the others," replied Muriel. "Go easy on her, Yuri, it's only her second day in the country."

"You got her passport?"

"Of course. It's in my safe at home."

Pascal followed Yuri through a door further down the hallway. Inside, sitting on a leatherette sofa like patients in a doctor's waiting room, were four short-skirted women. The youngest was a frightened eighteen-year-old Romanian who looked decidedly out of place in her seedy surroundings. The smell of cigarettes, cheap perfume and baby oil hung in the air and the other three women were watching a home renovation show intently on an outdated television set. Their security roughneck, Jack Lynch, sat in an armchair in a far corner and casually acknowledged the men's presence with a sullen nod of his lumpy head.

Yuri loomed over the girl who, from the moment she'd arrived, had taken to cuddling a leopard-skin cushion for comfort. She had spent the previous night praying to God for her safe return to Bucharest, where she would return to her family home and do everything in her power to resolve the petty differences she'd had with her parents.

"What is your name?" Yuri asked, blowing cigarette smoke over one shoulder.

"Daniela," she replied softly.

Yuri liked that she was trembling visibly. He turned to his colleague. "Hey, Pascal. Maybe get food from café? I will be upstairs for one hour."

Pascal nodded and smiled. The other women didn't move their lifeless eyes from the television screen.

"Daniela, do you know who I am?" Yuri asked, stubbing out the cigarette on the palm of his hand.

She hugged the cushion tighter. "No, sorry, I do not."

"I am your boss. This mean I own you. Come."

The girl looked at the other women who merely shrugged their shoulders and looked away dispassionately. Muriel entered the room and indicated to Daniela that she needed to go with the big Ukrainian.

"Come!" he said more forcibly, grabbing her in his iron grip and yanking her to her feet. Daniela burst into tears and cried for her mother.

"Which room?" Yuri barked to Muriel.

"Room number four. She has the key."

As Yuri carried the young Romanian up the staircase as easily as if she were a sack of feathers, Jack Lynch seized the opportunity to speak with Pascal on his own.

"Pascal, could I have a word in private?" he asked furtively. Jack was a big man with a twisted nose and an executioner's stare. Unlike Pascal, he had spent most of his adult life in and out of Her Majesty's prisons and had initially been grateful for the opportunity to live in a poky room on the top floor of their brothel.

"What is it?" Pascal asked.

"Listen, have you seen today's newspaper? Because I'm guessing you ain't."

"I don't read, so make your point."

"Look at this, yeah?" Jack said, unfolding the *Hackney*

Chronicle. "You and Yuri, larger than life. Photos and everything, splashed all over the fucker." He brushed a tattooed hand over their respective photographs, which stared defiantly out of a double-page spread. Pascal was aghast. He'd assumed that this story had died years ago.

"You two have got yourself a big fucking problem here. Police are reopening the case, asking for people to come forward. You need to make sure that your alibis are as tight as a duck's arse."

Demons screamed inside Pascal's head. "You did good to tell me. I will keep this newspaper and will talk with Yuri. But you need to keep your mouth shut, yes?"

"What's it worth?" Jack said menacingly. "A little extra money will go a long way to buying my silence, if you catch my drift."

Inside, Pascal was apoplectic with rage; outwardly, his alien mouth formed a psychopathic smile. "Jack, you need to think carefully, my friend. When you came out of prison, did we not give you a job and a roof over your head?"

Jack took a pace forward. "Look, the room's barely big enough to swing a fucking cat and I'm the one having to turf out drunken punters when they start acting up. I've got all the risk and you're trousering all the dosh."

"This is because I am your boss," Pascal hissed, his patience taut and ready to snap.

But Jack, now that he'd opened Pandora's box, wasn't prepared to hold back. "Listen, I ain't some mug that you can dick around. All that stuff I hear about you is bullshit as far as I'm concerned. Don't mean nothing to me, mate. You push my buttons, monkey boy, and I'm gonna let my fists fly."

"So let your fists fly. I would like to see what happens," Pascal said, his cadaverous face lighting up like a lantern.

Anticipating trouble, Muriel clapped her hands in the way that an emperor's lackey summons food and ushered the ladies out of the room.

Jack, as a matter of honour, threw the first punch but before it was able to reach its target Pascal's elbow had smashed into his face, destroying his nose.

"Whoo-hoo!" Pascal cheered, clapping his hands jubilantly and dancing on the balls of his feet. "That must hurt, no?"

Jack let rip with a fusillade of expletives and charged at the African, snorting blood like a wounded bull. Pascal snapped the man's head back with two rapid-fire punches that sent him crashing into a bamboo screen.

"Muriel, do not let anyone in!" he ordered as he dragged Jack's insensate body face-down along the carpet and onto the linoleum surface of the hallway. As Jack began to gather his senses, Pascal withdrew the knife from his jacket.

"No, Pascal!" Muriel yelled. "Do not, I repeat, *do not* kill him!"

Pascal put a dark finger to his one remaining lip to shush her. "I won't kill him," he grinned, his voice eerily calm. "You really think I want to go to prison? Watch this—"

As Daniela's muffled screams crawled down the stairwell, Pascal straddled Jack's back, facing his feet and pinning him to the floor. Jack's instincts kicked in and he began to buck but his attacker rode him and ably kept his balance. With a demonic determination, Pascal drove the blade through the man's trousers and deep into his anus three times in quick succession. Jack's head reared, as if pulled by reins, and an inhuman howl escaped his throat.

Pascal rolled off him, wiped the knife blade on the man's

shirt and patted him on his head as if they'd just enjoyed a play fight. Jack curled himself into a ball and whimpered in agony.

Muriel, despite having previously witnessed and experienced violence in all of its guises, was rendered speechless.

Pascal turned to her and grinned. "See, I did not kill him but for many months he will wish I did. Take him to the hospital. Make certain he does not speak about this, yes?"

"Of course," Muriel replied. "I'll say that he was attacked out on the street by a total stranger."

Pascal retrieved his holdall. "Here is some extra money, half for him, and half for you." He counted out two thousand pounds in notes and pressed them into her hand.

"More than enough for me. Not sure if it will be enough for him," she said, nodding towards Jack who was still in the throes of agony and squirming on the floor.

"Tell him that if he shoots his mouth off, I will kill him," Pascal replied matter-of-factly. "The money is enough."

"You'll need to hire new security," Muriel suggested.

"No problem. You leave that to us."

Muriel helped Jack to his feet; his face was a mask of pain and each movement agonising. As she led him to the front door, blood dripped from the seat of his trousers and dotted the linoleum with little red splashes.

Through a bloody grimace, Jack managed a few words of defiance as he shuffled out of the building. "Fuck you, you evil bastard."

"Let those fists fly, my friend," Pascal teased, flapping his hands daintily. "Let them fly."

When Yuri descended the stairs, having just violated a young woman whose life would never be the same, the last thing he expected to see was Pascal swabbing the hallway with a bloodied mop.

"Pascal, what you do?" he asked, with an exasperated shake of his head. "Every time I look away you do something crazy."

"Don't worry, this is not a problem," Pascal shrugged. "Jack wanted to fight, so we fight. Only a small stab wound. Muriel is driving him to the hospital. He will say nothing. I'm certain."

"You sure this, huh?" Yuri bristled, sensing that his freedom and his livelihood had been jeopardised because of his cohort's hot-headedness.

"Listen, Yuri, we have a much bigger problem. Wait, I will show you." Pascal fetched the newspaper and tapped a lacquered fingernail on the page that displayed their mugshots.

Yuri's face hardened the moment he saw the headline. Because of Pascal's illiteracy, he read the words out loud, spitting them as if they were poison. Henry's name was at the bottom of the report.

"Henry Drummond. This must be son of priest," Yuri growled.

"The little pig?" Pascal replied, remembering the child standing in the driveway of the vicarage that morning.

"Not little now. He is reporter for newspaper. Can make big problem for us. We must find where he live."

With fingers unsuited to a tiny keypad, Yuri stiffly typed Henry's name into Google Images, whereupon a grid of photographs depicting a Scottish author from the Victorian era flickered into view. Scrolling further down, a familiar face caught his eye: a recent head and shoulders thumbnail of Henry, taken by the newspaper's staff photographer.

"Him. I know him," Yuri snarled, jabbing a chunky

finger onto the screen. "He is new boyfriend of girl next door. I not believe this."

"Then we are lucky, no?" Pascal grinned. "We can wait for him and take him to the warehouse. Make him disappear."

"I not think so. For sure police will come to us first."

"So what else do we do? We just do nothing, huh?"

"If we kill him, police know for sure who is guilty. Pascal, use brain for once."

"So? Let the police think it is us. This is what they think anyway. If there is no body, there is no evidence. Come on, Yuri. This fool will be a problem, I promise you."

"I need to think about this," muttered Yuri, secretly countenancing the tempting idea of also taking Amber to the garage in the event of them snatching the boy. "Right now you need to clean floor. Are you sure Jack do not die?"

"Yuri. I promise."

"And where are other girls?"

"In their rooms, I think."

"OK, you clean, I will tell girls to have day off."

*

Pascal spent the rest of the morning and early afternoon trying to involve the Ukrainian in his plan to kidnap Henry. Yuri was still in two minds when he dropped Pascal off at his apartment block and told him that he would give him an answer after sleeping on it.

When he turned into Ferdinand Road, Yuri spotted a BBC television crew gathered outside his house. Eager eyes tracked his vehicle and fingers were pointed as he slowed to a crawl. A woman wearing a trench coat trotted over to his car clutching a microphone. Yuri thought better than to hang around and took off with a screech of tyres.

Mr Beardsley, with his ever-present necktie peeking out

from under a thick winter jacket, stood on the pavement and stared reproachfully at the Ukrainian as he sped past.

Yuri, after parking on a neighbouring road, and with fury leaking from every pore, grabbed his phone and speed-dialled Pascal. “I made decision,” he snarled. “We need to take care of business.”

CHAPTER THIRTY-FOUR

The Shoulders of Giants

Henry's usually trenchant work colleagues honoured his lead story with a spontaneous round of applause befitting a Nobel Prize winner but then offset their veneration by obliging him to do the coffee run.

In the course of the day, he'd taken a phone call from Amber who was decidedly edgy that a BBC news crew had camped outside her neighbour's house. He also received a text message from Vishnu, who wanted to meet him for dinner that evening to discuss his manuscript.

After work, Henry joined Vishnu at a dimly-lit Bangladeshi restaurant where Mr Jalil, the toad-faced owner, was not only known to treat his customers with hostile suspicion but also to eavesdrop on their private conversations.

Henry entered the restaurant with his usual harried expression. While shaking Vishnu's hand, he noticed a white stripe of regrowth in the parting of his liquorice-black hair, lending it the appearance of badger fur.

"Have you eaten here before, Henry?" Vishnu enquired.

"No, I'm afraid I haven't."

"The service is appalling," said Vishnu, lowering his voice. "But the food is exquisite."

"Ready to order, please?" a waiter interjected, before they'd barely had time to sit in their seats.

"Perhaps you could give us a moment to peruse the menu?" Vishnu asked wryly.

"Suit yourself," the waiter replied, rolling his eyes.

Before getting on with the business in hand, Vishnu passed on his sympathy regarding the infamous murder of Henry's parents. He'd only learned of this tragic connection through talking with Fergus the previous day. "I mention this not to upset you, but to acknowledge the fact."

"No, that's fine," Henry replied, masking his sadness. "I've had a decade to come to terms with it."

"Well, if it's some small consolation, we Hindus believe that good people are reborn after their death. Our souls are thought to be imperishable."

"That's a lovely thought, Vishnu."

"Not just a thought, Henry. How can one billion Hindus be wrong? Come, let's choose food. Just look at the waiters, they have the eyes of a firing squad."

Over a meal of fiery curries, accompanied by pilau rice, naan bread and glasses of cold Cobra Lager, Vishnu extolled the virtues of Henry's novel and told him more than once that he had a unique voice.

"It's a veritable mélange of all that is great in a story. It's allegorical and it's pulse-pounding. The characters are chock-a-block with hidden depths and it's free of the scourge of unnecessary adverbs. How the hell did you write something this good at your age?"

"You really are most kind—"

"Kind doesn't come into it, Henry. I'd soon tell you if it was a steaming pile of crap. Some of your future technologies were bloody scary, and relocating a war-weary populace to an unchartered planet is always a guaranteed crowd pleaser. This book is going to fly off the shelves. I've never been more certain."

"So does this mean that you're actually going to send my manuscript out to a publisher?"

"Going to? I already have! I know which ones are always on the lookout for new sci-fi writers. One of the biggest hitters, having read your submission, has already offered their commitment. How cool is that?"

"Crikey, I don't quite know what to say—"

"More than just 'crikey', I'd hope. Very soon you are going to be a man in demand, Henry. Without wishing to seem melodramatic, you are standing on the shoulders of giants and you thoroughly deserve every good thing that comes your way."

CHAPTER THIRTY-FIVE

The King

Just as it is possible for an atom to exist in two locations at the same time, the household names and famous luminaries of Paradise were granted the astonishing ability to be in several places simultaneously. Nature, it seemed, had a way of turning quantum physics on its head to meet the ever-growing demands of people wishing to revere their once-earthly heroes. This gift of ubiquity meant that eminences such as Mahatma Gandhi and Eleanor Roosevelt could address an immeasurable number of their followers publicly without the need for them all to converge on one location.

And so it was that Florence and Poppy, among a local throng of twenty-thousand enthusiastic fans, were able to attend a live open-air Elvis Presley concert, which was concurrently being enjoyed by Paradise-wide crowds in their billions. As there were no time zones in the afterlife everyone with an interest, no matter where they lived, could watch this evening spectacle at precisely the same time.

The friends could barely contain their excitement. Seeing

the legendary Elvis Presley in person, thirty-three years old again and wearing a tight black leather suit, was the stuff of dreams. Snake-hipped and once more at the peak of his powers, Elvis belted out many of the songs that had made him famous. His gloss-black hair shone under a cluster of spotlights as he prowled the stage, stopping occasionally to exchange some good-humoured banter with his musicians. When he sang 'Are You Lonesome Tonight?', the ladies were certain that he'd especially pinpointed them in the crowd with a flirtatious wink that sent them into squeals of delight.

"Isn't this just the best?" Florence shouted above the roar of the crowd.

"I love it!" Poppy shrilled, catching the eye of a caped man dressed in a Tudor doublet and hose, whose roguish smile caused the tips of his moustache to move as if pulled by invisible wires. "Hey, Florence, am I being ridiculous, or is that Sir Walter Raleigh?" she queried.

"How would I know? Why don't you go over and ask him?"

"You know what? I think I might just do that."

While Poppy introduced herself to someone who appeared to be a sixteenth-century explorer, Florence kicked off her shoes, felt the grass between her toes and danced under a midnight-blue sky. The night was proving to be a welcome distraction from the ceaseless fears that she held for Ulysses and Henry. She closed her eyes as moths orbited her body and stroboscopic lights flickered through her eyelids.

Elvis launched into another song, whipping the crowd into a fever with his bluesy vocals when he suggested that one night with an unspecified female was what he was prayin' for.

At the end of the show, after bowing to rapturous applause, the King of Rock and Roll sent himself up by saying, "Thank ya very much, thank ya very much," in a self-deprecating Southern drawl that trailed off into a series of chuckles. Soon, the stage lights dimmed to black and Elvis was gone. At the same time, across the length and breadth of Paradise, billions of happy spectators departed from an unimaginable number of venues.

Florence and Poppy held back and sat upon the grass, hugging their knees, wishing to savour every last second of this magical evening. It transpired that the Tudor gentleman wasn't Sir Walter Raleigh, but both he and Poppy hit it off instantly and arranged to meet for a drink the following day.

Most of the audience were intent on being somewhere else and had already melted into the night. Despite the number of years that they'd collectively lived in Paradise, it still amused Florence and Poppy to watch people disappearing in fits and starts like genies as each one visualised their next destination. A person in Paradise only had to think of their home, or any other terminus known to them, to be transported there, departing in a flurry of molecules, leaving just a fleeting silhouette of vapour in their place.

In a similar way that simple pleasure can be derived from popping bubble wrap, the friends cheered *olé* each time an individual vanished into thin air.

"*Olé*!" Florence exclaimed.

"*Olé*! *Olé*!" Poppy chuckled. "You know, when they go *pouf* like that, they remind me of those powder-filled balloons that I used to shoot with an air rifle at the funfair… *Olé*!"

After getting through more *olés* than could commonly

be heard at a bullfight, the novelty wore off. The friends, lying with their backs to the turf, gazed up at the stars and considered just how fortunate they were to be given such a wonderful second chance at life.

CHAPTER THIRTY-SIX

Men at Some Time Are Masters of Their Fates

Padding soundlessly through a fathomless darkness, Ulysses closed his eyes and pictured turquoise oceans and sun-kissed beaches. With Hassan's descriptive words of encouragement to guide him, he also visualised bosomy hills and clear blue skies. Mustering the figurative glint of light on Chekhov's broken glass, he gazed into the half-remembered irises of Florence's eyes and imagined her fingers, soft and delicate, against his cheek.

When he opened his eyes, the distant light that had eluded him for so long was ever nearer and a knowing smile had crept out from underneath Hassan's thick moustache. "Positive thinking, Ulysses. Keep it up."

"So, how is it that you can reach me so effortlessly," Ulysses asked, "yet I can't do the same?"

"Because my soul is undiminished, whereas yours is very much like a deflated balloon. I have no doubt that for a while after your death you would have been able to shift a piece of paper or snuff out a candle, but now that your soul has withered such simple tasks would be impossible to achieve."

"But you're no more tangible than I am, Hassan. Look, I can pass my hand straight through you."

"Ah, but that's where you are wrong, old chap. I am as solid as I was in my previous life and warm blood flows through my veins. Of the two of us, it is only you who is intangible."

"And when I step into Paradise, my old self will return?"

"Yes, most certainly! Your heart and soul will burst into life and your mood will swell like a soufflé. I'm amazed that, after all you've been through, you still doubt this."

"I guess I've become disillusioned. I was blindly loyal to a god who never came to me in my time of need."

"And this is what has held you back, Ulysses. You have put your faith in a blue-eyed, human god who doesn't exist. The real God, a higher energy, was ready to receive you several years ago."

"So tell me honestly, Hassan, did you stop praying to Allah once you arrived in Paradise?"

"Yes, my friend, I did. Does a starving beggar keep begging when he has been offered a hearty meal? Trust your instincts, not your beliefs."

Ulysses hung his head. "I've also foolishly clung to the belief that I could be there for my son should he ever need my help—"

"Ah, I might just be able to offer you some encouragement in that respect—"

"Go on," Ulysses said, with heightened interest.

Hassan went on to relate that, upon entering Paradise, the mantle of an angel was bestowed upon him to honour the good deeds he'd accomplished in his earthly life. He explained that the role was weighted with exclusive powers and came with the expectation of civic responsibility. It was an honour only bestowed on the few, and one that required a great degree of selflessness from the recipient.

"So, the story that will interest you is *this*," Hassan continued, raising a prophetic finger in the air. "It happened in 2007, seventeen years after my death. For reasons only known to the cosmos, an awful premonition came to me: a large truck bomb detonating in a busy market in central Baghdad. As you can imagine, the sights and sounds were beyond terrible. Such carnage would cause even the most devout worshipper to doubt their god."

"Yes, I remember seeing it on the TV news," Ulysses winced. "Truly abominable."

"Well, I recognised the place instantly. It was the Sadriyah market, the very one that my twenty-seven-year-old son, Zamir, visited each Saturday to buy fruit and vegetables for his mother."

"Oh God, I'm so, so sorry," Ulysses gasped, pre-empting what had happened next.

"No, please. No need to feel sorry. Let me explain. Somehow, in a similar way that I can be with you now, I was capable of visiting my son in a dream. I begged him not to go to the market that day and, when he opened his eyes, I swear that for a split second he saw me!"

"He saw you?"

"Indeed. And whether it was pure coincidence or not, Zamir didn't visit the market that day."

"And he's still alive today?"

"As alive as a tadpole. Going through a mid-life crisis and driving his wife crazy."

This wondrous news gave Ulysses a much-needed boost; as a result, he pushed on in the direction of his terminus with renewed vigour.

"Bravo. That is just what I wanted to see, old chap," Hassan beamed. "Beyond that distant light is another universe and a fresh start. And can you even begin to imagine how pleased Florence is going to be?"

CHAPTER THIRTY-SEVEN

Devotion's Visage

Yuri's mother, Iryna, despite having achieved her lifelong ambition of earning her rightful place in what was ostensibly the Kingdom of Heaven, still continued to pray to her masculine, humanesque god as if her life depended on it. On a balcony overlooking a cheery field of sunflowers, she'd even created a small shrine replete with a pomp of burning candles and some Christian iconography.

"Why do you do this, Iryna?" her father Leonid asked, worried that she was taking her devotion too far. "You've already had your fear of the unknown answered. Look around you. Without a doubt these are the Elysian Fields the ancient Greeks dreamt of."

"I pray because I'm not complete without God," Iryna insisted, clutching a string of rosary beads to her bosom. "I love him with all my heart and his son, Jesus Christ, is my saviour."

"But can't you see that God's plan is already revealed and that you've already been saved? Your prayers have no relevance here. Please, just accept the wonderful life you've been given and abandon all this praying nonsense."

Because of the choices they'd each made upon entering Paradise, fifty-three-year-old Iryna was now a great deal older than her father, who was once again a stocky thirty year old with a Cossack moustache. Iryna remained the age she was at the point of death, not being someone who wished to interfere with her god's grand design.

But, despite prayers being something of a fool's errand in the afterlife, her certitude was by no means an isolated instance. Throughout the centuries churches, mosques, synagogues and temples appeared across the length and breadth of Paradise to fulfil the needs of the resolutely devout. Leonid likened his daughter's fanatical allegiance to that of Hiroo Onada, a Japanese WWII soldier who, long after the cessation of hostilities, continued to fight a one-man war in the Philippines' jungle, refusing to believe the leaflet drops that confirmed the surrender of Emperor Hirohito thirty years earlier.

These places of worship, though not as well-attended as they would have been on Earth, nevertheless enjoyed the love and respect of a considerate society that was unencumbered by the canker of religious prejudice. Mortal spirits, once reborn in Paradise, found that they retained almost all of their human emotions but no longer harboured feelings of hatred, conceit, anger or contempt. Disagreements between people were efficacious, never acrimonious, and the only modes of transport available to the populace were bicycles and rowing boats. Furthering this Arcadian vision, motor cars and aeroplanes were conspicuous by their absence. In Paradise, one only had to think of a desired destination to arrive there, and people from different nations could converse easily without the need for an interpreter.

"Leonid, let her be," Iryna's equally youthful mother

said. "Be happy that we have such a righteous daughter, albeit one who is nearly twice our age."

"Ha! You can never let that go, can you?" Iryna smiled, kissing her twenty-eight-year-old mother on both cheeks.

Iryna couldn't understand why her father was so distracted by her dedication to God, especially as he had been a regular churchgoer himself until his death at the age of seventy-one. He'd recently even gone so far as to recommend courses in yoga and transcendental meditation, in the hope that Iryna might channel her time and energy into something more useful. At the heart of it all she knew that her parents wanted her to find companionship and happiness, especially as the only love she'd ever known came in the form of an alcoholic husband who often beat up her and their nine-year-old son for the most spurious of reasons.

It was after one such night that Iryna, nursing two broken ribs, slipped sleeping tablets into her husband's vodka. Then, as he snored on the sofa, she packed a suitcase for herself and a backpack for Yuri, who had been thrashed earlier with a belt strap by his father until his skin was raw.

Before stealing into the night, Iryna took the pickaxe handle that her husband kept by the front door and used it to strike him about his body. Yuri looked on fascinated as his father gasped and squirmed like a fish caught in a net. When his mother stopped to catch her breath, Yuri snatched the bludgeon and thwacked it across his father's kneecaps, causing the man to shriek in stupefied agony. If it wasn't for his mother's swift intervention, little Yuri would have willingly caved in his father's face.

Iryna left that night under a hostile sky and caught a sleeper train to Odessa. There she started a new life with her son and never saw her bastard of a husband again.

Clearly being someone for whom old habits die hard Iryna had, until recently, retained a misguided sentiment for Yuri, feeling that she'd failed in her duty as a mother and a Christian. As if to punish herself, she'd elected to remain the same careworn woman that she'd been at the end of her earthly existence, thinking herself not worthy of the second chance she had been given.

As helpless to stop him now as she ever was in her previous life, Iryna watched her once-affectionate boy continue to be a damnable brute, his cruelty knowing no bounds. With this in mind, Iryna closed her eyes and channelled her thoughts toward her English friend, Pamela Manette. In Paradise, once two people had become acquainted they could connect telepathically and converse with each other just as easily as if they were using a telephone, and Iryna felt herself obligated to Amber's grandmother.

"Hello, Pamela. Would you like to meet up today?" she asked through biospheric channels.

"Absolutely," her friend chirped, as effervescent now as she had been before a lightning bolt blew her out of her boots "How about we meet at Lady Bracknell's Tea Room in the English Sector? Let me look up the coordinates... Yep, got them. I'm pasting them to your mind now."

"Received. Oh, looks so nice. Is thirty minutes too soon?"

"No, that's fine, love. Gives me enough chance to put my lippy on. See you there."

Thirty minutes later, Iryna found herself standing on a pavement outside the tea shop, a hip, Victorian-style café offering homemade cakes and traditional loose-leaf teas. Pamela was already inside; she'd bagged a leather Chesterfield armchair and was waving energetically on the other side of a large window pane to attract Iryna's attention.

"Hello, my darling," Pamela said, swamping her Ukrainian friend with an affectionate hug. "So lovely to see you."

"You too." Iryna, dressed in a pea-green cardigan wrapped around a mud-coloured cotton dress, felt unadorned and dowdy whenever she was in Pamela's vibrant company. Each time they met, she secretly resolved to upgrade her drab wardrobe.

Grandma Pamela, since being reunited with husband Malcolm after his earthly body had succumbed to an asbestosis-related cancer in 2001, was now a youthful forty year old again, but would have preferred to be even younger. Malcolm, however, whose pragmatism outweighed what little vanity he possessed, had already decided upon the age of forty for himself and so Pamela followed suit. The golden opportunity to adjust one's age only arose at the once-yearly meeting with their guardian angels; Pamela had repeatedly pressed upon her husband that knocking another ten years off their ages would benefit them in all kinds of wonderful ways.

"Where is your lovely dog?" Iryna asked, speaking Ukrainian but being heard in perfect English.

"Sherlock, bless him. He's at home with Mal. He's already been out for a walk and a poo… Oh, that's Sherlock who's had the poo, by the way, not Malcolm. Although I'm guessing he's probably had a poo as well. Ugh, too much information, I'm sure."

Iryna giggled, which was rare for her. "You are too funny, Pamela. You really lift my spirits."

"Well, when you see the homemade cakes that they serve

here, your spirits will really be lifted. Come, have a look, they are absolutely yummy."

The two strolled over to display cabinets that showcased a selection of sponge cakes, brownies, baguettes and pastries. None of these were priced since there was no need for currency in Paradise. Natural resources across the 196 continents were inexhaustible, and industries and enterprises were run altruistically by people who formerly had a passion for their chosen professions on Earth. The friends ordered a pot of Earl Grey tea and two large slices of lemon-drizzle cake.

"You don't have to walk on eggshells, Iryna. I'm already guessing what's on your mind," Pamela said, as they sank into their armchairs like two setting suns.

"Yes, it can't be swept under the carpet any longer. It's obvious that I'm worried about Yuri and his bad intentions toward your granddaughter, so I cannot imagine what you are thinking."

"Well, I'm like a cat on a hot tin roof. So is Malcolm. But there's really nothing we can do, is there?"

"Perhaps we can go to the angels, or even the archangels—?"

"Oh, we've tried that, my love. But of course there are billions of people here who are all desperate to safeguard their loved ones' futures. What makes us any different?"

The waitress arrested their conversation, bringing a large tray laden with crockery and two sizeable portions of cake. She ceremoniously laid everything on an upcycled table and wished them *bon appétit* as steam from the teapot cavorted in a shaft of sunlight that streamed through the window.

Iryna poured the tea through a strainer and thought long and hard about what she needed to say. "My son needs to be stopped. I know this means that I will never see him again but I am beyond caring. He must be stopped."

CHAPTER THIRTY-EIGHT

Rising at Thy Name

"Sebastian, I can't seem to find those lovely earrings that you bought me. Have you seen them anywhere?"

"I expect you've lost them, Ophelia." Sebastian sighed dismissively. "And you've barely had them a week."

"Well, I don't see how I could have lost them. They can't be anywhere but in this apartment."

"I don't know why I bothered," he sighed. "There goes a month's wages down the drain."

"Sebastian, don't be so mean. If it turns out that I've lost them, I'll replace them myself. Which jeweller did you get them from?"

"Look, hun, don't worry. They're just earrings. I'll get you another pair."

"But I like those ones."

"Well, you should've been more careful then."

"I shan't stop looking until I find them."

"Good for you."

*

At the start of his evening shift at Café des Rêves, Sebastian was polishing wine glasses behind the restaurant's bar counter, languidly holding each one up to the light to check for smudges. Working only as hard as it suited came naturally to him; the rest of the team, including the restaurant manager, had abandoned all attempts to rope him into vacuuming carpets, laying tables and preparing for service.

His partial exemption from duty was largely due to the preferential treatment bestowed on him by the owner's libidinous wife, Jasmine, who only had to look at Sebastian to begin salivating like one of Pavlov's dogs. The staff didn't need to possess the analytical faculty of a Belgian detective to deduce that the two of them were secretly rutting like wild animals after everyone else had gone home.

Jasmine breezed in, wearing a fur-trimmed coat, a pair of over-the-knee suede boots and a short dress intersected by a gold chain belt that swayed to the rhythm of her hips. In her mid-forties, she still possessed a body that writhed nakedly in the mind of every heterosexual man she met.

"Have no fear, Jasmine's here!" she bubbled, pushing sunglasses to the top of her head and fussing with her chestnut-brown hair. "Can anyone tell me how many people are booked in tonight?"

"Thirty-six," said Sebastian, quick as a flash, before anyone else could answer.

"Well done, that man. Finger on the pulse as usual."

"Yes, I'm quite the suppository of knowledge."

"I think you mean repository, darling."

"Uh, possibly."

"Wine. I need a glass of wine. Seb, I'm coming over."

"And which wine would you like, Jaz?" he asked from the other side of the counter.

"Stay right where you are, hun, I'll come round and pour it myself, babe."

The rest of the staff threw each other knowing grins and carried on with their duties while Jasmine slunk behind the bar counter. Hidden from view, she grabbed Sebastian's cock and began to massage it through the material of his trousers.

"Aww, I haven't had this inside me for a few days," she whispered. "Your little girlfriend keeping you satisfied, is she?"

"She does her best."

"Yeah, but she's not as dirty as me, is she, babe? Doesn't do the things that I do for you, I bet."

"Perhaps not."

"Ooh, things are on the move. You want me to take care of that?"

"Now might not be the right time." Sebastian grinned, scanning the room to see if anyone was watching.

"Stay behind after work then. God, I bloody need it."

"Me too."

"So what's this about you getting engaged? How come I get to hear it from my staff and not you?"

"If you were to poison your husband, thereafter inheriting all of his money, I'd marry you instead," Sebastian said with a facetious smile, his cupidity knowing no bounds.

"God, don't tempt me. It'd be worth it to have you fucking me every night."

"Now wouldn't that be nice?"

Jasmine continued to covertly work Sebastian's clothed erection with her fingers while he remained poker-faced and vigilant. "You and me, Sebastian, we need to book a hotel room. Do it properly, rather than shagging in dark corners of the restaurant."

"Then you'll be pleased to know that my girlfriend is going to the Cologne Christmas Market with her parents next week and *I've* got the run of her apartment for a couple of days."

"Yum! That's what I love about you, Seb. You're a delightfully sneaky bastard. Let me know when and we'll both take the time off."

"Much as I'm enjoying the attention, Jaz, you do need to prise your hand off my dick. Customers are beginning to stream in."

"I'm coming back for *him* later," she purred, giving his bulge an affectionate pat before pouring herself a large glass of Chablis.

"Oh, I nearly forgot," said Sebastian, moving his cock out of the way so he could retrieve something from his trouser pocket. "I bought you these, as a gift."

Jasmine opened the small velveteen box that he handed her. "Earrings!" she squealed, a little louder than she'd intended. "Darling, they're lovely. D'you know what? You are *so* going to get it tonight, babe."

CHAPTER THIRTY-NINE

Shall We Not Revenge?

Odessa, Ukraine, 1992

"Yuri, please tell me that it's not so!" Iryna wailed, upon discovering that her eleven-year-old son was now the bearer of a crudely-drawn swastika tattoo that sat, inky and loathsome, upon his reddened chest.

Her first thought was to slap him across his defiant face but instead she held his cheeks in her hands and tried to reason with him. "Don't you see, Yuri? This brands you as nothing but a racist. Have you forgotten that in the eyes of God all men are equal? Who is it who puts these poisonous ideas in your mind?"

Earlier that day, Yuri had become the youngest addition to a street gang of skinheads whose induction rule was that each new member must have this insignia carved into their skin by whoever was recruited before them. Unfortunately for Yuri, his tattooist was cack-handed Igor Brutka who unwittingly incised the swastika into the rookie's skin back to front, much to the amusement of the other delinquents who kept this detail to themselves until after the ink was rubbed in.

Iryna's pleas fell upon deaf ears. In the absence of a fine, upstanding husband to assist her efforts, Yuri was soon lost to a Slavic subculture of violence and petty crime.

Yuri took to thug life like a duck to water. By the time he was twelve, he had proved himself time and time again in numerous skirmishes with other gangs, garnering a reputation for gamely standing his ground and fighting even when outnumbered. The older boys awarded him the nickname of 'Little Bull' and, because of his youthfulness, he was often used as bait to lure rival gang members into vicious ambushes.

Despite his descent into an adolescence of thuggery and lawlessness, Yuri still attended school and was smart enough to steer clear of drug use and glue-sniffing, sensing that there was real money to be made from a future career in crime. He aligned himself with an older boy, sixteen-year-old Boris Timko, who encouraged him to educate himself and who also spoke admiringly of Mishka Yaponchik, alias 'Mishka the Japanese', a legendary Odessan gangster who emulated the disciplined way in which the Japanese *yakuza* went about their business.

Yuri hung on Boris's every word, knowing that the rest of his fellow gang members would all end up as drugged-up nobodies before reaching adulthood. Boris, though, had something about him and his advice to be smart yet ruthless would later stand Yuri in good stead.

But it was also at the age of twelve that something pivotal happened to Yuri, which would twist his mindset for years to some.

In the height of summer, Yuri and his cohorts were reclining on abandoned car tyres, drinking cheap vodka and warm beer on a litter-strewn patch of wasteland just a stone's throw from the city's docks. It was mid-July, as hot as Hades; the searing sunshine had melted asphalt and burned any remaining moisture from the sky. With the mercury hitting the mid-nineties, an air of indolence pervaded the atmosphere. A street musician, wearing an embroidered blouson shirt, played his accordion with no real conviction and a stray dog, finding it too hot to even bark, sought shelter in the shade of a rusted car. Frenetic clouds of midges flickered above rancid refuse bags while Yuri's gang idled away the day, engaging in boastful banter and becoming steadily drunk. They croaked like parched frogs, exaggerating recent glories above the thrum of traffic noise as gauzy dragonflies darted about their heads. Usually, the briny smell of the Black Sea hung in a cooling breeze this close to the coast but the air today was thick as treacle and only a miasma of putrescence filtered into the boys' dry nostrils.

Inevitably, on a day such as this, the crow of their conversations died on their tongues and wilted on their chins. Everything was far too much of an effort and nothing of any substance was taking place. But then, from the other side of a sun-baked road and wading through a lake of heat haze, there approached a thickset teenage girl with wild, rat-tail hair and a murderous demeanour. She lumbered into their territory like a story-book ogre; it would have been easy to imagine the ground shaking under the thud of her boots.

The boys were transfixed and took in every detail of her appearance: there was a semblance of a moustache above her unsmiling lips, and her nostrils flared wildly like those of a horse ridden into battle. Her name was Olga Brutka; she was a sixteen-year-old gypsy who was strong as a blacksmith and as wrathful as a Gorgon. Yuri and his pals looked at her open-mouthed, wondering what her intentions were. Even the dog forgot about its fleas and stared at her with quivering trepidation.

"Which one of you sissy boys beat up my younger brother?" she demanded, rolling up the sleeves of her tracksuit top and revealing a large scorpion tattoo upon her left forearm.

The boys laughed at her chutzpah and one rather unwisely chose to throw a can of beer at her head, whereupon she lifted him up onto her chest and summarily hurled him into the nearest clump of stinging nettles. This provided the boys with some welcome light relief from their tedium and they laughed even louder.

"I'll ask you again," she snarled. "Which one of you sissies beat up my brother?"

"So who is your brother?" asked Boris with an inquisitive smile. "We beat up lots of boys. You need to be more specific."

"Vitali Brutka."

Upon mention of this name, all eyes and grins were suddenly on Yuri who'd brutally beaten the boy in a fight two days earlier.

"Ah, so it's you. Stand up and fight me, tough guy," Olga demanded.

"I don't fight girls," said Yuri, discharging a stream of cigarette smoke and nonchalantly leaning back onto his tyre.

"Well, I'll allow you to make an exception in my case. Get up!"

"Hey, give him a break. He's only twelve," Boris said. "And you're going to get yourself hurt, coming onto our turf and making threats."

Olga was undeterred. "Look, my problem is only with

him. No need for anybody else to get involved. Is there honour in your gang or not?"

"OK, that seems fair," said Boris with a deferential nod. "A one-on-one scrap and you have my word that none of us will get involved. Hey, Yuri, are you ready to fight for your honour?"

Olga removed her hooped earrings and hid them in a pocket. She took two steps back and beckoned Yuri forward, as if guiding a car into a parking space. "C'mon, sissy boy, where's your pride? After all, I'm only a girl."

"No biting or gouging," Boris cautioned. "A good, clean fight."

Yuri sensed the shadow of his father pass over him and a bee hummed in his ear. He got to his feet and took one last drag of his cigarette before flicking it to the ground. His T-shirt was clammy and it clung to his wet back; he removed it and began to circle his opponent like a gladiator. She mirrored his movement, turning as haltingly as a second hand on a clock face. The difference in their age and size was all too apparent to everyone watching from the sidelines.

Seeking to gain an early advantage, Yuri charged at Olga, keeping his centre of gravity low to the ground. This gambit proved ill-considered as she smashed a large knee into his face and sent him crashing into the dirt. Yuri, his senses addled, scrabbled to pick up his teeth, which lay scattered like eggshells on a beach. Olga, intent on doing him harm, set about his body with a quiet determination as he floundered on the ground.

Dusty flashes of the sun and blue sky interchanged with the smell of grass and dog shit as Yuri convulsed and tumbled under a barrage of punches and kicks. His mouth filled with blood, choking him, and he was vaguely aware of the mocking cackle of seagulls as they wheeled overhead.

"OK, stop! That's enough!" Boris yelled, pulling Olga by her hair and pressing his flick knife against the skin of her neck. The blade glinted in the sun. "He's done. You've made your point."

She staggered backwards, dizzy and breathless, taking in huge gulps of air.

Yuri struggled to get to his feet and allowed the blood to drip from his mouth, finding it too painful to spit. He regarded the triumphant grin on Olga's sweaty face and the scorpion tattoo on her arm.

"Things will be very different the next time we meet," he vowed, though his threat seemed somewhat feeble given that it was enunciated with a soggy lisp.

"Yeah, yeah, kiss my tits and make a wish, loser," she chuckled, hooking her earrings back into her lobes. "Thanks, though, to the rest of you for keeping out of it. You boys have acted with honour."

"This is true," Boris concurred. "But if you show your face around here again, you'll be leaving with a beating – or worse."

"That's fair. My family are always on the move anyway. You won't be seeing me again." With these parting words, Olga shook Boris's hand and lumbered away, leaving Yuri to lick his wounds.

"Don't lose heart, Little Bull," Boris said, placing an arm across Yuri's begrimed shoulders. "That freak would've beaten any one of us in a fist fight."

Boris's solicitude fell on deaf ears. As far as Yuri was concerned, the humiliation that Olga had just wreaked upon him would continue to poison his psyche for decades. A cauldron of hatred had already begun to bubble in his core. "I won't rest until I get my own back on that bitch," he snarled, running his fingers along bloody gums that had recently held teeth. "I can't bear the thought of her shooting her mouth off about this."

"Well, Little Bull, do you remember what I told you? Do you remember the favourite saying of Mishka the Japanese?"

"That the dead have the shortest tongues?"

"You've got it. The dead have the shortest tongues. So there is your solution for dealing with people who can't keep their mouth shut. Something to bear in mind as you go through life."

*

Odessa. New Year's Eve, 1999. Approaching nineteen years of age and looking anything but a teenager, Yuri was a different proposition to the twelve-year-old boy beaten up by a girl just seven years earlier. Natural growth and the habitual lifting of heavy weights in austere gymnasiums had turned him into a formidable young man accustomed to seeing fear in the eyes of anyone who crossed him. His mother had recently died from a heart attack and he'd moved on from gang fights and petty crime to become a salaried enforcer for a large drug gang. Along the way, he'd survived numerous attempts on his young life and his granite face now bore the cross-hatched scars of several knife attacks.

Against his better judgment, he'd been dragged to the New Year's Eve celebrations in Dumskaya Square by two of his associates. As anticipated, he detested the whole scene with its jubilant crowds of carousers in their stupid hats dancing to Euro pop and whooping like children at the laser light show. He left abruptly without saying as much as a Happy New Year to anyone.

As he walked, he allowed himself a moment of sentiment, summoning a childhood memory of his mother returning home from a New Year's party, waking him from his sleep to smother him in cognac kisses.

Though the night air was brittle with frost, Yuri didn't wear a jacket over his T-shirt, preferring to let his muscles make an intimidatory statement. He headed for a down-at-heel bar, which skulked in the shadows of a dingy side street that was used mostly as a latrine.

A clump of cheerless men, their cigarette tips floating like fireflies, scowled at him from an unlit doorway as he approached. He hoped that they might put their hostility into action as he muscled his way through, but they didn't. He bulldozed himself into a gap at the bar counter, uninterested in the salutation of drunken strangers.

The bar staff were working frenziedly to keep up with demand; there were three in total, two men and one hulking female. It was then that a thunderbolt of recognition struck Yuri and set his senses tingling. The same scorpion tattoo he'd purposely consigned to memory was there on the barmaid's beefy arm. She was older, of course, a woman in her early twenties, but she looked much the same apart from her hair, which was now cropped as short as a man's.

Yuri couldn't believe his luck; the last time he'd enquired as to her whereabouts, Olga and her itinerant family had moved to Kiev.

He studied her as she exchanged playful banter with a regular then, when she wheeled away, he caught her attention by waving banknotes in outstretched fingers.

She saw him, one more man in an endless line of thirsty punters. "So what can I get you, love—?" Olga stopped in her tracks, her words dissolving into silence as she did a double take. She folded her arms and looked at him askance, doubling her chin into her chest. "Hey, don't I know you?" she bubbled, her eyes brightening. "Don't tell me that you're the same boy I roughed up several years ago! You are! Look at you, all grown up."

"We meet again, Olga," Yuri said flatly, his voice several octaves lower than when they'd last met.

"No hard feelings then?" she asked a little warily, offering a conciliatory handshake.

"None at all," Yuri replied, appearing to accept her olive branch with good grace.

A confusion of flashbacks crowded his mind. He recalled her standing over him, cackling like a mad witch, and also remembered with shame the look of horror on his mother's face, asking how many boys had attacked him that fateful day. *Revenge is a dish best served cold*, he thought to himself and a faint, deviant smile buckled his lips.

"Wouldn't want to take you on now," she joked. "Look at the size of you. Built like a tank... And those scars... Anyway, please forgive me but I'm afraid I can't remember your name—"

"Yuri."

"Well, Yuri, to let bygones be bygones the drinks are on me tonight."

In between serving other customers Olga, relieved to expunge some of the guilt she felt about the wildness of her youth, sought to impress upon Yuri that she was no longer the same person. She'd been living in a loving relationship with a woman for the past two years and had also turned to God.

"Look, I'm ditching this place around eleven thirty to go to a millennium party. It's only a ten-minute walk, you can come if you want."

"I'd like that," said Yuri. "So I guess you're only asking

me because you're too scared to walk on your own at night?"

"Ha! You know different to that," she breezed, pouring him another free drink. "Hey, I'll introduce you to Sofiya, my partner."

Less than two hours later Olga, her teeth scraping against hard, frosty cobblestones, stirred from unconsciousness to find that she was being savagely raped from behind. She couldn't see Yuri's face but could smell the vodka on his ghostly breath, could hear his bestial grunts and the hiss of his insults. Squirming for her life but compressed under his weight, she received a hard wallop to the back of her head and a grenade of hot pain exploded in her skull. She didn't feel the second, third or fourth blows. Instead, her soul could only float on the periphery and watch helplessly as Yuri smashed a house brick onto her head time and time again until it crumbled in his hand.

She departed the scene and hovered high above the moonlit waters of the Black Sea, pausing only to enjoy the fireworks that heralded an auspicious new century. Then she stepped into a celestial corridor and headed for the light.

CHAPTER FORTY

The Fish that Climbed a Tree

Ulysses felt certain that some of his defunct senses were returning to him because suddenly he smelled Paradise in the way that a mariner smells landfall.

"We're nearly there, Hassan!" he yelled, his confidence buoyed.

"In reality I'm already there, Ulysses old chap. But yes, I believe that you are on the home stretch and I'm delighted for you."

"What's expected of me when I arrive?" Ulysses asked. "I don't want to make a mess of things."

"Come as you are, you'll be absolutely fine. It'll take care of itself."

Hassan explained to Ulysses that he would very likely be greeted by whichever archangel was seconded to him, most probably Voltaire. Then, in an incidence of name-dropping, he reeled off a list of archangels whom he'd personally met at the continental summits that were held each year.

"Oh, I've rubbed shoulders with Omar Khayyam, Benazir Bhutto and Martin Luther King," he said, star-struck. "I've also shared the same room as Socrates, John Lennon, and Louis Pasteur."

"How do these people get chosen? And by whom?" Ulysses asked.

"Natural selection," Hassan replied. "These things just happen organically, as you will see in due course."

"And the continents?" Ulysses queried, his mind spinning. "Are they the same as the ones that I'm familiar with?"

"Not quite. There are no continents. Instead there are 196 sectors," Hassan elucidated. "Each one corresponds to a country on Earth, but this creation remains fluid. As countries change on Earth, the sectors here similarly adapt. As more and more people enter Paradise, the sectors grow to accommodate them."

"So there's an English sector, a Scottish sector, and so on and so forth?"

"Correct. But of course each nation is way, way bigger than the ones you were used to. And all of the wonders of the world, natural and man-made, still exist: the Grand Canyon; the Great Barrier Reef; the Great Wall of China—"

"Wow. Hassan, I just can't get my head around this. It all just seems so outlandish and so unreal."

"No more outlandish and unreal than the planet you've left behind. How would you even begin to explain such a miracle to someone from another galaxy?"

"Quite. I do see your point."

"Of course, this could all be a dream within a dream, if we are to believe the words of Edgar Allan Poe."

"I suppose you've met him too?" Ulysses said with a twinkle in his one eye.

"Ha! Unfortunately not."

Then, walking through an eddying mist, Ulysses suddenly found himself standing at what he assumed were the gates of Paradise.

"See, Ulysses!" Hassan beamed. "See what a positive outlook and some self-belief has brought you. You've made it to Paradise! I couldn't be happier."

Almost as if summoned by a bell, Voltaire stepped regally from the light dressed in an embroidered velvet coat and fussing with the ruffles of his shirt cuffs. "*Bonjour*, Ulysses," he said, the impish smile never far from his face. "I'm so pleased that you didn't become just another *fantôme*, it really would not have become you."

"Oh, Voltaire, I am so incredibly relieved to see you again. I feared that this moment would never come."

"Please. Call me François," Voltaire replied, before kissing his charge's gossamer cheeks.

Hassan stepped decorously to one side and wished his friend good luck. "Ulysses, you are indeed the fish that climbed that tree. See you on the other side, old chap. I shall tell Florence the good news."

"Thank you, Hassan. I couldn't have done this without you." Ulysses watched his friend dissolve and disappear from view.

Voltaire extended a guiding arm towards the phosphorescent light. "Shall we?" he invited.

The air around them changed, ionised as if a storm were about to break. There were no orchestral choirs, nor were there any adoring cherubs floating overhead as Ulysses and the tattered flag of his soul stepped through a quivering curtain of light and into the promise of a new life.

CHAPTER FORTY-ONE

Speak Less than You Know

Brian McKay, a detective working on the recently reopened vicarage murder case, rapped repeatedly on Yuri Voloshyn's door and at the same time tut-tutted at a disarray of cigarette butts that littered the Ukrainian's porch. "Untidy bastard," he grunted to his fresh-faced colleague who hadn't even joined the force when the killings took place.

Yuri threw open the door, an angry slab of humanity dressed only in his boxers. The younger detective was seized suddenly with the urge to gallop up the road while the senior detective nonchalantly held up his warrant card.

"What you do banging on door?" Yuri growled, his Slavic cheekbones reddening. "Is early in morning, you piece of shit."

"Lovely to see you too, Yuri. I don't know if you remember me? I'm Detective Sergeant Brian McKay. I interviewed you some years ago with regard to the murders at the vicarage on Sowerberry Road—"

Yuri folded his arms and filled the width of the door frame. "So?"

"So, I've just popped round to let you know that we're treating it as a cold case. Having another look at it, so to speak."

"What this to do with me?"

"Maybe nothing, Yuri. But I would still like to invite you down to the station for a friendly little chat. Only if you've got nothing better to do, of course."

"You arrest me now?"

"No, not at all. You are what we like to call 'a person of interest', Yuri. You're not even under caution at this stage."

"So, you have nothing. Same like before," Yuri grinned.

"Well, you do know that not wanting to help us with our enquiries could be seen as an admission of guilt?"

"You must think I am born on yesterday," Yuri chuckled. "If you arrest me then we talk. Right now, I go back to sleep."

"Well, I must say it's been nice talking to you, Mr Voloshyn."

"Suck this," said Yuri, grabbing the front of his boxers before preparing to slam the door.

"Oh, Yuri? Yuri? Mate, before you go—"

Yuri sighed irascibly. "What?"

"Where on Earth did you get that swastika tattoo done? Looks like a frigging child did it!"

Yuri slammed the door in McKay's face.

Upon hearing the detectives' laughter on the other side of the door, he had to stop himself from tearing outside and beating them both to a pulp. As soon as they'd driven off, he phoned Pascal to warn him that he was also likely to receive a visit.

Of late, Yuri had been implacable. The renewed interest in the murders had put him firmly back in the frame and rubbed salt into old wounds. His comfortable life, the one he had once dreamed of as a street kid in Odessa, had been rolling along just nicely until the vicar's son took it upon himself to throw it all into jeopardy.

The dead have the shortest tongues, he reminded himself.

*

The first snowflakes of winter were falling soundlessly from the sky when Amber, wearing only a towelling dressing gown, stepped from her kitchen to throw an empty egg carton into the recycling bin. Yuri, sitting cross-legged on his kitchen doorstep and smoking a cigarette, called over to her. "Hey, pretty lady!"

"Oh, hi," Amber replied nervously, after initially pretending that she hadn't seen him.

"We need to have chat," he yelled, his voice the sound of a bluebottle trapped behind a curtain.

"Er, OK."

"What is matter, Amber?" Yuri asked, drawing nearer. "You look like scared rabbit."

A snowflake settled on Amber's eyelashes and the frozen tarmac nibbled at her bare toes. "No, I'm fine, Yuri. What do you want exactly?"

Yuri caught a glimpse of curvy flesh under the folds of her gown and a surge of blood fattened his cock. Uncomfortable in the glare of his piercing eyes, Amber drew the robe across her chest and folded her arms. He savoured her discomfort and thought about all that was waiting for him within touching distance.

"Your boyfriend, he make trouble for me. Police come to my house. Maybe he should be careful what he write in newspaper?"

"Look, Yuri, I really don't want to be having this conversation—"

He raised his voice, just as she was about to turn away. "Hey, you want to know something very interesting?"

"Go on—"

"I know what you did."

"Sorry?"

"I know what you did that night. So, if boyfriend make trouble for me, I make trouble for you."

Amber's jaw slackened and her blood congealed. She'd succeeded in putting the whole nightmarish episode to the back of her mind and now Yuri was showing his hand. A farrago of thoughts cartwheeled through her consciousness, making her stomach convulse. She immediately wondered where he was storing the body and what his motives were. Most of all, she worried about Henry's safety. "Uh, I'm getting cold," she muttered, breaking eye contact. "I'd better get back inside."

"Such a pretty girl," Yuri droned, moving forward and deftly slipping a chunky hand inside the fold of her robe.

"Don't touch me!" she raged, slapping him hard across his cheek.

The vulnerability of her anger prompted his erection to come alive. It throbbed against his pants and beat a drum, demanding to be deployed. A smirk and a red handprint bloomed on his face.

Mr Beardsley, returning from a gentle morning run, caught the sound of Amber's raised voice and saw her unease. "Is everything OK, Amber?" he called out from the pavement, jogging on the spot and looking at Yuri with acute suspicion.

"Yeah, yeah, I'm fine, Mr B. Just a difference of opinion, that's all."

"If you say so," Beardsley yelled back. "Give me a call if you need me."

*

Once inside, Amber phoned Henry, concerned that events might be taking a sharp turn for the worse.

"Hello, Amber," he said in a buttoned-up voice that told her he was with company.

"Hi, Henry. Is it OK to talk?"

She heard him excuse himself from whoever he was talking to and, after a breathless trot, he was able to speak freely. "Sorry, I was just interviewing the Hackney Players about their Christmas panto," he puffed. "Fire away."

"I'm sorry to bother you, but I'm really worried. Yuri was visited by the police today and it's rattled his cage. So now he's had a go at me, being all creepy and making threats—"

"Threats? What kind of threats?"

"Um, are you sure that no one can hear our conversation?"

"Positive. I'm out of earshot."

"Well, he said that he knows what we did. Said that he could make life difficult for us if we make it difficult for him."

A hollow feeling ballooned in Henry's stomach. "Oh, God. I feared that this might happen, or that he would try to blackmail us. In retrospect, I wish I'd never run the article."

"What are we going to do, Henry? I feel sick with nerves."

"Maybe I could talk with the police? Say that I've had a change of heart because the investigation is dragging up bad memories. Tell them I'd rather they closed the case."

"Would you do that?"

"I don't see that we've got much choice. That gorilla has the upper hand here. The only thing that might work in our favour is that the police would wonder why he hadn't come forward sooner."

"Are you coming here tonight? I really don't want to sleep on my own with all this going on."

"Of course. I'll come round after work. What time do you finish?"

"I won't be home until eleven thirtyish. I'll leave the key under the plant pot near the kitchen door."

The news photographer hoisted an arm, signalling for Henry to return to the fold. "Plant pot, kitchen door. Got it. I'm afraid I've got to go. See you later, Amber."

"Hey, thanks for being so calm, Henry. It's a real comfort, especially as Mr Beardsley is away visiting family for most of the weekend."

"Trust me, I'm really not that calm. I'm just trying to be pragmatic. Look, I really must get back to my interviewees. Keep it together and I'll see you tonight after your shift."

Henry returned to the ensemble of actors and their stage director, offering his apologies, which they accepted with good grace. It immediately occurred to him that this companionable group of people couldn't, in their wildest dreams, imagine that their mild-mannered interviewer was also an accessory to murder.

*

Yuri saw Amber's dappled silhouette through the frosted glass of his kitchen door and immediately bounded upstairs to better observe her from the landing window.

The snow was still falling, settling softly on windowsills and the tops of hedges, quilting everything with pillowy drifts. Amber scurried to the car, squinting into the wintry flurry, wearing a coat that flew open to reveal the tight uniform that Yuri liked to see her in. Thus aroused, he loosened his jeans to allow his hand access to his stiffening penis. He followed the sway of her breasts as she swept snow from the windscreen. Guttural groans rasped in his throat and his hand began to work more feverishly.

Amber scurried to lock the kitchen door, making further tracks in the snow. Then she did something that really caught Yuri's attention. Under his gaze, she got down onto her haunches and hid the door key beneath a terracotta plant pot.

"Amber, you are very helpful girl," he said to himself, immediately forgetting all about the needs of his burgeoning cock.

After watching her car disappear up the road, Yuri ambled over to the plant pot to capture the key. He unlocked her door to see if it was alarmed. As he'd suspected, nothing happened, not one decibel of sound. Delighted with his fortuitous discovery, he locked the door and drove to the local hardware store to get a duplicate key cut, all the time relieved that his mother hadn't lived to see what he'd become.

Upon his return, he slipped the original key under the plant pot, trusting the falling snow to cover his footprints. Happier than he'd been for quite some time, he spent the rest of the day contemplating his extreme good fortune.

CHAPTER FORTY-TWO

Like a Child From the Womb, Like a Ghost From the Tomb

No sooner had Ulysses stepped over the threshold of Paradise than his skeleton began to ossify. Regenerated bones cambered, creaked and clicked into position while a gelatinous stack of organs added ballast to the vacuum of his rangy body. He once more felt blood coursing through veins and his lungs puffed up like naan on the walls of a tandoor. As a finishing touch, a filo of tepid skin gloved his hands and clothed his body.

"My good man, the colour is restored to your cheeks," Voltaire said, with the air of someone who had witnessed such a transformation a thousand times.

With his olfactory senses fully restored, Ulysses found the Frenchman's perfume wonderfully intoxicating. The clothes he was murdered in now clung reassuringly to his frame and gravity weighted him down. He could feel the soft wool of his cable-knit sweater under his fingertips, the clerical collar against his neck and the leather eye patch against his orbital bone. For the first time in over a decade

Ulysses could test the solidity of the ground beneath him. Even seeing his shadow again was reassuring.

Overcome by it all, Ulysses sobbed noisily into his hands, at which point Voltaire held him in a hug that carried human substance. "Well done, my friend. You have caused me more concern than any other person under my guardianship but nevertheless you have arrived safely. Welcome to Paradise, Ulysses."

Steadily familiarising himself with his new surroundings, Ulysses realised that he was standing in a capacious, Renaissance-style marbled hall, domed with frescoed ceilings. Having been starved of natural light for such a long time, he was overjoyed to see a profusion of it flooding through a colonnade of porticos, beyond which he glimpsed the beautiful vistas of Paradise.

In the centre of the room, far from anything else, was a large gold-leafed desk, at which sat a young man dressed in Victorian clothes. The fellow wrote with a quill and looked over with watchful interest from a fancy, high-backed chair that might have doubled as a throne. He couldn't have been any more than twenty years old.

"Who's he?" Ulysses whispered.

"None other than Sir Charles Darwin," Voltaire replied.

"Charles Darwin? Surely not? He's far too young. I've seen him in photos. Old man with a big white beard—"

"Ah, but he chose to be a young man again. I'm told he preferred the red hair of his youth to the baldness of his dotage. Vanity torments us all, even in the afterlife."

"Ahem, Francois! May I remind you that I have also recouped the ears of my youth, and that the acoustics in this room are extraordinarily good," Darwin retorted, his words echoing off marbled surfaces. "Come. Let us process

Mr Drummond before his maltreated soul dissolves into gases yet again."

While Voltaire chaperoned him to the desk, Ulysses tried to make some sense of the implausible fact that he was being attended personally to by such historical icons. He, of course, wondered why they didn't have better things to do and put his thoughts into words. "It really is a great honour to meet you, Sir Charles, but—"

"Charles will suffice," Darwin interjected.

"But, you see, I'm confused. Surely someone such as yourself wouldn't spend each day processing all and sundry like a check-in agent at an airport? Am I being duped by some fanciful trick?"

Darwin raised both eyebrows and smiled at Voltaire. "Ah, you were correct, François. He is indeed a doubting Thomas."

"As was I when I first arrived," Voltaire replied. "In my considered opinion, this further demonstrates Ulysses' perspicacity."

"Indeed. But he has also proved the axiom that even intelligent people are liable to make irrational decisions."

Ulysses, baffled as to why these esteemed luminaries were discussing him as if he weren't there, chiselled into their conversation. "Excuse me, chaps. Will I be able to see my wife today?"

"Oh, so sorry, *mon ami*," Voltaire apologised. "Please forgive our indecorum, but I have told Monsieur Darwin so much about you. If you are amenable, we have already agreed to invest you with some ancillary powers."

"You see, Ulysses," Darwin continued, "as archangels, we are favoured with the capacity to bestow the mantle of an angel on whoever we feel to be worthy. If it's not too soon to ask, would you like to become an angel?"

"Me, an angel? Well yes, of course. It would be an honour," Ulysses replied without a moment's hesitation.

"Excellent. I heartily applaud a man who doesn't dither," Darwin beamed, before going on to explain to Ulysses that around 150,000 humans die each day and that the incoming footfall of their departed souls was managed by archangels.

"Here in Paradise there are more than one million archangels of all genders, many of whom were not at all famous during their earthly lifetimes. The prevailing reason that I am here today is because Voltaire was especially keen for me to meet you. Aside from this rascal and myself, there is an inexhaustible supply of angels to suit all nationalities and religions. You can therefore be assured that I am not at all your mythical St Peter, standing at the gates of Heaven."

"So what happens now?" Ulysses asked, keen to reunite with Florence.

"What happens now is that I will ask you just two questions. All that is required of you is to answer them. Then you will be free to enjoy a new life of unbridled joy."

Voltaire pushed an ornate Louis XIV-style chair up to Ulysses for him to sit on as Darwin began the induction process. "Now, Ulysses, which part of Paradise would you prefer to reside in? Keep in mind that the countries here are ostensibly the same as they were on Earth."

"Er, obviously I'd like to live wherever my wife is."

"That would be the English Sector—"

"The English Sector it is then. Crikey, this is extraordinary."

"Let me preface my second question by stating that no decision is ever cast in stone. Preferences can easily be changed at a later date."

"Thank you. That's most reassuring."

"You have the option of being whatever age you wish to be. Cast your one good eye upon me, Ulysses. Do I not exist in the first flush of youth? Am I not living proof that you can be any age you choose?"

"Um, what age did Florence decide upon?"

"Forty, evidently."

"Perfect. Well, I'm two years older than Florence, so I'll remain at forty-two, please."

"Ah, precisely the age you are now, or rather the age at which you expired. So, no need for cell reconstruction. Which is a shame as I was hoping to enthral you with my capacity to rejuvenate you."

"Uh, a kind offer, but my and Florence's lives were at their happiest in the days leading up to our, um, murder."

"So be it. Congratulations, sir. That concludes your induction into Paradise. You will have a plethora of questions but these will all be answered in the fullness of time. Would you be so good as to sign your name here? I'm sorry that I have nothing to offer you but a quill pen. I feel that it befits the formality of the occasion."

As Darwin fussed with his thinning sweep of russet hair, Ulysses applied a scratchy signature to a parchment scroll and succeeded in splashing droplets of ink all over it.

"You are not yet aware of this, Ulysses, but you are forthwith wholly incapable of succumbing to destructive emotions such as anger and avarice. So what do you say to that?"

"A wonderful state of affairs," said Ulysses approvingly, feeling an incoming breeze against his cheek.

"And, by the powers invested in me, you are also recast as an angel. But without those ridiculously unnatural wings, of course."

"Amazing. Thank you, thank you so much, Charles. If

you don't mind, I'll process all of this later. Right now I'm just so excited at the prospect of seeing my wife again. Is she here?"

The tear that fell from the vicar's remaining eye reminded Darwin vividly of the emotions he had felt when his beloved Emma was returned to him years after his own death.

"You will see her very soon," the naturalist said, pressing his youthful hand into Ulysses' palm. "And I should like for you and Florence to meet my wife and family once you are settled. You have found a new friend here today. If ever you need to call on me, just think of my name and if I'm available I will answer. This method of communication is one of Paradise's peculiarities, one that you will swiftly become accustomed to."

"Thank you, Charles. It's been a pleasure."

Voltaire bade Darwin a good day and took Ulysses by the arm, leading him toward a resplendent panorama of green fields and blue skies.

CHAPTER FORTY-THREE

I Wish You All the Joy You Can Wish

Having typed up a local news story about an elderly gentleman whose failing eyesight had led him to post Christmas cards into a council dog-poop bin, Henry made his way to the back of a queue at the bus stop, ducking under the batwings of wet umbrellas as he did so.

It was already crow-dark; squiggles of neon light shimmered on the wet pavements and the cold December air pricked at his cheeks. He grumbled to himself on account of his socks and trouser cuffs being sodden after he'd carelessly stepped into a mound of slush by the side of the road. It had snowed earlier but now only a faint mizzle hung in the air, spinning silvery cobwebs on the hair and shoulders of everyone in the queue.

He spotted Reverend Tulloch, his father's replacement at St Cuthbert's, coughing like a bronchitic camel and having his back slapped by a stout Welsh lady who told everyone not to worry because she used to be a nurse. Henry had never thought to visit the church since his parents' murder, still subscribing to the belief that Christianity as a concept suffered from a distinct lack of scientific insight. And yet, paradoxically, he remained convinced that mankind's mastery of time travel was inevitable and that its secret was likely to be unlocked any time soon.

When the bus arrived more passengers alighted than there were people in the queue. Taking advantage of the space created, Henry clambered up to the top deck and sat right at the front, as he had done when he was a schoolboy. With nothing better to do, he whiled away the time by absentmindedly examining the contents of his trouser pockets, sifting through door keys, coins, an asthma inhaler, a menthol nasal stick and a tube of lip balm. In the process, he unearthed a forgotten boiled sweet, which he unwrapped from its sticky wrapper and popped into his mouth.

He'd spent much of his day mulling over Amber's phone call and shared her consternation as to the significance of Yuri's veiled threats. He ran through several permutations, trying to second-guess what someone in Yuri's position might do next, but couldn't conceive of any retaliation that wouldn't also incriminate the man himself.

One thing that did occur to Henry, leaving him fraught with worry, was that Yuri might secretly return Danny's stinking carcass to Amber's garage and thereafter alert the police. This was the worst-case scenario in his theoretical checklist and he hoped against hope that Yuri wasn't daring enough to implement such an audacious plan.

Earlier in the day, immediately after interviewing the pantomime actors, Henry had attempted to effect some damage limitation by phoning Detective Sergeant Brian McKay to see if the murder case could be sidelined or postponed.

"Henry, has either Pascal Makuza or Yuri Voloshyn put the frighteners on you?" asked the detective, knowing full well how both men operated. "If they have, you can confide in me."

"No, not at all," assured Henry. "It's just that this dredges up bad memories for me. I wondered if it might be better to keep such things in the past."

"I do understand that, Henry, but your article has brought your parents' murder back into the spotlight and opened up some new lines of enquiry. Thanks to you, we've had several new leads. So you've done your bit, son. Just relax and leave the rest to us."

"Er, OK," Henry muttered with despondent resignation.

"And don't forget, Henry, I can clearly remember you sitting in the police station that day, dressed in a school uniform, grief-stricken and all alone in the world. I promised you then that we'd get these bastards and d'you know what? I think we will this time."

After stepping from the bus, Henry tramped to his apartment on Peggotty Road with the intention of packing an overnight bag then taking a taxi to Amber's house. The lights in Micawber's bookshop were being switched off for the evening and he offered Susan, the proprietor, a cheery wave while making a mental note to add her to his Christmas card list.

Misto's was already heaving with a tumult of gleeful customers, attended by a quintet of servers in Santa hats. Henry fondly remembered the first time he'd set eyes on Amber in the coffee shop, never imagining then that someone like her would ever be interested in someone like him. With a self-indulgent chuckle he relived with cinematic clarity the glorious moment she wrote 'pompous prat' on Sebastian's coffee cup. Almost as if it had happened yesterday, he recalled the disgruntled look on Sebastian's face set against the puckish mischief of her smile.

Nearing the house, he happened across Mr O'Connor, whose face was reddened by the cold as he struggled to squeeze a large spruce tree through the front door. Henry hurried to offer assistance. "Mr O'Connor, it might be best to drag it through stump first," he suggested.

"Ah, well said, Henry. Yes, let's try it the other way round."

Even though the tree was neatly squished into an arboreal version of a fishnet stocking it was catching on the door jamb and showering the threshold with a scattering of blue-green needles. Together they turned the tree around and heaved it through the door.

"That's just grand," said Mr O'Connor, dusting his palms. "Are you one for celebrating Christmas, Henry?"

"More than you might imagine," he replied. "I never celebrate my birthday on account of my parents being murdered the same day, so it goes without saying that I appreciate this time of the year all the more."

"Good boy. That's the spirit. Ooh, talking of spirits, what do you say we share a few whiskies to celebrate the lead up to Christmas?"

"Er, I'm not much a fan of whisky."

"Wine then. I've got a decent bottle of Shiraz waiting to be uncorked. We could drink to Francis de Sales, the patron saint of writers and journalists."

"OK," Henry agreed, secretly keen to expunge all thoughts of a missing corpse and a murderous Ukrainian.

As they climbed the stairs, Oscar leapt onto Henry's back, draping him like a stole. Inside the apartment, Mr O'Connor's parrot squawked, "Get the kettle on. Get the kettle on," and then enthusiastically whistled *The Flintstones* theme tune.

"I do love your parrot," Henry chuckled, allowing the cat to relinquish his grip and drop to the sofa.

"Ah, he's always in fine form," Mr O'Connor agreed, fishing for a corkscrew in the cutlery drawer. As if on cue, the parrot shouted, "Wilmaaa!" at the top of his avian lungs.

The living room was already very festive: Christmas cards monopolised every square inch of shelf space, and Mr O'Connor set a spiral of lights blinking on an artificial tree with a flick of a switch.

"The real tree, the one you just helped me with, will stay in the hallway," he explained, placing a wine bottle and two glasses on the coffee table. "Each year the sight of a Christmas tree warms my sentimental heart. Whenever I step through the front door, it's like a scene straight out of *It's a Wonderful Life.*"

"I'd love to help you decorate it but unfortunately I'm staying over at Amber's tonight. I could definitely assist at some point over the weekend though, if you're not in any rush?"

"Hey, no problem. Liam and I usually do it together, but it'd be lovely to see you two lovebirds. And in any case, I've yet to properly meet your girlfriend. Perhaps we could all go out for lunch afterwards, once the tree is in its pomp?"

"Sounds like a great idea."

Mr O'Connor skewered his corkscrew into the neck of the bottle at an oblique angle but nevertheless succeeded in removing the cork, which emerged as a ragged semblance of its former self. The wine glugged, billowed and clucked like a soft-beaked hen as it was poured generously into each glass.

"Cheers, Henry. Here's to your book!" Mr O'Connor said, with great vivacity. "You're flying a winged horse, my boy. May it be the best-seller that I expect it to be."

"To my book!" Henry cheered, before feeling a huge twinge of guilt in the light of his landlord's greatest literary achievement being cruelly taken from him. "I feel bad crowing about my book when your own dream was so unfairly dashed by your wife."

A discernible sadness rose in Mr O'Connor's eyes. "Ah, it is what it is," he said. "I console myself with the knowledge that I've had more than my fair share of success in the writing world. But oh Lord, that one would've beaten the pants off the lot of them. And to think that she was once a good Catholic girl from County Limerick. Jesus, I'd forgive every wicked thing she's ever done if she would return it to me." He gazed into his glass and tried to keep it together. "Anyway, let's not dwell on the things we can't change or we'll go insane. Where will you be spending your Christmas, Henry? If you haven't made plans, you're more than welcome to join us. We could use the company."

With all the secret tensions that had beleaguered his topsy-turvy life of late, Henry hadn't given much thought to where he would enjoy the holidays. Amber, because she was estranged from her mother and stepfather, had already suggested they spend Christmas at her house.

"I would love to join you, Mr O'Connor," Henry said, his eyes lighting up. "Could Amber come too?"

"Of course. It would be my pleasure. And for the umpteenth time, quit with the Mr O'Connor. It's Fergus to my friends. Now, are you sure that your family won't be put out?"

"Well, I've declined an offer from my maternal grandparents to join them in Bali. I did that last year but it wasn't the least bit Christmassy. I also need to remain in England so that I can meet with the publishing team in the new year. I've told my other grandparents that I might not be coming down to Epsom and they were fine with that. After putting up with me for ten years, I rather think that they'd prefer their own company."

Fergus set his glass on the coffee table. "Now, speaking of your book, has Amber been let loose on it yet?"

"Yes, and thankfully she loved it, but she also said that I sometimes use fancy words where simpler ones would have suited."

"Ha! Everyone's a critic. She's right, of course. Hey, show me a writer who isn't sometimes guilty of literary overkill. This is where a good copy editor is worth their weight in gold. In my first novel, when I didn't yet know my arse from my elbow, I used the word 'pulchritudinous' to describe a beautiful woman. Sweet Jesus, how pretentious!"

"Ouch," Henry winced. "Now you mention it, I do remember you using that word."

As Fergus recharged their glasses, a frown darkened his face, like a passing cloud. "Henry, have you heard any more from that weasel, Sebastian?"

"No, I haven't, thank goodness. But knowing how he operates, I should imagine he's landed on his feet. People like him always do."

"Well, it goes without saying that he's not welcome here again," said Mr O'Connor, bristling with indignation. "That fella behaves with a moral turpitude that makes Rumplestiltskin look saintly! Honest to God, I didn't like that boy from the moment I first clapped eyes on him."

"Oh, that reminds me," said Henry. "I phoned his mother to keep her in the loop, and I also asked her what she wanted me to do with the remainder of the money she'd given me."

"Oh? And what did she say?"

"She said that I was welcome to keep it."

"And have you?"

"No, I gave what was left of it to a charity."

"Good lad. And for that singular act of selflessness, you can live here rent-free from now on."

"No, I couldn't—"

"Ah, away with you! Shut up and drink your wine."

By the time the bottle was drained they'd compared science fiction novels, past and present, and philosophised as to whether a tree that falls in a forest with no earthly creatures around to hear it actually makes a sound.

With 'The Toreador Song' from *Carmen* blaring from a quartet of speakers, Henry caught the time on Mr O'Connor's mantelpiece clock and announced that he really should be making a move.

"I need to be at Amber's house before she arrives home," he explained.

Fergus creaked to his feet and fished a bottle of dark spirit from a walnut-veneered drinks cabinet. "Now, I know that you don't care for whiskey, but would you join me in just one tot of rum before you dash off?"

"Sure," Henry replied, remembering with regret that he still hadn't packed his overnight bag or even ordered a taxi on one of the busiest Friday nights of the year.

"A toast!" Mr O'Connor cheered, encouraging Henry to clink glasses. "May we both live to be a hundred years old, with one extra year to repent!"

CHAPTER FORTY-FOUR

Journey's End in Lovers Meeting

Having once gained a History of Art degree in her former life, Florence often helped out at the art gallery in her home sector, working closely with curators to ensure that paintings, statues and art installations were exhibited to their best advantage.

Paradise's gift of immortality meant that some of the greatest artists in history were able to continue their creative passions without having to contend with the ravages of old age. Such a benefaction meant that fingers were no longer destined to become arthritic and that eyes could never be clouded by cataracts. Renaissance artists, who'd entered the afterlife way back in the fifteenth or sixteenth centuries, continued to paint for hundreds of years, all the while being inspired and influenced by the art movements that superseded them. As a result, new masterpieces were created in abundance, something that was unimaginable in the artists' former lifetimes.

That wasn't to say that everyone on Paradise cherished the benefits of eternal youth. Many people (usually those without an imagination, it had to be said) tired of watching the sun rising and falling each day and so chose to be reincarnated, an option afforded to everyone.

Florence was assisting with preparations for a forthcoming exhibition where the work of celebrated artists would be beamed hologramatically across Paradise. The actual physical exhibits were displayed in a replica of the Louvre, which was immeasurably larger than the one on planet Earth. Paul Cézanne, whose work had evolved profoundly in the hundred-plus years spent in the afterlife, collaborated with Modigliani, Picasso, Kahlo and Warhol to create an eclectic collection of paintings that were set to enthral art lovers everywhere.

So as not to be disturbed, Florence had temporarily subdued the telepathic receptors in her brain while she was in a meeting with the curators. Once it ended, she received her missed messages in their order of urgency. The first was from Hassan, his voice feverish with excitement:

"Florence! Please get back to me just as soon as you get this. Fantastic news! Ulysses has arrived safely—"

Just as she was beginning to grasp the joyful significance of his exuberant proclamation, Hassan cut back in. "Florence. So pleased you've picked up. It's true! Ulysses has returned safely. He's just been processed."

Tears welled in Florence's eyes and her heart performed a somersault.

"Oh, thank heavens. Oh, thank God!" she babbled, leaning against a gallery wall to steady herself. "Is he OK?"

"Fit and well, and looking like his old self again. And guess what? None other than Charles Darwin himself was there to check him into Paradise. How about that for a red-carpet welcome?"

"Gosh, when can I see him?" she asked, her heart thudding against her ribcage.

"You can see him right now. He's with Voltaire, waiting in the reception hall as we speak."

"Oh, Hassan, I really can't thank you enough," Florence squeaked, bursting into a paroxysm of sobs. "I know that he couldn't have made it without you."

"Florence, it has been my great pleasure. My reward will be to see the two of you back together again. I'm on my way there now, so I'll see you shortly."

Florence dug in her handbag for a tissue. "Yes, I'll be there just as soon as I've dried my eyes. I must look a frightful sight."

"Oh, and Florence—?"

"Yes?"

"It is customary on such an occasion to invite all interested parties – forebears and the like. A blanket message should cover it."

"OK."

*

Ulysses' one eye squinted into the sunlight, not accustomed to its dazzle after several wasted years. An ornate marble fountain with a floral-shaped basin babbled next to him and spritzed him with a cooling mist. Paradise had seemed beautiful enough when he'd first glimpsed it through the arched walls of the reception hall but only when he stepped out onto a paved piazza did he truly appreciate its splendour.

In the distance he beheld a breathtaking vista of purple, snow-capped mountains rising above a patchwork of green fields. To his left, immaculate vineyards rolled as far as his eye could see and fruit trees, heavy with blossom, were perfectly reflected in the mirrored surface of a vast lake. Just bearing witness to a vault of blue sky again was enough to make his heart swell with joy. He tipped his head back and inhaled air redolent with the incense of honeysuckle and jasmine. As the lilt of birdsong lifted his soul, he thought himself a stubborn fool to have ever resisted such a wondrous reawakening.

"Beautiful, is it not?" Voltaire remarked, revelling in his charge's astonishment. "Created by nature and perfected by the hand of time."

Ulysses' lips moved but not one syllable slipped through so Voltaire allowed him time to gather his thoughts. The Englishman held a hand against his own forehead and words began to sputter from his mouth like water from an air-locked tap.

"What was I *thinking*, François? Were my actions really as selfless as I'd intended them to be? Was I acting out of a sense of duty, or was I vaingloriously doing my own thing and achieving nothing in the process?"

"Your actions were indeed selfless, my friend. You didn't want to abandon your son, so you placed him and your god before yourself. This is not the inclination of a selfish man, *monsieur.* Your sense of devotion was perfectly admirable."

"Even though it was a blind devotion?"

"Pah! I wave my cuff at hindsight as if it were a bothersome fly. Life can only be lived forwards, Ulysses. All that matters is what you do now."

"But my son—"

"Your son has since become a man. And know this. My own mother died when I was just seven years old. I was heartbroken, of course, but my wonderful godfather, a free-thinker, took me under his wing and life continued in a most cordial fashion. It would appear that Henry is similarly sheltered by his free-thinking landlord."

"Oh, that's so good to hear. I've totally lost contact with

everyone, so I'm pleased that his landlord is looking out for him. He did seem to be an agreeable chap."

"And you really must meet my godfather, Ulysses. He is possessed of a sharp wit that you might like. And we rather resemble brothers now, given that he elected to be the same age as me the year after I arrived."

At that moment, almost as if it were a trick of the light, Ulysses saw Hassan materialise from thin air. The Iraqi appeared directly in front of him, like a photograph developing in a darkroom, causing him to step back in shock.

"Hassan! Wow, that's some trick!"

The Iraqi's face was still flickering like a light bulb when he spoke. "Not a trick, old chap. Just one of the many things that you will quickly become accustomed to."

Hassan stepped forward to shake Ulysses' hand and kissed the Englishman on both cheeks, encasing him in the hug first promised when he was found lost in the wilderness. This was the affirmation Ulysses sorely needed: from the scratch of Hassan's stubble through to the muscles across his back, his friend was indubitably real. And, despite Ulysses' original misgivings, everything around him was reassuringly authentic. Paradise had already begun to feel like home.

Florence was the next to appear in a whisper of displaced molecules. She was panda-eyed, her mascara having run, and still held a work file, such was her haste. They rushed into each other's arms and Florence buried her face in Ulysses' chest while a vortex of butterflies fluttered about their heads.

Ulysses began to sob uncontrollably, prompting his wife to hug him even tighter. "Oh, Ulysses, you stubborn fool. I feared you'd never make it," she sputtered.

"I'm here, I'm here," he assured, choking on the tears he'd just unleashed. "How could I have been so stupid?"

"I don't know. You just are," she answered, looking up at him and managing a smile.

"They've made me an angel," he proudly announced, not yet knowing what the privilege entailed.

"I couldn't have cared if they'd slung you in a corner and put a pointy hat on your head. I'm just incredibly relieved to have you back again."

"And look, I chose to remain the same age," Ulysses said, wiping his eye on a sleeve.

"Good job too. I wouldn't have been best pleased if you'd decided to be fifteen again."

As if they were proud parents, Voltaire and Hassan looked on approvingly, each with a huge smile upon his face. No sooner had Florence and Ulysses become reacquainted than a succession of people popped up like mushrooms caught on a time-lapse camera. Soon a large crowd of well-wishers had assembled, blocking any immediate view of the countryside.

Among the throng, Ulysses swiftly recognised the rascally grins of the men who were formerly in his army platoon. No longer the casualties of war, they boisterously swamped him in bear hugs, ruffled his hair and ribbed him about his eye patch.

As quickly as he was able in a sea of bodies, Ulysses became acquainted with his forebears, some still dressed in the fashion of their eras; among them, he met noblemen, silversmiths, weavers, furriers, rat catchers, a spirited suffragette and a family of trapeze artists. Overcome with emotion, he was reunited with all four of his grandparents and also a favourite uncle who'd died after choking on a chicken bone.

Florence, finding an innate ability to orchestrate this impromptu meet-and-greet, ushered someone forward. The man in question was undeniably dashing, his face as familiar to Ulysses as his own. Upon seeing this particular ancestor in the flesh for the first time, Ulysses' eye grew wide as that of a Cyclops.

"Oh, good lord! Captain Ulysses Drummond, I presume?"

"My dear Ulysses," Captain Drummond replied, his bathing costume still damp from a swim he'd been enjoying. "I have followed your life with the utmost interest."

"Oh, dear. I've made rather a lot of mistakes, I'm afraid."

"Ha! You forget that you are addressing the crown prince of calamitous mistakes, Ulysses. We have much to discuss but for now the rest of us should take our leave so that you can spend time in Florence's company."

With that, Captain Drummond shepherded the crowd away from the happy couple. One by one the assemblage diminished in number, each vanishing in a succession of vaporous puffs. Ulysses' grandparents, as young now as they were when he was a child, told him how proud they were of his achievements and how much they loved Florence. They, along with Voltaire and Hassan, said their goodbyes and faded like sandcastles in the path of a wave, leaving Ulysses and Florence alone together for the first time in over four years.

"Is Paradise everything they claim it to be?" Ulysses asked, looking adoringly into his wife's eyes and flashing his buccaneer smile.

"Everything and more," she gushed, placing a reassuring hand against his cheek. "I've got so much to tell you. Oh, and guess what? I've even seen Elvis."

"Elvis? You've *actually* seen Elvis Presley?"

"Yes! As clearly as I'm seeing you now."

"And how is Henry?"

At that moment, Florence's smile dropped from her face and her voice adopted a more serious tone. "Ulysses, we need to talk about Henry—"

"Why? What's happened?"

"I think he might be in terrible danger."

CHAPTER FORTY-FIVE

Softly Like a Thief

Because the fifteenth of December was the penultimate Friday before the Christmas break, Henry had to suffer a ninety-minute wait for the next available taxi and so continued drinking rum with Mr O'Connor until his tongue had almost forgotten how to form words. His earlier decision to pack his overnight bag before this second bout of drinking had proved to be provident because, by the time the cab arrived, his coordination was all out of kilter.

"Ha-ha, sweet Jesus, you're as drunk as a skunk," Mr O'Connor chuckled as Henry clung to the banisters while he blundered down two flights of stairs.

Henry somehow avoided tripping over the spruce tree they'd earlier abandoned in the hallway and flapped his way to the front door as if wearing swimming fins. "Don't forget, Fergus, that I'm going to help you with the Tristmas chee," he slurred "I'm quite the whizzy wizard, y'know, when it comes to taubles and binsel."

The taxi driver, whose engine had been idling for quite

some time, was evidently losing his patience and sounded his horn twice in quick succession.

"Come on my son. Let's get you into the car before that bugger drives off."

"Son. You called me *son*, Mr O'Connor," Henry mumbled, with tears in his eyes. "I would just love it if I were your son, especially as I don't even have a dad."

"Ah, God, I'd be as proud as a peacock to have you as a son, Henry."

"Would you?" said Henry, his lips trembling.

Illuminated by his cabin light, the taxi driver shouted at them to hurry up.

"Jesus, would you wind your neck in, you crabby devil?" Mr O'Connor scolded.

"Can you please just get a move on?" said the driver, chewing gum like a cow chews grass. "We're rushed off our feet tonight."

"You're not even on your blessed feet! Just give us a minute here, will you?" The Irishman turned his attention back to his young friend. "Now Henry, listen to me. May your own dear father forgive me, but I already think of you as my second son. You're welcome under my roof for as long as I have air in my lungs."

Henry was visibly reduced to tears, which led the irritable cab driver to sit back with a look of sudden remorse on his face. Fergus helped his charge into the back of the taxi and thanked the man for his patience. "Henry, just be comforted that your father will be up there watching you from Heaven right now. Can you even imagine how proud that man must be?"

"I don't believe in a heaven," Henry sulked, folding his arms.

"Oh, sure there's a heaven, son. And it's never so full

that it can't accept you when your turn comes. Anyway, I shall leave you with that thought. Goodnight, Henry."

"So where are we headed?" the driver asked.

"Sevenry-flee, Fer'nand Road," Henry slurred, trying his level best to sound sober.

"Huh?" grunted the driver, looking into his mirror, hoping that lip-reading might be the way forward.

"Seventy-three, Ferdinand Road," Mr O'Connor clarified.

"Precisely what I shed," Henry retorted, trying to untangle his tongue.

Fergus bade Henry goodnight before slamming the door shut and slapping the car's roof as if it were a donkey's backside.

"May the road be downhill all the way to her door!" he trumpeted as the rear lights of the taxi disappeared up the road.

*

Henry spent the journey blathering to the back of the taxi driver's head, even going so far as to witter on about existentialism though he was unable to say the word. The cabbie chose to ignore his drunken gibberish, treating it as if it were the murmuring of insects, until he came to a stop outside number seventy-three. After initially spilling his money across the floor of the taxi, Henry paid the driver and lugged his overnight bag clear of the vehicle.

"Make sure you drink a pint of water, mate," the cabbie advised, before heading off into the night.

"Will do," Henry replied by way of a delayed reaction, his voice only heard by a glum moon and the stars in the sky.

He glanced at his watch: it read 11.04. This meant that, despite being waylaid, he'd arrived at least half an hour before his girlfriend was due home.

Henry clumped up the driveway and found Amber's door key under the terracotta pot. Frost sparkled on the surface of the tarmac and his wintry breath caught in the beam of the security light. He billowed back and forth, trying to engage the key with keyhole while the garage doors glared at him, evoking a memory in Henry's mind of Danny's decapitated body.

Oh, for heaven's sake, you can do this, Henry thought as his fingers struggled to perform the simple task of unlocking a door.

He was pleased to discover that Amber had set the heating on a timer and the temperature inside was agreeably balmy. Other than that, the house was deathly quiet.

His appetite heightened by intoxication, Henry scoffed a dictionary-sized slice of lasagne straight from the fridge and then artfully hid the empty dish under a gingham tea towel. Happily replenished, he lumbered up to Amber's bedroom, scuffing walls with his overnight bag as he went.

His phone pinged. A text message from Amber:

Are u there? Should b home in 30 mins xxx

Henry, who didn't approve of abbreviated words, smiley faces or acronyms, responded in a more formal manner:

Yes, I'm here. I'm afraid that I arrived quite late, as I was earlier dragged into a drinking binge with my landlord. As a result, I have not prepared food. I must also warn you that I am rather squiffy. Really look forward to seeing you, though. x

Henry was all fingers and thumbs and so it took an age to compile the message. Nonetheless, he found typing to be an easier task than speaking and was duly impressed with the sobriety of his text. He even deliberated as to whether he should add the kiss, or not.

By way of contrast, Amber's reply was almost immediate:

Ha! So funny when ur drunk! Have already eaten, food not a prob. See u soon! Luv u xxx

Prior to his new life with Amber, Henry had tended to excuse himself from inessential displays of affection. But, with a capability worthy of Aphrodite herself, she had somehow coaxed him from his shell. As a consequence, he'd become more demonstrative in her company. As far as he was concerned, her love was like water in a desert and he drank of it deeply.

In anticipation of her arrival, Henry scrupulously brushed his teeth and changed into a comfortable, rather homely, pair of cotton pyjamas. When Amber eventually breezed into the kitchen, she was met by the sight of him smiling like a dolphin and struggling to keep his eyes open.

"God, just look at the state of you," she said, giving him a cursory hug.

"I'm sorry, Amber, but I don't think I can keep awake much longer. I've consumed far too much alcohol."

"Yeah, you said."

"But I have drunk a pint of water. The taxi driver told me to do that."

"Good for him."

"You're angry with me, aren't you?"

"Of course I'm not angry with you. You're like a child when you're drunk. Get yourself into bed," she said, flicking him with the same tea towel that he'd draped over the lasagne dish. "I'll join you later."

"OK."

As Henry stumbled up the stairs, finding them as difficult to navigate as Columbus did the Sargasso Sea, Amber made certain that the back door was locked and returned the key to her key ring. By the time she retired to bed, Henry was already fast asleep, snoring as peacefully as Rip Van Winkle.

*

In the calm dead of night, Amber roused from her slumber imagining that she'd heard a noise emanating from downstairs. She glanced at the *crème de menthe* numerals of her clock and saw that it was 3.12am. The pause of her breath hung in the eerie stillness. Guessing that the noise was likely to be something outside, an urban fox or some other nocturnal creature, she drifted back to sleep.

Woken again, just seconds later it seemed, she heard the ghostly creak of a floorboard leeching in from the landing. She tried to rouse Henry by shaking him violently but he didn't stir. "Henry," she hissed into his ear, "I think there's someone in the house." Unfortunately, as Henry was sunk in the depths of an oceanic slumber all he had to offer was a faint grunt.

Amber's immediate instinct was to phone Mr Beardsley but then she remembered that he was away for most of the weekend.

She sat up in bed and listened keenly. Another creak, this time unmistakable, cawed in the inkiness of the night. Terror rose inexorably in her chest and grew as thickly as bindweed.

She pinched Henry's skin as hard as she could in a renewed attempt to wake him.

"Huh? What're you doing—?" he croaked.

"Shush. I think there's someone here," she said as loudly as she dared. "Listen. Did you hear that?" A different noise: a squeak this time.

Henry didn't appear to be getting involved so Amber slapped him hard across his face, jolting him out of his stupor. Her voice had become insistent. "Henry. You need to wake up," she rasped. "There is *someone* in the house."

Sobered by the imminence of danger and beginning to regain control of his faculties, Henry sat up as if he'd risen from the grave and craned his neck to listen. At first there was silence, broken only by the distant growl of a motorcycle. Then he heard a noise similar to the snap of a twig – a click of cartilage perhaps? Discernible proof of movement.

Muffled footsteps, soft as a cat's, padded into their bedroom and the purr of their trespasser's breath betrayed his presence. The couple stared, terrified, into the murk, neither one daring to switch a lamp on. A spectral silhouette hovered over a wicker chair that occupied one corner of the room. The shadow slunk into the seat, causing the wicker to rustle and scrape under its weight.

Amber and Henry were caught in a vortex of dread. Henry slipped quietly from the bed and stood barefoot in the dark, paralysed by fear. Amber, similarly petrified, felt the blood rumbling through her veins. A faint chuckle from the direction of the chair rippled into the darkness. Then, for theatrical impact, the intruder switched on a torch he'd aimed under his chin, instantly illuminating his hideous face as if it were a Halloween pumpkin.

"Sur-prise!" Pascal cheered, his cadaverous head seeming to float ghoulishly in mid-air.

A scream froze in Amber's throat and Henry's hands began to shake.

Louder creaks echoed from the landing, undisguised this time. Footsteps approached the bedroom door and another predatory shadow stole into view. A large hand hit the light switch, throwing the room into revelatory brilliance. Amber, who was spilling from her silk chemise, dragged the duvet up to her neck.

Yuri took pleasure in seeing her terror. He regarded her intently, his head cocked to one side, as if she were a curiosity that needed to be studied. Amber looked at the African's disfigured mouth and shivered in the chill of his gaze. She petitioned Yuri with her eyes in the faint hope of some kind of reassurance but the black gloves and the shoe covers he wore suggested that this was more than a sick prank. The Ukrainian didn't take his eyes off Amber, even when Henry found the courage to shout at him.

"I'm the one that you want," he blustered, his voice trembling. "So go ahead, teach me a lesson. Beat me up, do what the hell you want, but please keep Amber out of this."

"Whooh! He's brave this one," Pascal chuckled, bouncing in his seat and clapping his hands in mock applause.

Without preamble, Yuri declared their intention as he shifted his glare towards Henry. "When you write story, you make problem for me and problem for my friend. So now we take you somewhere and we execute both you." He said this as casually as a journeyman might explain his job role to a stranger.

Execute. The word jabbed its recipients like a cattle prod.

Henry, who had never fought anyone in his entire life, impulsively pulled a drawer from the bedside cabinet and swung it at the Ukrainian's head with as much ferocity as he could. Yuri capably blocked the attack with his forearm and punched Henry hard into his solar plexus, forcing the air from his lungs and causing him to squeal as if impaled with a spear.

In his ringside seat, Pascal whooped with laughter and kicked his legs with delight. Even Yuri raised his eyebrows and allowed himself a rare chuckle. "I let you catch breath, boy, and maybe you try again?" he smirked, offering the drawer back to Henry who was doubled up in agony.

"Please don't hurt him," Amber pleaded. "Please don't do this. Yuri, I'm begging you. If you leave us alone, we won't say a word. I promise."

Yuri loomed over her, ominous as an iceberg. "Impossible to leave you alone," he growled, with an intensity that curdled her blood. "I want you so long. Too late to stop."

Amber tried to disarm him by exaggerating her vulnerability, hoping to appeal to his human nature, but it made not one jot of difference. He continued to stare at her, pausing only to hammer a large fist against the back of Henry's neck, rendering him unconscious and sending him crumpled to the carpet.

The Ukrainian signalled to his companion, prompting Pascal to produce a syringe from a jacket pocket.

"No-ooo! Please, no-ooo!" Amber wailed, backing up against the headboard, dragging the duvet with her.

Yuri held her down with his gloved hands. She twisted and thrashed but to no avail. He shoved a pillow into her face as she blindly kneed him in the ribs and tore at his neck. Pascal, his grinning teeth like clothes pegs, slid the needle into her left arm and in a matter of seconds she was limp and swallowed by darkness.

The African prepared a second needle, which he used on Henry. Yuri, remaining on the bed, removed one glove and slipped a bare hand under Amber's chemise.

"No, Yuri. You have much time to do that later," Pascal cautioned. "We must leave here before daylight."

The Ukrainian stepped from the bed and scolded the African with his eyes. "You not tell me what I do," he grunted, thrusting his barrel chest forward.

"I am not telling you what to do, my friend," Pascal

replied. "But when we get to the lock-up, you can fuck this girl and do what you want. This is not the place, yes?"

Yuri threw Pascal a sullen look followed by a curt nod that signalled an end to the conversation. He hoisted Amber's flaccid body in a fireman's lift and headed for the stairs. Pascal followed, dragging Henry by the legs so that his head bounced lifelessly upon each stair.

"Check that we don't leave something in bedroom," Yuri instructed, lowering Amber onto the kitchen table, her auburn hair cascading off the edge. "I will move her car, then drive van to door."

Using Henry's prostrate body as a springboard, Pascal raced up the stairs, taking them two at a time.

Yuri found Amber's keys near the door and drove her car off the driveway, checking that the coast was clear. He reversed his van as noiselessly as he could, aligning it with the kitchen door and killing the headlights. Once both bodies were stowed in the rear of the van, the Ukrainian ticked off a checklist in his mind. Satisfied that they'd left no trace, he and Pascal removed their overshoes and locked up.

It was decided that Pascal would drive the van to their warehouse in the East End, a decision that didn't sit well with Yuri given that the African didn't own a licence and had only learned how to drive by stealing cars in his teens. The Ukrainian was to follow in Amber's Peugeot.

"Pascal, be careful. Must not drive crazy, yes?" Yuri warned.

Pascal rolled his eyes, an adolescent nagged by his mother. "Do not worry. If the police stop me, I have this," he smirked, revealing his handgun.

"Then be sure you are invisible," Yuri said wearily,

knowing that there was a chance that Pascal could bring them both down with his psychopathic indiscipline.

The journey took a little over thirty minutes. Yuri followed Pascal's tail lights; against all the odds, the African drove with a consideration that belied his usual inclinations. The killers arrived at the forecourt together, their headlamp beams ballooning and merging against the lockup's shuttered door. Pascal punched in the key code and, after the door had rattled open, he drove the van inside and quietened the engine. Yuri left Amber's car parked outside and followed in on foot, flicking a bank of light switches once the door closed.

"You know, these two woke up and made a noise, like *so*," Pascal said, slapping the side of the van in the same way that the captives had, halfway through their journey.

"You think anybody hear them?" Yuri asked as the banging resumed from within the vehicle.

"No, I think they are too weak to make much noise. It's all cool."

Yuri took the keys from Pascal and unlocked the van doors to reveal Henry and Amber, dislocated from reality and sitting in fearful disarray.

Amber's grandmother, Pamela, and Yuri's mother, Iryna, looked on helplessly in a heightened state of anxiety from their parallel reality.

"Out!" Yuri ordered the couple. Henry, still dressed in his pyjamas, was first to emerge, blinking into the glare of fluorescent lighting. Reeling, and trying to focus, he staggered in an ungainly semi-circle. Yuri clapped his hands with delight. "Ha! You do dance for me."

Henry surveyed his surroundings but saw no means of escape. At that moment, the unmistakable scent of his mother's perfume filtered into his nostrils, helping him to find an inner calm. Suddenly, during this most frightening of moments, he felt unruffled, pragmatic. He closed his eyes, breathed deeply, and mentally prepared for a violent death.

Amber clambered down from the van, lost her footing and spilled onto the concrete floor. She shivered as if in the grip of palsy as Henry helped her up but nevertheless managed a weak smile.

Henry was determined to do anything in his power to secure her safe release. "Guys, I'm ready and willing to accept my fate," he said, holding his hands up in a placatory manner. "But Amber has done nothing to either of you. She doesn't deserve this."

As Pascal ambled towards Henry he started a slow handclap. "She is here to die," he leered. "After she has watched you die first."

Yuri clumped over to a work bench and returned twirling a reel of duct tape on one of his fat fingers. "You should keep mouth shut, boy," he snarled. "Because of big mouth you force us to kill you both."

"Oh, just do what you bloody want, you piece of shit!" Amber yelled defiantly, her bleary eyes suddenly blazing with hatred.

"Thank you," Yuri smiled, touching the scratches she'd left on his neck. "I will do that, for sure."

For her show of bravado Pascal backhanded Amber hard across the face, ripping her lips. Then he stood eyeball to eyeball with Henry, daring him to retaliate on her behalf.

"Please. This is madness," Henry begged. "Let her go. Please just let her go."

Pascal, striking like a cobra, punched him flush on the jaw with a fist as hard as a hoof. Henry crashed to the ground, two of his teeth scattering like dice.

Amber brushed past the African, spat blood into her hand and daubed it onto Yuri's impassive face. "Are you proud of yourself, tough guy?" she taunted. "Is this *really* what you're about? You two are just pathetic."

A smile played at the edges of Yuri's mouth. "Right now we leave you here. We all need beauty sleep, yes? When we come back, you will see what I am about. This is promise."

Pascal retrieved two wooden chairs from a jumble of office furniture stacked between pallets of contraband. He forced Amber to sit down and took the duct tape from Yuri. After yanking her arms behind the chair he lashed Amber to it, lapping her with several revolutions of the reel, way more than was necessary.

"Hey, not go crazy," Yuri urged, noticing that Pascal had already used nearly half of the tape.

Pascal fastened Amber's ankles to the chair legs, ensuring that it was impossible for her to move a muscle.

"Please, I can barely breathe," she croaked.

"Not worry," Yuri replied. "He will not tape mouth. And if you want to scream, go ahead. Nobody outside can hear you."

Pascal manhandled Henry into the other chair and circled him with the tape, winding it around his arms and body several times until he was similarly secured. When the African began to whirl the reel about Henry's thighs, the tape reached the end and pulled feebly away from the spool.

"See. You use too much on girl," Yuri grumbled.

"Relax. They cannot go anywhere," Pascal grinned, kicking the cardboard reel across the warehouse floor.

"Sleep well, children," Yuri said facetiously. "We will be back."

Before he left, Pascal stopped to fire up a propane

blowtorch. He waved the jet of flame close to Henry's bloodied face, singeing his eyebrows. "*This*, my friend, is your destiny."

Pascal and Yuri switched off the lights and departed the lockup in a clatter of mechanical noise. They drove off in the van hours before the first glint of dawn, leaving the young couple trussed up in their nightwear, helpless and shivering, inhaling the night's dark dread.

CHAPTER FORTY-SIX

Whose Guilt within Their Bosom Lies

Once the guests at Ulysses' welcome party had decamped, Florence didn't waste time bringing him up to speed with the latest developments in their son's life. He was, of course, thunderstruck to learn of Henry's involvement in the concealment of a murder and was shocked that his wife saw fit to condone such behaviour.

As they strolled through a sun-dappled olive grove, she bandied the words 'justifiable' and 'manslaughter' to reinforce her argument. "But that's not even the worst of it," she continued.

"It gets worse?" Ulysses gasped.

"I'm afraid so. Henry took it upon himself to write an exposé of the events surrounding our murder in his newspaper, the result being that those two lunatics have now got him firmly in their sights."

"No-o! Why couldn't he have just let sleeping dogs lie?"

"My thoughts exactly. He's equally as stubborn as you,

darling, but at least he's got Amber by his side. She really is a remarkable girl."

"This being the young lady who dispatched someone with a spade?"

"Ulysses, don't be so melodramatic. Need I remind you that you killed enemy soldiers in Iraq?"

"Ah, yes, you do have a point."

Ulysses, not yet knowing the lay of the land, asked Florence if there was anything that could be done to reverse this calamitous state of affairs.

"Believe me, I've tried," she said in a low voice. "I've sought help from archangels and even joined forces with the Ukrainian's mother in the hope of some divine intervention. It seems as if nature and fate are the only governing forces here."

Closing his one good eye, Ulysses remembered the searing pain he had experienced as two swings of the African's machete almost severed his legs at the ankles. He also recalled the shrill of Florence's screams before they floated from their mutilated bodies, becalmed by the sweet sedative of death. Knowing what these two men were capable of, he was anxious to protect his son. He recalled Hassan mentioning that he'd visited his son in a dream and wondered if his own advancement to angel status might afford him a similar opportunity.

Florence looked up at Ulysses and, seeing the consternation on his face, realised that it was too soon to burden him with such an abundance of bad news. "I'm so sorry to land you with this, darling. You've barely arrived and I'm already raining on your parade."

"Not at all," he replied. "Better to be slapped with the truth than be kissed with pretence."

"Come," she said, grabbing his hand. "I'll take you to your new home. I know you'll be amazed."

"More than I have been already?"

"Much more."

Encircled by a kaleidoscope of butterflies, Florence wrapped her arms around her husband. Burying her head in his chest, she visualised the coordinates to their house. "Hold on tight," she grinned. "You're going on a journey."

Hugging his wife, and tingling with static, Ulysses found himself captured within a zoetrope of flashing images until a complete change of location materialised in front of him.

"Really strange the first time, isn't it?" Florence said, entertained by the expression on her husband's face. "And look. How about *this* for a surprise?"

Lost for words and disoriented, Ulysses entered a state of sudden befuddlement. Standing before him, exactly as it had existed on Earth, was their ivy-clad vicarage. He spun on his heels, expecting to see the pavements of Sowerberry Road, but instead of a residential street there existed a panorama of green fields upon which only the shadows of passing clouds moved.

"Did I choose well?" Florence asked anxiously.

"It's perfect, simply perfect," Ulysses sputtered, just as Bagheera the cat made a timely appearance.

Florence stood on tiptoes to plant a kiss on her husband's cheek. "Welcome home, darling. We've both missed you."

Their home was a carbon copy of the one on Earth, except that there were no television sets, computers or mobile phones. Florence explained to Ulysses how her social life was so much better without the ball and chain of electronic devices. She told him that, in the absence of television sets, the citizens of Paradise felt less need to stay in their houses and therefore ventured outside to socialise. Without mobile phones to preoccupy them, the more recent arrivals were delighted to find that their interactions became more natural and spontaneous. With the zeal of a prophet, Florence extolled the virtues of the setup, saying that people were inclined to read more books and that the art of writing by hand continued to flourish.

"*And* there are no cars, aeroplanes or trains," she said with a triumphant air.

"Really? How do people get about?" Ulysses asked lamely.

"You experienced it earlier," Florence explained. "Of course, you could still ride a bike or go for a walk if you fancied it."

Now that he was replete with flesh and blood again, and because he hadn't slept in ten years, Ulysses felt a sudden wave of heavy-lidded tiredness wash over him. "Please don't think me rude," he said, yawning like a lion, "but I am *so* tired. Would you mind if I had a lie down? Then, when I'm energised, we'll put our heads together and see what we can do about Henry."

Florence allowed herself a moment to ruminate. "Well, in addition to Amber's grandmother, Pamela, I would like you to meet Iryna. She's the one I mentioned earlier, the mother of that Ukrainian monster. Perhaps between us we could work some magic."

"Sounds good," he said sleepily. "Don't be offended, Florence, but I really must hit the sack. And please wake me up before nightfall. Er, we *do* have nightfall here, don't we?"

"Ha. Yes, we do. Catch forty winks, darling, and I'll see you later."

As soon as his head hit the pillow, Ulysses fell into a deep, curative sleep. Six hours later, he was woken by

Florence and the smell of fresh coffee. It was loud with rain outside and night had begun to descend on Paradise.

"Yup, we have rain here too," she smiled, placing a cup of coffee next to the bed.

"Uhh, it's getting dark," he protested, struggling to prop himself up. "Aren't we seeing the Ukrainian brute's mother?"

"I think it sensible that you get some more rest, don't you?"

"But time is against us. Shouldn't we press on, for Henry's sake?"

Florence placed a hand against his chest. "You won't be fit for anything unless you eat and get a good night's sleep. I've contacted Iryna and we're seeing her first thing tomorrow. Now, I've prepared sandwiches if you're interested."

"That would be lovely, darling," he enthused, distracted by the thought of food. "I'm totally famished."

*

The following day, as they prepared to leave after breakfast, Florence gave her husband a crash course in teleportation and furnished him with the coordinates for Iryna's house.

"Iryna can only speak Ukrainian but you will hear her in English," she explained. "Of course, her lips are out of sync with the words so it's rather like watching a foreign-language movie that's been dubbed in English."

They stood an arm's length apart; after seeing images strobe by, they materialised almost in unison at the Ukrainian's front door.

"Easy, isn't it?" Florence grinned as she pressed the doorbell.

"Certainly beats my Volvo."

Iryna opened the door, her face rueful. "I'm deeply sorry

for the sins of my son," she babbled, clasping Ulysses' hands before he had the chance to speak. "I am so ashamed, I just don't know what to do."

"Well, let's go inside," he soothed, slipping into vicar mode. "We'll chat about it over a cup of tea."

Iryna led them upstairs to the balcony and disappeared to fetch refreshments while Florence looked down on a field of exuberant sunflowers that received her as if she were Eva Perón on the balcony of the Casa Rosada.

"So beautiful," she sighed, as Ulysses joined her. "I wonder what William Wordsworth would make of such a magnificent sight."

Ulysses was concerned that Iryna was being overly hard on herself. "She's disproportionately penitent given that she's not to blame for her son's actions."

"Well, she feels responsible. As would you, if Henry was skulking around London like a latter-day Jack the Ripper."

"True, very true."

Iryna appeared with a tray upon which sat three tea glasses, each one nestled in its own pewter holder. In addition, it conveyed a bowl of sugar lumps, a ramekin of lemon slices and a hand-painted teapot. Still ridden with inordinate guilt, she poured the tea obsequiously, finding it difficult to maintain eye contact with her guests.

"His father was a bastard," she announced abruptly. "They say that the apple doesn't fall far from the tree but his father wasn't even around when my Yuri turned rotten."

Ulysses, in an attempt to assuage her guilt, sought to offer some Christian comfort. "Iryna, there really is no need for you to shoulder the blame."

Not yet accustomed to the translation process, he spoke slowly and artificially until Florence revolved a finger, motioning for him to speed things up.

Iryna couldn't believe the consideration afforded to her by her guests, given the sequence of events that had occurred overnight. "But your son, and his beautiful girlfriend, they are in real danger. Now that Yuri has captured them he is capable of anything—"

"Hey, say that again," Ulysses blustered, setting down his glass. "*Captured*, you say?"

"No-oo!" Florence wailed, holding her head in her hands.

Iryna was thrown by their obvious surprise. "Oh no, sweet mother of God. You haven't seen the latest—"

"No, I haven't," Florence interjected. "I was so preoccupied with getting Ulysses settled in that I didn't think to check on Henry. Now I'm almost scared to ask what has happened."

Iryna steepled her fingers, as if in prayer. "Please forgive me for saying this, but Yuri and his accomplice broke into Amber's house while they were sleeping and kidnapped them both."

"Where are they now?" Ulysses asked, his voice terse.

"I – I'm so sorry. They took them to a warehouse near the docks."

"Have they been hurt?" Florence asked.

"Not hurt, as such. But my son and the African are returning today. Really, what can I do? I'm sick to my stomach and Yuri's evil haunts me every day. I have tried everything. Everything."

The burden of guilt had become too much; Iryna held a crucifix to her bosom and collapsed in a fit of sobs. Florence and Ulysses comforted her while sharing her feeling of helplessness.

Able to rewind and review the latest situation, watching recent events unfold as easily as if they were viewing a horror movie, Ulysses and Florence's sense of powerlessness became even more pronounced. Iryna couldn't bear to relive it and instead busied herself with household chores to take her mind off her son's villainy.

An impromptu session, where they held hands and hoped to contact Yuri by channelling their thoughts, proved unproductive. When it was time to leave, the trio were at a loss as to what they should say to each other.

"He wasn't always like this, you know," Iryna sniffled. "Yuri was a good boy – for a while. In fact, when he was aged nine, just after we moved to Odessa, he loved to help the priest tidy up the church after mass. I have never seen him as happy as he was back then."

*

At that precise moment, as Yuri prepared to leave his house to return to the lockup, an unsolicited memory, vivid and evocative, supplanted all his other thoughts. Lost in the moment, he closed his eyes and recalled the proud look on his mother's face as he snuffed out the flames of the church candles one by one with his wet fingertips, exactly as the priest had shown him. He remembered dipping his fingertips into the melted wax and evoked the simple pleasure of seeing it solidify on his skin.

He looked at the framed photograph of his mother and stopped to touch her face. Then, turning away, he snatched the van keys from the dresser and envisaged what he would do to Amber Manette.

CHAPTER FORTY-SEVEN

Inferno

Because he'd assumed the faculties of an angel, the prophecy of his son's murder came to Ulysses in a lucid vision. As if in a dream, he was conveyed transcendentally from the vicarage and found himself gazing down from the roof joists of a cold warehouse. Below him was his son, totally oblivious to his shadowy presence and roped to a chair. Near to Henry, on her knees and pleading for his life, was his girlfriend.

Ulysses scanned the warehouse for Yuri but the Ukrainian was nowhere to be seen. The African was there, though, laughing with his head thrown back, baring a grate of hideous teeth.

Try as he might, Ulysses couldn't free himself from the ceiling. He was as stuck as a fly caught in a spider's web and, when he tried to call out, not one sound leapt from his tongueless throat. He observed Pascal lifting a jerry can from the floor and, to his horror, saw him douse Henry in petrol. Then, in no more than one darting second, a blowtorch ignited the puddle at his boy's tethered feet, twisting Henry into a human bonfire. Ulysses screamed, but his voice was as silent as a stone.

Raging against his worthlessness, Ulysses could only look on helplessly as Henry bucked and jerked within his own flaming pyre. Hot jets of fat spurted from his charred flesh and, while his body spat and crackled, Pascal Makuza, gloried in his terrible death.

CHAPTER FORTY-EIGHT

Captivity Is the Greatest of All Evils

Apart from one grimy skylight that faced away from the moon, the lockup was a sullen, windowless structure. Amber and Henry were left trussed in complete darkness save for a narrow strip of silvery moonlight that crept under the shuttered door. There was no audible indication of life outside the four walls of their prison, no voices nor nocturnal conversations, just the murmur of vehicles passing in the distance. After hollering for several minutes until their vocal chords were raw, they arrived at the realisation that nobody would be able to hear their cries.

Henry was parched and dehydrated from the glut of alcohol consumed the previous evening. In addition, his chest felt tight and he was in need of his inhaler. A sharp whiff of petrol haunted the shrieking shadows and Amber's teeth chattered from the cold.

"Amber, I am so sorry that you've been dragged into this," he brooded, addressing her silhouette. "I'm not sure how, but I'm going to do everything in my power to get us to safety."

Amber, however, as people often do in a crisis, had

discovered an inner fortitude in her hour of need. "Don't waste time worrying about me, Henry," she said tremulously, still groggy from the anaesthetic. "There is no way that I'm going to let these bastards beat us. Can you think of a way to get us out of this place?"

"Well, before they turned the lights off I noticed the only way out is via the rolling shutter or the wooden door. My legs are free so I could shuffle over there, but with the chair fixed to my back I won't be able to reach the control button with my head."

Amber's grandmother, listening in the inky periphery, soundlessly willed them to escape despite having scant faith in their prospects. Henry, evoking the determination of the Count of Monte Christo, searched the darkness for inspiration but the fact that he was trussed to a chair offered him little in the way of encouragement.

Despite this being the depths of winter, Amber noticed the inky silhouette of an uncommonly large butterfly flittering in the light sabre of moonlight beneath the roller door. The creature repeatedly buffeted the metal shutter, generating a chiming sound with each beat of its onyx wings.

As if in receipt of a revelation from a divinity, Amber was immediately blessed with a new-found certainty. "Henry, you said you could make it to the electronic door?"

"Uh, I'm pretty sure—"

"Well, if you're able to get to the shutter, you could rattle it with your feet. And if you can rattle it with your feet, a passer-by would be sure to hear."

Henry pondered this proposal in the darkness and liked the sound of it. "Amber, that's a brilliant idea!"

He wasted no time in waddling towards the fringe of light, bearing the chair like an uncomfortable papoose, forced to walk with his head low to the floor. Amber watched him shrink into the darkness with the gait of a tyrannosaurus rex and cheered him on. Despite stubbing his bare toes against a number of unseen objects, he made steady progress and reached the shuttered door with more ease than he'd dared hope for.

"Well done!" Amber yelled, heartened by the sight of his crooked silhouette against the door. "Kick that shutter with all you've got, Henry. Someone will definitely hear you!"

Henry returned to an upright seated position and clattered his bare heels against the metal roller door with such gusto that he nearly upended himself. Encouraged by Amber, he established a percussive rhythm and generated a din cacophonous enough to raise the dead, yelling loudly as he did so.

"There's no one about," Henry croaked, his voice hoarse after several minutes of shouting. "God knows where we are."

"It's probably not even five o'clock in the morning, Henry," Amber yelled. "You mustn't give up, it's our only hope."

The exertion had taken its toll on Henry. Without access to an inhaler, his breath had become ragged and he was light-headed, almost to the point of passing out. In addition, his mouth was raw due to two teeth being uprooted from their gums. Nevertheless, he continued his onslaught with a renewed vigour, kicking furiously against the metal panels until his heels blistered. After each bout he slumped in his chair, too exhausted to continue, but Amber urged him to rally.

After the slow misery of two unfruitful hours, his kicks had lost all potency and privately he had given up hope.

The soles of his feet were bloodied and Amber's cries were fading to murmurs.

While Henry readied himself for another despairing stab at attracting attention, he heard the echo of footsteps accompanied by a man's tuneless whistle. "Hey! Hey!" he bellowed, kicking at the shutters for all he was worth. "Help! He-elp!"

Auspiciously, the whistling stopped and the footsteps drew nearer.

"Yes! Come! Come! We need help!" Henry shouted with a renewed vigour.

"Ha! You locked yourself in, mate?" asked the voice on the other side of the door.

"Thank God! Oh, thank God!" Henry blurted, overcome with relief. "I'm with my girlfriend. We've been kidnapped and are being held captive by two gangsters. Please, we need you to call the police—"

"Is this some kind of wind up, mate? Because I've got better things to do than prat about."

"No, absolutely not, absolutely not," Henry countered, desperation rising in his chest. "My name is Henry Drummond. We have been taken from our bed in the middle of the night. They've taped us to chairs and they're coming back to kill us. Please, *please* do something—"

"Yeah, right. Nice one, mate," the voice chuckled. "You must think I was born yesterday. Let me guess, you're some posh student twat who likes to play pranks on members of the public, yeah?"

"No! Please, please! This is real. I'm begging you," Henry beseeched. The words tore at his dry throat. "I totally get where you're coming from but our lives are in danger. Please, you are our only hope!"

"Yeah, 'course I am. Well, good luck with the rest of your day, mate. Some of us have work to do."

"No-oo! No-oo! Don't go! Pleeeease!"

"Oh, piss off, you muppet."

Amber added her shouts from the back of the warehouse but her voice didn't carry.

"No! No-oo!" Henry pleaded, feverishly kicking at the metal door with his raw feet, but the sound of the man's footsteps faded into silence.

"He's gone?" asked Amber, with disbelief in her voice.

"I'm afraid so," Henry replied, hanging his weary head on his chest.

"Bastard," Amber blazed. "What a bloody, ignorant bastard!"

Henry sporadically continued to make a din until the first emanation of daylight crept into the nooks and crannies of the warehouse and through the skylight. The ill-starred couple had to suffer the ignominy of urinating right where they sat. The few pedestrians that passed within earshot seemed oblivious to Henry's attempts to hijack their attention.

In the half-light that now existed, objects emerged from the shadows. Henry remained at the front end of the lockup and scanned the area for anything sharp that he could use to cut their bonds. He spied a large handsaw hanging from a wall, its blade freckled with rust, but it was too high for him to reach and possibly too cumbersome anyway.

As he duck-walked back to Amber, his back screaming in protest, he continued to search the ghostly dimness for anything that could be of use. He was delighted to spot a small craft knife on top of a cardboard box. "Amber, I've found a knife. It's perfect!" he exclaimed.

"Omigod. Can you reach it?" Amber asked, desperate to be freed from her chair. "I can't feel my fingers, Henry. I don't know if it's the cold or whether it's because the bastard's taped me up too tight."

"I think I can grab it with my teeth," he said, leaning forward so that his chest was resting against the box.

The knife, though, was tantalisingly just out of range. Henry nuzzled himself into the cardboard, bending it under his weight, and then successfully managed to drag it nearer using his forehead. "I've got it!" he whooped, celebrating a small victory.

Amber didn't want Henry to get ahead of himself and mess things up. "OK, let's keep calm and think about how we're going to do this. You won't be able to cut my tape unless we're both lying on the floor. Agreed?"

"Er, agreed," he replied, looking at the knife in the way that a dog looks longingly at a tennis ball.

"So, I'll force myself to fall sideways onto the ground and when you're back here, you do the same, yeah?"

"Yes, that makes perfect sense."

Henry collected the knife with canine precision and rocked the chair back onto its four legs. Looking faintly piratical with a blade in his mouth, he jockeyed his chair in Amber's direction.

"For God's sake, don't drop it, Henry," Amber quavered, her heart rate quickening. "Free my arms first and then I can use the knife to cut the rest."

Once Henry was beside her, Amber steeled herself for her fall. "Henry, now listen. Keep your neck tucked in, yeah? Otherwise you'll crack your head open when you hit the deck. Follow what I do."

"Don't you gurry agout me," he assured her while biting down on the knife handle.

"OK, here goes." Amber shifted her body weight so that her chair rocked precariously before descending to the floor with a thud. "I'm fine, I'm fine," she announced, her shoulder having borne most of the impact.

Henry's own attempt at chair tipping was rather inelegant by comparison. The jolt of the crash whipped his head hard against the concrete floor and caused the knife to spill from his mouth. "Argh. I bashed my head," he groaned.

"Never mind your bloody head. Have you still got the knife?"

Henry scuffed across the floor like a decrepit snake and retrieved the craft knife with his teeth. Emitting several throaty grunts, he manoeuvred himself in a position to access the tape that bound Amber's wrists. Biting hard into the knife's plastic handle, he cut at the band of tape that stretched taut between her arms. Contrary to even his most optimistic hope, the tape yielded to the blade.

"It's loosening, it's loosening," Amber said excitedly, as Henry frantically nodded his head up and down, slicing a series of lacerations through the duct tape.

Suddenly, the tension was lost and Amber was at last able to move her arms freely. Her hands were numb, as if they'd been anesthetised, and she slapped them together to get the blood flowing.

"Quick, let me have the knife," she instructed as the feeling returned to her fingertips. "Omigod, Henry, you are just bloody brilliant."

Still lying on her side, Amber cut through the layers of tape that were wound about her torso and then moved onto the ones that held her to the chair legs. As soon as she was able to stand, and with mounting excitement, she sliced into Henry's ligatures.

The last cut caused a wave of unbridled relief to wash over her. “Yes! Bloody yes! We’ve done it!” she cheered, pulling loose strips of tape from her torn chemise. “Quick, let’s get out of here before those sodding lunatics return.”

Ignoring their aches and pains, they walked to the front of the warehouse. Henry, not wanting Amber’s euphoria to cloud her judgment, issued some calm guidance. “Listen to me, Amber. When I hit the button to open that shutter, we need to run as fast and as far as we can, OK?”

“Oh, don’t you worry,” she replied with a triumphant grin. “I’m not hanging around here a second longer than I need to.”

CHAPTER FORTY-NINE

A Stay of Execution

After a few hours' sleep, Yuri and Pascal began their day by eating breakfast at a truck stop before setting off with sadistic intent. They'd almost reached the lockup when Muriel phoned from the massage parlour, her voice sonorous through the van's hands-free speakers.

"What you want, Muriel?" Yuri answered, rounding a corner and visoring his eyes against the sudden glare of a yawning sun.

"Yuri, I could urgently use your help. We've got a drunk geezer here threatening the girls and kicking off. I told him to leave but he won't budge."

"Yes! Let's go," Pascal shrilled, his eyes lighting up.

"No, just I go," Yuri interjected, exasperation in his voice. "I will be there in thirty minutes, Muriel."

"OK, but be as quick as you can, yeah? The girls have locked themselves in their rooms and he's smashing the bloody place up."

"Motherfucker," Yuri snorted. "I am come now."

Yuri couldn't risk sending Pascal, knowing that he would only make a bad situation worse. This niggling development meant that his anticipation of enjoying Amber's body was temporarily derailed, leaving him noticeably disgruntled.

"Pascal, you walk to warehouse from here. I will deal with this piece of shit and come back."

"Why am I not coming with you?" Pascal asked almost petulantly.

"Because you will kill him or do something stupid. Then we have big problem again. Don't argue with me, I just not in good mood."

"So what do you want me to do with the girl and the boy?"

"Do nothing. And not damage girl, leave her to me."

"And the boy?"

"Him, I not care. But we kill them later with bullet. No petrol. No fire. Just like Body Snatcher say. You listen to me or not?"

Pascal nodded and opened the door. Yuri, as was often the case, had to speak to his associate as if he were addressing an unreasonable child. Pascal stepped silently from the van with a sour look on his face and zipped up his bomber jacket against the cold. At times like these he could have cheerfully plunged his knife into Yuri's throat.

"Be good," Yuri urged through his opened window, more in hope than expectation. Then he slewed the van in the opposite direction and drove at breakneck speed to the massage parlour.

CHAPTER FIFTY

We Are Our Choices

Henry pressed the green button and, to his and Amber's relief, the shutter doors began to rattle and hum. Amber smiled at Henry as they prepared to bolt outside, hoping to put some distance between them and the warehouse. But as the door made its clattering ascent, a man's running shoes and tracksuit bottoms came into view. Henry wondered, for one fraction of a second, if this was the person with whom he'd spoken earlier. Then he saw a clutch of purple-varnished fingernails attached to two dark hands, one of them holding a pistol.

Pascal Makuza dipped under the rising shutter and in the same movement bowled Amber to the ground. Holding the gun to her head, and with a murderous hostility in his eyes, he ordered Henry to stop the door's progress. "Hey, boy. Press the red button now or she dies."

Henry had no choice but to comply. No sooner had the door clattered shut than Pascal hammered the butt of his gun into his forehead, splitting it open.

"Arrrgghh!" Henry roared. An explosion of stars detonated in front of his eyes and a thunderbolt of hot pain shot through his skull. He went down on one knee, wishing that he hadn't left the craft knife at the other end of the lockup.

Pascal kicked Amber in the ribcage, causing her to jackknife, and pulled Henry up by his hair. After switching on the lights, he herded them away from the door.

"Move!" he ordered, shooing them forward with his pistol while at the same time wondering how they'd managed to free themselves.

Amber, despite being doubled over with pain, glanced at Henry with great concern; a runnel of blood was streaming down his face and dripping from his chin. Despite this, he managed a resigned shrug and something resembling a smile.

The African continued to bark orders and shoved Henry in his back to steer him forward. A ghostly contingent of Pascal's Rwandan victims grouped around him and caterwauled into his ears, their withering shrieks as soundless as raindrops on an ocean.

Pascal removed his jacket; underneath was a tight T-shirt that emphasised his gym-forged biceps. He wound a silencer into the barrel of his gun and thought about using the blowtorch on Henry's face, then he remembered with frustration that Yuri hadn't yet arranged for the Body Snatcher's visit.

*

Having received a second call from Muriel saying that the intruder had already gone leaving a trail of destruction, Yuri arrived at the massage parlour in a foul rage. Once inside, he saw that Muriel's left eye had disappeared under a livid bruise as shiny as an aubergine.

"Yeah, his parting gift to me," she said matter-of-factly.

"Who is this man?" Yuri asked as hot fury coursed through his veins.

"Not your average drunk, Yuri. This lump was connected, you could tell. Gun in his waistband, tattoos up his neck. Albanian mafia, if I were to guess."

"So what he want?"

"First he said that one of the girls had stolen money from him and he began to slap her about. Then, after I'd got the others to safety, he went crazy. I mean just look at the place—"

Yuri surveyed the damage and calculated how much the repairs would cost. It was as if a small cyclone had torn through the communal living room; shards of wood and glass lay like jetsam and stuffing spilled from the slashed bellies of upholstered chairs.

"And that's not the worst of it," Muriel continued. "He said that he would come back with his associates and take the girls away. Yeah, he was drunk, Yuri, but I don't think this was some idle threat."

"Not a problem. We can deal with this."

"Really, Yuri? You seriously want to lock horns with these people? Well, I certainly don't want to be around when it all kicks off."

The Ukrainian allowed himself a moment of introspection and, not for the first time, started to doubt that his heart was in this line of work any more.

Muriel, sensing his inner conflict, offered some sage advice, borne from years of being on the wrong side of the tracks. "Yuri, if you don't get out while the going's good, you'll end up in prison or in a coffin. I'm just so tired of this shit. Aren't you tired of it too?"

"I have to go," he said, changing the subject. "Have job to do with Pascal."

"You know he'll be the death of you?" she warned, holding a bag of frozen peas against her swollen eye.

"Yes, I know this."

As he reached for the front door, a black butterfly landed weightlessly on the wall, pulsing its wings. Without breaking stride he flattened it with his hand and strode out of the building.

*

Pascal, with the gun resting in his lap, sat opposite Amber and Henry and reapplied lacquer to his fingernails. When his phone rang, he grabbed it pincer-like to avoid smudging the wet varnish.

"Ah, this is Yuri." Pascal beamed at the couple in a manner that suggested they were all great friends having a cosy get-together. "Hello, Yuri, all cool here," he said, answering the phone.

When someone who was ominously referred to as the 'Body Snatcher', cropped up in the conversation, Amber and Henry looked at each other with heightened trepidation. As Pascal minded his captives while he chatted, his dark eyes shining like beetles, Henry covertly glanced at the craft knife that lay abandoned and out of reach on the concrete floor.

The African returned the phone to his pocket, using the tips of his fingers. He ran his tongue along his awful teeth, keen to arrest his captives' gaze. "Today is your lucky day," he said, addressing Amber with a cruel smile. "Yuri will be here soon and I know how much he *likes* you."

"Go to hell, you sicko," she said with an air of defiance that made Henry wince.

Pascal cleared his nasal passages and spat the contents at her bare feet. The whites of his eyes were as pink as the vitiligo on his dark skin, and his shit-eating grin never left his face for a second. Amber camouflaged her discomfort by staring at him unflinchingly, not wanting to gift him any kind of deviant satisfaction.

Given that she was in a gangster's killing room, Amber saw no need to beg for mercy or burst into tears. As far as she was concerned, their fate was sealed no matter how hard she tried to court sympathy. She looked at Henry in an attempt to draw courage from their solidarity. The blood on his face had dried to resemble rust and a lump the size of a duck egg rose from his forehead. He managed a weak smile and surreptitiously drew Amber's gaze to the knife that lay on the floor.

"Hey, boy. I'm watching you," Pascal teased, noticing the knife and secretly hoping that Henry might have the audacity to try something heroic. After blowing on his fingernails for more than a minute, he stroked his gun as if it were a cat. Then, for his own amusement, he stood up and casually turned his back on them, an intentional invitation for one of them to attack.

Henry glanced at the knife and judged the distance between himself and his captor. His head was pounding from the blow he'd received. He looked at his girlfriend intently and spoke to her as if he were uttering his last words on Earth. "Amber, I want you to know that I love you more than I love life itself."

Hearing this, Pascal chuckled quietly to himself.

Amber's stomach knotted and her pulse quickened. Her eyes screamed at Henry not to do what she guessed he was about to do.

Henry slipped from the chair and gathered the knife while Pascal cocked one ear and continued to gaze in the opposite direction. With Amber powerless to stop him, Henry launched his brave attack, aiming to open the

African's neck with one swift slash of the blade. Before the weapon was anywhere near its intended target, Pascal spun inside the arc of Henry's swing and sent him over his shoulder with an effortless judo throw.

"Whooh!" he cheered, collecting the fallen knife from the floor while Henry lay groaning in pain. "You thought you could kill me with *this*?"

Amber, while Pascal was distracted, leapt from her chair and tried to wrest the knife from his hand. He flung her contemptuously to the floor and spat in her face. She looked over at Henry; what a pitiful pair they were, him in his blood-stained pyjamas, her in a satin chemise that accentuated her vulnerability.

Pascal, rather than continuing to wait for Yuri, decided upon a change of plan. "You," he said, directing his gaze at Amber, "will wait for Yuri. But *you*, my friend are about to die a painful death."

Pascal tugged a dirty length of coarse rope from a hook on the cinder-block wall and used it to tie Henry to his chair. He scuttled off, returning with a jerry can in one hand and a blowtorch in the other.

"No-oo! Please no!" Amber wailed, getting on her knees to beg for her boyfriend's life.

"I told you before, newspaper boy," Pascal hissed through his awful grin. "*This* is your destiny.

CHAPTER FIFTY-ONE

Do I Dare Disturb the Universe?

Beneath an anaemic winter sun that festered in a hoary sky, Yuri drove his van onto the concrete forecourt outside the lockup and parked it next to Amber's car. Distracted by his acute need to satisfy his predatory impulses, he failed to notice the tall man who sat waiting for him on a low boundary wall.

"Hello, Yuri," the man said. "We meet again."

The greeting surprised Yuri. He spun round, expecting a gun to accompany the voice. The sight that met him was infinitely more unnerving. "No, it should not be. It should not be," he babbled, thunderstruck at suddenly finding himself face to face with a man whom he knew to be dead.

"Be not afraid," said Ulysses, returning the Ukrainian's consternation with a genial smile.

"Afraid—?" Yuri muttered, unable to comprehend what was happening.

"Be not afraid. This is commonly what angels say when they first approach a human."

Yuri nervously lit a cigarette without once taking his

eyes off his supernatural visitor. "Is not possible," he said, jabbing a fat finger at Ulysses. "This cannot be. You are—"

"Dead?"

"For sure," Yuri grunted, blowing smoke from his nostrils. "I not know what you do to me. This is mind trick." He studied the visitor more closely. Everything about him was exactly the same as it was on the day of his murder: the leather eye patch, the clerical collar under the cricket sweater. He noted that the vicar hadn't aged a day. It was as if he'd been frozen in time and somehow brought back to life.

"No trick, I assure you," said Ulysses, remaining perched on top of the wall.

Yuri pressed the heels of his palms into his eyes, hoping that this hallucinatory apparition would disappear. When he looked again, the vicar was still there, larger than life and peering into his soul. "This is crazy," he said again, torment rising in his voice. "What you want from me, priest?"

"I don't want anything from you, Yuri. But I urge you, with all of my being, to spare the lives of my son and his girlfriend."

"Too late to change me, priest. I have done many bad things in my life."

"Never too late, Yuri. I've been talking with your mother. She tells me that you were good once."

"You talk with my mother?" Yuri asked, incredulity rising in his voice. He slapped his hands against his head; sparks flew from the cigarette he was holding.

"Yes, I've met with Iryna," Ulysses said nonchalantly. With Yuri open-mouthed and rooted to the spot, he continued. "Iryna said that when you were nine years old you were a happy boy. You used to tidy the chairs away after the church service. She even mentioned that you loved to put the candles out with your fingers—"

"Mama," Yuri murmured involuntarily, remembering in a daze how carefree his life was back then. "Oh, God. You do meet my mother … is she in Heaven?"

"She is, Yuri, but even now you continue to break her heart."

"She can see me?"

"Every bad thing you do."

"And she is safe?" Yuri asked with genuine concern, flicking his cigarette to the ground.

"Yes, she's safe."

Making a conscious decision to regain his composure, Yuri removed an assortment of keys from a jacket pocket and selected the one that corresponded to the entrance door. He addressed Ulysses obliquely, too ashamed to look at him. "Priest, tell my mother I miss her."

"I will," Ulysses nodded, hoping to prolong their dialogue.

Barbs of despair raked his body as he watched the Ukrainian unlock the door, powerless to prevent him from going inside.

"Tell her I love her," Yuri said, looking at the ground and battling his demons. "Tell her am sorry for what I do."

Without uttering another word, the Ukrainian opened the door and disappeared into the warehouse.

CHAPTER FIFTY-TWO

I Love Nothing in the World so Much as You

Pascal neatly arranged the petrol can, a box of matches and the blowtorch on the warehouse floor in the way one would organise provisions for a day trip. Almost as an afterthought, he remembered the fire extinguisher and strutted off to fetch that too.

Without any preamble, he began to splash petrol onto Henry's pyjamas. The cold liquid took his victim's breath away and the fumes stung his eyes. Amber remained on her knees, face streaming with tears, pleading with the African to show mercy.

"Be strong, Amber," Henry urged, seeing the light disappear from her eyes. Even as he said them, his words seemed woefully inadequate.

Amber jumped to her feet, snatched the blowtorch from the floor and scrabbled for the matches, desperate to try anything. "Please, please," she begged, brandishing the blowtorch with feeble conviction and backing away as her captor walked towards her.

"Give those to me," he smirked. "Yuri will not be happy if I fuck your face up before he arrives."

"Amber, it's fine," Henry soothed, seeing how fearful she was about the blowtorch. "Just let him do what he wants. I'm ready."

Her voice stumbled over her sobs. "I would rather die than stand by and let this bastard hurt you."

With a fighter's ease, Pascal snatched the blowtorch from her grasp and slapped her hard across the face, whipping her head back. She staggered, regained her composure and glared at him with contempt.

Seeking to control his inner tumult, Henry closed his eyes and thought of his mother. Despite a ten-year distance, he could still recall the soft lilt of her voice and the security blanket of her smile. He wondered at that moment if he would see her again, wondered if there might be a Heaven after all.

Pascal fussed with the matchbox with a demonic eagerness, swelling Amber's anguish.

The faint clunk of a vehicle door immediately outside drew everyone's attention. After a brief pause Henry, with his eyes still firmly shut, vaguely heard Yuri Voloshyn having a muted conversation with someone.

Pascal ordered Amber to sit in a chair. "If you try anything stupid when my friend comes in, I will hurt you. Do you understand?"

Amber nodded submissively, hoping that Yuri's arrival might bring about a different sequence of events.

Yuri slipped in via the entrance door, locking it behind him. He took a moment to stand in quiet contemplation, muddled by what he had just experienced.

"What is the matter, Yuri? You look like you have seen a ghost," Pascal piped, allowing himself a girlish giggle.

Seeing his cohort brandishing the blowtorch was enough to jolt Yuri from his trance. "Pascal, fuck you. We agree we kill him clean with bullet. Why you do this when my back is turned?"

"I was thinking just one last time," the African demurred.

"No," said Yuri with finality in his voice, puffing out his gorilla chest. "Already Body Snatcher is on way. Have not time for this."

Pascal glanced at Henry's wet pyjamas with sullen disappointment.

Yuri was deflected from his displeasure by the sight of Amber; a smear of blood sullied her face and her curves were barely concealed under her flimsy shift. His cock came alive and began to creep across his pants in anticipation. "Give me gun," he instructed Pascal. "I kill him now, then maybe have time to fuck this girl."

Pascal dutifully handed him the gun, its silencer shiny under the fluorescent lights. Yuri checked the magazine and reloaded it into the grip with a sharp click. Henry closed his eyes and braced himself. In his thoughts he was ten years old again, standing on the gravelled driveway of the vicarage. He sought to give his mother the farewell kiss he'd childishly denied her on the day she was murdered.

"No-o, please no-o!" he heard Amber plead, but he was strangely at peace in the jaws of death.

"I love nothing in the world so much as you," he declared, opening his cherubic eyes to gaze at her for one final moment.

Amber, sinking to the depths of her being, surrendered a thousand unrealised dreams and grieved for the motherhood she would never know.

Yuri raised the gun.

Henry scrunched his eyes. Then, flinching, he heard

the muffled rattle of a gunshot. Immediately an inhuman noise, blood-curdling and deafening, tore through the air. A second shot rang out, its detonation echoing off the hard surfaces of the warehouse.

Henry opened his eyes to see Pascal writhing on the floor and screaming like a keening seagull. His tracksuit bottoms were soaked with blood above each knee and his eyes were wild with a rabid hostility.

"You make too much trouble for me," Yuri growled, digging the heel of his boot into Pascal's wounds, causing him to thrash about and shriek even louder.

The Ukrainian turned to Henry and offered him the gun. "You want to kill him?" he asked. "I can untie you."

Pascal, ablaze with ferocity, was trying to lift himself from the floor. Henry shook his head and declined Yuri's offer. Amber was outraged, sensing he was passing up a golden opportunity to save their lives.

"I want you to know that Pascal murder your mother and father," Yuri explained. "Not me. Is important you know this."

Henry nodded compliantly, unable to find the right words.

Without a moment's hesitation, and with chilling efficiency, Yuri knelt on Pascal's heaving chest and put a bullet between his eyes. The African jolted then lay motionless, his head haloed by a spreading pool of blood.

Unseen and jubilant, the Rwandan ghosts finally found redress in Pascal Makuza's death. They danced about him rapturously and started to jostle his damnable soul towards the howling tempests of Hell.

Yuri, with an aerosol of blood spatters on his grim face, turned his attention to Henry as he sat tethered and helpless in his chair. Amber, shaking with fear, threw herself upon her boyfriend as if she might somehow shield him from harm. She was flung aside as easily as a child.

"Please, Yuri, pleeease," she beseeched, her voice trembling with shock. "If you have any decency, you would let us go. And I promise you we won't say a thing. Not a thing—"

Henry, as atheists are inclined to do when caught in the eye of a storm, actually said a silent prayer and asked a god, whom he consciously didn't believe in, to ensure Amber's safe passage out of this nightmare.

Yuri started to untie Henry's petrol-soaked rope and muttered to himself in Ukrainian, over and over again. "Son of priest, I give you chance," Yuri intoned, his lips moving no more than a ventriloquist's. "I will give you gun. Then, if you are man, you will kill me."

"I can't do that," Henry answered.

"Then know this. If you not shoot me, I will fuck your girlfriend and after that, for sure I will kill you."

"Henry, for Christ's sake, take the bloody gun," Amber urged, her eyes bulging with frustration.

"See, she already know how to kill," Yuri said approvingly, remembering the dead body in her garage. A thin, knowing smile broke on his blood-stippled face. "So, here is gun. Is loaded and ready to fire but when you shoot, you must put *here*." Yuri pressed the barrel of the gun hard against his own forehead, leaving a red circular imprint on his scarred skin. "If you not do this, gun will kick and you will miss."

When the Ukrainian handed Henry the weapon, Amber breathed a sigh of relief. But then, in an unexpected instant, Yuri swept her up to his chest and threw her to the floor, winding her and causing her chemise to ride high above her naked hips.

Henry felt the weight of the gun in his hand and was

unnerved by its destructive potential. Yuri unfastened his trousers and released his engorged cock. Amber glared up at him and clawed wildly at his face.

"Stop!" Henry yelled, pressing the gun against the Ukrainian's bloodied head. "Don't make me do this!"

Yuri pinned Amber to the floor and saw his mother in his mind's eye. The shamed look on her face was too much for him to bear. Crossing himself as if he were in church, he snarled, "Do it! Shoot me!"

The gun trembled in Henry's hand.

"Go on, shoot the bastard!" Amber stormed, fighting against Yuri as he forced her legs apart.

Henry pulled the trigger. The gun's violent recoil jerked his arm into his shoulder socket and Yuri crashed to the floor like a felled oak. Amber disentangled herself from his heavy legs and threw herself into her boyfriend's arms. Terrified that he might accidentally discharge the gun, Henry tossed it onto Yuri's dead body.

"We're alive! We're bloody alive!" Amber shouted jubilantly between sobs. "I thought we were done for."

Henry, wincing with pain, was already thinking more pragmatically. He was troubled that the Ukrainian had met his death without revealing the whereabouts of Danny's rotting corpse.

Before either of them had time to ponder their next move, they heard a vehicle pull up outside. Almost immediately Yuri's phone began to ring, lighting up his trouser pocket.

"Aww, no," Amber wailed, filled with sudden dread. "Who the hell is that?"

Henry grabbed the gun from where it had come to rest on Yuri's belly. It felt a little more comfortable in his hand now. "Let's find out," he said valiantly.

As they walked towards the shuttered door, Henry pushed Amber behind him. His prime concern was for her safety but he noted that she was carrying the craft knife and looked ready to use it. The person on the other side repeatedly hammered a fist against the shutter to announce their presence. Henry looked at Amber and checked that she was set. She nodded and gripped the knife. He pressed the green button; the door rattled into life and began to rise.

"What the fuck is going on in there?" a man's voice demanded. His trouser legs and then his midriff gradually came into view.

Henry held the gun like he'd seen actors do in movies and Amber steeled herself for a violent fight, staying within touching distance of her boyfriend.

"Omigod!" Amber shrieked when the man's dour face appeared. Standing in front of them, wearing a V-neck sweater over a shirt and tie, was her neighbour, Mr Beardsley.

"Jesus, Amber, are you OK?" he asked, slipping under the moving shutter before scanning the warehouse and spotting two dead bodies. "I saw your Peugeot outside and feared the worst."

Amber's eyes widened, as did the gape of her mouth.

Mr Beardsley continued with practised authority. "I think that we need to shut these doors, don't you?" Henry stood stupefied, rooted to the spot. "Come on, dopey. Get the door shut and hide that gun away, there's a good boy."

Henry complied, although he wasn't quite sure why. Amber's face was a picture of confusion.

Exuding calmness, Mr Beardsley ambled over to the bodies and examined them, careful not to step in their blood. "Quite the stone-cold killers aren't we?" he grinned, the fluorescent lighting reflected in his spectacles.

Amber continued to stare at her neighbour with incredulity. "Mr Beardsley, I don't understand—"

"I can see how this would come as a shock, Amber, but I work with the criminal underworld to make dead bodies disappear."

"B-but that's terrible," Amber gasped.

"Well, I'm pretty sure you were glad of my services when I spirited away that dead boyfriend of yours."

"You?"

"Me and Yuri, actually. I roped him in to help me get the body into the boot of my car. Call it police intuition, but I sensed that something was up. You two up half the night, backwards and forwards to the garage. Not really much of a surprise to discover Danny's corpse, to tell you the truth—"

"And where's the body now?" Henry interjected.

"Oh, you've got no need to worry about that, matey. Sorry to appear a bit crass, Amber, but he's been eaten by pigs, shitted out and then used as fertiliser. You're both very much in the clear where his death is concerned."

Far from being upset by this revelation, Amber was only too pleased to discover that Danny was gone forever and had finally proved to be of some practical use.

Mr Beardsley continued. "I guessed straightaway that Danny must've killed poor little Sherlock. I loved that dog. You were fully justified in doing what you did."

"Thank you, Mr Beardsley. I'm certainly not wracked with guilt."

"So what happens now?" Henry asked, not wanting to relinquish the handgun in case Mr Beardsley wasn't quite the ally he appeared to be.

"Well, I'd love to hear all about how a young couple in their nightwear have managed to take out two hardened killers but I do need to crack on. Yuri merely told me that there were two bodies to collect. He neglected to mention that one of them would be you, Amber. Of course, the penny dropped when I saw your car outside."

"How do we know we can trust you?" Henry asked, trying to hold the gun as expertly as James Bond.

"Son, you need to put the gun down," Mr Beardsley instructed, his voice as arid as a desert. "You see, I've got a shooter of my own and you'd already be dead if that was my intent." After a reassuring nod from Amber, Henry placed the loathsome handgun on the floor. "Good lad. Now take a few steps back. Those things are dangerous in untrained hands."

The Body Snatcher picked up the gun and together they dragged the bodies out of sight so he could reverse his van into the warehouse before dropping the shutter. He slipped into a hooded disposable boiler suit and, over the course of the next few minutes, produced a butcher's saw, hoses, sprays, plastic sacks, caustic powders and two industrial-sized bottles of bleach. "You two have taken quite a bashing," he noted, perplexed as to how this bizarre scene had unfolded.

He spread a plastic tarpaulin across the concrete floor, instructing Amber and Henry to remove what little clothes they stood in, and provided them with a wet sponge. "Don't worry, I shan't look," he promised, busying himself with a UV light, looking for stray blood spatters.

Mr Beardsley deposited their nightclothes into a plastic bag and, while averting his gaze, handed them each a disposable boiler suit. He rifled through Yuri's pockets and found Amber's car keys, which he sprayed with a chemical and patted dry. "Your keys, Amber," he said with a self-assured smile. "You two lovebirds will no doubt be pleased to know that you are free to go."

Henry hesitated. Despite knowing the evil of the man, he looked down at Yuri's lifeless body with a deep sense of regret.

"Hey, don't go feeling sorry for him," Beardsley said, his surgical mask hanging below his chin. "He was a monster, make no mistake. He wanted to blackmail both of you over Danny's death but I soon nipped that in the bud. Leave here with a clear conscience, otherwise this sort of thing will eat away at you."

A wave of relief brought tears to Amber's eyes. She wanted to give her neighbour a huge hug but was mindful of the need to avoid contamination. "I don't know how I can ever begin to repay you, Mr Beardsley. It's going to take a while for this to sink in but I want to thank you from the bottom of my heart."

"Yes, thank you," Henry added.

"Tell you what, you can bake me another one of your cakes, Amber. Now go, both of you, skedaddle."

Shepherded through the wooden entrance door by their liberator, Henry and Amber were met by an icy draft of December air.

"Go on, enjoy life," Mr Beardsley urged, ready to lock the door behind them. "It's the week before Christmas. Forget this ever happened."

Barefoot and dressed as if they were setting off to attend a chemical spill, the couple trooped to Amber's car, stopping only to share a tearful embrace.

As they drew apart Henry, on this day of extraordinary surprises, saw something that shook him to his core. Fingertip-written in the patina of grime on the passenger door, were these words: *'Be a blessing to someone today, Henry'.*

CHAPTER FIFTY-THREE

The Earth Has Music for Those Who Listen

Amber, high on the opiate of life, gabbled excitedly throughout the journey home while Henry dabbed at the tender protuberances of his battered face and urged her to keep her eyes on the road. With a renewed appreciation, they marvelled at the splendour of the sky and the grandiloquence of the world they had nearly been forced to leave. On the afternoon of Saturday, the 16th of December, Amber reversed into her driveway feeling as if fate had granted them a new beginning.

"I'm so dehydrated I could drink a river dry," rasped Henry, poking his tongue into a raw trench in his gums.

Amber declared that she was looking forward to a soak in a hot bath. "You need one too," she suggested. "We absolutely reek of petrol."

Once inside, she flicked on the central heating and they crowded the hallway mirror to survey the extent of the damage to their faces. Aside from having badly split lips, their expressions were lost under purple atolls of bumps and bruises.

"Oh God, what *do* we look like?" Amber gasped, breaking into a chuckle that reassured Henry she was recovering from their ordeal with extraordinary ease.

"I guess that we look like extras in a zombie movie," he joked, a misshapen smile returning to his desecrated face.

"This all feels so unreal, don't you think?" Amber added, addressing his reflection in the mirror and shaking her head.

"I need water," Henry croaked, heading into the kitchen where he filled two large glasses and handed one to his girlfriend. Drinking proved painful and could only be achieved by sipping from the corners of their mouths. Amber fetched a blister strip of painkiller tablets and popped two into his palm before climbing the stairs to run herself a bath.

Ten minutes later Henry was sitting atop the closed toilet seat lid, watching Amber as she luxuriated under a sparkling cloud of bubbles. Their phones, once switched on, came alive in their hands with a symphony of missed communications. Henry listened to some anxious voicemail messages from his paternal grandmother, worried that he hadn't answered her regular Saturday morning call, and a further three from Mr O'Connor who was also a recipient of Constance's telephonic concern. Amber caught up with a succession of messages from friends and a caustic one from Sally Umbridge, the restaurant manager at ¡Arriba! who expressed her annoyance that Amber hadn't turned up for work today.

"I am extremely disappointed, Amber," the voice scolded. "At the very least, I expected the common courtesy of a phone call."

Amber allowed herself a grin. "If only she knew," she quipped, balancing a pom-pom of foam on her nose.

"Aw no," Henry interrupted. "I promised Mr O'Connor that I was going to help him decorate his Christmas tree this weekend." As he spoke, he was greatly surprised that such an insignificant event could so readily eclipse the horrors they'd endured. He scratched his head, confused by his unfamiliar nonchalance.

As his girlfriend gabbled in the bath, he countenanced the impossible and imagined his father stooping to write on the car door before wiping a blackened fingertip on his handkerchief. Amber, seeing that he was happily lost in thought, stopped talking and mirrored his smile.

This anomalous air of normality continued into the afternoon. Henry and Amber, bemused as to why they weren't experiencing any early symptoms of post-traumatic stress, ate lunch, watched a Cary Grant movie and fell soundly asleep together in front of the TV.

*

Rather like a character in a Michelangelo fresco, Ulysses looked down from above and was delighted to see that his curative powers had proved beneficial.

"Bravo, Ulysses," Hassan congratulated. "Those two will be just fine. I believe, my friend, that your mission is accomplished."

*

Under the cover of darkness, having disposed of their bodies, Mr Beardsley entered Pascal and Yuri's homes to remove anything that could link him to their criminal activities. From both properties he also appropriated significant amounts of cash, enough to grant him a very comfortable existence. It was three o'clock on Sunday morning before he was able to retire to his bed, exhausted, but secure in the knowledge that he'd done all he could to keep himself and the young couple from going to prison.

Gerald, you're getting far too old for this malarkey, was his last conscious thought before he drifted into an untroubled sleep.

CHAPTER FIFTY-FOUR

Those that Are Betray'd

For the next three days, the Earth still rotated on its axis, the Sun and the Moon kissed all they surveyed and the star-cross'd lovers' lives continued to chug along with reassuring ease.

To account for their facial damage, they cobbled together a story in which they were mugged by a gang of thugs as they walked home from the local fish-and-chip shop. This cock-and-bull story gave rise to a whole series of well-intentioned questions from whoever it was told to but nevertheless served its purpose. Henry continued to report for work but Amber was signed off for two weeks, her bruised face and damaged lips not fitting the look of an enthusiastic server in a themed restaurant.

Detectives visited Yuri's house on three occasions but left each time after banging on doors and peering through windows. Mr Beardsley visited the couple one tranquil evening for a convivial chat over tea and cake, bringing with him a holdall stuffed with banknotes, which he tried to gift them as restitution for the horror they had endured.

In predictable unison, Amber and Henry declined his offer without hesitation.

"Go on, take it, there's fifty grand there," Mr Beardsley exhorted, giving the holdall a shake. "And that's not even half of the total haul."

"Extremely kind of you," Henry replied. "But I'd prefer not to benefit from ill-gotten gains."

"Same goes for me," Amber agreed.

"Well, I applaud your conscientiousness," said Mr Beardsley, zipping up the bag. "A rare commodity these days. I have no such compunction and look forward to bolstering my retirement."

*

Ophelia's anticipation of a two-day trip to Cologne with her parents, taking in the Christmas markets, was dashed when their flight was cancelled at the eleventh hour. They were already at Heathrow Airport, relaxing in the Lufthansa club lounge, when news of the cancellation broke sending a squabble of crestfallen travellers scurrying to the departure monitors.

"Ah well, not to worry. These things can't be helped," breezed Ophelia's father with his customary composure in the face of adversity.

"Oh, Simon, don't be so blasé," Harriet interjected. "Ophelia was so looking forward to going."

"And we'll make it up to her at Christmas, darling. Ophelia, I take it that Sebastian is staying with us over the festive period?"

"Oh, he is. Just for two days. And he's really looking forward to it."

"Good. I'm keen to get to know him better. I suppose that this is his busiest time of the year?"

"Extremely busy. He's got a double shift today and he's working the next four days, including Christmas Eve. I feel so sorry for him."

"Well, I'm certain, if he's interested, that I can find him something better paid within our organisation. In fact, we have a position opening up that would suit an intelligent, personable young man such as him."

"Oh, Dad, that's wonderful! He'll be delighted. Can I tell him?"

Simon looked at Harriet and received a tacit nod of approval. "Of course, Ophelia. He's almost family."

Simon had sent their chauffeur home earlier after he'd dropped them off at the airport so he commandeered two taxis, one for his daughter and one for themselves.

Ophelia tried to call Sebastian to let him know about her unanticipated change of plan but his phone was switched off. She knew he was far too busy serving corporate groups attending their Christmas parties. She would be a welcome surprise for him when he returned home tired from his evening shift.

*

Although her taxi driver had to contend with the festive chaos of London traffic, Ophelia reached her apartment block in reasonable time. She'd decided that, after emptying her suitcase, she'd slip into some comfortable clothes and sit down to watch an afternoon movie with a cup of tea.

Stepping out of the lift, she was confounded to hear the pulsating thrum of loud music emanating from her apartment. *Huh? He didn't go to work after all?* she mused, unlocking the door.

Perturbed, she walked into a tumult of head-splitting rock music and almost tripped on an upended bottle of red wine that had bled much of its contents into her white carpet.

What the hell?

Ophelia called out Sebastian's name but she might as well have whistled into a gale, such was the deafening volume of the music. After first peering into the living room and then the kitchen, she meandered into her bedroom. Her hand rushed to her mouth as a scream died in her throat. The repugnant scene that greeted her was likely to live in her memory forever.

In full pornographic view, in the sanctuary of her own bed, a woman's spray-tanned buttocks were bouncing up and down on Sebastian's lap as if they were bestride an inflatable banana boat. Ophelia recognised the woman immediately as Jasmine, from the restaurant. Without let up, the pair continued to copulate with enthusiasm, oblivious to Ophelia's horror-struck presence.

She spotted a Champagne bottle reposing in a bucket of ice. The rattle of the bottle being withdrawn went entirely unnoticed and, with righteous efficiency, she hurled the bucket's entire contents over their rutting bodies.

"Wuaaaarrrgh!" Sebastian roared, as if gored by a bull. Both his and Jasmine's eyes were suddenly as big as lemons. "It's not what it seems," he shouted above the din while Jasmine, wearing Ophelia's missing earrings, tried to hide under the duvet.

"Don't you even dare!" Ophelia blazed, having the presence of mind to photograph them with her phone. "I want you out of here by the time I return this evening. Do you understand?"

Sebastian nodded weakly, knowing what damage the photograph could do.

Having issued the ultimatum, Ophelia stormed out of her apartment, determined that Sebastian wouldn't witness the tears caused by his betrayal.

CHAPTER FIFTY-FIVE

'Twas the Night before Christmas

By mid-afternoon on Christmas Eve a blizzard of snow, soundless and downy, was descending on London. Amber and Henry were travelling in a taxi en-route to Peggotty Road where they were to celebrate Christmas with the O'Connors. The pavements were teeming with festive cheer; drunken revellers gambolled from one pub to the next in a city that remained uncowed by the dual threat of terrorism and cirrhosis.

In the week since their brush with death, the couple had continued to sleep dreamlessly. Though the lump on Henry's forehead protruded like the boss of a shield, the contusions on their faces had faded to a jaundiced yellow. Their driver, a garrulous Cockney who sported a sweater emblazoned with a cartoon reindeer, noticed their bruises and quipped, "Wot? You two 'ad a fight didja?"

Henry felt compelled to expound their cover story of the street gang that mugged them on their way home from the fish-and-chip shop, prompting the cabbie to shout, "Bleeding liberty! Wot's the world coming to when these fugs are even mugging ya for your fish and chips?"

"Er, no, they didn't mug us for our fish and chips," Henry explained. "They mugged us for our money, as convention dictates. It just so happens that we were on our way home from a fish-and-chip shop. The fish and chips have absolutely no bearing on the story."

It was at this point that Henry dearly wished that he'd come up with a better explanation while Amber sought to suppress a fit of giggles by biting her hand.

The cabbie rounded the corner into Peggotty Road, passing a succession of houses that were festooned with a pageantry of garish lighting. Stopping outside Mr O'Connor's place, he left the engine idling and scuttled out of the car to help them with their suitcase.

"Sir, I would like to wish you a very merry Christmas," Henry said, adding a generous tip to the fare.

"Ah, nice one! I 'ope you both 'ave a very 'appy Christmas," the driver replied, sounding decidedly Dickensian.

"Thanks. You too," said Amber, stepping from the taxi into a frantic swirl of snowflakes.

Fergus O'Connor opened the door and welcomed them inside with a bustle of generous hugs. Henry had already seen the O'Connors' Christmas tree in all its glory when he'd returned home to collect a change of clothes. Amber had not and, unwinding a long knitted scarf from her neck, was mesmerised. "The tree… Oh, it's beautiful, Mr O'Connor," she enthused.

"Thank you, Amber. And please call me Fergus. You're making an old man feel even older."

The spruce dominated the hallway entrance and seemed to have had every ornament known to man thrown at it. Amber stamped her boots on the doormat to shake off their dusting of snow and tinkled one of the tree's ornamental bells. The sound made her think of an angel getting its wings.

"So are you both recovered from that nasty mugging?" Fergus asked with fatherly concern.

"Oh, we're fine," Henry answered, staring at the floor while Amber nodded sheepishly.

"Terrible what goes on these days," the landlord tutted with a rueful shake of his head.

"Yes, terrible," Henry mumbled.

"So what did you think of our wonder boy's novel then?" Mr O'Connor asked, helping Amber out of her coat.

"Biggest pile of rubbish I've ever read," she declared with an orator's flourish.

"Ha! Love it," Fergus chuckled with a twinkle in his Irish eyes. "Ah, praise be to God, you're just what this place needs at Christmas."

It gladdened Henry to see his girlfriend back to her old playful self again; it seemed inconceivable that just eight days earlier she'd watched him shoot a man's brains through the side of his skull. At the same time, he wondered what Fergus would think were he to discover that there were two killers in his midst.

Wild-haired and smelling of joss sticks, Liam appeared barefoot on the staircase dressed in a pair of harem pants and a tie-dye T-shirt. He shyly shook Amber's hand while Mr O'Connor made the introductions. After a brief chat, Liam politely excused himself and drifted back to his fragrant abode.

"Hey, I'm holding a little shindig this evening," Fergus announced, carrying their suitcase to the door of Henry's flat. "A few of my friends, mostly local luminaries and ne'er-do-wells, will be in attendance. You're both very welcome to join us."

"What time does it start?" Henry asked.

"From six pm. Drinks, nibbles and nonsense. Reuben and Vishnu will be there too."

"Sounds fun. Count us in," Amber piped up, speaking for them both.

Throughout the afternoon, the snow fell as softly as a poet's tears and only stopped once the night had spread its black cape over London. Peggotty Road slept under its wintry blanket and the scrape of metal spades against icy pavements was the only sound heard.

Amber's phone was as animated as a pinball machine, such was the abundance of Christmas greetings from her friends. Henry was the recipient of three communications. The first was a phone call from Detective Sergeant Brian McKay, who was disappointed to report that Yuri Voloshyn and Pascal Makuza had both suddenly disappeared without trace. "I hate to say this, Henry, but we think they've done a runner and might have even left the country," he intoned glumly.

The second communication was a FaceTime call from Bertie Wong, who was in the embryonic stages of organising a surprise book launch for *Planet Foretold* at the Mandarin Oriental Hotel in Hong Kong.

Henry held his phone in a way that allowed Amber to share the call. "So, let me know what dates you are available," Bertie said, his winning smile dominating the screen, "and I will arrange for you and Amber to fly here first class with Cathay Pacific. My treat."

"Please no, that's far too generous," Henry whined, while Amber kicked him in the shins and squealed with excitement.

"Not at all, it's my absolute pleasure. And see if you can

persuade Mr O'Connor to come too. Fergus Munro has a huge fan base here in Hong Kong."

"I-I don't know what to say," Henry sputtered.

"Just say yes. I've got a lot of movers and shakers interested in your novel, Henry. The anticipation here is off the scale so get over here whenever your calendar permits. You'll be doing me a favour."

Henry was left humbled by his friend's kindness. "Thank you, Bertie."

Bertie's face moved closer, almost filling the screen. "So, it's been Christmas Day here for three hours already. I'm partied out and need to hit the sack. Merry Christmas guys."

"Merry Christmas, Bertie!" Henry and Amber shouted in unison.

The third communication of the afternoon was a text message from Verity Fox-Gudgeon, cautioning that Sebastian had arrived on her doorstep unannounced, looking for somewhere to stay. When she refused, he had snatched the keys to her Aston Martin and drove off in it. The message continued thus:

...if you do have the great misfortune to run into my beloved son over the festive period, could you please advise him that my sufferance only extends so far. I am making it known that if he hasn't returned my car by the 26th of December, I shall report its theft to the police. Other than that, Henry, I should like to take this opportunity to wish you and yours a very fine Christmas. Kind regards, Verity.

"That creep is a first-rate arse," Amber fumed after reading the message. "Whatever did his mum do to deserve a son like that?"

"It also suggests that Ophelia must have come to her senses and finally turfed him out," Henry added. "There is no way that he would have willingly walked away from such a well-feathered nest."

"Well, I hope so," Amber harrumphed. "She deserves so much better than that rat."

*

Mr O'Connor's doorbell shrilled just before six o'clock and he hurried to the hallway, anticipating the arrival of his first guests. Opening the door, he was instead greeted by the magical sight of a decorated float in the middle of the road upon which stood a troupe of carol singers who scissored the night air with their melodious voices.

Silent night, holy night
All is calm, all is bright.
Round yon virgin, mother and child
Holy infant, tender and mild
Sleep in heavenly peace,
Sleep in heavenly peace.

Drawn by the euphony of the carolling, Amber, Henry and even Liam herded around the doorway to observe the spectacle. Homeowners opened their doors up and down the street. Meringues of snow sparkled on the moonlit roofs of parked cars.

"Ah, sure, it's truly beautiful," Fergus bubbled, his eyes misting with remembrances of Christmases past.

Once the singing had subsided, everyone scrambled to drop coins into a charity collection box carried by a teenage girl dressed as an elf. As she left, a much older elf trotted into view, waving his arms wildly and moving at a speed not especially suited to the conditions. Unsurprisingly, he slipped on the pavement and clattered into the gate, suffering the loss of his green hat and one latex ear.

"Jesus, it's not the weather to be running the one

hundred metres," Fergus said, helping the man to his feet. "Are you OK?"

"So sorry," the chap replied, putting his ear back on. "I was trying to catch your attention—"

"Well, you did just that."

"Are you Mr O'Connor?"

"I am."

"Then I've just been asked to give you *this*."

With a furtive glance, as if espionage were afoot, the man passed Mr O'Connor a padded envelope.

"What's this?" Fergus asked, perplexed. In the meantime the float had moved much further down the road, where the carolling resumed.

"Er, the nun over there asked me to give it to you—"

"The nun?"

The man, who by now was desperate to catch up with his crew, pointed to a nun who stood ghostlike on the other side of the street. "She said that you would be happy to receive it. Look, I really must catch up with the others."

Mindful of his tumble, the man took his leave, departing with a stride more befitting a geisha than an elf.

Fergus O'Connor tucked the envelope under one arm and rubbed his cold hands together. The mysterious nun remained as still as a statue, her gaze unremitting. Fascinated, if not a little spooked, Amber, Henry and Liam peered over Mr O'Connor's shoulders from the warmth of the hallway. The paleness of the nun's face was captured by a streetlight, an anaemic mask set against the black shadow of her habit.

With a jolt to his heart, Fergus finally recognised the woman by her witch's nose. "Dear God in Heaven," he exclaimed. "That's my wife! And she's become a nun! Look, Liam, it's your mother!"

Liam gasped. He felt compelled to run towards her, barefoot through the snow, but he knew that his mother would have returned to the house before now if she truly wanted to see him.

Mrs O'Connor acknowledged her husband and her son, blessing them from afar with the sign of the cross. Then, with a beatific smile, she faded into the shadows and began to glide soundlessly back to the convent.

"Well, did you *ever* see anything like it?" Fergus said, his jaw dropping like an anchor.

Reuben and Vishnu arrived on the scene, clambering out of a black taxi cab with gift-wrapped bottles of spirits and shouting their hellos.

"If this is how you gentiles celebrate Christmas, standing in the snow in your house slippers, don't expect me to join in," Reuben joked.

"Nor me," Vishnu grinned.

Mr O'Connor barely heard them for he was still agape at the event that had just taken place. He opened the envelope. It yielded a memory stick and a handwritten note. "Follow me… Please, everyone follow me," he said, as if lost in a trance.

As he ascended the stairs, an intrigued procession of people trailed in his wake. Up in the gods of the house, he entered his study and slotted the memory stick into his computer's USB port. A file header appeared on the monitor.

"Oh sweet mother of God," he gasped, clamping a hand to his quivering mouth. "It's my missing book, *The Sea at the Edge of Time.* God love her, she's brought it back to me—" His voice trailed off into a fit of sobs and everyone gathered around to share in his tearful exultation.

"Dad, read the note," Liam urged.

Fergus fished his reading glasses from a shirt pocket, unfolded the note and read it out loud, his tears hitting the paper and streaking the ink.

"Dearest Fergus,

I hope that you and Liam might one day find it in your hearts to forgive me. The story of me leaving you for another man was a complete fabrication on my part. I was plagued by demons and had somehow become a terrible wife and mother. Because of this, I desperately needed to save the two of you from myself. I've since realised that robbing you of your story was both spiteful and despicable, I really wasn't thinking clearly at the time.

I've found peace in the arms of God, a remedy for all my ills.

If I could ask you to grant me one kindness it would be to remember us as we once were.

You are both forever in my prayers.

Katie."

Reading the note, Fergus fondly remembered his young wife on the very day he learned she was carrying his baby, dressed for Sunday mass in a tweed skirt and jacket paired with white-satin gloves. He passed the note to Liam while everyone else congratulated him on his timely benefaction.

"Look. It's all here. It's all bloody here, all 120,000 words of it," he croaked. "May our merciful Father bless you, Katie O'Connor."

CHAPTER FIFTY-SIX

The Sword of Hercules

Hungover, yet inordinately happy with life, Fergus O'Connor gazed out of the downstairs' kitchen window upon a Christmas Day morning that was bright as a Promised Land. The snow blanketing his rear garden lay crisp and virginal, save for the trident motifs of a blackbird's meandering footprints.

The previous night's revelry had continued into the early hours. Fergus's guests, by and large, were an artistic bunch including a toupee-wearing TV soap actor, who called everyone *dahhling*, and a trombonist formerly with the London Philharmonic Orchestra.

Reinvigorated by three espressos in quick succession, random highlights of the evening came to him in precipitant flashbacks, most memorably the acute look of alarm on Henry's face when Vishnu mooted that he would be expected to attend television interviews and book signings. For Fergus's own part, he'd trotted out his time-worn anecdote about the night he foolishly challenged Peter O'Toole to a drinking competition at the Colony

Club in the 1970s, only to wake the next day wrapped in a tiger-skin rug with his eyebrows shaved off.

Because the downstairs' kitchen was commodious and housed a large table, Fergus commandeered it each year for their Christmas lunch. It was while he was sliding a large turkey into the oven that he considered his estranged wife's withdrawal from society, managing to keep sacred vows but at the same time having to hold that tongue of hers.

"God love you, my dear Katie," he said out loud with an expansive flourish, as if his words could somehow flutter through the snowy streets of Hackney and into the inner sanctum of her convent.

Several hours later, as the grandfather clock in the hallway chimed two pm, Fergus was ready to serve a bacchanalian feast that Amber and Liam had helped him prepare. Henry, whose culinary capability could best be described as minimal, had ironed a white linen tablecloth and spread it across the table. He put to good use the cutlery and plate-laying skills taught to him at boarding school and, with a rare pride in his work, deftly folded napkins into bishops' crowns.

Liam provided almost all of the fruit and vegetables from his allotment and, apart from the turkey (a concession to cater for the trinity of meat-eaters), the O'Connors had created an eye-catching Christmas lunch that was free from animal products.

An armada of hot food plates, held in oven mitts, sailed beneath billowy clouds of steam and were set along the length of the table in parallel lines. Shedding his customary bashfulness, Liam delighted in heralding the vegan produce, championing garlic-roasted root vegetables sprinkled with rosemary, a butternut squash stuffed with mushrooms and a large dish of Brussels sprouts flavoured with balsamic vinegar, all surveyed by a crispy pyramid of salty roast potatoes. Set upon a work surface, with steam rising from its crest, was the pneumatic turkey, its blistered skin as brown as that of a Greek fisherman.

Oscar the cat slalomed in and out of people's legs while the parrot remained upstairs perched in front of the television, happy to strike up a conversation with Bing Crosby and Danny Kaye.

Before the feasting commenced, crackers were pulled to loud whoops, paper crowns donned and trite jokes read out from narrow slips of paper. Amber and Henry slid each other a knowing glance; a discreet nod was all that was needed to attest to the absurdity of recent events.

Fergus, who had worn his elasticated Christmas pants in anticipation of an expanding waistline, stood up from the table and chimed a fork on his wine glass to grab everyone's attention.

"Now I know you're all mad keen to tuck into the food, which we are blessed to receive, but it has become something of a tradition in this house that I first read a passage from *A Christmas Carol*."

All eyes were upon him. With reading glasses perched halfway up his nose, he acknowledged Amber's captivating smile and looked at Liam and Henry with barely restrained pride.

"It's the speech that Fred delivers to Scrooge, after his uncle responds to his festive greeting with a 'Bah! Humbug!'. I believe that his words beautifully represent the seasonal goodwill that we should all hold in our hearts."

Henry listened intently, at the same time resisting the urge to pop a roast potato into his mouth.

Fergus continued. "With apologies to the late, great Mr Dickens, I shall paraphrase the speech for brevity:

"I have always thought of Christmas-time to be a kind, forgiving, charitable, pleasant time; the only time I know of, in the long calendar of the year, when men and women seem by one consent to open their shut-up hearts freely, and to think of people below them as if they really were fellow-passengers to the grave, and not another race of creatures bound on other journeys. And therefore, uncle, though it has never put a scrap of gold or silver in my pocket, I believe that it has done me good, and will do me good; and I say, God bless it!"

After his recitation, and with the tantalising smell of food lingering in everyone's nostrils, Fergus raised his glass. "A Merry Christmas to us all. God bless us, every one!"

"Merry Christmas!" his audience cheered, unfolding napkins and ravenously helping themselves to food while Fergus carved into the mountainous turkey.

The meal was a resounding success. The host, with his belly tight as a drum, offered his gratitude to whoever invented the elasticated waistband and Amber keenly jotted down some of Liam's vegan recipes. In between licking his own backside, Oscar was fed scraps from the table and the once-human spirit that lived inside him enjoyed a very happy Christmas indeed.

Henry felt it incumbent on him to say a few words of his own and was set to make a speech when the jarring sound of a pressed doorbell tore through the hallway. "Oh, that's *my* bell," he announced, rising from his chair, mystified as to who would want to call round on Christmas Day afternoon.

"If it's Santa Claus, tell him he's a day late," Fergus quipped, jabbing the air with a fork.

Henry jettisoned his napkin and headed for the threshold of the house with an acute sense of curiosity. The door opened with a shudder, spilling a crust of snow onto the mat. There, with his flop of hair as forlorn as his demeanour, stood none other than Sebastian Fox-Gudgeon.

"Merry Christmas, Henry," he croaked, preferring to keep his cold hands jammed into his coat pockets.

"What do you want, Sebastian?" Henry asked flatly, noticing that the stolen Aston Martin was parked further up the road.

The frigid air nipped at Sebastian's ears and reddened his nose. "Good to see you, Henry. How's that book of yours doing?"

"I shall repeat myself, Sebastian. What do you want?"

"Well, that's a fine way to greet a friend! Food smells rather good. Aren't you going to invite me in?"

Henry poked his tongue into a furrow that had recently held teeth. "I'm afraid you're not welcome here, Sebastian."

"Not welcome? Why ever not?"

"Well, stealing money and then trying to frame someone for your thievery would be an obvious starting point."

"Oh, for God's sake, how bloody petty!" Sebastian snapped, his hauteur bubbling to the surface. "Ever heard of live and let live, Henry? I'm reduced to sleeping in a car and have barely eaten in the last few days. And listen to this, last night I had no other option but to take a shit in a carrier bag. The very least you can do is to allow me in."

"I'm afraid I can't do that, Sebastian."

"I had to *shit* in a carrier bag, Henry—"

"Still not letting you in."

Flames of anger ignited in Sebastian's eyes. "For God's sake, man, where's your humanity? And on Christmas Day as well. Are you seriously telling me that there's no room at the inn?"

"Oh, please! You can hardly compare yourself to the Virgin Mary or Baby Jesus, Sebastian."

"But I've nowhere else to go," Sebastian whimpered, changing tack.

Henry didn't respond and for a moment pondered his landlord's message of seasonal goodwill to all men. Sebastian sensed a glimmer of hope, a softening in Henry's resolve.

"Who is it?" shouted Mr O'Connor merrily from the far end of the house. "Whoever it is, tell them that they're very welcome to join us!"

Henry's moment of hesitation caused a sly smirk to dance across Sebastian's lips. Like a latter-day Count Dracula, he waited to be invited in. "You and I, we go back a long way," he said, peeling a wolfish grin and switching on the charm. "I just need to crash for a few days."

Henry, much less trusting than before, saw that Sebastian's scheming countenance was starkly at odds with the snow's fairy-tale innocence: a viper in a wintry Eden.

"You're not coming in," he said decisively.

"What? Do you even realise how bloody selfish you are?" Sebastian raged. "I've got the Sword of Hercules hanging over me and you don't seem to care about anyone but yourself!"

Henry allowed himself a smile and his eyes darkened. "It's the Sword of Damocles, idiot." Then, with an immense feeling of satisfaction he abruptly, and conclusively, slammed the door in Sebastian's face.

"If you only knew in your own heart how many hardships you were fated to undergo before getting back to your country, you would stay here with me and be the lord of this household and be an immortal."

– Homer

ACKNOWLEDGMENTS

This book could not have been written without the support of Julie, my unflappable wife, who banned me from using our dining room as a chaotic workspace and exiled me to my cramped office with its fit-for-purpose desk and filing cabinets. Incredibly, this moment of pure madness proved to be wholly justified; who knew that an office was better suited to writing a novel than a dining room?!

I am also indebted to publishing editor, Karen (Genghis) Holmes for her expert guidance and grammatical diligence, and Catherine Cousins, publishing director of 2QT, who works tirelessly for her authors.

As an eclectic reader and movie fan, I drew inspiration for writing this book from Homer's *The Odyssey,* the works of Charles Dickens, Wodehouse's *Jeeves and Wooster* (Henry and Sebastian), Shakespeare's *Romeo and Juliet,* Leone's spaghetti westerns and the Christmas classic *It's a Wonderful Life.*

No actual animals – or humans – were harmed in the making of this story.

MY WRITING DAY.

I'm surprisingly disciplined when it comes to writing, and type from 5am until 5pm four days a week. Word counts don't come into the equation; I write with as much care and splendour as I am able, fuelled by Earl Grey tea and chocolate hobnobs, and only stop when my brain curdles or my tummy growls at me. Personal hygiene, male grooming and interaction with human beings almost cease for the duration; you do have to commit!

I endeavour at all times to elicit a variety of strong emotions and get a kick out of making the absurd seem probable. Adding to the mix, I see no reason why humour cannot rub shoulders with evil and trepidation. And I do foul up.

My wife Julie, an avid reader with the analytical eye of a Belgian detective, is the first person I turn to for an unvarnished appraisal. Trust me when I say that she doesn't hold back. My first draft was returned to me graffitied with directions and suggestions, the most crucial ones capitalised and reinforced with exclamation marks. My gratitude goes beyond words.

I have slung a superabundance of literary devices at this

book, hoping they might register subliminally: one of the more obvious examples is Ulysses being asked by Hassan to play dead on the battlefield, a scene mirrored by Amber, who asks Henry to pretend to be wounded as she pulls her kicks outside the burger restaurant.

Cynics among you might accuse me of adding Henry's prodigious penis to the storyline purely for gratuitous titillation. And of course you'd be absolutely right. Guilty as charged! But in a literary sense, I support Chekhov's famous principle that if in the first act you have hung a pistol on the wall, then it should be fired at some point. Henry's *membrum virile* is that loaded pistol.

I do hope you enjoyed my book. If you did, could I ask that you leave a review on Amazon or Goodreads, or both? Even one line will help a poor unfortunate wretch, such as this humble author.

Thank you for reading. I had fun writing it!

Much love, Kevin

CPSIA information can be obtained
at www.ICGtesting.com
Printed in the USA
BVHW031724051218
534859BV00001B/37/P